SDW
5/16

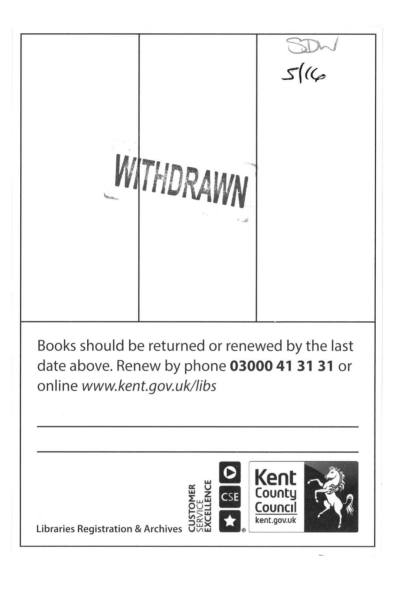

WITHDRAWN

Books should be returned or renewed by the last
date above. Renew by phone **03000 41 31 31** or
online *www.kent.gov.uk/libs*

_____

_____

D0275120

THE POISONOUS SEED

When a customer of William Doughty's Bayswater chemist shop dies of strychnine poisoning after drinking medicine he dispensed, William is blamed, and the family faces ruin. William's daughter, Frances, determines to redeem her ailing father's reputation and save the business. She soon becomes convinced that the death was murder, but unable to persuade the police, she turns detective. Armed only with her wits, courage and determination, Frances uncovers a startling deception and solves a ten-year-old murder. There will be more deaths, and a secret in her own family will be revealed before the killer is unmasked, and Frances will find that her life has changed forever.

THE POISONOUS SEED

THE POISONOUS SEED

by

Linda Stratmann

Magna Large Print Books
Long Preston, North Yorkshire,
BD23 4ND, England.

British Library Cataloguing in Publication Data.

Stratmann, Linda
    The poisonous seed.

    A catalogue record of this book is
    available from the British Library

    ISBN   978-0-7505-4266-1

First published in Great Britain in 2011 by The History Press

Copyright © Linda Stratmann, 2011

Cover illustration by arrangement with The History Press

The right of Linda Stratmann to be identified as the author of this work has been asserted in accordance with the Copyright, Designs and Patents Act, 1988

Published in Large Print 2016 by arrangement with
The History Press

Magna Large Print is an imprint of Library Magna Books Ltd.

Printed and bound in Great Britain by
T.J. (International) Ltd., Cornwall, PL28 8RW

*This book is dedicated to the two people who inspired
'Chas' and 'Barstie' with appreciation and affection,
and my thanks for taking it in such good part!*

CHAPTER ONE

Police Constable Wilfred Brown strode briskly along Westbourne Grove, his boots thudding heavily on the wooden paving. A few days before, dirty yellow fog had swirled thickly across London, turning daytime into twilight, burning eyes and lungs, and dissuading all but the most determined or the most desperate to venture out of doors. The return of daylight had brought the Grove back to life again, but it was still bitterly cold, and he carefully warmed his fingers on the top of the bullseye lantern that hung from his belt. Last month's Christmas bazaars had become this month's winter sales, and the Grove was choked with carriages, a lone mounted policeman doing his best to make the more persistent loiterers move on. The constable wove a determined way through armies of large women in heavy winter coats fiercely clutching brown paper parcels, vendors of hot potatoes and mechanical mice, and deferential shop walkers braving the cold to assist cherished customers to their broughams. The chill air was seasoned with the scent of damp horses and impatient people. Despite the appearance of bustle and prosperity, there were, however, signs that all was not well in the Grove. The bright red 'Sale' posters had a sense of desperation about them, and here and there were the darkened premises of businesses recently closed. On the north side of the Grove, the unfashionable side, opposite the sumptuous glitter of Whiteleys, Wilfred found his destination, the murky yellow glow of the morning gas lamps softening the gilded lettering of William Doughty & Son, Chemists and Druggists. He pushed open the door and the sharp tone of an overhead bell announced his entry into the sweet and bitter air of the shop, where the glimmer of gaslight polished the mahogany display cases, and within their gloomy interiors touched the curves of porcelain ointment pots, and highlighted the steely shine of medical instruments.

It was a small, narrow shop, in which every inch of space was carefully utilised. There were cabinets along its length, filled with neat rows of bottles and jars, and, above them, shelves reaching almost to the ceiling arrayed with more bottles, lined up like troops on parade. In front of the counter there was a single chair for the benefit of lady customers, and an iron stove filled with glowing coals, gamely supplying a comforting thread of warmth. Behind the counter were deep shelves of brown earthenware jars, and fat round bottles with glass stoppers, some transparent, some opaque blue or fluted green, each labelled with its contents in Latin. Below were dark rows of wooden drawers with their own equally mysterious inscriptions. Nowhere, he observed, was there any speck of dust.

Wilfred paused as a tall young woman in a plain black dress and a white apron finished serving a customer; a delicate-looking lady who shied away at the sight of his uniform and left the shop as quickly as she could.

He stepped forward. 'Good morning, Miss. May I see the proprietor?'

The young woman looked at him composedly, lacing her long fingers in front of her, a subtle glance noting the striped band on his left cuff that showed he was on duty.

'My father is unwell and resting in bed,' she said, her tone implying, in the nicest possible way, that that was the end of any conversation on *that* subject.

Wilfred, who stood five feet nine in his socks, was unused to meeting women tall enough to look him directly in the eye and found this rather disconcerting. Recalling that the business was that of Doughty & Son, he went on: 'Then may I see your brother?' He could have kicked himself as soon as the words were out.

Miss Doughty could not have been more than nineteen. She was not pretty and she knew she was not. The face was too angular, the form too thin, the shoulders too sharp. She was neat and capable, and her hair was drawn into a careful knot, threaded with a narrow piece of black ribbon. Her one article of adornment was a mourning brooch.

Her eyes betrayed for a brief moment a pain renewed. 'My brother is recently deceased.' She paused. 'If you require to see a gentleman, there is a male assistant who is on an errand but will, I am sure, return shortly. If not, then I should mention that I have worked for my father for several years.'

Wilfred, who could already see in her the makings of the kind of formidable matron who at forty years of age would be enough to terrify any

11

man, took a deep breath and launched into his prepared speech.

'You may have heard that Mr Percival Garton of Porchester Terrace died last night?'

'I have,' she replied. Bayswater was a hive of talk on all subjects, and several customers had arrived that morning eager to tell the tale, each version more dramatically embellished than the last.

Frances Doughty had never met the Gartons but they had been pointed out to her as persons of eminence. They were often, in good weather, to be seen taking the air, an anxious nursemaid following on with the children, of whom there were now five. Percival was something over medium height, with handsome features impressively bewhiskered, his figure inclining to stoutness, while Henrietta, with a prettily plump face, was ample both of bosom and waist. Frances had observed the way that Henrietta placed her hand on her husband's arm, the little glances of confidence that passed between them, the small acts of consideration that showed that, in each other's eyes at least, they were still the same graceful and slender creatures they had been on the day of their wedding. There was a delightful informality about Henrietta's pleasure in her husband's company, while Percival, at a period in life when so many men were pressed down by the cares of business and family, showed the world a smooth and untroubled brow. Bayswater society had judged them a most fortunate couple.

'Is it known how he died?' asked Frances.

'Not yet, I'm afraid. We are making enquiries about everything he ate and drank yesterday, and it is believed that he had a prescription made up at this shop.'

'I'll see.' She moved behind the wooden screen that separated the dispensing desk from the eyes of customers, and emerged with a leather-bound book which she placed on the counter. As she turned to the most recent pages, Wilfred saw that it was a record of prescriptions.

'Yes, here it is.' She pointed to some faint and wavering script that he felt sure was not hers. 'Yesterday evening – a digestive mixture.'

'I'm not sure I can read that, Miss,' said Wilfred, awkwardly. 'Is it in Latin?'

'It is. I'll show you what it means.' She fetched two round bottles from the shelf behind her, one clear and one pale blue, and placed them on the counter, then added a flat glass medicine bottle and a conical measure. 'First of all, two drachms – that is teaspoonfuls – from this bottle, tincture of nux vomica.' She pointed to the clear bottle which was half full of a brown liquid. 'The tincture is a dilute preparation from liquid extract of nux vomica which in turn is manufactured from the powdered seed. Two drachms' – her long finger pointed out the level on the measure – 'are poured into a medicine bottle this size. We then add elixir of oranges' – she indicated the pale blue bottle, which was only a quarter full – 'to make up the total to six ounces. The elixir is our own blend, syrup of oranges with cardamom and cassia. Many people take it alone as a pleasant stomachic. The whole is then shaken till mixed. The dose is one or two teaspoonfuls as required.'

'This nux vomica...' he left the question unsaid

13

but she guessed his meaning.

'The active principle is *strychnia,* commonly known as strychnine.' She saw his eyebrows climb suddenly and smiled. 'In very small amounts.'

Wilfred frowned. 'What if he took more than the proper dose?'

'I can assure you,' said Frances firmly, 'the amount of *strychnia* in this preparation is so small that Mr Garton could have swallowed the whole six ounces of his mixture and come to no harm. Also,' she turned through the pages of the book, 'It is known that Mr Garton does not have an idiosyncrasy for any of the ingredients, as he has had the mixture several times before without ill-effect.' She pointed out the entry for a previous prescription, this one in a neat legible script. 'And this is not freshly made-up stock. As you can see from the levels in the bottles, we have dispensed from this batch many times in the last few weeks.'

Wilfred nodded thoughtfully. 'Are you – er – learning to be a chemist, Miss? I've heard there are lady chemists now.'

She paused, and Wilfred, to his regret, saw once again a sadness clouding her eyes. 'One day, perhaps.' It was not the time to explain. Frances recalled the long evenings she had spent in diligent study to prepare for the examination that would have admitted her to the lecture courses of the Pharmaceutical Society, and the incident that had put a stop to her ambitions; her brother Frederick's fall from an omnibus and the injury which had sent poisons coursing through his blood. There had been two years during which she had nursed him, two years of fevers and chills

14

and growing debility, three operations to drain the pus – procedures which would have killed an older man – the inevitable wasting of strength, and decline into death at the age of twenty-four. It was a time during which her grieving father had dwindled from a hale man of fifty to a shattered ancient, becoming a second invalid requiring Frances' constant care.

'Can you advise me how much of the mixture remains in the bottle?' asked Frances. 'I really do doubt that he drank it all.'

'We do have a slight difficulty there,' admitted Wilfred. 'The maidservant was so upset she dropped the bottle and most of the medicine spilled out. We are hoping that what is left is enough for the public analyst but we have no way of knowing how much he took.'

'I see,' said Frances. 'All the same, I believe you may safely rule out Mr Garton's prescription as being of any significance in his death. When is the inquest?'

'It opens at ten tomorrow morning, at Providence Hall, but I doubt they'll do more than take evidence of identification and then adjourn for the medical reports. If you'll take my advice though, I suggest you ask your solicitor to watch the case. You never know what might be said.'

There was a sudden loud jangling of the bell and a dapper young man with over-large moustaches burst into the shop, his eyes wide with alarm. 'Miss Doughty, I met a fellow in the street and he told me–' He halted abruptly on seeing Wilfred and gasped, 'Oh my Lord!'

'Constable, this is Mr Herbert Munson, my

15

father's apprentice,' said Frances evenly. 'Mr Munson, I would beg you to be calm. The constable is merely enquiring about the prescription made for Mr Garton yesterday.'

Breathlessly, Herbert dashed to the counter and glanced at the book. 'Yes, of course. I remember it very well, I was here at the time, and I can assure you that everything was in order.' He threw off his greatcoat. 'I'll make up some samples of the stock items for you to take away. The sooner this is settled and we are cleared of suspicion the better.' He busied himself behind the counter. Despite the chill weather he was sweating slightly, and had to make an effort to steady his hands as he poured the liquids. Frances remained calmly impassive as she helped to seal and package the bottles.

'We would appreciate it, Constable,' said Frances, handing Wilfred the parcels and looking him firmly in the eye, 'if you could let us know the outcome of your enquiries.'

'Of course, Miss Doughty.'

'And should I wish to speak to you again, where can I find you?' Frances had already observed his collar number, and now produced a notebook and pencil from her apron pocket and solemnly wrote it down.

'You'll find me at Paddington Green station at either six in the morning or six at night. Just ask for Constable Brown.' He smiled. 'Good day to you, and to you Sir.' As Wilfred trudged away his thoughts turned, as they so often did during his long hours of duty, to his wife Lily, the sweetness of her face and temper, her diminutive rounded form innocent of any sharpness and angles, more

16

rounded recently since she had borne him their second child (not that he minded that at all), and how she had first melted his heart by the way she had gazed up trustingly into his face.

In the shop, Frances was deftly tidying everything away while Herbert sank weakly into the customers' chair and dabbed his brow with a handkerchief. At twenty-two he was three years older than she, and had been apprenticed to William Doughty for a year. With the death of William's son Frederick, Herbert had, without saying a word, assumed that he would in time be the heir to the business, a position which would probably require marriage to Frances. That she held no appeal for him either in form or character hardly mattered, and the fact that she would rather have been doomed to eternal spinsterhood than marry him was something he was unaware of. Slightly built and four inches shorter than Frances, he had deluded himself that his large moustaches made him an object of female admiration, and enhanced them with a pomade of his own mixing. Frances had never liked to tell him that in her opinion he used too much oil of cloves. When he was agitated, as he was now, the pointed tips quivered.

'They're saying that Mr Garton was poisoned by your father!' he gulped. 'It's all over Bayswater! They know Mr Doughty has been ill and they're saying he made a mistake and put poison in the medicine! But I can *swear* it was all right!'

'Then that is what the analysis will show,' said Frances, patiently. 'You know what Bayswater is like; by tomorrow there will be a new sensation

17

and all this will be forgotten.'

'We'd best not mention it to Mr Doughty.' He suddenly sat up straight. 'In fact, I *insist* we do not!'

Frances, who was sure she knew better than he what was best for her father, bit back her annoyance. 'I agree. I hope the matter may be disposed of without him being distressed by questioning.' She removed her apron. 'If you don't mind, Mr Munson, I shall see how he does.'

There was no direct connection between the shop premises and the family apartments above, so it was necessary for Frances to leave the shop by the customers' entrance and use the doorway immediately adjacent. Ascending by the steep staircase, Frances found the maid, Sarah, in the parlour, wielding a broom with intense application, strewing yesterday's spent tealeaves to collect the dust. Sarah had been with the Doughtys for ten years, arriving as a dumpy and sullen-looking fifteen year old. With unflagging energy and a fearless attitude to hard work, she had become indispensable. Now grown into a brawny young woman, solid, plain and unusually stern, she showed a quiet loyalty to the Doughtys that nothing could shake, and a tendency to eject by the back door any young man with the near suicidal temerity to court her.

'Mr Doughty's still asleep, Miss,' said Sarah. 'I'll bring him his tea and a bit of toast as soon as he calls.'

Frances eased open the door of her father's room. He was resting peacefully, the deep lines that grief had carved into his face softened by

18

sleep, his grey hair, which despite all Frances' attentions never looked tidy, straggling on the pillow. For two months after Frederick's death he had been an invalid, rarely from his bed, and the Pharmaceutical Society had sent along a Mr Ford to supervise the business. Frances had given her father all the care she could, but when he eventually rose from his bed, he was frail and stooped, while his mind was afflicted with a melancholy from which she feared he might never recover. Since the death of her mother, an event Frances did not recall as it had occurred when she was only three, all William Doughty's hopes for the future had rested on his son, and nothing a daughter could do was of any consolation. Frederick's clothes were still in the wardrobe, and despite Frances' pleas, William would not consent to them being given to charity. Often, she found him gazing helplessly at the stored garments and once she had found him clutching the sleeve of a suit to his face, tears falling copiously down his cheeks. Only once before her brother's death had she seen her father weep. She had been ten years old, and had asked many times to be taken to her mother's grave to lay some flowers. After many weary refusals he had relented, and on a bleak winter day took her to the cemetery where she saw a small grave marker, hardly big enough to be a headstone, bearing simply the words 'Rosetta Jane Doughty 1864'. To her horror, her father had fallen to his knees beside the stone and wept. When he had dried his eyes they went home, and she had never mentioned the matter to him again.

It was Frederick who had talked to her about

their mother. 'We had such jokes and merriment!' he would say, eyes shining. 'Sometimes we played at being lords and ladies at a grand ball, and danced until we almost fell down, we were laughing so much.' Then he took his little sister by the hand, and whirled her about the room until William came in to see what all the noise was, and suggested that they would be better employed at their lessons.

In the December that followed Frederick's death, William had once again assumed his duties in the shop. In truth, he was there only as the nominal qualified pharmacist. His professional knowledge was intact, but his hands were weaker than they had been, with a slight tremor. The work of preparing material for the stock of tinctures and extracts fell largely to Herbert and Frances. In the stockroom at the back of the main shop there was a workbench where the careful grinding, sifting and drying of raw materials was carried out, the mixing and filtering of syrups and assembling the layers of the conical percolator pot. Although William observed the work, he seemed unaware that by unspoken agreement, Herbert and Frances were also watching him. He had confined himself to making simple mixtures from stock and filling chip boxes with already prepared pills. The sprawling writing in the book recording Garton's prescription had been his. Behind the counter it was usually Frances' nimble fingers which would wrap and seal the packages so William could hand them to customers with a smile. It was the only moment when he looked like his old self.

Gazing at her sleeping father, Frances noticed,

with a tinge of concern, the small ribbed poison bottle by his bedside, which contained an ounce of chloroform. He had taken to easing himself to sleep by sprinkling a few drops on a handkerchief and draping it over his face, declaring, when Frances expressed her anxiety, that if it had benefited the Queen it could scarcely do *him* any harm.

She closed the door softly and returned to the parlour. 'Sarah, I don't know if you have heard about Mr Garton.'

'I have, Miss,' she said grimly. 'I had it off Dr Collin's maid. I don't want to upset you, but they're saying terrible lies about Mr Doughty.'

'I know,' said Frances with a sigh.

'I've heard that it's Mrs Garton herself, who's accused him. Well I've said that the poor lady is so beside herself she doesn't know what to think.'

Frances sometimes wondered if the servants of Bayswater had their own invisible telegraphy system, since it seemed that once any one of them knew something, so the rest of them instantly knew it too. 'My father mustn't be troubled with this,' she said. 'He's too unwell.'

'I know, Miss, I'll never say a word.'

Despite what Frances had said to soothe Herbert's panic, she remained deeply concerned, but there was nothing she could do except write to the family solicitor Mr Rawsthorne asking him to attend the inquest, and hope that the post-mortem examination on Percival Garton would show that he had died from some identifiable disease.

The winter season with its coughs and chills was normally a busy time in a chemist's shop, but as the day went on it became apparent that the

21

residents of Bayswater were taking their prescriptions elsewhere, while medicines made up the previous day and awaiting collection remained on the shelf. There were some sales of proprietary pills and mixtures, but Frances had the impression that the customers had only come in out of curiosity. Some asked pointedly after the health of William Doughty, and those ladies who were in the shop when he made a brief appearance later in the day, shrank back, made feeble excuses and left. William frowned and commented on the lack of custom, implying by his look that it was somehow the fault of Frances and Herbert. He seemed to be the only person in Bayswater who did not know of his assumed involvement in the death of Mr Garton. Herbert went out in the afternoon for a chemistry lecture, and returned in a state of some distress. A Mrs Bennett, a valued customer of many years, had stopped him in the street and explained at great length and with many blushes that she wanted to take a prescription to the shop and she did so like the way Herbert prepared her medicine and could he promise her that if she brought it in he would do it with his very own hands?

'I didn't know what to say!' whispered Herbert, frantically as he and Frances made up some stock syrups in the back storeroom. 'She's one of our best customers and she's afraid to come into the shop!' For the sake of the ailing man, Frances and Herbert did their best to behave as if nothing was the matter, and at four o' clock William muttered that they could see to the shop for the rest of the day, and went back upstairs to read his newspaper.

Early the following morning, Constable Brown

returned, and this time he was accompanied by a large man with a bulbous nose and coarse face who he introduced as Inspector Sharrock.

'Is Mr Doughty about?' said Sharrock, glancing quickly about the shop. 'We need to speak to him.'

'He is unwell,' said Frances. 'He is in his bedroom, resting.' Out of the corner of her eye she saw Herbert starting to panic again.

'Can't help that,' said Sharrock, brusquely. He strode up to the counter and thumped it loudly with his fist directly in front of Frances. Herbert jumped and gave a little yelp. Sharrock jutted his chin forward, with an intense stare. It was meant to intimidate, but Frances, standing her ground and clenching her fingers, could feel only disgust. 'Either he comes down here or we go up to him. You choose.'

The last thing Frances wanted was her father waking up suddenly to find strangers in the house. 'I'll fetch him,' she said, coldly. As she passed Wilfred he gave her a sympathetic look, which she ignored.

It took several minutes to prepare her father for the interview she had hoped to avoid. He was tired and seemed confused, but she explained as best she could about Garton's death and, amidst protests that he hardly knew how he could help, he agreed to speak to the police. She saw that his clothing was tidy and smoothed his hair, then brought him downstairs. When they entered the shop Sharrock put the 'Closed' sign on the door, and ushered William to the seat. 'Is this your writing, Mr Doughty?' said Sharrock, thrusting the open prescription book under William's nose, and tapping the page with a large blunt finger.

'I expect so,' said William, fumbling in his pocket for his spectacles, getting them onto his nose at the third attempt and peering at the book. Sharrock pursed his lips and gave a meaningful glance at Wilfred. 'Yes – that is my writing.'

'And did you prepare the prescription for Mr Garton?'

'Well – I – imagine I must have done. Yes – let me see – *tinctura nucis vomicae, elixir aurantii* – I believe he has been prescribed this before.'

'The thing is,' said Sharrock, 'our enquiries show that the medicine you made for Mr Garton was the only thing he had on the night of his death that was not also consumed by another person. And the doctor who examined the body is prepared to say that the cause of death was poisoning by strychnine. What do you say to *that?*'

William frowned, and his lips quivered, but he said nothing.

'Come now, Mr Doughty, an answer if you please!' Frances, trembling with anger, was about to reprimand the policeman for bullying a sick man, but realised that to plead her father's condition would only increase the suspicion against him. She came forward and stood beside her father, laying a comforting hand on his arm.

'Really, Inspector,' said William at last, 'I can't say anything other than that the mixture would not contain enough *strychnia* to kill anyone.'

Sharrock, towering over the seated man, leaned forward and pushed his face menacingly close. 'Is it possible, Mr Doughty, that you made a mistake? Could you have put in more of the tincture than

24

you thought? Or could you have put in something else instead? Something a lot stronger?'

'Inspector, I must protest!' exclaimed Herbert. 'I myself was here when the mixture was made up, and it was exactly as prescribed.' He drew himself to his full height – not a long journey – and as Sharrock stood upright and gazed down at him he quailed for a moment, the tips of his moustaches vibrating, then recovered. 'I will say so under oath if required!'

Sharrock smiled unpleasantly. 'And that is what you will have to do, Sir. I must tell you that we are working on the theory that Mr Garton was poisoned due to an error in the making up of his prescription.'

'I am sure you will find that is untrue,' said Frances quietly.

Sharrock glanced briefly at her but didn't trouble himself to reply. Instead he tucked the prescription book firmly under one arm, strode over to the shop door and turned the sign back to 'Open'.

'Inspector,' said Frances, following him before he could depart with the book. She held out her hand for it. 'If you please.'

He smiled his humourless smile. 'I'll hold onto this for the time being. Evidence. We'll take our leave now. You'll be hearing from the coroner's court very shortly. And if you'd like to take my advice, I'd say Mr Doughty looks unwell. He ought to rest.'

As Sharrock departed with Wilfred trailing unhappily after him, Herbert turned to Frances and mouthed 'What shall we do?' She shook her head in despair and returned to her father's side, taking the cool dry hand and feeling it tremble.

'He was right,' said William, in a sudden miserable understanding of his condition, 'I am unwell. I may never be well again. Perhaps I *did* poison Mr Garton.'

'No, Sir, I will swear you did not!' exclaimed Herbert.

'Come with me, Father,' urged Frances. 'You need rest and a little breakfast.'

He sighed, nodded, and went with her. Once he was comfortably settled, with Sarah keeping a careful eye on him, Frances returned to the shop.

'What did Inspector Sharrock have to say while I was fetching my father?' she asked.

Herbert shuddered. 'He wanted to see everything we have which contains *strychnia*. When I showed him the pot of extract of nux vomica in the storeroom he was very interested indeed. I told him that was where we always kept it, but he didn't believe me. He tried to imply that we usually kept it on the shelf amongst the shop rounds, and only moved it into the stockroom after Mr Garton's death to make it look less likely it could have been used in error.'

'What an unpleasant man,' said Frances.

'Miss Doughty, I want you to know that I have the most perfect belief in your father!' exclaimed Herbert. 'He is the kindest and cleverest of men!'

'Thank you Mr Munson. I value your support, and if, as you say, you observed the mixture being made, then that settles any question I might have of an error occurring here. We must wait to hear the public analyst's report, and hope that it reaches some firm conclusions. The constable informed me that most of the medicine was spilled, which is very troubling. If the inquest was to leave the matter open, it might never be resolved in the public mind.'

'What if Mrs Garton poisoned him?' suggested Herbert. 'Have the police thought of that? Perhaps she put poison in his medicine and then blamed it on your father! Wives do murder their husbands, you know.'

'Yes,' said Frances dryly, casting Herbert a pointed look, 'I am sure they do.' She paused, thoughtfully. 'But if the Inspector is determined to find my father at fault then he will not be looking for other explanations of Mr Garton's death. It is easy for us to form theories, of course, but we know almost nothing of the Gartons, their household and their circle, and only a very little of what happened on the night he died.'

'That is true,' admitted Herbert, 'But there is nothing to be done about that. It's not as if you can turn detective.'

'I think,' said Frances, with a sudden resolve, 'that is exactly what I may have to do.'

CHAPTER TWO

Having decided to become a detective, Frances soon realised that she had no idea of how to go about it. She was naturally anxious that detective work might lead her into areas inappropriate for both her sex and class, but with the reputation of the business at stake, decided that considerations of propriety might have to be cast aside. She knew that there were private detectives who advertised their services in the newspapers, but recoiled from the idea of entrusting family business to a stranger. Even had she been able to find a reliable, recommended man, her father, parsimonious to a fault, would never have sanctioned the considerable expense involved.

At the breakfast table next morning she sat deep in thought, reviewing all that she knew about Percival Garton, mainly what had been learned from the local gossips, who had flooded into the shop on the previous afternoon with rumours eagerly transmitted over their teacups. A wealthy man of independent means, and in his late forties, Garton had lived in Bayswater for more than nine years. Seized with violent convulsions at about midnight on Monday 12th January, he had expired an hour afterwards, in great agony. Garton had been born in Italy where his parents and sisters still resided, but his younger brother Cedric had been visiting Paris and was travelling to London to represent the family at the funeral. Frances took out her notebook and jotted down all the facts she knew. So engrossed was she that she quite forgot to take breakfast. A looming shadow at her side was Sarah, with a disapproving look, and Frances, feeling suddenly shrunk to the size of a nine year old, hastily helped herself to a boiled egg and bread and butter.

Frances then turned to her father's collection of books, relying principally on the *British Pharma-*

copoeia, *Squire's Companion to the Pharmacopoeia* and *Taylor's Manual of Medical Jurisprudence*. She did not believe for one moment that her father could confuse the concentrated extract of nux vomica with the more liquid tincture, and the fact that Herbert had observed the making of the mixture put any error of that kind beyond possibility. Despite Inspector Sharrock's insinuations, the extract had always been kept in the back stockroom, and to use this instead of the tincture would have been a deliberate act, not a moment of inattention to detail. Even if by some incomprehensible mischance, the extract had been used, one or two teaspoonfuls of the resulting mixture would still not have contained a fatal amount of *strychnia*, but Frances knew too well that people often took additional doses of medicine in the mistaken belief that if a teaspoonful did them good, then four would be four times as beneficial.

The timing of the attack also interested her. The symptoms of poisoning by *strychnia* could be apparent within minutes of it being taken, but only if it was present in its pure form. When taken as tincture or extract, onset could sometimes be delayed by an hour or two. She would have to wait for the analyst's report to confirm what, if anything, had been found in the medicine.

Her thoughts led her into darker waters. If the medicine had been correct when it left the shop, then poison might have been introduced into it later. This could scarcely be an accidental act. Self destruction did not appear likely in a man of Garton's obviously contented demeanour, and even if he had possessed some terrible secret which had led him to take his own life, he would surely have chosen something like Prussic acid rather than endure the long agonies of death by *strychnia*. Could it be possible that Percival Garton had been murdered? Wealthy men often had enemies, or friends and relatives jealous of their wealth. Supposing Garton had had an enemy who wished to poison him, someone closely enough acquainted with his habits to know that only he drank from the medicine bottle, someone whose presence in his house would not have been remarked upon, and who was therefore able to gain access to the bottle long enough to tamper with it. Frances realised that it was vital she follow the journey of the bottle from its leaving the shop to reaching Garton's bedside; who handled it, who knew where it was located, where and for how long it might have been left unattended, where and when it was opened; and discover, if possible, how much of the mixture he had taken.

A policeman or a real detective would have had no difficulty in finding the answers to these questions, but Frances knew that she was not in a position even to make enquiries. Still, she felt that by addressing the situation she had made some progress, and decided to start by questioning the one person she felt able to approach – Herbert. She joined him in the shop, and found him gloomily surveying the empty premises. Frances felt suddenly chilled with anxiety. Surely the loyal customers would have returned by now.

'It was one of the maidservants who brought the prescription,' said Herbert, in answer to her question. 'She waited, and took it away with her. I don't know her name, but it's always the same one they send.'

Frances nodded. 'That would be Ada. She's been with the family for many years, and has always struck me as very sensible. I shall have to speak to her.' Frances knew Ada to be a simple, honest young woman who had held a touching respect for William Doughty ever since he had provided a remedy for some trifling but painful ailment. She would now prove to be a valuable connection with the Garton household.

Herbert looked astonished. 'Do you think any person from that house will agree to an interview? It would be highly irregular.'

'I think Ada would be willing to talk to me, but I don't know any of the other servants. I have been thinking – there are some important questions that need to be asked, and I was wondering if *you* would consider approaching them. You could say that you are from the newspapers.'

Herbert gaped at her in undiluted horror. 'That is quite impossible! I flatter myself that I am well known in this neighbourhood, and I would be recognised at once. Supposing the Pharmaceutical Society was to find out that I had done such a thing? My prospects would be quite gone, and the business damaged beyond repair.'

Frances said nothing, but had to admit that Herbert was right. It was a ridiculous and dangerous idea. Despairingly she realised that the two people whom she would most have liked to interview were, in any case, utterly beyond her reach. It would have been highly improper to approach Mrs Garton, and Dr Collin would tell her no more

31

than she could glean from the newspapers.

After some further thought she composed a note to Ada and sought out Tom, the errand boy, to deliver it. Tom had worked for the Doughtys for three months but in that time had made himself entirely at home. His predecessor in the post had ended a brief and undistinguished career by being arrested for thieving, and Frances had scarcely formed the resolution to find a replacement, when Tom appeared, looking as if he had been born to the job. A small boy in that indeterminate period of life between nine and eleven, he resembled Sarah sufficiently to make it obvious that he was a member of her family, though in what way he was related to her the Doughtys had never liked to enquire. They were aware that Sarah came from a substantial brood, a family whose tendrils spread across most of the East End, and found it convenient to assume that he was a nephew. Tom shared Sarah's room and made himself generally useful at little cost, since he seemed to be able to feed himself more than adequately by scavenging. Mindful of his need to appear clean and neat in the service of a chemist, Sarah would every so often seize him by his collar, dunk him to his shoulders in a tub of water, and scrub him till his face glowed brightly enough to put Messrs Bryant and May out of business, a process that always elicited some unusual verbal expressions which Frances found both amusing and educational.

Frances found Tom in the stockroom, munching at a piece of bread almost as large as his head, and sent him off to the Gartons' house in Porchester Terrace with the note.

The next idea to occupy her thoughts was how the medicine bottle might have been tampered with. When the bottle had left the premises it had been sealed with a cork, which had first been mechanically compressed to ensure a secure fit. The bottle had then been wrapped in a sheet of white paper, the original prescription placed in a special envelope which was laid at the side of the bottle, and the whole tied with pink string. The knots of the string had then been sealed with wax, and an impression of William Doughty's own business seal.

'How easy do you think it would be for someone to introduce poison into the bottle before it was unwrapped, but without Mr Garton noticing?' Frances asked Herbert. She felt sure she knew the answer but wanted his opinion to confirm what she was already thinking.

He frowned. 'I would have thought that anything done in that way would leave some signs. How would they re-tie and re-seal the package? And once the cork was taken out it would be very obvious that the bottle was not as it left the shop.'

'Could someone have injected poison with a syringe? Then they wouldn't need to unwrap the bottle.'

There was a pause as Herbert thought about this. 'That's the kind of thing one reads about in sensational novels. Not that *you* read such things, of course. I suppose it is possible for a person of experience, but it would need a very strong needle, and would leave a hole in the paper and the cork.'

Tom returned about half an hour later with a reply in one hand and a corner of piecrust in the other. Frances unfolded the paper, and perused the contents. Ada would be able to speak to her at five o'clock. She decided to say nothing of this to Herbert.

Business remained slow and Frances could easily be spared to attend the opening of the inquest at Paddington coroner's court, William and Herbert's attendance not being required on this occasion. Providence Hall was a meeting house on Church Street near Paddington Green. Wearing her winter coat and black bonnet with a demure veil, she travelled there alone, and on foot. It was not a long walk for an active young woman, and Frances had grown too used to her father's insistence on frugality to even consider taking a cab. The hour that would be required on her return to brush mud and worse debris from her skirts, was of no concern to him. The air was cold, and heavy clouds threatened snow, but the brisk journey warmed her. There was a vestibule outside the main hall where Frances waited to speak to Mr Rawsthorne. Hovering there was a thin gentleman with a sour expression whom she recognised as Mr Marsden, a local solicitor. He was deep in conversation with a handsome, overly mannered man in his early thirties, whose pale hair and tawny skin suggested a life spent in warmer climes, and Frances wondered if this could be Cedric Garton. To her relief, Mr Rawsthorne appeared, and she at once greeted him.

'My dear young lady!' exclaimed Rawsthorne, a middle-aged man with kindly eyes who had been her father's advisor for as long as Frances could remember. He pressed her fingertips sympathetically. 'And how is Mr Doughty?'

'Improving daily,' Frances reassured him.

Rawsthorne spread his hands wide with un-feigned delight. 'I am so *very* pleased to hear that! He has given me a great deal of anxiety, and I am vastly relieved at your good news.'

'Tell me,' said Frances, 'the gentleman talking to Mr Marsden, is that Mr Garton's brother?'

'I believe that is Cedric Garton.'

Frances cast another look at Cedric, who seemed to be so enamoured of his own profile that he constantly posed to show it off to its best advantage. It suddenly occurred to her that since Cedric Garton did not know her by sight, he was her best and probably only source of reliable in-formation about the personal life of the dead man. She could approach him under a pseudonym and ask questions, and after the inquest he would return to Italy none the wiser. But what pretext could she use? The idea she had suggested to Her-bert, that of posing as a newspaper reporter, was, she felt, barred to her. It was most unlikely that she could convince Cedric that she was engaged in such a profession. She was aware that there were lady journalists for she had often heard her father speak of them disparagingly. They were, as far as she knew, mainly concerned with writing articles on literary matters, or subjects in the feminine sphere of life. Frances did not know of any lady who wrote about murder, and, if there was one, suspected that she would not be a girl of nineteen. Had she been a young man, thought Frances, she might have succeeded in such a deception.

'I regret,' said Mr Rawsthorne, 'that very little

will be achieved today. The medical reports have yet to be completed, and we cannot expect a verdict until next week. I must tell you, however, that I have heard it is very probable that the doctor will conclude that Mr Garton died of poisoning with strychnine.'

They entered the meeting room where two rows of plain chairs had been placed ready for the jury, a long table and a rather more comfortable chair for the coroner, a decidedly hard-looking chair at one end of the table for witnesses, and, in the body of the hall, rows of seating, such as might be provided for those attending a talk or a concert. Less than half the seats were filled, and Frances thought that several of the men, with well-worn suits and an air of boredom, were from the newspapers.

As Rawsthorne predicted, the proceedings took only a few minutes. Cedric, who revealed that he had no occupation other than travelling and amusing himself, stated that he had last seen Percival a year ago when visiting London, and formally identified the body as that of his brother. The enquiry was adjourned for a week.

The shop was still quiet when she returned. She reported events to Herbert, but he seemed to have something weighing powerfully on his mind, which made it impossible for him to meet her gaze. At last, he spoke.

'Miss Doughty – I understand your emotions at this time, but I have given matters a great deal of thought and it seems to me that there is a way in which this difficulty may be resolved. I suggest that your father should retire from business. He could take a holiday in some pleasant climate. I'm sure it would do him good. We could easily find a reliable man to supervise the business until I am qualified.'

Frances was silent for a moment, but she could feel a momentary rush of anger which she tried to quell. 'My father is not an old man, he is simply unwell. You have seen for yourself how much improved he has been in the last weeks. This business is his life, and his daily attendance here is instrumental in restoring him to health. Take him away from it, and he would fret. And have you no consideration for his reputation? Would you have him live out his life under a cloud of suspicion? Surely if he was to retire now, it would be taken as an admission of fault? You yourself have said that there was no fault.'

Herbert said nothing, but there was a point of red on each cheek, which had not been there before.

A new and uncomfortable thought occurred to Frances. It was a difficult subject but she had to have the answer before she could continue. 'I am afraid I must ask you this, and it may give you offence, for which I apologise. I know your loyalty to the business, and it has occurred to me that your statement to the police that you saw the mixture made, while greatly to our benefit, may not be precisely – true. If not, I will not condemn you, but for my own information, I beg you to tell me the truth now.'

'I understand why you have asked this question,' said Herbert, stiffly, 'and I invite you now, if you have any doubts as to my veracity, to bring me a Holy Bible this very minute, and I will place my hand upon it, and swear to you that I was indeed present when the mixture was made, that I observed it being made, and that it was entirely according to the prescription.'

'Thank you,' said Frances, 'I will not trouble you further on that point.'

For the remainder of the day the atmosphere in the shop was even frostier than that in the street.

At five o'clock, Frances met Ada in the anonymity of early darkness, on the Bayswater Road, where it skirted the edge of the heavily wooded enclave of Kensington Gardens. Their dark garments and obscured faces lent them the air of conspirators. Frances was sorry to make use of the maid's innocent regard for her father for her own purposes, but feared that it might be only the first such adventure of many.

'I shouldn't be talking to you, Miss Doughty,' said Ada, glancing about her fearfully, as Frances obligingly steered her into the shadows. 'I can't stay long. I told them my brother was took ill and I was fetching him some medicine. "Don't go to Doughty's then", they said. Sorry, Miss, but that's what people are saying.' She pulled a shawl about her face. Frances suddenly wondered how old Ada was. Under thirty, in all probability, but she seemed tired and her face and hands were rough and red, making her look older, and there was a wheezing in her chest that did not bode well.

'I don't want you to get into any trouble, Ada, but it's all I can think of doing to help my father. The police have questioned him cruelly, and he has been very ill.'

38

'He is a kind and generous man,' said Ada. 'I'm sure he hasn't done anything wrong.'

Frances plunged quickly into the questioning. 'Ada, when you collected the medicine for Mr Garton, who did you hand it to when you returned?'

'No one, Miss,' said Ada promptly. 'I put it on the night table in the bedroom.'

'Unopened?'

'Yes.'

'What time was that?'

Ada frowned. 'I can't say exactly – just before seven, I think, maybe ten minutes before.'

So, thought Frances, the bottle had been left unattended for some hours before it was opened. 'Can you tell me about that night? Did Mr and Mrs Garton dine at home?'

'No, Miss. They took the carriage and went out at seven. They dined at Mr and Mrs Keane's in Craven Hill. Mr Keane and Mr Garton are great friends; they often dine at each other's houses.'

'I suppose they were getting ready to go out when you returned?'

'Yes. Master was in his dressing room and Mistress was saying good-night to the children.'

'Did Mr Garton seem his normal self?'

'Oh yes.'

'And were there any visitors to the house while they were out?'

'No, Miss.'

The available time for Mrs Garton to have tampered with the bottle was hardly sufficient, thought Frances, and the risk of detection surely far too great. 'When did they return?'

'It was just after eleven. They looked into the children's room to see how they were, and retired for the night.'

'How did Mr Garton seem to you then?'

'I thought–,' Ada paused. 'He looked like he'd dined a bit too well, if you know what I mean. I saw him put his hand to himself, just there.' Ada indicated her abdomen.

'Did he say anything about it?'

'Mistress looked at him in a worried sort of way and he smiled at her and said he was all right, but he thought he had had too much pudding.' She smiled, sadly. 'Master liked his pudding.'

'What happened after that?'

'I raked out the kitchen fire and laid it ready for the morning, and then I washed and went to my bed. That was just before midnight, and I was asleep soon after. I woke up when all the commotion started. There was Mistress calling out for help, and Master groaning in pain. We were all in an uproar. I ran into the room and saw him–,' she gave a little gasp at the memory. 'Oh it was a terrible thing to see – the expression on his face – a smile like Old Nick himself, if you'll pardon me for saying it and his body all bent back.'

Frances sighed. Ada had described the rictus and convulsions that attended poisoning with *strychnia*.

'Do you know what time it was when you were awoken?'

'Just after midnight, I think.'

'And where was the bottle of medicine then?'

'I don't know Miss, it was all a lot of shouting and confusion and I can't rightly say.'

40

'Who else in the household saw what was happening?' asked Frances.

'Well, Mr Edwards – that's Master's manservant – he came in and Mistress told him to go and fetch Dr Collin. Then Mary, the nursemaid, looked in, but Mistress sent her to go and make sure the children weren't disturbed. Then she sent me to get a towel to bathe Master's face.'

'What about the other servants? What did they do?'

Ada pulled a wry face. 'Flora, she's the kitchen maid, she was so frightened by the screaming, she thought there were burglars in the house, and she put the bedclothes over her head and never came out till morning. Susan, Mistress's maid, she sleeps though any amount of noise and I had to go and wake her up. Then – Mrs Grange, the cook, and Mr Beale the coachman – they–,' she hesitated, 'they didn't arrive till a bit after everyone else.'

Frances decided to gloss over this irrelevant indecency. 'I believe you have been with the Gartons for several years.'

'Nine and a half years, ever since they came to Bayswater.'

'And the other servants?'

'Flora has been with us two years but the others, like me, were engaged when Master and Mistress took the house.'

'Ada, this is very important, did you see what happened to the medicine bottle later on? What about after you came back with the towel?'

Ada shivered, and her lower lip trembled. 'It was an accident, Miss.'

41

'I am sure it was,' said Frances, gently. She said no more but waited until Ada felt able to go on.

'When I went in, Mistress had the bottle and was holding it to her nose to smell what was in it. She was crying and saying that Master had been poisoned by his medicine. Then Master went into another fit and she ran to him, and gave me the bottle saying I had to cork it up tight – but I was that alarmed – I dropped it.'

'Do you know how much medicine was in the bottle then?'

'No, Miss, I'm sorry.'

'And what happened to the bottle?'

'I picked it up and put the cork in and put it back on the nightstand. Later on Mistress gave it to Dr Collin and told him to take it to the police.'

'Can you guess how much was spilled?'

'I'm not sure, Miss. When I cleaned it up it was a mark on the carpet about the size of my hand.'

'I don't suppose you know when Mr Garton took his medicine or how much he took?'

'I did hear Mrs Garton tell the doctor that he took it at about a quarter to twelve. I don't know how much he took, but she said he told her it had a bitter taste and was different from the other bottle he had.'

Frances felt her heart sink. Could her father's trembling hands have put more than the usual amount of tincture into the mixture? But even if he had, it would still have been far from lethal.

Ada looked around again. 'I must go, Miss, I'm sorry.'

'Ada, please, just one more moment, I need to know – did Mr Garton have any enemies? Were

42

there people he argued with, and who might have wanted to do him harm?'

Ada stared at her in astonishment. 'Oh, no, no one like that! Master was a very kind man with the nicest manners you could imagine. He was very well liked by everyone who met him.'

'And Mr and Mrs Garton; they were on good terms?'

'Oh yes, Miss, they were very affectionate. The poor lady is quite distraught. Goodbye, Miss.'

'Goodbye, Ada, and thank you for speaking to me. If there is anything else you remember–,' but Ada had disappeared into the darkness.

When Frances returned to the shop, Herbert was busy preparing an ointment, working a greasy yellow mass on a marble slab with a spatula. Presumably, thought Frances wryly, customers were still happy to purchase items for external use. She wanted to talk to Herbert about what she had learned but was reluctant to reveal that she had made an appointment with Ada and instead told him that they had met in the street by accident. She was not used to telling untruths and the words fell from her lips awkwardly, but he seemed not to notice. Perhaps, she consoled herself, it was all part of being a detective, a small sin committed to achieve a far greater good.

'I don't believe there was enough time for Mrs Garton, supposing she is our suspect, to have put poison in the medicine without leaving obvious signs of tampering in the time between the bottle being brought in and their going out,' said Frances. 'If poison was put in the bottle it must have happened while they were out.'

'Such a thing is not beyond what an intelligent servant might do, but for what reason?' observed Herbert.

'There is another possibility,' said Frances. 'Mr Garton might have had something at the house of Mr and Mrs Keane. Not at dinner, which everyone ate, but a drink, perhaps, just before he got into the carriage?'

'Then he would have suffered an attack on the way home or shortly afterwards.'

'Not necessarily. If the *strychnia* is present as nux vomica, sometimes the onset is delayed.' Herbert frowned thoughtfully, and conceded the point. 'Now, as we seem to have no customers at present, I shall go to the police station and see what more I can find out from Constable Brown.' Herbert opened his mouth to protest, but she had already departed.

By the time Frances arrived at Paddington Green Police Station, it was dark and the glow of the tall gas lamp that stood outside was curiously comforting. The building was square and heavy, a four-storey fortress with a deep basement, and a series of pointed crenellations on the roof. As a child she had imagined it to be a castle like those in Frederick's history books, and wondered if a king lived there. Frances had never entered the station, or imagined she would ever do so, but any concern at encountering the criminal classes of Paddington was necessarily thrust aside. She took a deep breath and ascended the steps to the front door. Inside she found what she assumed to be a waiting area. There was a tall deep counter, manned by a sergeant, with shelves of books and ledgers behind it. In front, there were wooden benches, where a few individuals were seated, some slumped over and dozing, others holding an animated conversation as to which of two persons had struck the other first. Voices dropped as she entered, and she realised that she was the only woman there, and the only person apart from the sergeant with any claim to neatness and cleanliness of dress. Ignoring the stares, Frances marched straight to the counter and asked the sergeant if she might see Constable Brown.

Eyebrows were raised. 'Not a personal matter, is it?'

'No, of course not!' she exclaimed, blushing. Really, what had he taken her for? 'It is a police matter.'

The sergeant looked dubious, and went through a door at the back, and a few moments later, Wilfred appeared. Without his helmet, the constable looked younger than Frances had at first supposed, no more than twenty-five, with deep chestnut hair and whiskers that needed no pomade. 'Good evening, Miss Doughty. Inspector Sharrock is out, we can talk in his office.' He conducted her to a small and dingy room, with a greatly worn desk and chairs, and shelves reaching up to the ceiling stuffed higgledy-piggledy with papers, parcels and boxes of every size and description. Frances saw with some dismay that Sharrock's desk was piled high with assorted papers in no particular order, and wondered if his mind was in similar disarray.

'I was hoping that you might have some further information about Mr Garton's death,' she said.

'I believe–,' Frances hesitated as she did not want to reveal that she had interviewed Ada, '–this is only local gossip, you understand – that Mr and Mrs Garton dined with some friends shortly before he was taken ill.'

'They did, yes, they dined with Mr James Keane, the banker, and his wife, who have been good friends for many years.' He smiled, anticipating her next question. 'You can be sure that we looked very closely at everything that was served to him there. We found that he did not eat any dish that was not also eaten by another person, and there was no drink that only he tasted.'

'I see,' said Frances, disappointed. How naïve she had been to think that any idea of hers had not already been thought of and addressed. 'And are you able to tell me Mrs Garton's account of the events of that night?' She saw him hesitate. 'Come, now, it will all be made public at the inquest next week, it will do no harm to tell me now.'

'I suppose not,' he conceded. 'Mrs Garton told us that she and her husband returned home at about eleven. The bottle of mixture was then on the night table where the maid had left it.'

'Was it still wrapped and sealed?'

'Yes, it was. Mr Garton didn't take any immediately, but some time after he had retired to bed, he complained of indigestion, and decided to take a dose.'

'What time was this?'

'About midnight, or shortly before. He got out of bed, unwrapped the bottle, and drank some of the medicine.'

'Did she say how much he took?' asked Frances, anxiously. 'One teaspoonful? Two?'

'It seems that Mr Garton was a gentleman who did not like teaspoons,' said Wilfred, ruefully. 'He found them too awkward to use. He drank it straight out of the bottle.'

'Of course,' she said pointedly, 'the mixture is quite harmless even if he had overdosed himself.'

'Yes, and I can tell you that the assay of the samples you provided from the shop has found nothing out of the ordinary. However–' he paused, unsure if he should go on, then took pity on her. 'I suppose you will hear of it soon enough. Dr Collin has said that on the basis of preliminary tests he believes it will be proved that Mr Garton died of poisoning by strychnine and that the medicine was responsible.'

She looked away, unable to meet his eyes. For a moment her throat was constricted with emotion and she dared not try to speak.

'Would you like to sit down, Miss?' Wilfred cleared some papers from a chair. It was not like Frances to admit weakness, yet she was suddenly very grateful to take advantage of that seat and recover her composure.

'Inspector Sharrock believes,' said Wilfred uncomfortably, 'that when the mixture was prepared, your father, quite by accident, used extract of nux vomica and not tincture.'

'Ridiculous, of course!' exclaimed Frances. 'I will never forgive him for his cruel treatment of my father!'

'I think it was a bit too much, though I shouldn't say so,' Wilfred admitted. 'Inspector Sharrock isn't so bad as you think, though, he's hard pressed right now, six little 'uns at home and Mrs Sharrock none too well.'

'Then I sincerely hope that she is soon fully recovered so her husband can attend to his duties in a proper manner,' said Frances, sharply. Anger had given her renewed energy, and she rose to her feet. A new thought had crossed her mind, that while the Gartons were out, someone had removed the innocent bottle dispensed by her father and substituted one with poison in. 'I would like to see the medicine bottle,' she demanded.

He was surprised, but after a moment, said, 'I'm afraid that isn't possible. The bottle isn't here, and even if it was...'

'Then what about the wrapper? Do you have that?'

His look of alarm told her what she needed to know. He hesitated. 'I suppose I can show it to you, just so long as you don't touch anything.' He brought a box down from a shelf and placed it on the desk.

Frances peered in at the contents. The box contained the envelope enclosing the original prescription, the pink string, and the sheet of plain white wrapping paper. 'Where did you find these?' she asked.

'They were in the waste paper receptacle.'

Ignoring the instructions to touch nothing, Frances lifted all the items from the box. This was probably the only chance she would ever have to examine them and she wanted to make the most of it. Wilfred almost jumped, and quickly glanced over his shoulder to check if Sharrock was in the vicinity, which he was not. 'Please!' he exclaimed.

'You're not allowed to do that, Miss! Put them back!' He was in a terrible quandary, wanting to snatch the articles from her but realising that this might make matters worse.

'I'll only be a moment,' she said. 'They won't come to any harm and you can watch what I do.' He accepted her terms, but was clearly unhappy.

The prescription was exactly as recorded in the shop's book by her father. The wax, which bore the undeniable impression of the Doughtys' own seal, was intact, and still adhered to the string and wrapping paper. The string had been cut either with scissors or a pocket-knife, and the paper was creased but undamaged. Gently, she opened out the wrapper. Pushing aside some heaped documents – they could scarcely be less tidy for her actions – she laid it flat on the desk, scanning it minutely.

'What are you looking for?' asked Wilfred.

'Evidence of tampering,' said Frances. She sighed. 'Of which I find none.' Regretfully she watched Wilfred return the items to the box and guiltily make them look as much as possible as if they had not been disturbed. 'Thank you,' she said at last. He looked at her with a sympathetic expression and she thought of asking him if she would see him at the inquest, but could not think of any reason why she would want to know this.

The following morning, the early post at the Doughtys' shop brought two letters, one each for Herbert and William, requiring them to attend the adjourned inquest to give evidence.

Time was short. If, as Constable Brown had said, the tests would support the police theory of a prescription error, Frances had only six days to identify some previously unknown enemy of Percival Garton who might have been his murderer. Even if there was no definitive proof that her father was at fault, the suspicion alone could mean the ruination of everything he had worked for, and a blot upon his reputation that nothing could ever remove. The only person she could talk to was Cedric, and if Herbert was afraid to pass himself off as a newspaper reporter she was not. There remained the difficulty of convincing Cedric that she was a lady reporter; it was something that could only be addressed in one way. It was a desperate and dangerous proceeding, but she must gather her courage and take the chance. Half afraid and half excited, Frances considered that it had, after all, been a good thing that they had not given her brother's clothes to charity.

CHAPTER THREE

With business still distressingly quiet, Herbert took the opportunity to retire to his room and study, leaving Frances to mind the shop. The only customers she saw were those openly touting for gossip, after which they shamefacedly purchased a tin of Holloway's Pills or a bottle of hair lotion. She busied herself with stocktaking and the accounts, and diverted Tom from his preferred state of idleness by asking him to dust, which he did with very ill grace.

She was thus engrossed when the door of the shop burst open violently and two men dashed in at a run. Frances looked up in alarm, but they seemed to be taking no notice of her. They were both just on the favourable side of thirty, and one, a plump, pink-faced individual dressed in venerable tweeds, began pacing briskly back and forth, blowing noisily through pursed lips, arms swinging at his sides. His shirt seemed to have lost its collar, though whether this was a recent development in its history was unclear, as was the tendency of its tail to escape the restraint normally acceptable in public. His bowler hat, a size too small, was dusty and crumpled at the brim.

'It won't do, Barstie, it just won't do!' he exclaimed. 'No, I know what you're about to say, but I won't do it! I won't give in!'

His companion, tall and slender, leaned against the doorjamb and gazed out into the street. His attitude was casual, but there was no mistaking a certain anxiety in his observation of passers-by. 'No need to get in a panic, Chas,' he said, soothingly. He was neatly dressed, but the coat, trousers and waistcoat had all seen better days and other partners, the shirt collar was frayed, and the crown of his silk hat was losing its bid to stay attached to the sides.

Chas was far from pacified. He seemed hardly to know which way to walk, turning first this way and then that, chewing his knuckles, and then when that didn't afford any relief, waved his hands wildly in the air. 'He's a thief, a crook! He's cost me money!' he exclaimed.

Barstie turned and smiled at Frances and

touched the brim of his hat. 'Excuse my friend, Miss. We've had a nice day out on the town, but unfortunately my friend met an associate who advised him that he had suffered a reverse in business, and it's rather upset his temper.'

Frances did not know what to make of the two men, except that they reminded her of a class of gentleman who often appeared in the works of Mr Dickens. At least she felt sure that they had not come to rob the shop, not that there was a great deal to take. 'Is there anything I can do to help you Sirs?' she asked.

Chas seemed to notice Frances for the first time, and abruptly changed the direction of his stride, darted over to her, and leaned heavily on the counter. 'Yes – you're to remember that we haven't been here!' then he dashed away, trailing a scent of tobacco and beer.

'I am very sorry to hear of your recent difficulties,' said Frances with controlled politeness. 'May I ask what line of business you are in?'

He whirled around to face her. 'Money,' he said. 'That's all there is. Money. Look at all your other businesses and whatever they say and do, be they a butcher or baker or–,' he looked around him having just noticed where he was, 'or a chemist – and there's only one commodity – money. See that?' he pointed to a bottle of Elliman's Universal Embrocation. 'If you know your business, Miss – and you look to me like someone who does – you would know to the farthing exactly how much that bottle cost and how much you can sell it for. And if you're clever enough – and I'm not saying you aren't because I know a great many ladies who are very clever with the shillings and pence, and there's many a house would be bankrupt without them – then you will know how much this premises costs, in rent and gas and coal, and then you will know exactly how much profit you will sell that bottle for, to the last tiny part of a farthing. That, Miss, is not a bottle of embrocation. It is money.'

'Would you care to purchase it?' asked Frances, sweetly.

Chas put his hands in his pockets, but seeming to find nothing of value there, frowned, and took them out again.

'We've had expenses,' said Barstie, regretfully. 'Tomorrow we may be men of millions, but today – we're a bit short.' He pressed his nose against the cold glass of the door. 'All quiet,' he said. 'I think it's time we were off.'

Chas rushed to the door, looked out, rushed back, and passed a sleeve across his forehead, staring at Frances. 'Right – got to go now – urgent business – not a second to waste!' Nevertheless, as he opened the door he paused, and looked back, almost as if he was treading water, arms flapping at his sides.'

'You're ... an uncommon-looking girl, if you don't mind my saying it!' He turned and hurried down the street so fast that he was obliged to hold his bowler to his head to prevent it sailing away. Barstie, with a shrug and a smile, touched the brim of his hat politely before he followed.

Frances shook her head and went back to the accounts. When she looked around to give Tom another task, she found that he had slipped away,

53

though when and where to she could not be sure. He did not come back for another hour, and when she tried to ask him where he had been, he scampered quickly out of the way.

When Herbert returned to the shop Frances was able to excuse herself, saying that she had household duties. After seeing that her father was resting, and reassuring him that his presence at the counter was not required, she entered the room where her brother had slept and studied and died.

As Frances touched the sleeve of her brother's suit she felt, for a moment, too full of emotion to move. Grief had been something she had not permitted herself to show openly. It was bundled and knotted tightly inside her, bound hard lest it break out and render her incapable of function. Merriment, too, was a thing of the past. She felt sure she would never be merry again. Her life was determined by duty; duty to her sick father, duty to the household, keeping the accounts correct to the last farthing and grain of rice, and the never-ending cycle of work in which she assisted Sarah where two pairs of hands were needed, battling the constantly encroaching London grime, boiling and pounding and starching and drying what seemed like acres of linen; and duty to the business, her father's one remaining treasure, the thing that gave meaning to his years of study and toil. From the earliest moment of the day, when she polished the mahogany counter, something that had been her task since the age of seven, to the last piece of mending as she sat by the parlour fire, her eyes beginning to close with sleep, it was her efforts and her attention that ensured the smooth running of home and business. Had Frances succumbed to her emotions, and neglected her duties, she would have despised herself, as being no more use than one of those elegant ladies who professed themselves exhausted after a little shopping, and called for a smelling bottle when in two minds over the best way to trim a hat.

She reassured herself that it was not disrespectful to her brother's memory to use his clothes for a masquerade to save the business from ruin. He would, she knew, have heartily approved. She had worn his clothing once before, some five years ago, as a delightful prank they had devised together. It was a Christmas entertainment, and they had copied some poems, jokes and comic dialogues from the newspapers and invited a modest audience to take tea. Some of the wittiest exchanges were between two gentlemen, and it had been Frederick's idea for Frances to play the part of a young man, and he had helped to dress her in his suit. It was a little long in the leg and wide at the hip but a few pins corrected that, and he laughed at her efforts to swagger like a boy. 'Now then, you must hold your body like this, and take a good long stride, not little trotting steps, and try and imagine yourself a fine fellow, a real roistering Jack, with all the girls sweet on you.' They invited a neighbour, and their father's sister Mrs Scorer, who had looked after Frances and Fredrick after their mother died, also their mother's brother, Cornelius Martin. Mrs Scorer, the former Miss Maude Doughty, had managed the household until Frances was thirteen, when much to the disgust of William, who had thought that this useful and thrifty arrangement would last forever, she insisted at the age of forty-five on marrying the first man who asked her, a coal merchant twenty years her senior who died two years later, leaving her £4,000 the richer. Mrs Scorer was a calm, organising sort of woman who seemed to despise tender affection – at least, she had never shown any to her niece and nephew. She was neither harsh nor kind, but believed in attending to practical wants in the way of food and clothing, without thinking very much about the individual concerned. Frances was very fond of her Uncle Cornelius. She recalled gloomy visits that must have happened after her mother's death, when he and her father had sat together for hours at a time and talked in low voices. As he departed, he had smiled at her and Frederick, and given them pennies and peppermints, so she thought he was not a sad person in himself, rather a man made sad by circumstances. Cornelius' wife, Phoebe, had died some years ago. He often spoke of her with affection and said how much he missed her company, and how he regretted that they had had no family. Occasionally he had taken Frederick and Frances out for the day, excursions which she had always anticipated with great excitement. She had never been disappointed. Sometimes they had ridden in a carriage, sometimes they had gone to Paddington Station and taken a train, always they had explored places that seemed foreign and wonderful, and then they had had tea. Her father had grudgingly allowed these adventures on the condition that they were educational in nature, with admonitions to Cornelius not to allow the children too much freedom. Aunt Maude had never attempted to conceal the fact that she viewed the absence of her charges with some relief.

At the Christmas of 1874, when Frances was fourteen and Frederick nineteen, their entertainment had been received politely. Uncle Cornelius had laughed at the jokes, and even her father had admitted that it was not without wit. It was their neighbour, an elderly, slightly deaf lady called Mrs Johnstone, a vision in yards of black bombazine wrapped in an Indian shawl, who concentrated most of her attention on the tea and sandwiches and asked afterwards who the 'other boy' had been.

Five years later, the trousers that had been too long were, if anything, a little short in the leg, but no worse than Frances had observed worn by young men who had seen a good thing in the pawnshop and wanted to wear it no matter what. It was as she considered how best to hide her hair in her brother's best round hat, that she heard a little gasp behind her, and turned to see Sarah in the doorway. It said much for Sarah's nerves that grasping a pail full of dusters and brushes, she had dropped none of them.

'Oh, Miss, I had such a fright just then!' she exclaimed.

'I'm sorry, Sarah,' said Frances, realising that the sight of a figure dressed in Frederick's suit would have caused a less sturdily unflappable woman to faint with terror. 'Come in, I don't want anyone else to see me in these clothes.'

Sarah obeyed and shut the door, then stood

looking at Frances, round-eyed with anxiety. Questions were quivering on her lips but remained unspoken.

'I hope you don't think this is just some silliness,' said Frances, awkwardly. 'I have decided that I must find out more about Mr Garton, to see if he had any enemies who might have wanted to harm him. If I do not, I am very afraid that the coroner will conclude that there was a mistake in the prescription, and then the inquest will blame his death on my father. I asked Mr Munson if he would pretend to be from the newspapers and ask Mr Cedric Garton some questions about his brother, but he refused, so I have determined to try it myself. I thought I would succeed better if I portrayed myself as a young man.' She sighed, suddenly realising how dreadfully alone she was in this task. Any member of her family, any of her small circle of acquaintances, would surely have been horrified at what she was about to attempt. Sarah, on the other hand, having got over her initial fright was now gazing at her calmly, as if studying how well she looked.

'I imagined Mr Munson would be a help to me, but I have been disappointed,' said Frances.

Sarah set her mouth in a firm line. 'It's not my place to say it, Miss, but Mr Munson–,' she hesitated. 'Well – it's not my place to say it.'

Frances raised her eyebrows. 'Sarah, I do believe you were about to say something very uncomplimentary about Mr Munson' she said.

Sarah gave a sniff of disapproval, and squared her broad shoulders. 'Yes, Miss, I do believe I was.' There was a smile of understanding between the two women.

'So – how do I appear?' Frances struck what she hoped was a masculine attitude.

Sarah took a few moments to look at her critically. 'It would do well for a pantomime, Miss.'

'Oh!' said Frances. She sighed. 'Perhaps it was silliness after all.'

'Well you ain't got the collar right for a start. Let me see what I can do. I got eight brothers, Miss and none of them could dress like a gent.'

Sarah put down the cleaning tools and began to work on Frances' costume in earnest, tugging here, adjusting there, and finally stepping back to survey her work. 'That looks more like it. Now you need to stand and walk right, or it'll never do. And let your voice go lower.' Some minutes of practice ensued. 'Have you decided, Miss, how you will try to meet with Mr Garton? I don't think it'll do to go up to the house.'

'No,' said Frances, frowning at this new difficulty. 'I hadn't thought of that, but you are right. I expect anyone from the newspapers will not be allowed in.'

'Why don't I get Tom to keep a watch and tell you when Mr Garton goes out? Then perhaps you can think up a way of speaking to him.'

'Yes, that is the best plan, I think. And Sarah, there's something else I need. On the night of his death Mr Percival Garton dined at the home of his friend Mr James Keane, who is a banker. I know nothing of Mr Keane's household. Can you think of any way that I could speak to someone there?'

Sarah thought for a moment. 'I'll see what I can do, Miss.'

When Frances returned to the shop she knew the moment she entered that there was an unusual visitor. An aroma reached her nostrils of something unsavoury – not exactly dead but in a state of decay – something which had not been pleasant to smell even in that distant time when it had been fresh. A man stood beside the door who seemed at first glance to be very aged, but who, on a further moment's inspection, could not have been a great deal more than twenty-five. His thin body was clad in black, greasy garments that looked as though they might have been stolen from a corpse, and his hair hung raggedly about a pale, narrow face seamed with grime. He leaned against the wall, head bent over his hands, picking at filthy nails with what appeared to be a filleting knife, a sly grin on his lips. There were, Frances was well aware, parts of London where this man could pass unnoticed, where the streets were no less dark and greasy, and smelt much the same.

Herbert was not standing at the counter, but cowered as far as he could be from the new arrival, his back pressed against the shelves, his body rigid with fear. 'Ah ... Miss Doughty ... perhaps you may be able to assist this gentleman. He is looking for some friends of his.'

'That's right, Miss,' said their visitor in an unexpectedly soft voice. 'Two associates, who, if I could discover their whereabouts, would find it to their advantage.'

'Perhaps you could tell me their names, or describe them to me,' said Frances, not sure that anyone could benefit from acquaintance with the

60

person before her.

'Charlie Knight is one; round-faced cove; and t'other is Sebastian Turner, likes to dress as a toff. I've heard they were in the Grove today.'

Frances paused, unsure what to say. She abhorred a direct lie, yet she felt disinclined to offer any information about her recent visitors. She was relieved from her dilemma by Tom's voice behind her.

'*I* seen 'em Mister.'

'Oh? Where?' The stranger uncurled himself swiftly, like a spider darting towards its prey. He wiped the knife on his hip, thrust the blade into a battered leather sheath and slipped it into his pocket.

'They was walking down the Grove this mornin', goin' to the station. I noticed them partic'lar – couple of fly gents with a sneaking look about 'em. I went after 'em for a yannep but they didn't have none. I heard 'em say they was goin' up to Birmingham on business.'

The man looked at Tom, thoughtfully. 'Do you know when they return?'

'They di'n't say.'

He lunged closer. 'You'll keep a lookout for me? Tell me when they come back? There'll be something in it for you when I get the news. And something for them, too.'

Tom nodded. He didn't ask the man where he must go in order to impart the news, and Frances had the uncomfortable feeling that Tom was well aware of where such a man might be found on those occasions when he wished to be. She studied Tom's face for a moment, trying to see if he was

61

telling the truth. He was the picture of artless innocence, a matter she thought highly suspicious, as that was not his normal expression. When she looked around again, the man had gone, and he had managed to depart without disturbing the shop bell. Wordlessly, Frances polished the counter for a second time that day, and wiped down that part of the wall where the man had leaned, wondering what the 'yannep' might be that Tom had wanted, and, like so many of his curious words, solved the mystery merely by sounding it in reverse.

That afternoon Ada scurried into the shop, looking guiltily around her as if afraid to be seen. 'Oh Miss, I was just passing and had to come in and speak with you. I can only stop a minute though; they mustn't know I was here!'

'Come into the storeroom, we can talk there,' said Frances, deliberately ignoring Herbert's frown of disapproval.

Ada followed her behind the counter, and for a few moments stood in awe of the deep shelves of grim brown bottles, giant carboys, and barrels and sacks of raw materials. There was a workbench, which held the larger pieces of equipment, and items such as infusions that needed to be left undisturbed. On that day, there were shining metal suppository moulds, sitting in rows with their glistening gelatinous contents. Everything was spotlessly clean and laid out neatly, and every stock container was labelled with care. Frances hoped Ada was thinking how hard it must be to make a mistake when all was in such good order.

'Well, Miss I expect you know that the police have been at the house for ever so long, asking questions about what Mr Garton ate and drank before he died, and poking about in the kitchen and pantry, not that they ever found anything wrong.' She paused, breathlessly. 'The thing is – Mr Edwards – Master's manservant as was – he remembered something after the police went. Master used to have a flask of brandy in the carriage – just to keep the cold out, you understand – and Mr Edwards said that as he stood on the step when Master and Mistress drove away, he was sure he saw Master take a drink.'

'That would have been at seven o clock?' said Frances.

'Yes, Miss. So Mr Edwards asked Mrs Grange if he ought to tell the police what he remembered, and she said he might if he wished, but she didn't think it signified, as if there had been anything in the brandy then Mr Garton would have been took ill a lot sooner.'

'Which is true,' admitted Frances. 'Did Mr Edwards go to the police?'

'I don't know, Miss. I don't think so. He's been given his notice so he's out a great deal looking for another position. The thing is, I was thinking about it and it came to me – even if what Mrs Grange said was right, and it can't have been anything Master had at seven o'clock – well – it was an awful cold night – he might have had some brandy later, on the way home.'

There was silence for a moment, as Frances digested this thought. 'That means that the brandy was uncontaminated at seven o'clock, and if there *was* anything in it, it must have been put there between seven and eleven that evening. Who would have known that the brandy was there?'

Ada frowned. 'I did, Miss, and Mr Edwards, and Mrs Grange, and Mistress of course, and I suppose anyone who travelled in the carriage with him.'

'But surely the carriage cannot have been kept waiting outside Mr Keane's house all the time your master and mistress were inside?'

'No, Miss, on account of the weather. Master didn't like the horses to stand in the cold for too long, so Mr Beale brought the carriage back then went out later to bring Master and Mistress home. But it was standing outside Mr Keane's house for a little while after seven, about ten minutes perhaps. Mr Keane's cook is very fond of Mr Beale and invited him in for a nip of something. He told us about it later. He got a boy to hold the horses while he was away, but it was that dark, anyone could have sneaked in, and you know what these boys are like, take your penny and run off, most of them.'

'Or of course, someone could have tampered with the brandy when the carriage was in Mr Garton's coach house.' Frances paced up and down thoughtfully. 'What has Mrs Garton said about her husband drinking brandy that evening? Does she remember it?'

Ada shook her head, sorrowfully. 'Poor lady hardly knows what day of the week it is, and that's a fact. She tries to remember, but all she can do is cry.'

'I think this could be very important,' said

Frances. 'You must go to the police and tell them what you have just told me.'

'Oh no, I daren't go near them!' exclaimed Ada, horrified. 'Everyone in the house has been told not to. I'd lose my place and my character, and I'd miss the children so much! Please don't make me do it!'

Frances tried to calm Ada, who hurried away with many a nervous glance over her shoulder, but it was clear that the police ought to be informed, and so she composed a note to Constable Brown. When Tom arrived back to say that Cedric Garton had gone out for a drive, she got hold of him before he could run away and gave him the note to deliver.

Later that afternoon, Sarah, who had been out buying fish for supper, returned with a brown paper parcel and an expression of quiet triumph. 'I can tell you all about Mr Keane,' she told Frances, and they hurried to the kitchen, where the fish was unwrapped and cut in pieces to be fried. 'Mr Keane is a gentleman of thirty-six or thereabouts, and has lived here more than ten years. By all accounts he's quite high up at the Bayswater Bank, but when he came here he was no more than a clerk and had no fortune at all. Then he courted Miss Morgan – she's the only daughter of Mr Morgan the fancy milliner. He's Thomas Morgan Ltd, now, with that big shop on the Grove. He was none too happy about the match but Mr Keane was a very handsome young man, and Miss Morgan very wilful and she *would* have him, and her father was very doting, so it came off. But I've heard say lately that Mr Keane is indifferent to his wife on account of her having become very fat, and she was no great beauty before, and Mrs Keane is very unhappy and takes wine a little too often, and Mr Keane and Mr Morgan only speak to each other when they have to. It's a very unhappy place, Miss, and there's many servants won't stop there for long. Two weeks ago, Mr and Mrs Keane had a terrible quarrel, a real upper and downer. One of the maids overheard it – she was polishing the keyhole of the study–'

'With her ear, no doubt,' said Frances, dryly.

'Very likely, Miss.' Sarah paused. 'Miss, I hope you don't think that *I*–'

'Please, go on,' said Frances.

'Well she didn't exactly hear what the quarrel was about, but she said that Mr Garton was mentioned a number of times.'

'What is this maid's name?' asked Frances.

'Ettie, Miss. Her brother Harry is a friend of John Scott who drives a delivery cart for Whiteleys who is the sweetheart of my cousin Mary what works on the fish counter.'

Frances decided not to try and follow these convolutions. 'I think I should like to speak to Ettie,' she said. 'I wonder how that might be arranged?'

'I've been thinking about that, Miss and it would need a bit of play acting which I know you won't mind, and a cake.'

'A cake?'

'Yes, Miss. Ettie likes cake, and so do the other servants, only they don't often get much in the way of leftovers as Mrs Keane is very fond of cake as well.'

Frances nodded in sudden understanding. 'So if there's a cake in the kitchen...'

'Yes, Miss. They'll all come for a slice.'

'Then,' said Frances, 'it should be a large cake, and made with best butter.'

Saturday morning's *Bayswater Chronicle* contained only a short paragraph about Percival Garton confirming that he was forty-eight years of age, had lived in Bayswater since 1870 and was the father of five children, the eldest of whom was eight. The weather remained cold, and there was a stiff breeze, with a dull sky threatening rain. Herbert was behind the counter with half his attention on the Pharmacopoeia, and Frances was trying to coax the stove into giving out a little more warmth when Tom appeared in the doorway. 'That gentleman you want to talk to, 'e's left the 'ouse and is walkin' up the Grove,' he said.

Frances gave a sudden shiver of terror. Having planned and rehearsed her role as a young reporter, she found herself giving in to a moment of weakness. She now saw that the imposture was both foolish and fraught with peril, and decided that she should not attempt it after all.

'What gentleman is this?' asked Herbert, suspiciously.

'That is not something you need to know,' said Frances, briskly dusting the stove-top.

'If it concerns the business then I *should* know,' he said firmly, putting the book down. 'I *insist* you tell me at once.'

Irked by his manner, Frances found a new

resolve. This might be the only chance she would ever have of interviewing Cedric Garton. She must not allow fear to stop her from doing what was necessary. Her hands shook as she folded the duster. 'Kindly mind the shop. I will not be out long.' Herbert looked deeply affronted at this snub to his masculine authority, but before he could reply she had put on her coat and left. He did not see her hurry to the family apartments where Sarah was waiting to transform her. The masquerade was about to begin.

CHAPTER FOUR

That morning, a passer-by on Westbourne Grove who saw a young man emerging cautiously from the private door beside William Doughty's chemist's shop might have thought him a queer sort of person. He first peeped out, turning his head this way and that, and then eased himself from the doorway like a butterfly squeezing from its pupal case. On the street, he again looked around him, as one familiar with the Grove who was, nevertheless, seeing it for the first time. Above middling height, he was thin, yet pleasingly broad of shoulder, with a strong jaw which would have looked out of place on a woman, but lent his masculine face an air of authority and determination. He was perhaps less than twenty, and must have grown too fast for his suit which was a little short in the leg. Setting off, he began at first with odd, short, almost girlish steps, which he lengthened to a self-conscious stride, moving up the Grove in the direction of Queen's Road. The walk seemed to do him good. He had appeared at first to be a young man with more cares pressing upon him than was appropriate for someone of his age, but as the perambulation continued, his body straightened, his shoulders moved back, and he breathed deeply, his confidence growing with each moment. When he crossed over the road, he dodged the carriages with alacrity, and smiled as if the act of running was a pleasure in itself.

As he neared the row of Whiteleys shops, he paused and looked around him once more. He was either an idle individual who had nothing to do with his time but waste it, or else he was waiting for someone. He walked slowly up the parade, then turned and came back again. He sauntered, he strolled, he lounged, he loafed, and finally stopped and looked in one of the windows, every so often glancing out of the corner of his eye at the throng of people who also haunted the Grove. He stared for a while at a display of ladies' mantles, then seemed to recollect himself with a start and moved to another window of gentlemen's hats, sticks and whips. Another gentleman, tall with a boyish lick of blond hair and suntanned face, was also walking along the Grove and stopped to gaze into the same window. His elegantly tailored suit of clothes was cloaked in a heavy dark coat with a fur collar, yet he was shivering.

'Damn me, but it's cold' he exclaimed.

Frances gave a start. No one had ever addressed her in quite that way before. Having seen Cedric

69

Garton walking towards her, she had been wondering how she might approach him, and now found that he had approached her. She swallowed and coughed to try and temper her voice. 'Indeed,' she said softly, still staring straight ahead.

'You look like a knowledgeable young fellow. I don't suppose you know somewhere hereabouts where one might go to keep warm?'

'There are restaurants and teashops on the Grove, and Whiteleys, of course. I have heard they do a very good luncheon, if you don't mind being bothered by the idle chatter of ladies.' She smiled to herself at this little characterisation.

Cedric looked around to check that no one was near enough to hear his words, and leaned towards her. 'I was hoping you might direct me to somewhere more private,' he muttered. 'Somewhere we might go together and become better acquainted.'

It took a moment or two for his meaning to become apparent, and when it did her heart sank. It was what Frances had dreaded, and worse. Not only had he seen through her poor disguise, he had taken her to be an immoral kind of woman.

'I am sure I don't know what you mean, Sir,' she said, intending it to be a firm reprimand although it came out as a nervous gulp.

He moved closer still. 'Come on, lad,' he whispered, in what he obviously hoped was a persuasive manner. 'I know what you're about. I've been watching you. You've been parading the goods up and down the street for everyone to see.' He smiled, understandingly. 'New at the game, I expect. Don't you worry about that; I know how to be kind to a young man if he can be kind to me.'

Frances was struck dumb, her mind in momentary confusion. Trying to understand what was
happening, she suddenly recalled an incident
some years ago when her brother had been snig-
gering at an article in the newspaper regarding the
trial of a man on charges which the paper was able
neither to name nor describe, but which involved
another man. Her father, sensing from Frederick's
half-stifled amusement that he was reading
something indecent, and seeing Frances looking
over her brother's shoulder, had snatched the
paper from him. When he saw the article his face
went pale with rage and he at once threw the offending item on the fire. Afterwards he had written
to the editor to complain about the publication of
such filth. Later, Frederick had told Frances that
there were such things as 'lady men' but all that
she could gather was that this was a class of person
in whose company a lady could be confident that
she would be in no danger of insult.

One thing at least was clear; by attempting to
importune someone he thought was a young
man, Cedric was risking arrest and imprison-
ment. The knowledge made her bolder. 'I think
you should know, Sir,' she said with great dignity
'that you have entirely mistaken me. I was hoping
to make your acquaintance, but it was for the
purpose of interviewing you for the newspapers.
I wished to speak to you about your late brother,
but it seems to me now that I shall be writing an
altogether different piece.'

She was pleased to see that this had the desired
effect. 'You would not dare!' exclaimed Cedric,
recoiling in alarm.

71

'If you think that, Sir, then you do not know the *Bayswater and Kensington Examiner!*' declared Frances, which was true because no such newspaper existed. 'We are fearless to print the truth, however shocking it may be.'

Cedric looked about him as if wondering whether to run away, but thought better of it. 'I will deny everything,' he said.

'Better still, Sir,' she said archly, 'I might be persuaded not to write of what has just happened here.'

With a sigh of resignation Cedric reached into his pocket.

'I did not speak of money,' said Frances, with an offended air. 'Grant me an interview about your late brother, and we will say no more of it.'

He groaned. 'I can't! Henrietta will never speak to me again!'

'I promise that your name will nowhere be mentioned.'

There was a long pause, during which they both stared into the shop window and shivered. 'Oh, very well,' said Cedric, at last. 'But let's get out of this damned cold!' They started to walk down the Grove together.

Frances was hoping they might find a teashop which sold the kind of pastries she regarded as a rare treat, but just then it began to rain, heavy cold drops which stung her cheeks. Cedric, brushing the offending water from his luxurious collar in alarm, said, 'Quickly! In here!' seized her by the arm and almost pulled her into the Redan public house that occupied the corner of the Grove and Queen's Road. Frances had never entered this or any other public house before. It was crowded with men in the coarse working clothes of cab drivers, artisans, and labourers, and a few faded-looking women, some without bonnets, whose profession she preferred not to contemplate. A small group of men in threadbare yet better quality attire were probably artists looking for inspiration in the coarse faces around them, or in the liquor bottle, or both. They favoured unusually colourful cravats, and brought flashes of bright green, orange and purple to the otherwise gloomy interior. The air was blue-grey with tobacco smoke, but it was warm, for a hearty fire blazed in the grate, adding the tang of burning coals to the already heady atmosphere.

'Dear God, what kind of place is this!' exclaimed Cedric.

'It is not the kind of establishment a respectable gentleman would frequent,' said Frances, faintly. 'I suggest we leave.'

Cedric glanced out of the window, where the rain was intensifying. 'It's got a good fire. The roof doesn't leak. Any port in a storm, as the sailor boys say.'

There was a row of compartments in front of the long bar with benches and a table in each. All were occupied, but Cedric stepped up to a morose-looking man who sat hunched in a corner by himself, smoking a pipe. 'My nephew and I wish to converse alone, Sir,' he said. 'We would take it as a great favour if you would seat yourself elsewhere.' The pipe smoker did not move apart from his mouth, which opened for an imprecation. 'And you may have a drink for your trouble,' Cedric added. Coins flashed, there was a mumbled 'thank you, Sir' and moments later Cedric and Frances had the compartment to themselves. Cedric wiped the benches with a large pocket handkerchief and they sat down.

'I would order something to drink, but I think this is the kind of establishment where I would prefer not to sample the *spécialité de la maison*,' observed Cedric. Frances hastily agreed. Cedric produced a silver case from his pocket, which he opened, and offered Frances a cigar.

'No thank you,' she said, not prepared to carry her performance quite so far. She took out her notebook and pencil, and Cedric gazed at her in amusement as she laid them neatly on the table before her. He lit his cigar and settled back. Having recovered from his shock he was now the more relaxed of the pair. 'I don't believe I caught your name, Mr –?'

'Williamson,' said Frances.

He leaned forward with what he probably hoped was an engaging smile. 'You can call me Cedric if you like.'

'I don't think so,' said Frances curtly.

He shrugged and settled back. 'Let the questioning begin.'

Frances opened the notebook and took up the pencil. 'I would like to know something of your brother's early life and character.' She was somewhat concerned that Cedric would be instantly afflicted with grief, but he seemed more regretful than anything.

'Well he was born in Italy, as we all were. Father was a wine merchant. Percy came to England

74

around the end of '56.'

'For what purpose?'

'Grandfather ran a small shipping business out of Bristol. When his partner died he needed a man to assist him. Percy was the man.'

Frances became aware that behind the bar, a middle-aged man, probably the landlord from the cut of his clothes, and a woman almost certainly his wife judging by the number of flounces on her costume, were standing side by side, pretending to polish glasses, their gaze fixed firmly on Frances and her companion. She pushed her hat more firmly down on her head. One of the barmen was ordered by his employer to come and hover expectantly by their table but Cedric waved him away casually, as if swatting a fly.

Frances realised her face was reddening. Cedric had noticed, and smiled at what he saw. Nevertheless she pressed on with her questioning. 'Why did he select your brother?'

'There was really no other choice. Father had his own business to attend to, I was too young, and he could hardly send one of the girls.'

'Was he pleased to come to England?' asked Frances, wondering if Percival Garton had resented the enforced uprooting.

'Oh yes. Not so much for the business – he found that rather dull – but he had always fancied himself as the English country gentleman. He bought a house in some out of the way village in Gloucestershire – what was the name, now – Tollington Mill, that was it – and I believe he enjoyed the life there. He used to write to us a great deal, and he never said much about trade, it was all about the house and the countryside and how they amused themselves.'

'How *did* your brother amuse himself?' asked Frances.

'Oh the usual kind of thing one does in that part of the world,' said Cedric, airily. 'Reading, walking. I'm not sure what else. It sounds dreadfully dull to me, but Percy liked it well enough. I remember he had a great fancy that he could be an artist, and he and another gentleman used to go on walks to view the countryside and make sketches. He sent us some of his drawings.'

'Did he have great talent as an artist?'

Cedric looked thoughtful. 'I would say – none whatsoever. But it pleased him.'

'Did he have many friends there? And in Bristol?'

'There were business acquaintances, of course, and the more gentrified of the village folk.'

Frances hesitated. After the opening enquiries, which had given her a picture of the man and his mode of life, the next question was going to be the difficult one. 'Was there anyone with whom he was on bad terms?'

Cedric reacted with surprise. 'Great heavens, no! Percy was never the sort one could take exception to, if you know what I mean. He was good company, undemanding on the intellect, a friendly, confiding sort of fellow, and from what Henrietta has said, the best of husbands

'When did they marry?'

'62, I think. Henrietta was a relative of Grandfather's old partner. That was how they were first introduced.'

Frances looked back at her earlier notes. 'So they were married quite some years before they came to Bayswater. That was in 1870, I believe. Are there older children away at school?'

Cedric paused, and spent a few moments tapping out the ash on his cigar. 'No, there are not.' There was something in his manner, the way he had suddenly dropped his voice and avoided her gaze, that told Frances it was a question he found uncomfortable.

She continued the gentle probing. 'What brought your brother to Bayswater? Was it business?'

The trace of awkwardness in his manner remained. 'Oh no, the business was sold just before they came here. Grandfather died in '64 and left everything to Percy. He did well, by all accounts, and by the time he came to London he had means enough to live off his principal.'

'But he had lost his desire to be a country gentleman?' she persisted. 'Given his tastes in that regard, I cannot understand why he came to live in London when there was no pressing need.'

Cedric drummed his fingertips on the table. 'There are private family matters which have no relevance here and I would not see anything published that would add to Henrietta's distress.'

'Would you accept my promise that I would publish nothing to distress a lady, especially one already labouring under such a burden of loss?'

'Ah, a promise of discretion from a newspaper man,' he said with a humourless smile, 'how that inspires me with confidence!'

Whatever she had uncovered, Frances could

77

not let the moment escape. She leaned forward suddenly. 'I am not the only person who will ask you these questions,' she said. 'Do you know that many people in Bayswater are wondering if your brother's death could have been something more sinister than an accident? Anything unusual in his past life might come under scrutiny.'

His expression told her that this was not an eventuality he would relish. 'That is, of course, an outrageous suggestion, but then I suppose we cannot control low gossip. What do *you* believe, Mr Williamson?'

She looked him firmly in the eye. 'I believe that every effort should be made to uncover the truth, whatever that may be.'

He favoured her with a wintry smile. 'But if a lie is more sensational then you will print the lie.'

Frances closed the notebook with a snap, and put the pencil down. 'There. There will be no record of what you say.'

He looked at her closely. 'So young, and yet so forceful. Well there was nothing irregular about the move to Bayswater. It was entirely a personal matter. A question of some delicacy, not for the public prints.' He stubbed out the cigar. 'I think I will have something to drink after all.' He looked around and waved an arm at one of the potmen. 'You! Brandy to this table! Two glasses, and mind they are clean. And bring a fresh bottle!' He turned to Frances. 'Not that viewing the label will be any guarantee of what is within.' There was a certain amount of scurrying about and whispering behind the bar before someone went down to the cellar. Brandy was not a commonly ordered drink, being more expensive than the other spirits, and the prospect of a sale aroused some excitement.

Frances decided not to protest, in the hope that the liquor would loosen his tongue. She had occasionally sampled wine and sherry but never brandy, and found alcoholic drinks a little heady.

The bottle arrived, and Cedric cleaned the dust off the label and nodded. 'I expect I have had worse than this, though I can't recall exactly when.' He poured two glassfuls and pushed one across the table to Frances, then took a good pull from his own. 'Oh my blessed aunt!' he said, shaking his head. 'I can't say I would recommend this as an after-dinner digestive, but it reaches all the right places on the way down.'

'You were about to tell me the reason why your brother came to London from the countryside,' said Frances.

'I was,' said Cedric, staring into his glass. He took another drink. 'I don't suppose you have met Henrietta?'

'No, I have only seen her in the Grove.'

'Well, you might not believe it to look at her now, but in her younger days she was considered to have a delicate constitution. If you were to see her engagement portrait you would hardly think it was of the same woman. She had that fragile look you see in females you would swear are not long for this world. When Percy and Henrietta had been married a number of years and were still without a family, they consulted a doctor who said that her health would never permit her to be a mother. After that they saw a great many more doctors, the best men in the country, and all of them said the same thing. And then they heard about a new man, with a clinic in London, who was reputed to be able to cure ladies with a similar complaint. Percy had been intending to give up business in any case, and they sold their house and came to London. So now you know. I can assure you that it is not something either of them chose to discuss except with immediate family.'

'Do you know the name of the doctor or the clinic?' asked Frances.

'No, I can't say I do, in fact I'm not sure Percy ever mentioned them. But the move bore fruit – quite literally. Less than a year after they came to London little Rhoda was born, and a miraculously robust child too, when one considers the poor health of her mother.'

'And, as I have observed myself, there are now five children.'

'Indeed. All in the very pink. I can *especially* testify to the new baby's splendid lung power. And motherhood has suited Henrietta. Percy used to say that she grew stronger with each one.'

'And what of your brother's health? Did he ever dose himself with proprietary medicines?' asked Frances, hopefully.

'No, apart from his indigestion he was always in excellent health. The last time I saw him alive he looked very well. And the only medicine I have ever known him take was that infernal mixture he got from the chemist.' Cedric was a little heated by this, and Frances changed the subject.

'Did they never consider a move back to the country?'

He shook his head and poured another brandy. 'I don't believe so. London to my mind was the making of Percy, although sadly it also meant his destruction. He was a less dull fellow here. I think he found more to engage his interest.'

'How did he occupy himself?'

'Well thankfully for the world of art, he gave up all claims of any personal prowess in that field, and began to encourage the works of others. He visited galleries and exhibitions, collected paintings and drawings, and became patron to a new artist who he said had considerable promise.'

Frances realised she had uncovered a new part of Percival Garton's life which could well hold valuable secrets. The world of art was unknown to her, yet she was easily able to imagine that it might conceal rivalries and enmities that could lead to murder. 'Can you tell me the name of this artist?'

Cedric shrugged. 'Fields or Meadows or some such. He exhibits at a gallery on Queen's Road.'

'Is Mr James Keane also interested in art?' asked Frances, wondering if the two men had had some falling out on that subject.

'I doubt it. I have met him on one or two occasions and found him insufferably boring. He has no intellect and no conversation. His only amusement is to make cruel comments to his wife, and his only talent is to have grown a beard more interesting than himself.'

'Yet he and your brother were great friends,' she reminded him.

'Apparently so,' said Cedric. 'Their attachment was always inexplicable to me, but they were often in each other's houses. Henrietta did not like Mr

81

Keane at all but tolerated him for her husband's sake, although she expressed some sympathy for Mrs Keane, who is a very unhappy lady. That said, I understand from Henrietta that Keane has been acting as a true friend since Percy's dreadful death, assisting with all the necessary arrangements.' He sighed. 'Poor Percy! Poor Henrietta! And the children! The distance between us meant that we could never be as united a family as we might have been, but all the same, it is a terrible blow, and I feel for them.' He gazed out of the window where the rain was still thudding down, stirring the gritty roadway into a brown, muddy slush. 'The doctor told me that Percy had suffered terribly in his final hours, yet when I saw his body, he looked so peaceful, just as I had seen him before, sleeping in his armchair after dinner.' He sighed again. 'Another drink? Oh – you haven't touched the first one! Come on, drink up, we may be here a while.'

Frances uttered a silent prayer as she raised the glass to her lips.

Some time later – and Frances could never be sure exactly how much later it was – she somehow made her way back home, and fortunately found Sarah there to assist her from the muddy suit, pour various remedies down her throat and put her to bed. Frances was not a person given to headaches, but all the headaches that had not troubled her over the years seemed to have combined into one large headache determined to have its day. Sarah informed Herbert that Frances would not be returning to her duties in the shop, as she had taken a chill from being out in the rain. Fortunately he did not enquire further, although there was an odd hint of satisfaction about him as if he felt that Frances was being suitably punished for her earlier slighting of his wishes.

Later that evening, Sarah crept up the stairs to see how Frances was, and found her mistress up and dressed. 'I have no patience for lying abed as you know,' said Frances, who still looked a little fragile about the eyes. 'I confess I was obliged to drink brandy as part of the masquerade. It must have been very bad brandy as it made me feel extremely ill.'

'Either that or very good brandy, Miss,' said Sarah, smoothing Frances' hair as she had often done when they had both been much younger. 'Perhaps next time you dress as a man you should profess to be a Salvationist.'

'Oh I hope I may never have to do it again,' said Frances fervently, 'although I did learn a great deal I might not have done otherwise.' Frances did not mention it but as she had lain in bed, watching the room slowly spin about her head, she had spent some time contemplating the terrible consequences had she been arrested in the street for public drunkenness while dressed in men's clothing. Her father would probably have turned her out of the house. She might have had to leave Bayswater, or even go abroad to avoid the shame. She felt sure that the images of this potential disgrace would haunt her for the rest of her days.

'If you feel well enough, Miss, you have a visitor. Constable Brown. Will you see him or shall I ask him to come back tomorrow?'

Frances felt suddenly enlivened. The young constable would surely only have called if he had important news relating to Percival Garton's death. 'I will see him, of course. Show him into the parlour, and I will be there straight away. And fetch him tea or coffee or whatever he might like, and a plate of biscuits.' Frances gazed into the mirror, which told a sorry tale of dissipation. She sighed and went downstairs.

Wilfred was warming himself at the parlour fire. Frances saw that he was off duty, as he had removed the striped band from his left cuff. He rose to his feet politely. 'Miss Doughty, I hope you are feeling better. Your maid told me you had a chill from being caught in the rain.'

'I am entirely well, thank you,' she said with dignity. She suddenly found herself imagining what might have ensued if it had been he who had found her in a state of inebriation and indecently attired. She sat down and gripped the edges of the table to control her trembling fingers. 'May I ask if you received the note I sent about Mr Garton and the brandy?'

He looked at her sympathetically, and was seated, resting his helmet on his knees. 'I did, and we're very grateful for your information. In all the search of the house no one thought there might be something in the carriage. I thought I had better come and tell you that the flask has been found, and was given to the analyst, and he has reported to us that it contains only brandy. No poison of any kind. I know you must be disappointed but I thought you would want to be informed.'

Sarah brought in a pot of tea and a plate of

biscuits on a tray. Frances was so distracted she did not think to pour the tea, and Sarah, seeing how she was, did what was required. Frances hardly looked at the cup of tea that was placed in her hand. 'I confess I am disappointed, but I have not altered my opinion that my father was not at fault. I assume that the analyst has by now confirmed the cause of Mr Garton's death?'

'Yes, he has. It was as we suspected, poisoning with strychnine.'

'And the medicine?'

'We expect his report very soon.'

Frances put aside her cup, the tea untasted, but Wilfred gratefully drank his and took a biscuit to go with it. After a few moments, Frances took her notebook from her pocket. 'I have been collecting information about Mr Garton, which may have something to do with the case. I have been wondering if he could have had enemies who might have wanted to poison him. Perhaps there is something here that you might find of value.'

Wilfred did not, as Inspector Sharrock might have done, admonish her for meddling in police business. He put down his cup and plate and took out his own notebook. 'Fire away, then.'

'Mr Garton came to England from Italy in 1856 to help his grandfather in his shipping business in Bristol, and lived in a nearby village called Tollington Mill, where I understand he enjoyed an easy, sociable life. He inherited the business on the death of his grandfather, sold it in 1870 and moved to Bayswater. Since then he has had no occupation but has taken an interest in paintings and drawings. If he has enemies they could date from his days as a man of business, although that was many years ago, or there may be something in his connection with the world of art.'

As she looked up from her notebook she realised that Wilfred was staring at her with an expression of profound interest. She felt a leap of hope. Slowly, thoughtfully, he put the notebook away. 'Tollington Mill,' he said.

'Yes. Does the name mean anything to you?'

He picked up his cup again, and sipped, thoughtfully. 'I doubt that it has anything to do with Mr Garton's death, but–'

'Constable,' she said eagerly, 'please tell me what you know.'

'The thing is,' he said, 'my father was a policeman and he always took a great interest in unsolved crimes. He used to read about them in the newspapers, and often talked about them. Fair upset my mother, but I used to drink it all in. I think he had a fancy that one day he'd catch a criminal who had puzzled the best heads in Scotland Yard and then he'd make his name. Only he never did.' Wilfred smiled, sadly. 'He did think he was close to it once, but it never came to anything. But I do remember him talking about something – I can't remember what exactly – but it happened in Tollington Mill. That's Gloucestershire, isn't it?'

Frances nodded. 'When was this?'

'I'm not sure, but it was well before I was in the police service, I know that, and I joined in '73.'

'So,' said Frances, 'it could have been when Mr and Mrs Garton were living there?'

'Yes, it could.' There were some moments of silence as Wilfred gave the matter some consideration. 'Let me think about it, Miss, and I'll see if I can find out some more for you. My father used to keep the newspapers if there were cases that took his eye, and I still have them.'

'And you'll tell me what you find?'

'I'll do that.' He finished his tea. 'Now I must get on. My wife will have supper on the table and I won't half catch it if I'm late.'

As he departed Frances was filled with a new excitement. Perhaps she had, after all, found a clue to the reasons behind the death of Mr Garton. She also felt a little stab of disappointment, although she could not readily identify its cause.

CHAPTER FIVE

No anxious mother with a brood of unruly children to feed, wash and dress in time to look their best for church on Sunday could have been put to more trouble, thought Frances, than she and Sarah were over her father. Coaxing him from his bed was an art in itself, for there seemed to be nothing that was sufficiently interesting or improving to tempt him from his preferred state of almost torpid melancholy. The simple acts of washing and dressing were, on his unhappier days, mountainous tasks too exhausting for him to contemplate, and Frances was often driven to despair that he would ever complete them, for she knew that once they were done he would feel more like his old self, relish his favourite breakfast of haddock poached in milk, enjoy the service at St Stephen's and even talk sociably with acquaintances as the congregation filed out.

Choice of clothing was a fraught matter as the weather was still dangerously frosty, with a chill wind, patches of ice underfoot, and precipitation threatened at any moment. All of William's garments had to be carefully aired in front of the fire before he put them on, and once he was dressed Frances wrapped woollen shawls about him, helped him into his overcoat, and added a favourite muffler, all despite his feeble protests, and to the utter neglect of every other person in the house who had to fend for themselves as best they could. When everyone was ready, Herbert called up a four-wheeler and William was tucked inside under layers of blankets. No new-born babe could have been better protected against the cold air.

One mercy, thought Frances, as they entered St Stephen's Church, her arm firmly linked in her father's, was that they would not encounter any member of the Garton family, who lived in the adjoining parish and therefore worshipped at St Matthew's. Nevertheless, the parishioners of St Stephen's included many persons of quality, some of whom might well have been acquainted with the Gartons, all of whom could not have failed to know of Percival's death and William Doughty's supposed involvement, since the rattling of afternoon teacups in the Grove carried messages faster than any device of Mr Morse. As they took their places, she sensed a coolness in the air which was more than just the temperature. There were odd little half-glances from persons on either side, some frankly curious, some wondering, some with a hint of pity. The inclement weather had resulted in the recent death from lung disease of some of the frailer members of the congregation, as well as two youths who had ignored warnings not to skate on a frozen pond. Reverend Day, in his sermon, understandably said kind words about the departed, regretting especially the loss of those still in the prime of life, and took for his text Romans chapter 6 verse 9, 'death shall have no dominion over him.' To Frances' dismay, and Herbert's embarrassment, although Percival Garton was not mentioned, William seemed to think he had been. 'Poor Garton!' he exclaimed, all too audibly, shaking his head, 'Poor fellow!' Frances tried to soothe him into quiet, without success. All around her, shocked looks were exchanged, and there were silent mouthed conversations, and more flickers of eyes in William's direction from under Sunday bonnets.

William was too wrapped in his own thoughts to be aware of the attention. Herbert, in his best dark suit and stiffest collar, his moustaches pomaded to a pungent gloss, squared his narrow shoulders and adopted a dignified air. When the congregation rose for a hymn he stared straight ahead and sang with what he fondly imagined to be a manly baritone. He actually reminded Frances in more ways than one of a seal she had once seen in the zoo. When time came for prayer and contemplation, Frances closed her eyes, and implored with all her heart for God to aid her father, for his name to be washed clean of suspicion, to inspire confidence and respect as it had always done, and for peace to enter his soul.

There was, in the Doughty household, a difficulty concerning Sundays, since William insisted on having a hot dinner on his return from church, a requirement incompatible with Sarah being able to attend service. She had to be content to say her prayers alone in the morning, between clearing away the breakfast things and starting to boil the joint. William, whose mind had in recent weeks only been able to focus clearly on the mundane, remaining curiously vague about anything of importance, would roundly insist each Sunday that the piece of mutton or beef about to be cooked was far too large for the household, and rail against the crimes of extravagance and waste. Every Sunday it would be patiently explained to him that the leftovers would be thriftily transformed into pies and hash and potted meat, and the bones into soup for the week ahead. Even when he appeared to be briefly mollified, it was clear that he did not believe what he was being told. He would mutter under his breath about the expense all through dinner and would not depart from the point until he was settled with his newspaper, and found something in its pages about which he might complain. He was especially troubled by the decline in trade, the war in Afghanistan and the state of Ireland. In the last two weeks, it had been nothing but Tay Bridge.

That Sunday, however, he was silent on the journey home from church, and throughout dinner. He seemed to be thinking deeply about something. What it was, Frances could not imagine, but she dreaded the time when his thoughts would suddenly burst out into some strange fancy born of his confused brain that would set the household out of sorts for the rest of the day.

When dinner had been eaten Sarah cleared away the dishes, then prepared and laid out the tea things for later, so she and Tom could visit her family in the afternoon. Frances saw her father settled comfortably before the fire with a blanket over his knees and, in an effort to calm him, gave him the dullest book she could find from his small collection of dull books, which she expected he would make a desultory effort to read before falling asleep. To her consternation, however, he was unusually restive. The sermon and its memories of those recently deceased had unsettled him, and he turned and said, 'Frances, bring me the Pharmacopoeia, the prescription book and the receipts book.'

Frances glanced at Herbert. He seemed unwilling to say anything and it was left to her to reply, 'I am afraid the police still have the prescription book, but I will bring you the others.'

'Still?' He seemed puzzled, then suddenly frowned and leaned forward. 'How have you recorded the prescriptions? I hope you have not been neglectful.'

Frances did not like to tell William that since the news of Percival Garton's death had become general, there had been no prescriptions. 'We have recorded everything, I assure you,' she said, and before he could question her further, she went to fetch the other books, ignoring Herbert's protests that this was unsuitable literature for a Sunday.

The receipts book was a leather-bound volume,

originally of blank pages, in which Frances, William and Herbert entered the composition and method of manufacture of all mixtures not described in the Pharmacopoeia. Some were copied from professional journals and others, such as the elixir of oranges which had formed the basis of Percival Garton's prescription, were William's own adaptation of a basic stock syrup. Frances brought the books to her father, and watched him pore over them. Every so often he would sigh deeply, but he seemed to come to no conclusion.

Sarah, in her Sunday best of a stout brown costume and thick dark coat, and a large brown bonnet with a decoration of ugly roses, her strongest corset creaking with every movement, had scrubbed Tom until his ears were almost raw, forced him into an ill-fitting but clean suit of clothes, then brushed and flattened his hair, plastering it to his head with what looked and smelt suspiciously like lard. As she dragged him towards the door she nodded to Frances, indicating the paper-wrapped package, which contained the cake she had made. 'I'll be back before you go out,' she said, making sure that this information was imparted out of Herbert's hearing. Herbert left shortly afterwards, to take tea with his family, he said, although Frances' sensitive nose often detected on his return from such excursions that he had a secret partiality to a glass of beer.

Frances stayed by the fire, reading her bible, and watching her father with anxiety, as he studied the books before him and muttered to himself, but eventually the warmth and the quiet soothed him to sleep. Quietly she laid the bible aside, removed her pocket book from her apron, and read through the notes, then she took up her pencil and began to make a list of everyone she could think of who might have had something to do with Percival Garton's death. She did not neglect to include those long dead such as his grandfather, whose lives could provide some clue as to the reasons behind his death; and persons as yet unknown – the artist he had encouraged, the gallery owner, or his neighbours in Tollington Mill, who might supply her with valuable information. She would have liked to know why Mr and Mrs Keane had quarrelled, and the reason for Garton's name being mentioned. Did James Keane suspect his wife of some impropriety with Garton? Was the dinner only a device for him to take revenge on his supposed friend? She suspected that a man who despised and neglected his wife would still feel the blow to his pride should she find solace with another.

On Sarah's return, Frances put on her coat and bonnet, tucked the wrapped cake under her arm, and set out to walk to the Keanes' house. The temperature was still hovering below freezing point, and ice puddles crunched under her feet. Normally she would have worn her warm winter coat in such weather, but today, as a part of her carefully planned approach, she had selected an old and much mended coat, quite insufficient to protect her against the cold. She hoped to look poor but respectable. Had she attempted such a thing only a few days ago she would have been trembling with anxiety, but her outing as Frank Williamson had somehow inured her to any feelings of that kind. Instead she occupied her time rehearsing in her mind the part she was about to play.

The villa where Mr and Mrs Keane resided was a handsome Georgian triple-fronted building set back from the street, and protected by thick hedges. The main entrance was a large, double oak door reached by a flight of stone steps and flanked by sturdy pillars. By the side of the house there was a short driveway leading to a coach house and stables, with servants' rooms above, and a narrow path which she knew must lead around the building to the domestic and trade entrance at the back. Everything was, Frances noted with approval, neat and spotless; the hedges trimmed, paths swept, steps scrubbed, and door handles polished. She followed the path, which brought her to a small, enclosed yard where everything again spoke of neatness and order, and knocked on a stout wooden door at the rear of the house. As she did so, the rain started to descend.

Moments later, the door was opened by a round-faced young woman in her twenties, wearing the plain dress and apron of a general servant. She had been hard at work, for her hands were red and she exuded a distinct odour of soap. Despite that she seemed to be in good humour. From Sarah's description, Frances knew this must be Ettie. 'We don't buy nothing at the door, sorry,' she said, eyeing the parcel.

'Oh, I'm not selling nothing,' said Frances. 'I'm from the bakery. I've got a cake to deliver.'

'Oh!' said Ettie, puzzled. 'Well, I'll take it then.' She held out her hands, but Frances had no plans to give up the cake so easily.

'Please let me in for a moment to warm,' said Frances, shivering. 'I've been out all day in this weather, and it's just begun raining again.'

Ettie paused. 'You poor thing, you look half starved,' she said sympathetically. 'Well, come in and sit down, but just for a minute, mind.'

Frances followed her into a large kitchen where a substantial range blazed with heat, and a delicious-looking joint turned on the roasting jack, exuding a savoury scent. Saucepans bubbled with soup and puddings, and at a long table, a rotund woman of about forty was kneading pastry, while a bowl of eggs, a jug of cream and a sugar loaf at her elbow spoke of custard tarts in the making.

'Delivery from the bakery, Mrs Grinham,' said Ettie, as Frances put the package on a chair and hurried over to the fire to warm her hands.

'I don't know of no delivery,' said the cook, pounding the pastry as if it was an unruly malefactor that needed to be flogged into submission. 'What is it then, and who ordered it?'

'It's a cake, that's all I know,' said Frances. She showed Ettie a piece of paper on which she had scribbled the address. 'This is the right house, isn't it?'

Ettie showed the paper to Mrs Grinham, who grunted. 'That's this house, right enough, only if anyone had ordered a cake I would know about it, and I don't know anything about it. If Master and Mistress want a cake they ask me to make one. Someone wrote it down wrong.'

Frances took hold of the paper and made a great show of studying it. 'What am I going to do?' she said, 'I was told it was wanted today, urgent! Even if I took it back and got the right address it'll be too late. I'll get into such trouble!' Sighing, she sat down, and then suddenly jumped up with a little scream. 'Oh no! The cake!'

Ettie came up to peer at the damage. Frances had sat squarely on top of the cake, which for all its wrappings was not looking as deep as it had once been. 'Oh dear!' said Ettie. Frances held her hands to her face and uttered a wail of misery. She was a little shocked to find that her main difficulty was preventing herself from laughing.

'Oh, there, there, maybe it isn't as bad as all that,' said Ettie quickly. 'Here, let me open it up and have a look.'

Ettie lifted the substantial parcel onto the kitchen table, untied the string and pulled aside the wrappings. It was pound cake, glistening with butter, scented with cloves, nutmeg and cinnamon, speckled with caraway, and frosted with powdered sugar. Sarah's burly arm could mix a cake which, however rich its ingredients, always turned out pleasingly light and digestible. Its very lightness had, however, been its downfall, and it was quite obvious that it had met with some accident.

'I can't take it back like that!' exclaimed Frances. 'Master will stop it out of my wages, and Mistress will beat me!' She sank into the now empty chair, shoulders shaking.

Ettie looked around at Mrs Grinham. 'What do you think we should do?' she said.

'It ain't nothing to do with us,' said the cook, with a derisive laugh. '*We* don't have to do anything. Let her take it back and catch the consequences.'

'Oh, but look at the poor creature!' exclaimed Ettie. 'I can't help but feel sorry for her.'

Frances sniffled into a handkerchief. 'What if I was to say it was stolen in the street? Do you think they would believe me?'

'They might,' said Ettie gently, although she hardly sounded convinced.

'If they asked, you could say I came in here all upset,' said Frances, dabbing her eyes.

'Well, that would sort of be the truth, wouldn't it?' agreed Ettie.

Frances blew her nose. 'I can't take the cake back like that. I'm sure it would taste very good, even if it is all squashed. You're welcome to have it. I never want to see it again!'

Mrs Grinham looked at the cake, critically. She seemed like a lady who would enjoy cake, but only if she made it herself. 'I'm sure it isn't half as good as one *you* would make,' said Frances.

Mrs Grinham looked up at Frances then back to the cake again, then she wiped the flour from her arms. 'Put the kettle on, Ettie, the pastry needs time to rest before I roll it out.'

'Will you stay and have tea?' asked Ettie. Frances quickly assented. A knife and plates were brought, and the kettle was soon boiling and a pot of tea made. Mrs Grinham ate a slice of the cake, and said it tasted better than it looked, but it ought to have been baked a little less, then she ate another slice just to make sure.

'I expect your Master and Mistress are great admirers of your baking,' said Frances.

'They are,' said the cook proudly, 'especially Mistress.'

'It is a great comfort to her, poor lady,' said Ettie, with a mouthful of cake.

'Now then, no gossip!' said Mrs Grinham, sharply.

'Oh but I love a bit of gossip!' said Frances, gulping her tea. 'Is it ever so shocking? Come now, I promise I won't tell!'

'Oh it's no great secret that Master and Mistress are very unhappy in each other's company,' said Ettie. 'He spends almost all his time away from home, and when he is here they have terrible quarrels.'

'I was once in a place where Master and Mistress quarrelled,' said Frances. 'He was a very jealous man, and thought that she was – well, I can't say the word, it wouldn't be polite.'

Mrs Grinham laughed scornfully. 'If you were to see Mistress you wouldn't think her a lady with many admirers.'

'Except one,' said Ettie, unable to resist a sly smirk.

'Oh, that's just a silly boy's fancy,' said Mrs Grinham. 'We won't talk of that.'

'So what do your Master and Mistress quarrel about?' asked Frances, pouring out another cup of tea and cutting more cake.

'I think it was all about money,' said Ettie.

'Oh?' said Frances, surprised.

'I know that when Master makes his remarks – the ones that upset Mistress – it's always about money.'

'What sort of remarks?' asked Frances, wondering how far she could go with her questions.

Mrs Grinham flashed her a suspicious look but Ettie continued innocently, 'I once heard him say that money could make a man seem to be great when he was not, but it could also destroy him.'

'That doesn't seem *very* cruel,' said Frances.

'Oh, but you should have heard the way he said it,' said Ettie, meaningfully.

Frances wondered if the man who Keane said might be destroyed was Garton. Perhaps, she thought, Garton and Keane had been partners in a business which had failed, or one had lent funds to the other which had not been returned, or still worse, one had cheated the other and been found out. All these were situations which could lead to murder.

Just then the inner kitchen door opened, and both Mrs Grinham and Ettie rose guiltily from their seats, licking cake crumbs from their lips. Frances thought it best to stand up too. She saw a dignified man of about thirty, impeccably dressed and looking every inch the better class of servant. He was carrying a framed portrait.

'If you are without employment, I suggest you busy yourselves with this,' he said, severely. 'Ettie, Mr Keane has asked that this drawing be removed from the frame and burnt. Then make sure the frame is well cleaned.'

'Yes, Mr Harvey,' said Ettie, taking the portrait.

Noticing Frances, Harvey tilted his head and looked at her severely down a long, tapering nose. 'Who is this?'

'Liza, from the bakery,' said Frances. 'I – had an accident with a cake'

He glanced down at the plate. 'Several slices worth of accident, I see,' he said.

There was a pause, then Mrs Grinham, who had returned to kneading pastry, said, 'Don't you worry, Mr Harvey, you'll be saved a piece.'

His eyelids fluttered briefly. 'I certainly hope so,' he said, and swept out.

Frances had a look at the picture. It was a cleverly executed pen and ink drawing of James and Mary Keane. James was standing beside his wife's chair, a tall man with abundant side-whiskers flaring to unusual proportions and framing a deeply bushy beard. Even that heavy growth was inadequate to conceal his expression of slightly stupid self-regard. The representation of his wife was less unkind. Corpulent, without a doubt, her face creased with unhappiness, yet it could be seen that had she been more slender, her appearance would have been pleasing if not actually pretty. Frances wondered why Keane would have ordered the picture to be burnt. She realised that up to that moment she was not, in her role of Liza the bakery girl, supposed to know the name of the family living there, but now she seized her chance.

'This is Mr and Mrs Keane!' she said. 'I didn't know this was *their* house!'

'How do you know Master and Mistress?' asked Ettie, surprised.

'They have been pointed out to me in the street as persons of very great quality,' said Frances. 'Oh!' she suddenly exclaimed, 'that means that it was here that–,' she clapped a hand to her mouth. 'Oh dear!' Ettie and Mrs Grinham stared at her. 'Only – I heard all about it, and – this is the house where Mr Garton dined the night he died!' There was a moment of frigid silence and Frances realised that Mrs Grinham was not best pleased by any suggestion that her cooking had been involved in Garton's death. 'Oh, please believe me,' said Frances hurriedly, 'I know that his dying couldn't have been anything to do with what he had here.'

'No, it was all down to that medicine he had from the chemist,' said Mrs Grinham. 'And if you ask me, the man what made that terrible mistake ought to be put in prison, or at least thrown out of business!'

'It might not be the chemist's fault,' said Frances. 'Maybe Mr Garton had an enemy who put poison in the medicine.'

'I don't know about that,' said Mrs Grinham dismissively. 'Mr Garton was a good, kind man, who would want to poison him?'

Frances was hoping to explore this idea further, but the moment was lost when a young woman came in from the yard entrance, her cheeks glowing red with cold. She immediately made for the fire, rubbing her hands to warm them. 'Oh, is that tea? Just the thing! And what a delicious-looking cake! You *have* excelled yourself Mrs Grinham!'

Ettie stifled a giggle.

'Please help yourself to a slice,' said Frances, trying her best to avoid Mrs Grinham's gaze. 'I've come from the bakery, and there was a bit of an accident about the delivery, and, well, I thought we might as well eat it up.'

'The bakery?' said the new arrival, surprised. 'Well, thank you, I'm sure.' She was slender and

101

fair, and about the same age as Frances, with slightly protuberant eyes under heavy lids which marred an otherwise pretty face. There was something familiar about her features, and Frances realised that she had seen her in the Grove more than once, though she had never entered the shop. Fortunately the girl did not appear to recognise Frances. She took off her coat and busied herself making a fresh pot of tea and cutting cake.

'We were just talking about poor Mr Garton,' said Frances.

'Oh, yes, that was a very sad thing,' said the girl through a mouthful of cake. 'And to think we saw him only about an hour before he died. I can hardly believe it!'

'Were there many people here that night?'

'No, just Master and Mistress and Mr and Mrs Garton. It was more like a family dinner than a grand occasion.'

'I expect it was a very good dinner; better than I'm used to,' said Frances, wistfully.

'Artichoke soup, and fried sole, then cutlets and boiled fowls and vegetables, and apple pudding and blancmange,' said Mrs Grinham, proudly. 'And that wasn't all because they were served tea and macaroons and sandwiches in the drawing room afterwards. They all ate very well and there was hardly a crumb left and *no one was took ill.*'

'I should think a gentleman like Mr Keane can afford the very best wines, too,' said Frances.

'He can,' agreed Mrs Grinham, 'though I have heard Mr Harvey say that he might save himself a shilling a bottle and not know the difference. But then everyone knows that Mr Keane came

102

from a very low family and only has his wife to thank for his position.'

'Perhaps,' said Frances hopefully, 'Mr Garton wasn't poisoned at all. He might just have had a spasm on the heart.'

While they considered this, a young Atlas of a man with long brown hair tied back in a switch and a mild expression entered the room. His clothes were rough yet clean, and there was a whiff of the stables about him, but his presence in the kitchen was tolerated.

'Here, Adam, what do you think of this?' said Ettie teasingly, showing him the portrait. 'Would you believe Master has said it is to be burnt?'

He frowned as he looked at it, then, without saying a word, he took the picture from its frame and tore it in half down the middle. The part with James Keane was consigned to the fire, but the other half he rolled up and placed carefully in his pocket. 'There, and if you tell anyone, it'll be the worse for all of you!' he said, his face flushing red.

'Now then, Adam, we know it's just your little way,' said Mrs Grinham. 'No harm in admiring a lady. Come, have some tea.' Ettie poured a large cup and Adam sat in a corner taking large noisy gulps, scorning the cake to munch at a piece of coarse bread. Whatever his thoughts he kept them to himself, and when he finished eating and drinking he wiped his hands on his trousers and went out.

Mr Harvey returned, and looked annoyed to see Frances still there. His eyes flickered around the room and Frances realised that he was inspecting its contents. She would not have been surprised had he decided to count the teaspoons. He raised an eyebrow at the fair girl. 'Ellen, I believe the table is yet to be laid,' he said curtly. She put down a half-consumed cup of tea and hurried out. Frances cut a slice of cake, put it on a plate, pushed it across the table in Mr Harvey's direction, and poured more tea. He hesitated. 'It's very cold outside, don't you think?' she said, innocently. 'Thank goodness for tea and cake or we would all catch a chill.'

'That is true,' he said, and sat down. There were a few moments of appreciative silence as he sipped tea and nibbled cake.

'I was just saying that poor Mr Garton must have been a very unwell man when he came here,' ventured Frances.

He stared at her. 'And what concern is that of yours?' he observed, sharply.

'None, only I thought it was a shame that some people think he ate something here that was wrong, when after all the gentleman was probably very poorly. I expect he came here with lots of medicines and pills.'

'None that I saw.' He paused. 'You seem to be taking a very particular interest in the matter.'

'Well it has created no end of a sensation in our household.'

'Perhaps you would do well to amuse yourself with more wholesome diversions than considering what Mr Garton may have had on the night he died,' said Harvey coldly. 'I believe that is a matter for the police.'

'The police must have been very troublesome to you, and very upsetting for Mr and Mrs

Keane,' said Frances sympathetically.

'They were, but of course they have their job to do, as have we all.'

Frances refused to take the hint. She poured herself another cup of tea.

'Poking their noses in everywhere!' exclaimed Mrs Grinham with more than a touch of outrage. 'Asking all sorts of questions – do we have medicines in the house, do we have vermin killers – hmph! I run a clean kitchen and we have nothing of that sort here!'

'I believe,' said Harvey, more for Mrs Grinham's temper than for Frances, 'that the police are now entirely satisfied that Mr Garton was poisoned because of a mistake by the chemist, and that is what the inquest will show.'

'Mr Keane must be very upset,' said Frances, 'what with being such a good friend, and their business must be all at sixes and sevens.'

'Gentlemen in their position are well able to manage their affairs, you'll find,' said Harvey.

So Garton and Keane had been business partners, thought Frances, or Mr Harvey would surely have denied it. She was about to ask what business they were in, when Ellen rushed in. She had changed her dress to a plain workaday garment and donned the apron and cap of a parlour maid. 'Mr Harvey! Master and Mistress are back!'

Harvey dabbed at his lips with a napkin, and rose. 'Well, Miss Liza from the bakery,' he said to Frances, 'you'd best be getting back to your employer. And I do hope for your sake that the art of baking has more to interest you in the future than it has done previously.'

105

As Frances walked home, she considered what she had learnt by her visit, and as soon as she was able, sat down to record her thoughts in her notebook. Herbert had not yet returned, and her father was still dozing, so she helped Sarah sort linens for the Monday wash. William still had the books he had been consulting on his lap, and it wasn't until he awoke that she was able to remove them and take them back to the shop. He was still silent, shaking his head every so often, almost as if there was a thought in his mind he needed to dislodge so he could examine it. It might have been no more than one of his strange fancies, but Frances had an increasingly uncomfortable feeling that there was something in her father's troubled memory which related to Percival Garton's death.

CHAPTER SIX

Monday 19th January was the day of Percival Garton's funeral. Frances considered attending but eventually decided that to do so would be highly improper, especially if she was recognised; also her household duties that morning did not permit her to be absent for any length of time. It was washday, and she would be employed for several hours, boiling water, then pounding, rinsing and wringing before everything could finally be hung to up dry. Yesterday's squally showers had passed on, leaving the day bright and clear, but it was so cold that anything hung outside would have frozen to the line, so all the linens had to be draped over clotheshorses in the kitchen where they dangled, filling the room with vapour. Usually when Frances and Sarah worked together it was a companionable time, when, while never forgetting that they were mistress and servant, they could still talk as two women united by their duties in life. On that day, Frances was largely silent. She imagined the service at St Matthew's and the interment at Kensal Green, with herself there as an observer, perhaps appearing as a darkly veiled figure of mystery, or even as eager young Mr Williamson the reporter, casting her eyes over the assembled throng. There would be the distraught widow, Henrietta, Cedric Garton, Mr Keane and his wife, and those of the household servants permitted to leave their duties. Perhaps there would be others she knew nothing of, social acquaintances, the artist whose career Garton had been encouraging, or business associates. Any one of the mourners might well be a murderer. Someone, whose outward demeanour was of familial grief or silent respect, was concealing a secret satisfaction at Percival Garton's death and congratulating him or herself on not being suspected. Whoever that individual might be, Frances knew that he or she was callously indifferent to the distress and possible ruin of the Doughty family. Frances wondered if, had she been present, she would have seen that moment when the murderer dropped his or her guard, and revealed a gloating pleasure underneath the mask of propriety?

One thing at least pleased her that morning, and she said as much to Sarah. Her father was looking more robust, and needed no urging to take up his duties behind the counter. At midday, when William sat down to a plate of mutton hash with more appetite than he had displayed in some time, Frances, with reddened hands and aching back, returned to the shop.

She was surprised to see a familiar figure there, deep in conversation with Herbert. During the worst times of her father's illness, Mr Ford had been responsible for supervising the dispensing of medicines. He was a man of about forty-five, broad and stocky with a bald pate, fringed with crisp dark hair. He was knowledgeable and experienced in his profession, courteous towards the customers, polite and helpful to both Frances and Herbert, yet she had disliked him almost at once. It had taken her a while to understand why this was so, but she eventually realised that it was the way he moved around the shop, and looked about him. Mr Ford did not see himself as a mere salaried individual, employed by the business for a few short months. Mr Ford was, in Mr Ford's mind, the future proprietor. He surveyed the premises as if he already owned it; saw the customers as his patrons, and Frances and Herbert as his staff, whom he could afford, from his lofty position, to treat with magnanimity. Mr Ford, when running his plump white fingers along the perfect shine of the mahogany display case, did so caressingly, as if it was already his. He had two sons, pharmacists in the making, to whom he wanted to leave an empire of shops, and the illness of William Doughty and the possibility of a sale made quickly and cheaply out of necessity had excited him.

Every so often he would ask questions which Frances thought impertinent and intrusive, about how the business was stocked, who were the best customers, what weekly profits were made, and, most tellingly, the amount of the rent and when the lease was due for renewal. These questions were largely directed at Herbert, even those which Frances could best answer. Though women could now qualify as pharmacists and even open their own businesses, this to Mr Ford's mind was an aberration he preferred to ignore. Frances had once mentioned to him the inspiring example of Isabella Skinner Clarke, who after years of fighting for recognition had been admitted to full membership of the Pharmaceutical Society only a few months previously. He had gazed at her in cold disdain, and indicated that, in his mind, the Council's decision had been 'inappropriate'.

Mr Ford had pretended to be overjoyed when William Doughty's improved health had enabled him to return to work, but his disappointment had not been well concealed. Recent events had clearly raised his hopes.

As Frances entered, the two men looked around, and there was no mistaking a trace of guilt on both their faces.

'Good morning, Miss Doughty,' said Ford, politely, 'I was just passing and called in to enquire after your father's health.'

'That is very thoughtful of you,' said Frances, with cool dignity, 'he is greatly improved.'

'I trust that he has not been unduly distressed by the terrible rumours that have been pervading the area. I must assure you that I, of course, do not

109

believe a word of them. Mr Doughty would be incapable of making such an elementary error.'

'I am most gratified by your confidence,' said Frances.

Whatever had been said before her arrival, the remaining conversation dwindled into a matter of exchanging politenesses and Ford soon removed himself as graciously as he could. Herbert bustled about, pretending to be busy. 'I suppose,' said Frances, 'you have no intention of telling me why he was really here?'

'I'm not sure what you can mean,' said Herbert, his tone indicating astonishment. 'He stated quite plainly the reason for his visit.'

'He did not state it to me,' said Frances. 'I believe he came to find out if the business was for sale. He imagines that the recent difficulties will enable him to buy at a favourable price. His approach has the subtlety of a vulture seeking carrion, but he will have a surprise, for we are very much alive and can repel him.'

Herbert was silent, and Frances wondered if Mr Ford's visit had been a matter of chance or whether Herbert had had something to do with it. Later that afternoon, William joined them in the shop, where he obtained a joyless gratification by complaining about how things had been run in his absence. He supervised Herbert in the making of a batch of pills, leaning over his apprentice's shoulder as he worked, making, as was his habit, little 'Um-hum' noises at each stage of the procedure, which meant it took twice as long as it should have and was no better done. He then turned to fussing over the accounts,

110

trying to find mistakes. Disappointed by the absence of mistakes, he was obliged to pretend that Frances' handwriting was unreadable, and assumed imaginary errors in order to have the satisfaction of taking her to task.

A note arrived from Mr Rawsthorne, stating that in view of the impending inquest proceedings he wished to visit the shop and see for himself where items were kept and how things were done. He arrived on the stroke of three with a bundle of papers under his arm, and a clerk to take notes.

He first shook hands with William. 'My dear old friend,' he said soothingly, 'do not worry yourself. I am here to learn what I can and promise you we will find out what happened. I have every confidence that the inquest will clear you of blame.' He turned to face Herbert and Frances with a beaming smile. 'Now, to make a start, I need to see the items which formed the ingredients of the mixture made for Mr Garton.'

Rawsthorne examined everything minutely, both smelling and tasting the contents of the bottles, and looking at the Pharmacopoeia and the receipts book, questioning William until he was certain that he understood the matter thoroughly. 'So,' he said at last, 'two teaspoonfuls only of tincture of nux vomica went into the bottle, which was then made up to six ounces with elixir of oranges.' Rawsthorne's clerk, a pasty-faced youth with ink-blackened fingers, unrolled a paper on the counter. He had listened to the conversation, his eyes flickering back and forth about the shop as if fearful that at any moment someone might emerge from the shadows and offer him a deadly poison. Possibly having no suitable pocket for pens and pencils, he favoured keeping them clamped between his teeth, although they also provided a suitable barrier against harm. Removing his sharpest pencil from this convenient holder, he began to write, rapidly, as if his entire future career depended upon it. 'And how much strychnine would you say was in each dose?' asked Rawsthorne.

William started to leaf through the Pharmacopoeia, and Herbert began to scribble numbers on a scrap of paper, but Frances had already done the calculations. Referring to her notebook, she said, 'The dose is one or two teaspoonfuls of the mixture. There is approximately one hundred and sixtieth part of a grain in each teaspoonful.'

'But we now know,' said Rawsthorne, nodding at Frances approvingly, 'that Mr Garton was very imprecise as to how much he took. He disdained teaspoons and drank from the bottle. This fact is very much in our favour as the habit may well have contributed to his death, in which case, it is his own negligence that is to blame, and the court can do no more than issue a stern warning to the public against similar behaviour. Now, assuming Mr Garton to have been only careless and not foolhardy, let us say that he may have taken as much as four teaspoonfuls. That would suggest he ingested one fortieth of a grain of strychnine. And, before we do any more arithmetic of this nature, I need to know the fatal dose of strychnine.'

'For a man in good health, between one and a half and three grains,' said Frances. 'Half a grain

112

has been known to be fatal, but only in very rare cases.'

'Well,' said Mr Rawsthorne, his eyes twinkling, 'I can see that Miss Doughty has all the answers, and I shall certainly apply to her first if I require any information!'

Herbert frowned.

'Now I have it from Mr Garton's medical attendant that there was no reason to suppose that he had an idiosyncrasy for strychnine, and that his indigestion was not a serious condition, and would not have made him more susceptible than the average man. Of course,' added Rawsthorne with a knowing smile, 'since Dr Collin was the man who prescribed the mixture for Mr Garton, he will be more than usually eager to assure us that, properly made up, it could have done him no possible harm. So, assuming that a minimum of one and a half grains would be fatal to Mr Garton, let us continue. How much strychnine is there in the entire bottle of mixture?'

'Six twentieths of a grain,' said Frances promptly.

'Which we know is not enough to slay even the most debilitated of men. So the mixture as properly made up could not have caused his death. Now let us move on, and it is necessary that we do so to consider what the police are saying they believe happened. They have suggested that a more concentrated article, extract of nux vomica, was used in error for the tincture. First, can you show me where it is kept?'

They all moved into the storeroom where the bottle of extract was pointed out. Rawsthorne

113

examined it carefully, and smelled the contents. 'Is it safe to taste a little?' They all nodded, and he cautiously dipped a finger into the bottle, and placed a touch of the thick liquid on his tongue, then grimaced. 'Very bitter,' he said. He held the 'bottle up to the light. I see also that it is almost full. Is this as it was on the date Mr Garton's prescription was made up?'

'Yes,' said Herbert. 'It is used only as the base extract from which to prepare the more dilute tincture, and we have prepared none in the last week.'

'And it is always kept here, and not in the shop?'

'It is,' said Herbert firmly.

'Hmm. You see, it is my experience that when mistakes are made it is because a bottle of poison has been placed on a shelf next to something innocent, and the two things look very similar, or a bottle has been improperly labelled, or not labelled at all. Many an individual would be alive today had these elementary matters been properly attended to. But here we have two bottles, one large and one small, two liquids which both look and smell distinctively different, especially to a man of experience, and are in different rooms. Clearly also, the tincture is the more commonly used article.'

Everyone assented.

'Then if any mistake were to be made it is far more likely that a commonly used item would be mistaken for one more rarely used, and in this case it is the commonly used tincture which was the correct ingredient. The theory that the extract was mistaken for the tincture therefore runs entirely counter to our natural intuition. Still, this is the official theory so we must test it. If we consider only the strychnine content, how much more concentrated is the extract than the tincture?'

'It is twenty times more concentrated,' said Frances, immediately.

'So, Miss Doughty, I am sure you will be able to tell me how much strychnine there is in four teaspoons of this mixture, had it been made with extract and not tincture.'

'Half a grain,' said Frances. 'The entire bottle would have contained six grains.'

'In other words,' said Rawsthorne, 'Mr Garton would have had to consume at least a quarter of the bottle, and possibly up to half, to obtain a fatal dose. All this is, of course, on the assumption that only two teaspoons of the extract was used to make the mixture, but as we have seen the bottle is almost full so it is hard to see how any more could have been used. Frankly, I think the police theory is a very poor one. First of all, we have the evidence of both Mr Doughty and Mr Munson that it was the tincture that was used, and secondly the mistaking of extract for tincture seems so very unlikely. I would also venture to say that had the extract been used, the resultant mixture would have been so bitter that he would never have consumed it in any quantity likely to be dangerous. The first sip would have told him that something was the matter. There is another theory, which has not been mentioned, that the mixture was made using the tincture, but contained a very much greater amount than two teaspoonfuls. Let us suppose therefore that the

115

mixture was made up not with two teaspoonfuls of the tincture but two ounces. I'm sure Miss Doughty will be able to do the arithmetic if she has not already done so.'

'Two ounces is eight times as much as in the prescription. Even if he took four times the correct dose he would only have taken two fifths of a grain of *strychnia*,' said Frances.

Rawsthorne nodded. 'Still less than a fatal dose. So here we have it in a nutshell: whether tincture or extract was used, any mixture which Mr Garton might have found palatable enough to consume in any quantity would not have supplied a dose of strychnine sufficient to kill him.'

'Then we are in the clear!' exclaimed Herbert.

'Possibly,' said Rawsthorne. 'Although I see this as the point where the difficulties begin.'

There were a few moments of silence. Frances, who knew that behind the avuncular manner and cheerful smile, the solicitor was a clever man, realised that the entire conversation had been carefully steered by him to this very point. Only one piece of information was wanting.

'Mr Rawsthorne,' said Frances, 'what does the analyst say about how much *strychnia* Mr Garton consumed?'

Rawsthorne nodded. 'Ah, I wondered who would ask me that. Obviously it is not possible to be precise about these things, but he believes that Garton took at least two grains and probably as much as three.'

'Dear Lord!' exclaimed Herbert.

'To take that quantity in the form of any

116

medicine containing nux vomica, he would have had to consume a large amount of an unpleasantly bitter mixture. Now as we all know, many medicines are bitter to the taste, and some people believe that the more unpleasant the taste, the more effective the medicine, but Mr Garton had had this medicine before, and was familiar with its flavour.'

Frances recalled something Ada had said. 'When Mr Garton took his medicine, did he make any comment about how it tasted?'

Rawsthorne nodded. 'He did. He told Mrs Garton he believed that it was more bitter than he was used to.'

Herbert hid his face in his hands and groaned.

'But not, I think, so bitter he could not drink it,' said Frances.

'That seems to be the case,' agreed Rawsthorne.

'Has the analyst said anything about the presence of the other constituents of nux vomica?' she asked. 'You should know that it contains another, less poisonous alkaloid, *brucia*. If, as the police suggest, the extract had been used, or if, as you have said, too great an amount of tincture, then not only would the *strychnia* content of the medicine be increased but the *brucia* also.'

Rawsthorne unrolled the bundle of papers under his arm, and examined them carefully, but the answer to this question was obviously not there. 'Thank you, Miss Doughty, I will make enquiries on this point,' he said.

'Does the report mention any dyestuffs?' asked Herbert. 'Vermin killers may be freely purchased by almost anyone at sixpence apiece, each of which contains sufficient *strychnia* to kill a man. To protect the unwary they are dyed with Prussian blue or mixed with soot, yet despite that one often hears of them causing death, either by accident or intent.'

'I see no mention in the report of those substances, but I will enquire,' said Rawsthorne. He paused, and surveyed the anxious faces that surrounded him. 'There is, of course, one other possible source of strychnine, the pure article, but I assume that you do not carry this as a rule.'

Frances shook her head, and Herbert said, 'It is not something we keep or use.'

Rawsthorne was bundling his notes when William said. 'Pure *strychnia!* Yes. We do have some, but – oh – it was a long time ago – a very long time...' All eyes turned to William as he ran his hands though his hair, trying to remember.

'Surely, Sir, we can have it no longer,' said Herbert. 'I have never been aware of such a thing here.'

'But there was – is, I think.' William began to search the shelves and behind a range of bottles found a small metal box. Frances recalled that the box contained samples of items that were never used medicinally but had been produced when her father had been training Frederick. As a precaution it was always kept locked and neither she nor Herbert had access to it. William rummaged in his pockets for what seemed for the anxious watchers to be a great length of time, before he found a bunch of keys. There was a further delay as the right key was identified, and the lid opened. The box contained a number of

118

small glass phials and paper packets. 'Long ago, now,' he muttered, 'instructional demonstration of methods. No reason to destroy the materials – one never knows when they could be required.' Frances made a mental note to go though the box at the earliest opportunity. 'It was not a large amount, about thirty grains, it was in a small phial with a label, well corked and sealed, of course.'

'When did you last see it?' asked Rawsthorne.

'Oh – I really couldn't say.' After a minute or two William stopped searching and sighed. 'I am certain it was there!' Herbert took the box and conducted a more methodical search but eventually looked up at the others and shook his head.

'Well, this is interesting,' said Rawsthorne, solemnly, 'and unexpected. Assuming that Mr Doughty is correct about the presence of pure strychnine in the box, then we must wonder why it is no longer there. Was it employed for some valid purpose or destroyed long ago, in which case it is no longer our concern? Or has it only recently disappeared? Miss Doughty, some more arithmetic if you please. Based on thirty grains of pure strychnine in Mr Garton's bottle and his taking four teaspoons of mixture, how much strychnine would he have consumed?'

Frances made the calculations carefully and then checked them again before she spoke. 'Two and a half grains.'

'Dear me,' said Mr Rawsthorne.

There followed several moments of silence.

'Mr Rawsthorne, I would appreciate your observations on our present position,' said Frances.

'Well, Miss Doughty, we were trotting along

very merrily until now,' said Rawsthorne. 'We agreed that any medicine containing enough nux vomica to account for what was found in the body would have been too unpleasant to take by accident in any dangerous quantity. We established that, however constituted, there could not have been a fatal amount of strychnine in Mr Garton's usual dose or even double that. It was my intention to suggest to the court that Mr Garton died of poison administered to him either in some article other than his medicine, or added to his medicine by a malevolent hand after it left here. That would have raised sufficient doubts to clear Mr Doughty of any suspicion. However, the presence of pure strychnine in the shop does add something of a complication.'

'A court might well be persuaded that a mistake is possible between the tincture and the extract, or in the amount used of either,' said Frances, 'but surely you are not suggesting for a moment that my father went to this box, unlocked it and added a deadly amount of pure *strychnia* to Mr Garton's medicine! That is not an error one might make.'

'I agree,' said Rawsthorne.

The clerk looked up from his writing and took the pens from his mouth. 'That's murder, that is,' he said, then quickly thrust the pens back into his mouth and went on writing.

'How dare you, Sir!' exclaimed Herbert, his moustaches vibrating. 'If it was not beneath my dignity I would strike you for such an insult!' The clerk, assessing correctly the probability of Herbert becoming dangerously violent, simply bared his teeth in a sneering smile.

'But it *is* murder,' said Frances earnestly. 'Not by any person here present, but Mr Rawsthorne, I do believe that Mr Garton was murdered. How and why and by whom I cannot tell you.'

Rawsthorne rolled up his papers. 'You may be correct, but my concern now is solely for Mr Doughty.' He turned to William and Herbert. 'I would advise you this, gentlemen, be scrupulously truthful in court but answer only those questions which you are asked. I am sure that the missing phial of strychnine has no relevance to Mr Garton's death, therefore it would do no harm if it was not to be mentioned. It never does to confuse a jury with too many facts.'

Rawsthorne took his departure, the clerk pausing in the doorway for an impudent look before he hurried into the waiting carriage after his employer. Herbert was almost speechless with agitation.

'Mr Munson,' said Frances softly, 'we need to discuss this further, I believe, but not just at present. Let me see that my father has some tea and I will return shortly.'

'I wish I had struck that – that–,' fumed Herbert.

'It would not have assisted us if you had.' Frances turned to her father, who required little persuasion that a hot cup of tea and some bread and jam would be just the thing to improve his sprits. It was tempting as they climbed the stairs to the parlour to try and press him about the missing phial, but Frances knew that such a course could only drive the memory deeper.

Herbert had calmed a little by the time she

returned. 'It is my observation,' said Frances, 'that my father is only afflicted by a difficulty in recalling things that have happened in recent months. His memory for more distant events is as good as ever it was. That would suggest that the phial of which he spoke was placed in the box some while ago, possibly even years, but has gone from there more recently. It may not even be missing. He may have moved it to a new place.'

'Then I suggest,' said Herbert, 'that I attend to the shop while you search everywhere possible. After all, you know his mind better than I.'

Frances assented, and Herbert took his place behind the counter, no doubt congratulating himself on having avoided a difficult and tedious task. Frances, who had been about to suggest that she do the search herself was well satisfied with the position and had already borrowed her father's keys. She took the view that it was best to alter nothing and so did not destroy anything in the box, but wrote out a list of the contents. She then carefully inspected every shelf in the stockroom, lifting out bottles and jars and peering behind them, passing her fingers over the darkest corners so as not to miss even a tiny hidden item. The sacks of raw materials were inspected, either to check that they were unopened, or if opened that nothing lay concealed within. She then turned her attention to the shop, and examined every shelf and display. An hour later she had to confess that if the phial had been moved it was no longer on the shop premises. When she told Herbert that she would search the private apartments he raised no objection and she went upstairs, but she knew it would be useless. Sarah was exceedingly diligent about cleaning and would at once have seen and brought to her attention any unusual item she found. Nevertheless, Frances told Sarah of what had occurred and Sarah promised that she would leave no tiny nook unsearched.

During her fruitless task, Frances had thought deeply about what Mr Rawsthorne had said. Had the report shown that Garton had died from an unusually small amount of strychnine, she might have been forced to consider that his death could have been due to her father's error, compounded by Garton's tendency to overdose himself, but the sheer size of the dose put that beyond possibility. In less than three days the inquest jury would convene to consider the facts, and could change both her and her father's lives forever. She had learned a great deal but nothing that pointed unerringly to a possible suspect. With no suggestion that Garton was the victim of romantic jealousy, she wondered how best she might discover more about his business interests. She picked up her notebook again and read it through. The only business anyone had mentioned Garton undertaking since his arrival in London was connected with the encouragement of art. The Queen's Road Gallery, where his protégé was said to exhibit, was just around the corner. Frances put on her bonnet and coat and went out.

CHAPTER SEVEN

The cold had intensified and Frances was obliged to walk briskly as she made her way up Queen's Road, where despite the freezing temperatures and darkening skies, work continued apace on Mr Whiteley's new buildings. A constant din of loud hammering resounded through the street, much, she knew, to the annoyance of the residents, whose protests had as yet fallen on deaf ears. Cynically, she felt sure that as Mr Whiteley was a substantial ratepayer, the members of the Paddington Vestry, which carried out public works and whose coffers he helped to fill, would drag their heels over the nuisance, in the hope that by the time they were obliged to attend to it, the buildings would be completed. Number 123 was the chemist's shop of Mr Lynn, an enterprising man some twenty years her father's junior. As she passed, she could not resist taking a look inside, and saw to her dismay that the premises was crowded with customers, not a few of whom she recognised as those who had previously been loyal to the Doughtys. She could not blame Mr Lynn for his success. The two shops had always maintained friendly relations and had even assisted each other on occasions when one had run out of stock of something the other required, or had directed customers to the other shop if necessary. It was not the downturn in trade that had sent people to Mr Lynn, and it was not for him to refuse them.

She found the gallery tucked away unobtrusively between some small private houses. It had clearly once been a two-storey private house itself, but the ground floor had been converted from a front parlour to a shop, and in the window was displayed a reproduction of one of the excellent works of Mr Frith. The conversion should have been an opportunity to give miniature charm to the location, so the painful lack of ornamentation, the complete absence of gilding, or Italianate scrollwork, gave the frontage a half-finished look, as if the proprietor had lost interest or run out of funds part way through the work. It was a sombre little shop, with only a small painted wooden board outside to convey its purpose. 'Bayswater Gallery. Paintings and drawings bought and sold'.

Frances was not a student of art, but she felt confident in her ability to detect whether or not a portrait was an accurate depiction of its subject. It was with no trepidation therefore that she pushed open the door and went in.

The display room of the gallery was, she thought, unusually dim, considering that patrons required the opportunity to examine the items on show. A small fireplace of feebly glowing coals was unequal to the task of supplying adequate warmth. The walls were of plain-varnished wood, and were hung with a small assortment of framed paintings. Other unframed pictures were on the floor, leaning against the wall like tiles waiting to be laid. There were only two customers, a lady and a gentleman, who were staring at a gloomy landscape, discussing in whispers not its artistic merit but whether it would match their furniture. At the back of the gallery was a desk and a high stool, where there reposed a sleepy-looking young man wrapped in a large overcoat against the chill. His hair was long, lank and unkempt, and the muffler wound about his neck up to the level of his ears was an alarming shade of purple. From time to time, he reached into his pocket and refreshed himself from a small flask he kept there. Frances thought he might have been one of the artistic men she had seen in the Redan public house, but since they had hardly glimpsed her she hoped that she would not, dressed as a woman, be recognised.

The gallery manager, if that was his position, was taking scant interest in the activities of the customers, and paid no attention at all to Frances, as she walked slowly about the room looking at the paintings. Eventually the couple departed, the young man marking the event by taking another sip from his flask. Frances decided to approach him.

'Sir, I would welcome your advice,' she said.

He rubbed his eyes and yawned. 'Buying or selling?' he asked.

'I may wish to commission a piece,' she said boldly. 'I have been advised by an acquaintance who has excellent taste in art, that there is a new artist I should consider employing for a portrait, whose works are exhibited here. However, and I must apologise for my stupidly muddled head, I have quite forgotten the name of the artist, and my acquaintance has gone abroad and will not return for some weeks. I think it may have been either Fields or Meadows.'

He nodded. 'Meadows. Don't know the Christian name.' Slowly, he unfolded himself from his seat. 'I can show you some drawings over here.'

He extracted three unframed drawings from the group stacked against the wall, and placed them in a row, then stood back with folded arms. All were in pen and ink and were of local scenes; beggars on the Grove, a summertime study of girls in flowered bonnets and muslins, and a fashionable lady riding by in an open-topped victoria. The first two pictures looked to have been done in recent months but the last clearly had not, as it depicted Queen's Road before some of the demolition, conversions and building of the last few years, which suggested to Frances that Mr Meadows was well acquainted with the area and had probably lived and worked there for some time. The penmanship was well done, and the style was oddly familiar. It took a moment or two before she realised why.

'Has the artist ever drawn a portrait of Mr and Mrs James Keane?' she asked.

'I don't know,' said the man. 'It's very possible, I suppose, as his associate Mr Garton was the artist's agent.'

Frances pressed a gloved hand to parted lips in the mock alarm used by purveyors of gossip to conceal delight at a choice morsel of news. 'Dear me!' she exclaimed. 'Not the same Mr Garton who died so tragically last week!'

'The very same,' said the young man, shaking his head regretfully. 'Tragic, as you say.'

127

'I was not acquainted with him myself,' said Frances confidingly, 'but I have heard say that he was a gentleman of very pleasing manners, and a great connoisseur of art. You must have known him very well. I expect he came here often on business.'

The manager yawned again, and she had to control herself so as not to recoil from the reek of cheap liquor on his breath. 'Hardly at all, as it so happens.'

'Really? I find that very surprising. Did he not call to see if Mr Meadows' pictures were a success with the public?'

'He called about once a month. He didn't say much to me. He mainly came to see Mr Keane.' He pulled his coat more closely about him and went to warm his hands in front of the fire.

Frances wondered if these meetings at the gallery related to mutual business interests. There was a door in the shadows at the back of the display area, which she had noted earlier but had not seemed to be of any importance, but which she now realised could well lead to a room where business was conducted. She decided not to be too prying, in case it aroused suspicions, and returned to her original enquiry. 'And what of Mr Meadows? I am most anxious to meet him to arrange a commission. Does he come here?'

'He has never been here, as far as I am aware,' said the manager indifferently, 'I have not met the fellow.'

'This must be a very difficult time for him with the loss of his patron,' persisted Frances, in a tone suggesting deep sympathy. 'One hopes that he will not be long in that position. Perhaps if he is fortunate, Mr Keane may be pleased to encourage him.'

'Possibly. Mr Keane is now managing some of Mr Garton's affairs. Perhaps Mr Meadows was bequeathed to him.' He sighed, ruefully. 'Which is more than I was.'

Frances was surprised by this comment, then suddenly saw the implication behind his words. Did Garton's death mean the end of the manager's employment? In which case Percival Garton had been more than just a patron of art, and an interested spectator. Either solely or in partnership with James Keane, he had been the owner of the gallery.

'Has Mr Keane decided to sell the gallery?' she asked.

'It's as good as done already. There are some items waiting to be collected and we close in two days. And there's an end to my wages and my rooms all at once,' he added gloomily. 'I live in the apartments above,' he explained.

'I am very sorry to hear it,' she said. 'It is as well that I came here today. I would like to make an appointment to see Mr Meadows to discuss the commissioning of a portrait. Would you favour me with his address?'

'I'm afraid I don't have his address. But if you were to leave a note here for Mr Keane, I will hand it to him, and I am sure he would oblige.'

'I think Mr Meadows must be a Bayswater resident,' said Frances, 'judging by these pictures.'

'I expect so.' The man tucked his hands under his arms to retain any warmth they may have absorbed from the fire, and went back to his seat. She took out her notebook to write a message but without any great anticipation of success. With the closure of the gallery imminent, this was probably her last chance to find out more. She wondered if there was anything of interest in the other room.

Frances began to shiver. 'Oh dear,' she said, 'it is so very cold in here.'

The manager was far from being what she would have called a gentleman, yet he did have the good grace to be concerned. Approaching her, he said, 'It is deadly cold today, come nearer to the fire. May I offer you something?' He reached into his pocket.

The last thing Frances wanted was a sip of whatever was in the flask. She knew from the professional journals that the public's belief in alcohol as something that warmed the system was a fallacy, but so popular was the concept that she had quite given up informing people of this, as it often led to ridicule.

'I think I may have a slight touch of influenza,' she explained, in a faltering voice. 'I am feeling a little faint. Perhaps if I could sit down for a few moments?' He glanced around at the high stool, and offered to conduct her to it, but she began to sway alarmingly. 'Oh no, please, I think I would fall down if I were to sit there.'

He hesitated. 'There's a comfortable chair in the office, but it isn't very warm.'

'Oh, yes, please,' she gasped, 'anywhere I might rest and close my eyes.'

He opened the door at the back of the gallery and, taking her gently by the elbow, led her inside.

A small window admitted just enough murky light to make out the interior. It was a small, wood-panelled office room, with a carved desk, two chairs upholstered in leather, and a roll-top cabinet. He tried to steer her towards the chair in front of the desk but somehow she managed to stagger into the chair behind the desk, and flop weakly into it.

'Is there a friend I can send a message to?' he offered. 'Or may I call a cab to take you home?'

Frances, who was now adding 'indisposed lady' to her cast of characters, smiled bravely. 'That is very kind of you, Sir, but I will be well with just a few minutes' rest.'

'Very well, Miss – er?'

'Williamson.'

'My name is Guy Berenger.' He paused, and gave her a puzzled look. 'I don't suppose we have met before?'

'I do not believe so,' said Frances, turning her head so the shadows fell upon her face.

'Only, I hope you don't think I'm being forward, Miss, it's the artist in me that is talking, but you have very distinctive features and I can't help thinking that your face looks familiar.'

At this awkward moment, there was the sound of the shop door opening, and he peered out of the office door.

'Berenger!' said a commanding voice.

'It's Mr Keane – I must go.' He hurried out, and closed the door behind him.

Frances realised that if she was to find anything of interest in the room she had possibly no more than seconds to do so. She pulled open the top

131

drawer of the desk, finding only ink and pencils. Another drawer yielded notepaper and a few coins. The other drawers contained folders of papers, which she had no time at all to look through. She then saw that the wastepaper basket had some pieces of crumpled paper in the bottom, and quickly took them out and stuffed them into her pocket. Hopefully, it would be assumed that a servant had cleared them away. She had just enough time to flop back into the chair as the door was flung open.

'What is this?' demanded a voice. James Keane stood in the doorway; his feet planted firmly apart, his chest thrust forward. His hair was dark and glossy and his handsome face was framed by a flamboyant set of side-whiskers and a beard, which curled strangely about its fringes. The intense blue of his eyes was made more so by a piercing gaze. Here was a man who assumed he was in command of any situation of which he was a part, but the artist who had captured his image in the drawing which Adam had consigned contemptuously to the fire, had seen beneath this presumption. There was, Frances knew, something essentially shallow about the man. He was all noise and bluster without, she was sure, the qualities of character or intellect to justify his outward show of confidence. In the gallery behind him, Guy Berenger stood, his hands clasped anxiously in front of him, his face a mask of concern.

'Excuse me, Sir,' said Frances, 'I was overcome by faintness and needed a few moments' rest. I feel I am suffering from a touch of influenza.'

Keane strode into the room and pulled open the

drawer containing the coins, in a manner which suggested he fully expected to discover that they were missing. Seeing that they were still there he said only 'Hmph!' slammed the drawer shut, and turned to her. 'Well madam, I cannot permit you to remain here. You appear to me to be fully recovered and I suggest you take your departure.'

Frances decided not to appear in too much of a hurry to leave in case that aroused further suspicions. She began to carefully ease herself from the chair. Berenger rushed forward and helped her up. 'Thank you, Sir,' she said, gratefully. 'I feel very much refreshed by my brief rest.'

Keane scowled at her. There were gentlemen whose hard hearts would melt at the sight of womanly weakness. Clearly James Keane was a man who regarded such an affliction as an insufferable personal inconvenience.

She favoured him with a polite smile. 'Before I go, Mr Keane, would you be so kind as to inform me how I might obtain an interview with Mr Meadows? The purpose of my visit here was to commission him to paint a portrait.'

'Meadows has gone to Paris, and is not expected to return,' said Keane, curtly.

'I am sorry to hear it, good evening.' As Frances made a dignified exit from the premises, she became aware of the smell of charring paper, and turned to see that Keane had walked over to the fireplace, taken some crumpled slips from his pockets, and thrown them onto the dull red coals.

She was eager to look at the papers in her pocket as soon as she was able, but found on her return that Constable Brown was waiting for her in the

133

shop. Herbert was regarding him coldly. Frances realised that, unaware that the young policeman was a married man, Herbert saw him as a rival for her affections, and was alert to the danger of either the business as it stood, or its value should it be sold, slipping away from him. She did not feel inclined to relieve Herbert's anxiety by informing him that Constable Brown had not come to court her, and greeted the policeman in a friendly manner. Out of the corner of her eye, she saw the moustache tips quiver like the strings of a violin.

Wilfred had a large scrapbook tucked under his arm. 'I brought this Miss,' he said. 'Some of my father's papers. I think you'll find them very interesting.'

As they settled in the upstairs parlour with tea, Wilfred opened the book on the table. 'I've got the *Illustrated Police News* here, and all sorts of cuttings from the local papers. I think he must have written to the police in Gloucestershire or someone he knew there to have all these things. It was a murder in 1870, a Mr John Wright who lived in Tollington Mill, and the Gartons were living there at the time, in fact Mrs Garton gave evidence at the inquest. One thing – I'm afraid the *Illustrated Police News* can be a bit – er – well the artist gets carried away sometimes, I think. I hope you won't be offended. I know some ladies who would be very upset by it. You're not upset, Miss?'

Frances gazed at the pictures on the front page, dated 27 August 1870, which included a gruesome murder in Kensington, a tragic drowning near Swansea, a scene of battle near somewhere called Metz, and a man strangling his wife in

Manchester. 'It's a very unusual style of journalism,' she said. 'It reminds one of tales told to schoolchildren to frighten them into good behaviour. I shall certainly avoid all of these places in future.' Turning the pages she discovered an account of the inquest on John Wright held on the 22nd. Cuttings of varying sizes from other publications were enclosed in the leaves of the scrapbook, and she unfolded them and laid them out on the table.

As Frances read the reports of the inquest in all its different guises, she thought how much like a jigsaw puzzle it was. Each writer had a different style, and had been permitted a different number of words, and each publication had its own ideas as to what the important facts were, or what their readers might want to know. Therefore no account of the proceedings contained all the facts, and even the wordiest sometimes omitted what was included in others. Each supplied a number of pieces which she had to put together, not in order to see the final picture, but to see where the places were that still needed to be filled.

The first and most important witness was Mrs Cranby, John Wright's housekeeper. She had been engaged by Wright when he had first leased Tollington House in June 1869. She knew nothing of his family, or any friends he might have had before his arrival, as he had never spoken to her of them, nor would she have expected him to do so. He was a quiet young man, with pleasing manners, who had at once made himself agreeable in the neighbourhood. As far as she knew, he had no business interests but was of independent means.

135

His chief amusement appeared to be country walks, and drawing, which two he usually combined, often in the company of Mr Garton, who was a near neighbour at Old Mill House. Mr Wright, she recalled, had only one peculiarity, he used to dye his hair black. She knew this because after his death a partly used bottle of dye had been found in his bathroom. Not that other gentlemen did not also dye their hair, but in her experience, it was done by gentlemen of more advanced years who wished to appear younger. Mr Wright had no reason of that sort as she estimated his age to be less than thirty.

On 3 July 1870, Mr Wright had told her that he planned to be absent on business for a month, and the house was to be shut up and the servants placed in rented accommodation until his return. He did not reveal the nature of the business and she did not enquire. All was carried out according to his instructions and he left that same evening. At the time of his departure he was wearing, as he usually did, a gold watch and chain. She also recalled that he carried a pocket book in which he kept banknotes, and a small memorandum book, and shortly before he departed she saw him placing these items in the inside pocket of his coat. She heard nothing more from him until 29 July, when she received a letter from Mr Wright postmarked Bristol. He said that he would be passing through Tollington Mill on the following day, as he had an appointment of some importance in the vicinity, and if the opportunity presented itself he would call upon her to give her further instructions. If he was not able to call that day, he promised to call in one week's time. Mrs Cranby had obligingly waited in for her employer but he did not call on 30 July, nor did he call the following week. Shortly afterwards the servants discovered that the rent of their accommodation, which had been paid by Mr Wright until the end of July, had not been renewed. Mr Wright had always been the most considerate of masters, and Mrs Cranby, unable to believe that even a man who dyed his hair would abandon his servants in that manner, had become anxious for his safety. She had made enquiries in the neighbourhood and found only one person who had seen Mr Wright recently, Mrs Garton, who had encountered him by chance on 30 July. After waiting another week and hearing no more from her employer, Mrs Cranby decided to go to the police. Her thought at that time was that he might have met with an accident.

The next time she saw Mr Wright was on 17 August, when she was asked to identify his body. Those newspapers with room for such details reported that when recollecting this event, Mrs Cranby became very distressed and was furnished with a glass of water.

Police Constable Alfred Cooper testified that he had been present when the body of John Wright was discovered on 17 August. On receiving information that a gentleman was missing, and being informed of his last known whereabouts, he and other constables had proceeded on foot along the country roads where the gentleman had most likely travelled, examining ditches and fields along the way. They had spoken to a passing shepherd who had informed them that his dog had become unusually excited when close by an abandoned quarry in the area, but he had not troubled himself to investigate the matter. On examining the quarry they had found, hidden under branches torn from some nearby bushes, the body of a man, who had clearly been dead for at least two weeks. Constable Cooper had searched the man's pockets to discover his identity and found a pocket book and a memorandum book with the name John Wright and the address Tollington House. There was nothing of value on the body.

The coroner asked the constable if he had in his possession the items found on the body of the deceased, and these were at once produced, creating, according to the *Daily Bristol Times and Mirror*, a 'sensation in court'. Of particular interest were the pages in which John Wright had kept a diary of his appointments. These revealed that Wright had spent the weeks between his departure and 29 July in Hertfordshire, though no addresses were given, and there were no clues as to whom he had met there. The Hertfordshire police were currently making enquiries. On 29 July, Wright had recorded the word 'Bristol' and on 30 July 'Tollington Mill, appointment with M 3 o'clock'. No one had as yet discovered where he had stayed in Bristol, or the identity of the person he had arranged to meet.

The next to give evidence was Mrs Henrietta Garton. She and her husband had become acquainted with Mr Wright on his arrival in Tollington Mill. He had made a favourable impression on them, and had dined with them at their home, Old Mill House, on several occasions. He had never spoken to them, either of his family or any business interests, and they had assumed that he was a man of independent means. Wright and her husband had a mutual interest in painting and drawing, and the two men would often go on walks in the countryside where they would make sketches of the landscape and houses, before returning to Old Mill House for tea. At the beginning of July – she could not recall the date – Mr Wright had mentioned that he would shortly be away on business for a month. He did not say where he was going. On 30 July – and she was sure of the date as it had coincided with the village fancy goods bazaar – she had met him in the street quite by chance. He was on foot, walking briskly, going, as far as she could see, in the direction of Thornbury. He had stopped for only a moment, greeted her politely, and apologised for not being able to remain longer, but he was hurrying to an appointment of very great importance. She had said only that she would not detain him further, but hoped that he would have the leisure to call on another occasion. She never saw him again. She did not think it especially unusual for Mr Wright to be on foot as he was a man who thought nothing of long walks, and the weather was very fine that day. At the time, she and her husband had been preparing to move to London and this they did on 10 August. She did not hear of Mr Wright's death until she read of it in the newspapers.

The last witness of any importance was Dr McPhail. There was, according to the *Gloucester Journal,* a hum of excited chatter in court at his appearance, and he was obliged, almost at once, to deny emphatically that he was the mysterious 'M' who had met Mr Wright on his last appointment. Dr McPhail had been the first medical man to see the body, and had later conducted a post-mortem examination. He testified that John Wright had died from a single blow to the back of the head with a heavy blunt instrument. He had not died where he lay, but at some other, unknown location. The body had been taken to the spot where it was found, thrown into the old quarry, and covered with branches. It was his opinion that both the murder and the hiding of the body would require some physical strength, and that the criminal was therefore undoubtedly male.

The jury, after a brief deliberation, recorded the verdict that John Wright had been murdered by some person or persons unknown, but that was not the end of the mystery, for even three weeks after his death no member of his family had come forward to claim him. The newspapers devoted columns of print speculating about his identity, and, there being no portrait of the man, artists were employed to draw his likeness based on interviews with witnesses in the hopes that someone would recognise him. The fact of his hair being dyed was regarded as highly suspicious, and while some artists depicted him with black hair, others shaded their drawings to suggest brown, or even blond. All the pictures showed a slim, clean shaven man, with nothing to distinguish him except youthful good looks, his facial features varying depending on whom the artist had interviewed.

'Who is to say which of these pictures is most

like the man?' said Frances. 'Do you think there is any connection between the murder of John Wright and Mr Garton's death?'

'Who can say, Miss? It could just be coincidence. But I do find it very interesting, all the same.'

The last cutting, dated a month after the murder, bore the headline 'Tollington Mill Tragedy: Distressing Family Secret.' A relative of John Wright had at last come forward and revealed that he was not, as had been supposed, a man of property, but an escaped lunatic whose brain had become deranged after suffering a fever. Although he appeared from both intellect and manner to be of sound mind, he suffered from the belief that he was the heir to a great fortune and that there were enemies plotting to cheat him of his inheritance. The little fortune he did have had been squandered on lawyers' fees, and his despairing family, afraid that he would plunge them all into debt, had had him declared insane and locked away. It was only in the last few days that they had realised that the murdered man was their unfortunate relative.

'What a very sad tale,' said Frances. She looked through the cuttings once more. 'It doesn't say in any of the papers why Mr Garton was not called as a witness,' she observed. 'It is mentioned that he and Mr Wright were friends, yet he seems not to have been questioned. Also it has been assumed that Mr Wright was murdered on the 30th of July, which, although probable, is far from proven. It could easily have happened on the following day or the day after. I accept that it is most unlikely that Mrs Garton could have murdered Mr Wright,

141

at least not unaided, as she would not have been strong enough, but where was Mr Garton at this time?'

'You suspect him?' asked Wilfred in surprise. 'For what reason?'

'Only that he himself has been murdered. It could have been a matter of revenge.'

'But it is nine and a half years since Wright's murder,' he reminded her, 'and Mr Garton has not been hiding himself away. If some relative of Wright suspected Garton, would they have waited so long to take revenge?'

'They might only now have obtained the proof they needed,' said Frances. 'Tell me, did the police ever discover who Mr Wright was supposed to be meeting on the 30th of July? The person whose name begins with M?'

'No, Miss, never.'

Frances took up her notebook and examined the list of names. The only persons on the list with that initial were Mr Morgan, James Keane's father-in-law, and Mrs Keane, who was called Mary, but there was now another name to add. 'Meadows,' she said.

'Meadows?' repeated Wilfred, mystified.

'The name of the artist of whom Mr Garton was patron. There are pictures of his at the gallery on Queen's Road, which I believe was owned by Mr Garton. I have been wondering if the clue to the murder of Mr Garton lies in his business interests, and Mr Meadows might be able to tell us something about that aspect of Mr Garton's life. I am told that Mr Meadows has gone to Paris, but I am afraid I do not have his address.'

She paused to allow Wilfred time to scribble the information in his notebook. 'I don't suppose the police have already interviewed Mr Meadows?'

'No,' confessed Wilfred, 'the police have only just this minute found out that Mr Meadows exists.'

After he had left, Frances reflected that it was too much to hope for that Meadows could be the M whom Mr Wright had been meeting. After all, her own uncle had a surname beginning with M and her aunt was called Maude, but she was hardly going to suspect them of involvement.

She had been so interested in the details of Mr Wright's murder that she had all but forgotten the scraps of paper in her pocket. Now she removed them and smoothed them out on the table. They were receipts for expenditure, and looked as if they had been kept crumpled in a pocket, possibly for some time. She wondered why they had not been put on the fire. It might have simply been a moment of carelessness. The thing that puzzled her was why anyone would dispose of a receipt for expenditure, to her mind an item of vital importance in any business or household account. One, with a November date, was for artists' materials, pens, paper and coloured inks. The other, also dated November, was for three months' advance rent of an address in Maida Vale. The landlord had helpfully provided the name of the person renting the property. It was Meadows.

CHAPTER EIGHT

The following morning, Frances wrote a note to Constable Brown advising him of the Maida Vale address where she believed the artist Meadows had lived. The rent receipt showed that on 1 December Meadows had fully intended to remain at the lodgings for three months. She doubted very much that Mr Keane had told the truth when stating that Meadows had gone to Paris. Much as she would have liked to go to Maida Vale, her duties did not permit such an excursion, and in any case, she felt that the police were best placed to demand information from the landlord. It was when she began seeking Tom to deliver the note that she realised she had not seen him for the last two days. After a brief search she discovered him in the kitchen, gazing wistfully at the locked door of the larder. Frances had every confidence in Sarah's honesty with the household stores but her father distrusted all servants and in Tom's case was certainly right. To her surprise, Tom was wearing a suit of clothes which, while obviously not brand new, was of more recent vintage than even his old Sunday best, and better she thought than any family hand-me-down might be.

'Well, Tom, those are splendid new clothes,' she said.

'Yes, Miss,' he said, puffing out his chest with a

grin. 'Don't I look spruce? Don't I look just the gen'leman?'

'Not too grand to deliver a letter, I hope,' she said. 'To Constable Brown at Paddington Green Police Station.'

Tom's eyes widened.

'Not afraid of the police, are you Tom?' she teased.

'I ain't afraid of no copper!' he exclaimed, taking the note. He smirked. 'Partic'lar friend of yours, this Constable Brown?'

'That's none of your business, Tom,' said Frances sharply, realising to her dismay that she was blushing. 'Now set about it quickly!'

'Best message carrier in London, that's me!' he said, and sped away.

Frances wondered whether the unpleasant Mr Keane had ever visited the address in Maida Vale. She was sure that he had something to hide. Mrs Keane would probably be the very last person to know of any doubtful business he might be transacting, but the servants could well have information about his comings and goings. With the adjourned inquest due to take place the next morning, she had little time to gather more facts. As she considered how she might do this, a new plan formed in her mind.

After the breakfast things had been cleared, Frances and Sarah worked together on starching shirts and aprons, which Sarah would iron later in the day. 'Young Tom looks very smart in his new suit,' Frances observed, 'I hope you have not been to too much expense.'

Sarah frowned. 'I hope you don't mind, Miss,'

she said awkwardly, 'but what with the business here being a bit quiet Tom has found some extra work with two gentlemen who have provided the clothes themselves. I am not sure who they are or what their business is, but I think he takes messages for them.'

'Well, if he is able to, then it shows an enterprising spirit, but I do anticipate that when the inquest is over we will be vindicated and then the unfortunate death of Mr Garton will not be laid at our door, and the customers will return,' said Frances, with more confidence than she felt. 'No doubt they will say that they believed in my father's innocence all along, and will try to gloss over their absence with some feeble and unconvincing excuse. We will be bustling again soon, especially at this season, and Tom will be much required.'

'Yes, Miss, I'll make sure to tell him,' said Sarah, loyally.

The work done, Frances rinsed the starch from her hands, and began a curious process of making her hair look a little dishevelled, as if she was a young woman in distress. Throwing on her old coat in a suitably careless manner, she set off to walk to the Keanes' house again. She was not concerned that there was any risk of encountering Mr Keane, as she doubted that he had ever set foot in his own kitchen, but hoped she would not fall under the supercilious suspicions of Mr Harvey. The kitchen was a haven of warmth as before, but only Ettie was present.

'Well, Liza, I didn't expect to see you again!' exclaimed Ettie. She looked tired and flustered, but not displeased to see the unexpected visitor. The scullery door was open and Frances could see that the breakfast pans were still heaped in the sink. 'Oh, we have had such a morning! Master and Mistress have been shouting loud enough they could be heard all over the house, and there has been best china smashed to pieces, and Mistress has got her hysterics again.'

'Oh, how dreadful!' exclaimed Frances, picturing in her mind's eye a small knot of open-mouthed servants clustered about a door, ears pressed close to the panelling.

'Mr Harvey went up to try and calm them, and has done what he can, which is not as much as he had hoped, and he is still with them now. He wanted to call the doctor to Mistress but Master wouldn't hear of it. And Mrs Grinham is laid up with the lumbago and not fit to move, and the new scullery maid has said she won't work in such a madhouse and has packed her bags and gone. We're lucky to have Ellen; she's been in service since she was twelve and can turn her hand to anything.'

'Oh, Ettie – I'm sorry if I have come at a difficult time for you,' said Frances.

'We have had our ups and downs here and no mistake,' said Ettie. 'And what about you, Liza; I hope you didn't get into trouble over the cake.'

Frances sat down and clasped a handkerchief to her face. 'Oh, you wouldn't credit it, Ettie, Master as good as accused me of stealing it. I was lucky he didn't call the coppers! And now I've no place and no character! I came here to see if Mrs Grinham would see me about getting some work.

147

I'll do the rough work, Ettie, I don't mind!'

Ettie patted her shoulder sympathetically. 'I tell you what, Liza, I'll put in a word for you as soon as she's up and about.'

'Oh, thank you Ettie, that's so kind.' Frances made a great show of wiping her eyes. 'Why don't I give you a little hand now?' There was a coarse apron, cap and sleeve protectors hanging up behind the door of the scullery, and Frances removed her coat and bonnet and transformed herself into a scullery maid, then set about seeing what there was in hot water, scouring cloths and soda. The polite injunction not to trouble herself about it trembled on Ettie's lips but remained unspoken. There was no mistaking the maid's look of profound relief.

Ellen emerged from the larder, her arms laden with bowls and jars which she set down next to some wrapped parcels on the table. She stood back and surveyed the produce. 'Luncheon will be cutlets, kidneys, potatoes and stewed leeks followed by a raisin tart,' she said. 'Only I don't know if they'll even want anything to eat.'

'The last time I saw Mistress she was crying and saying that Master thought she was a burden on the family and no morsel of food would ever pass her lips again,' said Ettie.

'In that case,' said Ellen, thoughtfully, 'I'd better make a sweet custard sauce to go with the tart.' She looked up and saw Frances in the scullery. 'Why it's Liza – I didn't see you there!'

'Liza has come to help us out, seeing as we're in such a state,' said Ettie.

'Oh that's very kind of you!' said Ellen rolling

up her sleeves.

'Come,' said Ettie to Frances. 'We'll do the pots together and I'll make us a nice cup of tea when we're done.'

Frances and Ettie began to scour pans, while Ellen made pastry. As she scrubbed with a will, Frances saw Ettie glancing at her approvingly. Years of wielding a heavy pestle and working thick ointments with a spatula had given her the strength to make nothing of the encrustations on a few saucepans.

'It's very upsetting when Master and Mistress quarrel like that,' said Frances, shaking her head. 'In the place I was before I used to brush the carpet outside the drawing room door and you couldn't help but hear all they said.'

'And then they accuse you of listening at key-holes,' said Ettie indignantly, 'something I would *never* do!'

'Nor me, neither,' said Frances, hoping that her grammar was suitably incorrect. 'Master was always going out all times of the day and night and he told Mistress it was on business, but do you know, it turned out he was seeing some fancy woman, and when she found him out, oh the things that were said, I couldn't repeat them!'

'Oh, there's many a gentleman looks respectable enough but goes out visiting that sort,' said Ettie scornfully. She paused. 'Now Mr Keane, we've never been sure what *he* does, but I've always sus-pected there's a woman in it somewhere. He often takes the gig and goes out alone, and Lord only knows where he goes or what he gets up to.'

Frances felt it appropriate to give a little gasp at

this point. 'Does your Mistress suspect him?'

Ettie gave a little laugh. 'Oh, I don't think Mistress cares one way or another. All their quarrels were over money.'

'Surely not?' exclaimed Frances, 'what with Mr Keane being such a wealthy man? Or perhaps he is one of those misers who keeps all his money for himself and grudges his wife if she wants to dress in the latest fashion.'

Ettie gave a rapid glance over her shoulder then leaned closer. Frances held her breath, feeling sure that she was about to receive a confidence. 'Mistress was saying how Mr Garton had left Master £50,000 in his will' – Frances thought it right to give a slightly larger gasp than before – 'and she said he ought to be able to spare something, and Master said he had thrown away quite enough money in the past and was not going to waste any more.' She pursed her lips with disapproval.

'How dreadful!' exclaimed Frances.

'Then she cried a great deal and said something about being ruined, and *he* said that the Garton family wanted the will overturned, so even if he wanted to part with the money, which he decidedly did not, he couldn't lay his hands on it until everything was settled and that could be months or even years. And Mistress cried so hard I thought she would burst.'

'Well,' said Frances, 'fancy that!' She frowned. 'Does Mr Garton have a very big family, for I never heard of any?'

'Oh they are all in Italy, except for his brother Mr Cedric who visits from time to time.' Ettie paused again, and Frances was silent in anticipation. 'I heard Mr Harvey saying that the family in Italy are not as prosperous as they once were, and Mr Garton has left them not a penny piece in his will. Last year, Mr Cedric wrote to his brother on purpose to ask him to provide a pension for their father who is very aged and infirm and has had to retire from business. But apart from what was left to Master, everything has gone to Mrs Garton.'

Frances puzzled over how Mr Harvey could have acquired such an intimate knowledge of the Garton family's financial affairs, but the information was detailed enough not to sound fanciful. 'But Mr Garton was such a kind man, by all accounts,' she said. 'Why would he be so cruel to his own father?'

'Well he might have been just about to change his will before he died,' said Ettie.

Frances pondered this. If true, and the new will would mean a serious loss for James Keane, this gave him a clear motive for murder.

The breakfast things done, and put away, and a refreshing cup of tea consumed, Frances started to peel potatoes and cut up leeks while Ettie took dusters and brushes and went upstairs to clean the bedrooms. Work progressed in a companionable silence until Frances asked politely, 'Have you been here long, Ellen?'

'About a year. Longer than most.' She smiled. 'Servants don't stay here, what with all the goings-on.'

'Doesn't it upset you, all the quarrelling?'

'Oh, I don't take any notice of that.' Ellen

started the vegetables cooking and arranged the cutlets in a large frying pan, then turned to Frances. 'Miss Doughty?'

'Yes,' said Frances automatically, and then, 'Oh!'

Ellen laughed, but in a pleasant way. 'I *thought* it was you. I saw you once or twice in the shop. I would have liked to have worked in a chemist's – all those pills and potions, it looks really interesting – only I never had the right schooling for it.'

Frances felt a great impulse to put on her coat and bonnet and leave at once. 'Have you told the others who I am?' she asked anxiously.

'No,' said Ellen, softly. 'I think I can guess why you come here, and I understand, I really do.' There was a sympathetic sadness in her eyes.

'I need to find out the truth about Mr Garton's death,' exclaimed Frances. 'My father is unwell and he can't look after himself and he is being destroyed with unfair allegations, and the inquest is tomorrow, and–,' she broke off, hardly able to speak with distress.

'That must be very hard for you, Miss, but what can you do?'

'I talk to people; I try to learn everything I can. Maybe someone will tell me something that will show the police that my father couldn't have caused Mr Garton's death!'

'You mean like a detective, Miss?'

'Yes,' said Frances. She was sure by now that the girl would not give her away. 'Ellen, is there anything that you know which might help me – you may have heard something by chance – what are people saying about Mr Garton?'

Ellen thought about it and gave a little gesture

152

of helplessness. 'Only that it's a great shame he is dead and how upset Master is.'

'And do they say that it was my father's mistake that killed him?'

Ellen bent her head in regret. 'I'm sorry, but what else is there to think?'

Frances sighed. She took her leave soon afterwards, not before asking Ellen to make sure and tell her if she heard anything of interest, which Ellen solemnly promised to do, though she did not leave Frances with any great hope that there was much to learn.

That afternoon, Frances received a note from Wilfred.

Dear Miss Doughty
Thank you for the address you sent me. I cannot imagine how you came by it, and I think it would be by far the best thing if I did not ask you, but if they were ever to appoint lady police officers then I would be sure to recommend you. The address was searched this morning, and there was no sign of Meadows or anybody else. The landlord said that the house was rented by a person of that name, but as he does not live on the premises he was unable to tell us who stayed there. We think that the rent was paid by Mr Garton. We did find some paint and ink stains, which suggest that the house could have been used as an artist's studio. After our conversation yesterday, I wrote to the Gloucestershire Police asking what they know about where Mr Garton was at the time of John Wright's murder. I will write to you or call when I have a reply,
Wilfred Brown

Frances and Herbert were making the best of a quiet time in the shop when, to her surprise, the door opened admitting two gentlemen whom she had not expected to encounter again.

'Good afternoon, good afternoon my dear Miss Doughty!' exclaimed Chas, tipping his hat, and Barstie did likewise. Frances saw that not only were both in exuberant good spirits but they were dressed rather better than the last time she had seen them and Chas had a folded copy of a financial newspaper protruding rather ostentatiously from his pocket. 'We must apologise for not introducing ourselves properly at our first meeting. My name is Charles Knight, and this is my good friend and business associate Sebastian Taylor. Both at your service!'

'Good afternoon,' she said. 'I think I should mention that shortly after you called a few days ago a – er – friend of yours came looking for you.'

They exchanged glances. 'Oh, Miss Doughty, I do hope you don't think for one moment that the Filleter is any friend of ours,' said Barstie, mournfully.

'A rogue and a villain!' declared Chas. 'An individual best avoided.'

'He seemed very anxious to find you,' said Frances, mischievously.

'Ah, well, perhaps we should explain,' said Barstie. 'The person in question was labouring under an unfortunate misapprehension at the time. He was of the belief that we were indebted to him in some way.' The two men threw back their heads and laughed as if the very idea was ridiculous. 'Quite incorrect, of course.'

154

'But as it so happened,' went on Chas, 'our business commitments at that time did not permit us to correct that misapprehension. Only a few short days were required to settle everything to the satisfaction of all, yet those few days he would not allow.'

'Which is where,' said Barstie, 'to our eternal gratitude, you assisted us.'

'I did?' said Frances in astonishment.

'You did indeed,' he assured her. 'By making shall we say a tiny innocent error in directions, the Filleter thought that we were elsewhere. This gave us the time we required to conclude our arrangements. And thus the reason for our coming to see you now.'

'We do not forget our debts,' said Chas, expansively, 'and most especially we do not forget our friends, especially a charming and intelligent young lady such as yourself, if I might be allowed to say so. We have come, Miss Doughty to ask you to tea.'

'There is a very pretty little shop on the Grove,' added Barstie, 'where a refreshing pot of tea and a dainty bun may be had. We would be honoured if you would accompany us.' Both men made a respectful bow.

Frances dared not look at the expression on Herbert's face, as she felt sure that if she did she would burst out laughing. 'That would be most pleasant,' she said. 'I am sure Mr Munson can manage very well in my absence.' There was an indignant spluttering behind her, as she put on her bonnet and coat.

The Grove was unnaturally quiet, the continuing cold and damp hazy air discouraging the crowds that usually thronged the street. In the teashop a warm fire blazed, and waitresses in neat uniforms darted back and forth with laden trays of steaming teapots and delicious-looking cakes. Condensation streamed down the windows where the curtains, which must have been crisp and white that morning now hung limp and grey. The diners consisted mainly of overdressed ladies refreshing themselves after an arduous morning, choosing layettes and linen, gratefully drinking cups of hot tea and stifling rattling coughs. Frances made herself comfortable, and Chas and Barstie ordered the tea and buns.

'Now Miss Doughty,' began Chas. 'If you do not think it impertinent, there is something I must say. We have over the last few days become aware of the distressing situation in which you find yourself, and may we say that if there is some small service we can perform to alleviate that situation, you have only to ask.'

'Thank you,' said Frances gratefully. 'This is a very trying time. You must know that the inquest resumes tomorrow and the entire future of our business depends on the verdict. We have already suffered greatly, and unless my father is entirely exonerated I fear we may never recover.'

'Are you confident of a happy outcome?' asked Barstie, as the tea and buns arrived.

'I–' began Frances, and for a moment her reserve unexpectedly left her and she felt tears start in her eyes, tears which, to her embarrassment, she was quite unable to hide or stop. 'There are terrible things afoot and I fear that my father is being made a scapegoat. I am speaking of murder!' Chas and Barstie gazed at her in some alarm. There was a certain amount of murmured sympathy, offering of handkerchiefs and pouring of tea. The plate of buns was pushed in her direction, and then, as that did not have the desired effect, bread and butter, marmalade, cocoa, and finally potted shrimps were ordered and appeared, as if the application of food and drink could soothe her distress. Frances sat there helplessly with tears pouring down her cheeks and wondering why it was, when she was able to quell her emotions with those who meant most to her, she was suddenly bereft of proper control in front of two men who were almost total strangers.

'Please be assured, my dear young lady,' said Chas, 'if there is anything in our power we may do to assist you, you have only to ask!'

'Thank you,' whispered Frances, drying her eyes.

'You believe that Mr Garton was murdered?' asked Barstie, in astonishment.

She nodded. 'But by whom or how it was done, or why, I can only guess.'

'This is all about money,' declared Chas. 'I can feel it – I can smell it – money! Take my advice, Miss Doughty, the important questions to ask are who has the money, where did he get it from, and who else lays claim to it. And don't trust to outward appearances or who makes the most noise. There's many a rogue in a carriage and pair with only someone else's money to his name.' He patted the newspaper at his side. 'Now according to rumours in all the financial prints, Mr Garton left £150,000 – a very nice sum. Where did it all come from, I wonder?'

'He inherited a shipping business from his grandfather,' said Frances. 'And I have been told that he left a third of his fortune to his friend Mr James Keane and the remainder to his widow. But he may have been about to change the will before he died, to leave a pension to his aged father.'

'What did I say?' said Chas triumphantly. 'Motive! Motive plain and simple!' he leaned forward excitedly. 'Who do you suspect – the widow?'

'I suspect Mr Keane,' said Frances, confidently.

'Ah yes, another gentleman of some standing in Bayswater. And where does *his* fortune come from, I should like to know?'

'Well,' said Frances, 'there is his position in the bank–'

To her surprise they both gave a short laugh. 'Mr Keane's position is to puff himself up and strut like a turkey-cock,' said Barstie, 'but the Bayswater Bank is a small concern, and if you were to go there and ask for an interview with the manager it would not be Mr Keane who appeared.'

'I think it is generally known that he owes the greater part of his wealth to his marriage,' said Frances. 'Mrs Keane is the former Miss Morgan, only daughter of Thomas Morgan, who has the great double-fronted fancy millinery shop on the Grove.'

'Well, now, that is *very* interesting,' said Chas. He leaned back, helped himself to a bun and munched thoughtfully.

'Mr and Mrs Keane had a great quarrel only this morning about money,' said Frances. 'I think

158

he is a very cruel man who will not keep his wife as she deserves. She begged him for some portion of the sum he was due to inherit, but he refused, and she was very distressed. He went so far as to say that he had thrown away a great deal of money in the past and would not do so again.'

'Did he now?' said Barstie softly and he and Chas exchanged knowing glances.

'She even spoke of being ruined for lack of means,' added Frances. 'A man who would treat his wife with so little regard is surely capable of murder.'

'Now,' said Chas, 'leaving aside all question of how you came by that information, which I am sure was not in any way demeaning to your reputation, do you recall hearing Mrs Keane say for what purpose she required the money?'

'I–' Frances frowned, trying to recall what Ettie had said. 'No, I do not.'

Chas raised an eyebrow. 'What do you think, Barstie?'

Barstie nodded. 'I think I know, Chas.'

'Well, gentlemen?' asked Frances, looking from one to the other.

'The thing is,' said Chas, pouring more tea, 'you need to know that a great many things go on in the financial world which never appear in the journals, or if they do they are revealed to the public a very long time after persons who move in those circles have had all the facts in their possession. I can tell you now that Mr Thomas Morgan is one of those tradesmen who has grown his premises to great proportions not on the profits he has made but on the expectation of profits to come. Such men are

159

often disappointed. They have a beautiful shop, a large shop, a shop exhibiting the very perfection of taste and fashion, but what they do not have is the customers to maintain the business. Sooner or later, they will be obliged to admit failure, and then the public, who have seen only the outer show, will be amazed. Men with financial brains, however, will only be surprised that it did not happen sooner.'

'What my associate is saying,' said Barstie, helping himself to the potted shrimps, 'is that Mr Morgan has been on the brink of bankruptcy for several years. In fact it is a curious thing, that he has advanced to the very edge of ruin several times, only to retire from the brink just as he was expected to fall.'

Frances suddenly understood. 'So Mr Keane has been helping him?'

'It would seem so. Of course, it is not something that either would speak of. The quarrel you overheard suggests to me that Mrs Keane was begging her husband for money, not for her own expenses, but to save her father from ruin.'

'That would explain it,' said Frances. 'Unhappy lady!' She looked down at the bun on her plate. It was studded with tiny pieces of cherry and angelica, and sprinkled with crushed sugar. She broke off a piece and nibbled it, Chas and Barstie looking on approvingly. 'And no wonder Mr Keane felt he needed the inheritance if he has been losing all his money helping Mr Morgan. That is surely a motive for murder. I had been wondering, too, if there had been any business dispute between Mr Keane and Mr Garton. Perhaps you have heard something of the sort?'

'I don't know of any interests they had jointly,' said Chas.

'Would you be so kind as to try and discover if there was anything in that way? I have been wondering if they were partners in the Bayswater Gallery.'

'Of course!' said Barstie. 'It will be our very next piece of business. And now, I think I would like to propose a toast.' He raised a teacup. 'I would like to drink to the very good health and success of Miss Doughty and her family.'

'To Miss Doughty and family!' agreed Chas, finishing his tea at a gulp.

At that moment, a small rather grubby but familiar-looking hand sneaked a bun from the plate on the table. 'Message for you Mr Knight,' said Tom, with his mouth full. He passed a letter to Chas, who almost tore it in half in his eagerness to see the contents.

'Right!' exclaimed Chas, leaping to his feet. 'Business calls! Miss Doughty, our good wishes to you. No doubt we will meet again before long!'

Chas hurried from the teashop, leaving Barstie to pay the bill and amble after him with a polite smile. Tom sat at the table and rubbed his hands in anticipation. 'Best not to waste this!' he said, heaping marmalade onto bread and butter, 'What a feast!'

'How long have you been working for those gentlemen?' asked Frances.

'Since las' week,' said Tom. He flashed a sly look. 'That Mr Knight – 'e thinks you're a tasty spot 'o jam. 'E wants you to be 'is Dinah!'

161

There were times when Frances was truly grateful that she did not fully understand some of the things Tom said. 'And what *exactly* is Mr Knight's business?' she enquired.

Tom was munching shrimps washed down with cocoa. ''E never said. I never as'ed. Best thing.'

Frances left him polishing off the remainder of the little tea. It had been a pleasant interlude, but at home she was once again plunged into gloom. Unless something unexpected occurred before the following morning, the inquest on Percival Garton could very well leave her father under a permanent cloud of suspicion. She found Herbert reading the January edition of the *Chemist and Druggist* with an expression of deep concern. Wordlessly he showed her the report of an inquest into the recent death of Lilian Selina Holt, just five years old. She had been given a poisonous powder sold in error by an untrained assistant aged fourteen who had been left in temporary charge of a doctor's dispensary. The jury had brought in a verdict of death by misadventure, but added that there had been gross neglect. The coroner had been severe. He had called the boy forward and cautioned him as to greater care in future, and said he hoped the incident would be a lesson both to the doctor and his assistant. Had the powder been sold by a chemist, he added ominously, he would hardly have escaped so easily.

CHAPTER NINE

The day of the resumed inquest on Percival Garton dawned cold and grey. William Doughty seemed blissfully unaware that his future existence as he knew it hung in the balance. Frances, both saddened and relieved at this observation, was not about to enlighten him. She opened the shop as usual at seven, but no one came in. Customers who had once been pleased to idle there over small purchases, anxiously beg William's advice, or just exchange the gossip of the day, now hurried quickly by, with furtive glances and whispered words. At half past nine, by mutual agreement Frances and Herbert put up the closed sign and locked the door. William protested, but Frances pointed out gently that as all three of them were to attend the inquest, there was no one to mind the shop.

'I don't see why *you* can't stay, Frances,' he grumbled. 'I am sure you know how to sell cough lozenges and blood mixture by now. We will lose customers if we are closed!'

Frances usually deferred to her father's wishes, but on this occasion she stood firm. She had no intention of not being present at the inquest. 'I must attend in case I am required to give evidence,' she said, 'and who is to look after you and ensure you are comfortable if not myself?'

William muttered something about losing

money, almost as if he had not observed how far the business had declined in the last week, but as Frances fussed about him, making sure he was warmly dressed for the chill, he grudgingly accepted her attentions, and allowed himself to be bundled into the four-wheeler where Frances and Herbert joined him. Frances felt grateful that it was only a short journey, not so much because of the cold but because Herbert, intent on making a good impression, had freshly pomaded his moustache, and the pungent scent soon filled the interior of the cab. As they reached Paddington Green and turned into Church Street, Frances looked out of the window and gasped, and Herbert exclaimed, 'Dear Lord!'

'What is it?' asked William. 'Why have we stopped? Who are all these people? Has there been an accident?'

Despite the inclement weather, the street outside Providence Hall was choked with crowds of men and women, all eager to get inside. Some of the men were waving press tickets, but the rest were simply trying to push or argue their way through the doors. Frances felt her heart sink. The court had not been busy on the day the inquest had opened, but since then Percival Garton's death had been the subject of sensational articles in the newspapers, and even letters to *The Times* about the safety of chemists' shops, the agitation further fuelled by the recent tragic death of little Lilian Holt. From now on, thought Frances, with sudden dread, William Doughty's plight would not be a private affair, but a public scandal, like a play to be acted out in front of an audience hungry for excitement.

'How will we get inside?' said Herbert in dismay.

Just then, they saw Mr Rawsthorne and his clerk emerge from the hall. The two men pushed their way through the throng and ran up to the carriage. 'Ah, you are here – splendid,' exclaimed Rawsthorne, breathlessly. 'Pray do not be concerned with this dreadful situation, we will be allowed in, the court officials have been instructed to admit us.'

As they descended from the carriage Frances felt grateful that the unruly crowd was so intent on getting into the building that they had not realised that some of the central persons in the affair were only yards away. As Rawsthorne led them towards the door, policemen and ushers created a path and they began to pass quickly through the mob.

'Oi oi oi!' yelled the clerk, who had stuck his pens into his hair and had decided to draw attention to the new arrivals from sheer devilment. 'Make way, make way! Important witnesses for the inquest!' He flashed a grin of sheer insolence at Frances.

Frances, her arm fast folded in her father's, was grateful for the thick dark veil she wore, but she could hear voices around her suddenly say, 'Look! That's the chemist!' and 'Here – let me see!' One even cried out 'Murderer!' and there were jeers and groans. All around she was stifled with the crush of bodies, then she received a great push in the side, and almost fell, but before she could be pushed again, she stuck out her

165

thin, sharp elbow like a shield, so when the man who had pushed her tried again, he ran upon it, clutched his ribs and howled.

'Did you see that?' he yelled, 'Did you see that?' but no one had seen it, and the police moved forward and they at last emerged from the crush into the foyer of the court, and the police were able to hold back the crowds.

Frances was too concerned about her father to care much about herself. She saw him to a seat that was out of the draught, and listened sympathetically to his grumbles about the rudeness of common folk. Herbert paced up and down, clenching and unclenching his fists, and appeared, as far as she could see, to be rehearsing his evidence.

'Well, the good news is,' said Rawsthorne, when he had regained his breath, 'that I am confident the inquest will be over today. Once it is done then I think in a short while the whole matter will be forgotten.' He smiled down at William, encouragingly. 'Please do not worry yourself, my dear Mr Doughty. I have known you long enough to realise that you are never happier than at the dispensing desk, and I trust that you will be at your post for many years to come.'

As they filed into court, Frances saw that the crowds were still milling about outside the door, staring and gossiping, still hopeful of gaining admittance in a moment of inattention. She made sure that William was comfortable, then, taking her seat, she gazed about her and saw a number of familiar faces. James Keane was there, his body stiff with pride. It was impossible to read his

166

expression, for his face was a mask of propriety. Beside him, a bulky figure in a sombre dress with a substantial veiled hat was undoubtedly his wife Mary. Inspector Sharrock was also in court, as was Dr Collin, a tall, lean figure with mild eyes and silver-grey hair and whiskers. Mr Marsden, the Gartons' solicitor, was present, seated beside Cedric Garton. Towards the back of the court, a flash of purple told her of Guy Berenger's presence, and she could also see Ada. There was one important person she could not see.

'Mr Rawsthorne,' she asked, 'is Mrs Garton not here?'

'Oh yes,' he assured her, 'she will give evidence later, but she will sit in a side room during the medical testimony, which it is thought would be far too distressing.' Frances nodded understandingly. For Mrs Garton to be present at her husband's horrid death was one thing, to listen to a cold discussion of the contents of his intestines quite another.

The jury took their places, and Dr William Hardwicke, Coroner for Central Middlesex, entered and was seated. He looked about the court with a critical eye, as if gauging the quality of those attending. 'Before we begin I wish to point out to those in attendance that this court will not tolerate the kind of exhibition that has taken place in the street outside,' he said sternly. 'Anyone behaving in an unseemly manner will be held in contempt, and liable to prosecution. I hope that is understood.' The pressmen scribbled rapidly. 'We will begin with the adjourned inquest on Mr Percival Garton, aged forty-eight, who

167

died at his home in Porchester Terrace on the morning of Tuesday 13th of January. This court has already heard evidence of identification from the brother of the deceased, Mr Cedric Garton, and I wish now to proceed to the evidence of his medical attendant, Dr Collin.'

Dr Collin rose and took his place by the coroner's table.

'Dr Collin,' said the coroner, 'in your own words, please relate the events of the night of 12th to 13th of January last and the subsequent events concerning the death of Mr Percival Garton.'

Collin had a soft, drawling voice. At the bedside of a patient those calming tones would utter gentle reassurances that all would be well, and had soothed many a fretful sufferer into much needed repose. Here, he spoke easily and convincingly. 'I was called to attend Mr Garton shortly after midnight. I had already retired for the night, but on being told of the seriousness of the case, of course I dressed and came at once. It would have been about half past twelve on the morning of the 13th of January when I reached him. He was then between fits, and lay in bed exhausted, his body bathed in sweat. He was able to speak, and said that he was thirsty. I called for a carafe of water to be brought, but before it came, he suffered a fit in which the convulsions were so violent that it was with very great difficulty that Mrs Garton and I were able to keep him on the bed. Mrs Garton, I have to say, showed enormous courage in her very obvious distress. My first impression was that her husband was suffering from tetanus, and I asked Mrs Garton if he had any recent injuries but she

168

said he had not. I soon observed, however, that the jaw was not affected as one might expect in tetanus, and I began to suspect poisoning with *strychnia*. All doubt was removed when the next fit supervened, his body adopting the characteristic posture in which it arched backwards, head and heels alone touching the surface of the bed. His face was livid, the eyeballs staring, his pulse almost too fast to count, his expression contorted in *risus sardonicus*.

'Throughout this ordeal, Mr Garton was, I may add, fully conscious, in great pain, and most dreadfully aware of his predicament. I attempted to treat him with an emetic, but the slightest touch brought on new spasms. I was about to apply chloroform on a handkerchief, but he suffered another violent fit during which he was unable to breathe, and he expired.'

Dr Collin paused, and for a while the only sound in court was that of rapidly scribbling pencils. 'On the 14th of January I carried out a post-mortem examination. I noticed at once that the body was unusually rigid, the hands clenched. The brain was considerably congested, the lungs normal, and the stomach was almost empty apart from a small amount of fluid. I gathered from this that prior to his death he had not had any solid food for several hours. It is my opinion that the cause of death was poisoning with *strychnia* and, given the severity of the symptoms, I would estimate that Mr Garton must have consumed at the very least two and very probably up to three grains or more.'

'Did you form any opinion as to the source of the *strychnia?*' asked the coroner.

'I questioned Mrs Garton very closely as to what her husband had consumed in the hours prior to his death. We know that he ate dinner, which commenced just after seven and was over by half past eight. No one else at the meal was affected, and indeed had he consumed *strychnia* at that meal he would have been taken ill much sooner than he was. I discount the meal entirely. During the rest of the evening he ate no more solid food but consumed only aerated water. This was from a bottle which was also used to serve others. I discount the water. According to Mrs Garton, he took nothing more that evening until he returned home and dosed himself with the mixture obtained from Mr Doughty's chemist's shop earlier in the day. The symptoms of poisoning commenced less than half an hour afterwards.'

Herbert glanced at Frances, his face creased with anxiety. Having listened attentively, she was obliged to admit that she had heard nothing in Dr Collin's evidence with which she could disagree.

The next witness was the analyst Dr Whitmore, who began by confirming that Percival Garton had consumed some of his medicine as he was able to detect oil of oranges in the stomach contents. He had also found *strychnia*, in a quantity that led him to agree with Dr Collin's estimate of how much the deceased had ingested.

'From your examination of the stomach contents have you been able to form any opinion of whether Mr Garton consumed an overdose of nux vomica, or was the *strychnia* present in any other form?' asked Dr Hardwicke. Frances realised that her hands were trembling and she

170

clasped them tightly together.

'One form of *strychnia* which is readily available to the public is vermin killers,' said Dr Whitmore. 'These are sold mixed with colouring such as Prussian blue or soot. I detected neither of these colourings in the stomach, and concluded that the *strychnia* did not come from such a source. I also examined the material for the presence of *brucia*. The quantity of *brucia* in the nux vomica seed is almost as great as *strychnia* but it is not nearly as poisonous. My tests led me to believe that the amount of *brucia* consumed by Mr Garton was less than one twentieth of a grain. I do not believe therefore that he consumed an overdose of nux vomica in any form, be it tincture, extract or powder.'

Frances could not resist a glance at Inspector Sharrock, whose theory had just been officially discounted. He was frowning with concentration.

The analyst went on: 'The amount of *strychnia* in the stomach and the severity of the symptoms can only, in my opinion, be accounted for by the deceased having taken a fatal dose of *strychnia* in its pure form. I have also subjected to analysis items of foodstuffs, wine, and other drinks that remained after the meal served to guests at the home of Mr Keane where Mr Garton dined shortly before he died. I found nothing of any note. I also examined the contents of Mr Garton's brandy flask, which he kept in his carriage, and that, too, I can absolve of any suspicion. I analysed samples of the ingredients used in composing Mr Garton's mixture taken from the shop of Mr William Doughty of Westbourne Grove, and found nothing suspicious. Finally I turned to the bottle of medicine which was prepared by Mr Doughty and from which Mr Garton took a dose shortly before his fatal attack. The mixture contained, as I would have expected from the prescription, a small quantity of nux vomica, which I believe to have been in the form of the tincture, diluted with stock syrup, and flavoured with oil of oranges and some harmless carminatives. In addition, however, I discovered some grains of pure white crystalline *strychnia*.' A low groan ran around the hall, and Frances knew that all eyes had turned to look at William and herself. 'The amount of mixture remaining in the bottle was an ounce, and I detected two and a half grains of *strychnia*. I have no doubt that if Mr Garton had consumed more than the prescribed dose of the mixture, as I understand was his habit, this would easily be sufficient to account for his death. I can offer no opinion, however, as to how the *strychnia* came to be in the mixture.'

As the court buzzed with chatter, Frances tried to take heart. As far as she was concerned, the analysis proved that the medicine had been made up according to the prescription. The mysterious presence of a lethal amount of pure *strychnia* was clear evidence of tampering after the bottle had left the shop.

'Silence!' called Dr Hardwicke. 'This is not a theatre; it is a serious business. Please show respect for the court.'

Ada was the next to make her statement. She crept to the chair with a terrified look, and had some difficulty in opening her mouth to speak, eventually admitting that she was Ada Hawkins, aged twenty-five and housemaid to the deceased. 'Now then, Ada,' said Dr Hardwicke kindly, as one might speak to a child, 'tell me all about the evening you went to the chemist's shop to get Mr Garton's medicine.'

'Well, sir, there isn't a great deal to say,' said Ada, who was trying to overcome her nerves by addressing the coroner directly. He obliged her by leaning towards her as if at a private interview. 'I gave the prescription to Mr Doughty and then I sat down. My corns were hurting terrible that night!' Hardwicke nodded sympathetically. 'Then I took the bottle – it was all wrapped up with paper and string and sealing wax as usual – and brought it home.'

'When you were in the shop, did you see the prescription being made?'

She shook her head. 'No, Sir. Mr Doughty and Mr Munson were behind the screen.'

'Now, Ada, this is a very important question,' said Hardwicke. 'Did either of those gentlemen at any time go into the storeroom behind the counter to fetch anything? Think carefully. Can you remember?'

Ada thought, her face twisted into a frown, then she sighed. 'I don't remember seeing anything. I was looking at my feet most of the time.'

'Did anyone else enter the shop while you were there?'

'No, Sir.'

'So,' said Hardwicke, 'you brought the medicine home. What did you do with it?'

'I put it on the night table in the bedroom,' she

173

said, more confidently.

'Still wrapped and sealed?'

'Yes, Sir.'

'And as far as you are aware no one touched it before Mr Garton took his night-time dose?'

'Yes, Sir.'

Ada gulped and looked as if she was about to babble an apology for dropping the bottle, but to her relief the coroner said, 'Thank you, Ada, you may stand down now.'

Ada rose and scurried thankfully to the back of the court. Hardwicke turned to the court attendants. 'Bring Mrs Garton to the court please.'

A policeman opened a door at the back of the court and, after a brief pause, Mrs Henrietta Garton emerged. She was a stately woman, her posture giving her an air of noble suffering that could not help but evoke small sounds of pity from the onlookers. She was dressed in the deepest of mourning, and thickly veiled so that her features could not be seen. Slowly, she sat upon the chair, where she rested like a statue, poised and dignified.

'Mrs Garton,' said Hardwicke kindly, though not at all in the way he had addressed Ada, 'I am aware that this must be very painful for you, and I will keep it as brief as possible, but the court must hear from your own lips about the night of your husband's death.'

'I understand,' she whispered.

'Would you say that up to the moment of his last fatal illness your husband was, apart from his tendency to indigestion, in good health?'

There was a pause, as if she needed to collect

174

herself. 'Yes.'

'When you returned home on the evening of 12th January, was the bottle of medicine standing on the side table, still wrapped, tied with string and sealed?'

'Yes.'

'And who unwrapped it?'

A deep sigh. 'My husband.'

'Can you say how much of it he took?'

Another pause. 'I – do not know. He drank directly from the bottle.'

'Did he say anything to you about the medicine?'

A small rapid intake of breath, as if stifling tears. 'He said it tasted bitter.' The sound of scribbling pencils rustled about the court.

'How soon after taking his medicine did he become ill?'

'About fifteen or twenty minutes.'

'Can you tell us how it came about that so little of the mixture remained in the bottle?'

She paused again, and sighed. 'My husband said he was sure there was something wrong with the medicine. I picked up the bottle and un-corked it and was smelling the mixture, when – oh it was a terrible sight – his whole body – the pain of it – his face – I gave the bottle to Ada and told her to take care of it, but the foolish girl dropped it, and some was spilt.' She began to weep, gasping and choking for breath, her bosom heaving. Hardwicke motioned an attendant to bring a glass of water to the lady. She lifted it to her mouth behind the veil, sipped, and after a moment was able to collect herself. 'Fortunately not all of it was lost and I asked Dr Collin to give the bottle to the police.'

'I know this is very distressing for you, Mrs Garton,' said Hardwicke, 'I will try to be brief.'

'Please,' she whispered, 'go on.'

Hardwicke nodded. 'Mrs Garton, do you know of anyone who might have wished harm to your husband?'

There was a soft gentle sobbing from under the veil, and she shook her head. 'My husband was the best of men. All who knew him liked and admired him.'

'And – I am sorry if this question is painful to you, but I am obliged to ask it – was your husband ever in a despondent mood? Did you ever have a suspicion that he might have been inclined to do himself harm?'

'Never!' she said firmly.

'Thank you, Mrs Garton, there are no further questions.'

With an imposing slow dignity, Mrs Garton rose, and returned to the room at the back of the court. It was as if everyone had been holding their collective breath, like an audience who had been watching a tightrope walker, and could only now exhale.

'Mr Herbert Munson,' said Hardwicke.

Herbert jumped up so fast he almost knocked his chair over and took his place. He was panting slightly and little beads of sweat stood out on his brow.

'In your own words Mr Munson,' said Hardwicke, briskly, 'identify yourself and tell the court about the making up of Mr Percival Garton's prescription on 12th of January last.'

Herbert nodded. The words came out in a torrent. 'Yes, Sir. My full name is Herbert George Munson and I am twenty-two and for the last year I have been apprentice to Mr William Doughty at his shop on Westbourne Grove. Shortly before seven on the evening of 12th January a young person I know only as Ada who is maidservant to Mr Percival Garton entered the shop with a prescription. It was for a mixture which has been dispensed to Mr Garton before. It consists of only two ingredients, tincture of nux vomica and elixir of oranges. The mixture was made from stock which had been used on previous occasions, and exactly as required by the prescription.'

Hardwicke nodded. 'So, Mr Munson, you are saying that only the two ingredients you have mentioned were in the bottle?'

'Yes, Sir,' said Herbert. 'And in the amounts specified.'

'Did either you or Mr William Doughty go into the storeroom to fetch anything while the prescription was being made.'

'No, Sir,' said Herbert emphatically.

'Did anyone else enter the shop while the prescription was being made?'

'Not that I noticed, Sir.'

'Does the shop carry any stock of *strychnia* in its pure form?'

Herbert trembled, and Frances saw the tell-tale quivering of his moustache tips. 'I have never seen any, Sir.'

'Thank you Mr Munson. You may stand down. I now wish to question Mr William Doughty.'

As her father took his place, Frances, for one

177

horrible moment of revelation, saw him as he appeared to others, a man whose prime had been destroyed by sickness and care. His hair, which despite her best efforts at smoothing and dressing it, was dishevelled, and there was a weakness in his left leg which dragged a little as he walked.

Hardwicke, himself a medical man, observed William carefully as he took his place.

'Mr Doughty, you are a qualified pharmacist and member of the Pharmaceutical Society?'

'I am,' said William.

'And how long have you been proprietor of the shop in Westbourne Grove?'

'Oh, upwards of twenty years. We are very well thought of in Bayswater.'

'In your own words, please, I would like you to tell me about the evening on which you prepared Mr Garton's prescription.'

William licked his lips and frowned. 'I – can you tell me the date – I am not sure – my memory...'

'That would be Monday the 12th January last,' said Hardwicke.

'Ah. Yes. Monday,' said William thoughtfully. 'And today is...?'

'Thursday 22nd January.'

William nodded. 'Yes. 22nd you say. January. Indeed.'

There was a long pause, as if William had forgotten the original question. 'Mr Doughty,' said Hardwicke, patiently, 'can you tell the court what you recall of the making up of Mr Garton's prescription?'

'I–,' William sighed. 'I think I have been asked

about this before. Is the poor fellow dead?'

A titter ran around the court, but one stern look from the coroner brought silence. 'Indeed he is, Mr Doughty, and it is his death we are enquiring into today,' said Hardwicke, gently. 'Do you recall making up his prescription on the 12th of January?'

There was another long pause. 'It is very strange,' said William sadly. 'There are so many things I remember well. Ask me anything from the Pharmacopoeia and I would answer you directly. I could tell off the order of the stock bottles on my shelves as if I was standing before them. But I can recall nothing of making Mr Garton's prescription.'

Hardwicke tried another tack. 'Mr Doughty, can you tell me from memory the ingredients of the mixture normally dispensed to Mr Garton?'

'Oh, indeed,' said William, promptly. '*Tinctura nucis vomicae* two drachms, *elixir aurantii* to six ounces. The elixir is our own receipt, you know,' he added with modest pride.

Hardwicke nodded at the coroner's constable, who brought forward the Doughtys' prescription book open at the 12th January, and showed it to William. 'Is that your handwriting, Mr Doughty?'

William peered at the book. 'I – yes, yes it is.'

'Let the jury take note,' said Hardwicke, 'that Mr Doughty has identified as his the writing in the book relating to Mr Garton's prescription made on the 12th of January. Now then, Mr Doughty, you have heard Dr Whitmore give as his opinion that the *strychnia* in Mr Garton's stomach was present in its pure form and that quantities of *strychnia* sufficient to cause death were found in the mixture prepared in your shop. You have already said that you can tell from memory what stock you have in your shop, so I am sure you can advise the court whether or not you have any pure *strychnia*.'

'I am sure that we have none,' said William.

'Thank you, Mr Doughty. I have no more questions.'

William was returning to his seat, and Frances was holding out her hand to guide him, when he turned back and added. 'Of course, there was some, about thirty grains, but it is no longer there, and I am very much afraid I cannot recall how it was utilised.'

There were gasps around the little courtroom, followed by a great hum of chatter. Hardwicke called for silence again. Herbert sat quite still with his eyes closed, and Frances was grateful for the veil which hid the shock and despair on her face. Her father took his seat by her side, possibly the only person in the courtroom indifferent to what was occurring.

'I wish to call the last witness,' said Hardwicke. 'Mrs Mary Keane.'

For a moment Frances wondered if she had heard rightly. Had she concentrated her mind so much on the Keanes that she was actually imagining hearing the name? But Mrs Keane arose like a great full-bodied sailing vessel on the swell of the tide and moved to take her place. Frances glanced at Herbert, who looked at her in astonishment and shrugged.

'Mrs Keane,' said Hardwicke, 'I understand

that you are a resident of Bayswater?'

'I am,' said the lady in an unexpectedly rich and resonant voice. 'I am the wife of James Keane of the Bayswater Bank.'

'Would you be so kind as to tell the court where you were on the evening of the 12th of January last?'

'I was in Westbourne Grove.' There was a dramatic pause, then, as if her words needed explanation, which to Frances' mind they certainly did, 'My doctor had advised me that gentle walking was beneficial to the constitution, and I had determined to follow his advice as soon as those dreadful fogs had cleared. It so happened therefore that shortly before seven o'clock, I was outside the shop of Mr William Doughty.' Another pause for effect. Frances, who was holding her breath, had the horrid realisation that Mrs Keane was enjoying this theatrical moment. 'I recalled that there were a few small articles of a trivial nature which I required, and so, on a moment's impulse, I entered the shop.'

There was a brief hum of whispered voices in court. 'Silence!' insisted the coroner. 'I do not want to have to say this again!' He turned to Mrs Keane. 'Can you tell the court who was in the shop at the time, and what was taking place there?'

'I could partially see that there were two gentlemen behind the screen. They were clearly occupied, and they did not see me. This young person,' she indicated Ada, 'was seated in front of the counter. She did not see me and she did not rise. She was staring at her feet. I thought she was an imbecile.'

181

Frances looked at Ada, whose face had coloured. She was shaking her head in dismay.

'I waited a moment or two,' went on Mrs Keane, 'and took a brief turn about the shop. I then saw the gentleman who I know to be Mr Doughty leave the counter and pass through a door directly behind him – I assume to some rear portion of the premises. As he did so he emerged briefly from behind the screen, and I saw that he was holding a medicine bottle. A few moments passed and then he returned, still holding the bottle, and rejoined the other gentleman behind the screen.'

Frances now had a full understanding of what the newspapers always described as 'sensation'. Everyone in court forgot the coroner's strict injunction and burst into excited chatter, while the pressmen wrote furiously, their eyes gleaming in excitement. Ada sat still with tears in her eyes, and Herbert turned to Frances and said, 'She was not there! I will swear it in any court! If she had come in I would have heard the bell!' In the midst of it all, James Keane sat utterly composed, a small smile of triumph on his lips.

'If this continues the court will be cleared!' exclaimed Hardwicke. 'Please restrain yourselves and recall the dignity of the occasion!' Gradually, the onlookers settled. 'Please go on, Mrs Keane.'

'Shortly afterwards, I left the shop. I did not speak to anyone there and I did not purchase anything.'

'Mrs Keane, you have said that no one in the shop noticed you were there,' a snigger ran around the courtroom, which was quickly stifled. 'But the shop has a bell, does it not? A bell which

182

alerts those behind the counter that a customer has entered? Did the bell sound?'

There was a long pause as if Mrs Keane had only just recognised the difficulty with her story. 'It did not,' she said at last. 'I can only assume that the bad weather had somehow affected it.'

'I see,' said Hardwicke. 'You may stand down, Mrs Keane.'

The lady returned to her seat, leaving Frances wondering what Mrs Keane hoped to achieve by offering such blatant lies to the court. She looked at the jury but saw no sign in their solemn faces to suggest whether they believed this travesty.

Mr Hardwicke addressed the jury. 'That, gentlemen, concludes the evidence, and it only remains for you to arrive at your verdict. The first point for you to consider is the cause of death, and I believe that the evidence of Dr Collin and Dr Whitmore offers only one possible conclusion, that Mr Percival Garton died from poisoning with *strychnia*. Moreover there is no reason to suggest that anything other than the medicine was responsible. The next matter for your consideration is why the poison was taken. In cases of this nature there are usually three possibilities. Poison may have been taken deliberately by the deceased. It may be administered by a third party with intent to kill or injure, or it may have been taken by accident, usually because of negligence or carelessness either of the deceased or another person. In this instance I see no shred of evidence that Percival Garton administered poison to himself with the intent to take his own life. Indeed, suicide with *strychnia* is rare, compared with the

183

other poisons, because of the unpleasant nature of the symptoms. The next possibility is deliberate administration by a third party. If you believe this to be the case then your verdict should be murder, and you may name the individual you consider to be guilty, or else lay it at the door of a person or persons unknown. While murder is not beyond the bounds of possibility in this case, you may consider that the evidence before you has not supplied one hint of any individual who might wish harm to Mr Garton. There is no suggestion that Mr Doughty regarded Mr Garton as anything other than a valued customer. He gains nothing by Mr Garton's death, in fact he loses. If you believe that Mr Garton's death may have been one of those unfortunate accidents which happen from time to time, you should bring in a verdict of misadventure.'

The jurors were glancing at one another and Frances suspected that this was their preferred verdict, one that would leave her father's position in a horrible limbo where he would be tried by the tongues of gossips.

'Yet it is more than that,' Hardwicke went on. 'If Mr Doughty did mistakenly put a deadly poison into Mr Garton's medicine, he did so not as an ignorant untrained person but as a man of experience, qualifications, a man occupying a position where he should inspire confidence and trust. You may wonder if such a gross error of judgement is likely for a man such as Mr Doughty, but it is apparent to us all today that the gentleman is unwell. His memory does not serve him as it once did. A mistake is therefore very possible. A verdict of misadventure may, despite the absence of any harmful intent, still lead to serious consequences for Mr Doughty, even a criminal prosecution, but I ask you to put that from your minds. Your task here today is to arrive at a conclusion regarding the death of Mr Garton. I now ask you to retire and consider your verdict.'

Hardwicke was ordering his papers, while there was a brief consultation amongst the jurymen. 'Sir, we feel it is not necessary for us to retire,' said the foreman. 'We have arrived at our verdict.' A paper was passed to Hardwicke, who perused it and asked the foreman to address the court.

The foreman rose. 'We find a verdict of death by misadventure, and we add that we believe that this was due to a mistake made by Mr Doughty. Given the gentleman's illness we would hope that any consequences will not be too harsh. We also find that Mr Munson was entirely blameless in the matter.'

It was over, thought Frances. Everything was over. The business, her father's reputation – all gone. The room seemed to darken before her and for a moment she thought she was about to faint, but she tried to breathe evenly and stay calm for her father's sake. The feeling passed. There was nothing to do but go home and sit quietly and consider what was best to be done.

'I am truly sorry,' said Mr Rawsthorne, as they left the court. The crowds were still there, not in such numbers as before, but all in hot debate about the verdict, and as Frances appeared with her father, they surged forward. The young clerk was about to call out for a path to be made, but to his consternation, his pens were suddenly scattered on the ground, and he was obliged to scramble for them. The police formed a barrier, and Frances, rubbing ink from her fingers, was able to guide her father to the carriage without too much discomfort. 'If there is anything I can do, you must tell me at once,' said Rawsthorne. He grasped William by the hand. 'You must rest and recover, old friend.'

On the way home, Frances was silent. Despite the jury's request for lenience, she knew that they were facing the alarming prospect that her father might be arrested. At the very least he would be expelled from membership of the Pharmaceutical Society. Would he even understand what had happened to him? How could she persuade him that he must not appear in the shop? Would the customers ever return?

William was tired, yet as she helped him up the stairs there was a note of agitation about him which suggested he would be unable to settle. It was useless to question him about the 12th – like all recent memories it seemed to be clouded in his mind. She saw that he had a warm drink, and hoped that this would soothe him into taking a nap.

When she returned to the parlour, Herbert was pacing the floor distractedly. 'I am convinced that the bell was working,' he said. 'It has always worked unless deliberately interfered with, as that malodorous person did the other day. And I would be prepared to swear that Mr Doughty did not go into the storeroom at any time during the making up of the prescription!' He waved his arms above his head in agitation. 'What is to become of us now? We are tainted with suspicion! And your poor father, what will happen to him? He has long enjoyed the admiration and respect of everyone in Bayswater. None more than myself! He has been kinder to me than a parent! His guidance and teaching will be of value to me for the rest of my life! I–,' he broke off and clenched his fists, and Frances saw to her surprise that there were tears in his eyes.

She certainly trusted Herbert's recollection of events, but was aware that in the event of a trial any court might consider his evidence tainted by self-interest. Her father's memory was clearly faulty, and anything Ada said might be disregarded as she was a servant. Mrs Keane, as the respectable wife of a local banker, could very well carry the day. The thing that most disturbed her was the unpleasant smile on James Keane's face, when everyone else in the court was struck by alarm and despair.

With chilling certainty, Frances now knew the true source of Mrs Keane's evidence. It was a lie from beginning to end, and she had been coerced into it by her husband. Frances had no doubt that Keane had murdered Garton, and had no compunction about sacrificing her father to avoid discovery. And Mrs Keane, married to such a brute, and in his power, had done his bidding. Had Keane promised to save his father-in-law from ruin in return for her testimony? The more Frances thought about it the angrier she became, until it was impossible for her to sit still and do nothing.

Frances stood up. 'Sarah – see that my father is

settled for his nap. I am going out.'

Sarah obeyed, but Herbert stared as she put on her coat. 'Are you going to consult Mr Rawsthorne?'

'No,' said Frances, 'I am going to see Mrs Keane and demand that she change her evidence.'

'But they are most unlikely to admit you to the house,' said Herbert.

'I will gain admission,' said Frances. 'I don't yet know how, but I will do it. I will do it if I have to stand in the street all night and make a public commotion.'

'This is hardly–'

'Hardly what, Mr Munson?' she cried so sharply that he recoiled. 'Hardly proper behaviour? I no longer care about that. If Mrs Keane has so far forgotten the niceties as to tell a lie that will destroy my father I think I may be excused for forgetting them too.'

'But our reputation!' he squeaked.

'As long as those allegations stand, we *have* no reputation!' Frances left the house and strode rapidly down the street, by now so possessed with anger that she could hardly see.

CHAPTER TEN

As Frances walked to the Keanes' house, her first passion of anger gradually subsided. She could not help arguing with herself and as she did so her decidedly unladylike strides became a more moderate pace. Was this desperate approach really the correct course of action, and yet, she asked, what else was there she could do? Appealing to the sympathy of Inspector Sharrock was hardly likely to be successful, and Constable Brown, who would understand her plight, was powerless to assist. As she neared the house, still with no plan in mind as to how she was to gain an interview with Mrs Keane, her steps became less determined, and she thought again. Herbert, she was forced to acknowledge, was right, there was no possibility of her being admitted to the house, let alone confronting Mrs Keane; the lady's husband would surely see to that. Frances knew she might enter though the kitchen and so make her way up the stairs, but that way she would be suspected of being a thief. Mr Keane had already seen her at the gallery, and entertained suspicions of her motives, how much worse would it be if she was found wandering in his house without permission? The consequences of such a situation to her family were too unpleasant to contemplate. Frances told herself she was doing a foolish thing, but at the same time she was unwilling to give up and go home without even trying to see Mrs Keane, since she would for ever afterwards be wondering if she might have succeeded had she gone on. There was, perhaps, just once chance – she must wait outside the house, unobserved, until Mr Keane departed, and then go boldly to the door. She would need some excuse to be brought into the lady's presence. Perhaps, given the tendency of servants in the house to stay no longer than a few months, she might claim to be applying for a position of lady's maid, something that would require a personal interview with Mrs Keane. The unhappy lady might be sufficiently bereft of female company to condescend to see her.

Frances calmed herself, smoothed her hair, and checked, as far as she could, that her garments were not in disarray, and walked slowly on. Whatever slight chance she had of admission to the house, it would be better if she did not come to the door resembling a madwoman. As she drew nearer to the Keanes' villa, she heard voices, and these were voices not in conversation, but raised, as if in anger. As she drew closer, it became apparent that the dispute was taking place in the cobbled yard outside the Keanes' coach house. So extraordinary was the sound, so unlike what one might expect to hear on a public street where persons of quality resided, that she hurried forward to see what was happening, and peered around the thick hedges that fringed the property. To her astonishment, she came upon a scene that would have been better suited to the popular stage.

The doors of the Keanes' coach house were open, and the brougham was out, the horse harnessed, with the coachman and Adam, the young stablehand, in attendance. Mrs Keane was dressed in a travelling cloak, and Adam was putting a large leather handbag into the carriage, but as soon as this was done, Mr Keane, his face red with fury, strode over to the carriage, pulled out the bag and threw it violently to the ground.

'Now go indoors and we will hear no more of this!' he exclaimed.

190

Frances noticed that Mrs Grinham and Mr Harvey were at the top of the steps leading to the front door, peering anxiously at the unseemly events, while Ettie and Ellen were half inside the house, peeping out, their faces pale in wide-eyed alarm.

'I will not remain in this house a moment longer!' said Mrs Keane, her voice if anything richer and more thrilling than at the inquest. 'You have made me into a criminal! I would rather live in want than stay here!'

'How *dare* you accuse me!' he raged. 'You did it willingly! You took pleasure from it!'

'Yes, I confess that much,' she admitted. 'To see everyone hang upon one's words as if they are a treasure, how many desire such a thing – but I have thought upon it since then, and now I regret it. You have destroyed my love, James. I must depart.'

'Do as I say!' her husband exploded. 'And you,' – he turned and barked at the house servants – 'get back into the house at once!'

Ettie and Ellen withdrew inside with squeals of alarm, but Frances saw their faces emerge from the doorway as soon as Keane withdrew his attention from them. Mrs Grinham and Mr Harvey stepped back less hurriedly to the doorway, but remained there, where Frances could still see them watching what was happening. The coachman shrugged and retired back into the coach house, but Adam stood quiet and still, a frown on his broad face, his fingers tightening into fists.

'Now get back inside,' snapped Keane to his wife. 'Have you no shame, behaving in this way in front of the servants? Practically on the public street in full sight of our neighbours? You are making a spectacle of yourself!'

Mrs Keane laughed unpleasantly. 'Oh, that I have done already and in a far worse way! I have reached the depths of iniquity, and you have brought me to it. My father told me I should not marry you, he said you were a rogue and a thief and a fortune hunter and he was right.'

He advanced upon her, and looked down contemptuously from his far greater height. 'Your father is a beggar unless you go back into the house and abandon this indecent adventure.'

She returned his gaze without fear, her head tilted back defiantly. 'I will not. I should have left before. My father will consider the price well paid for my happiness.'

He gave a derisive laugh. 'I doubt that very much. You will earn only his curse. You already have mine. Now get inside and let us continue our lives of misery.'

She shook her head. 'No, James. I cannot set foot in there ever again. Adam – put the bag in the carriage. I am leaving!'

Adam came forward to pick up the bag but Keane, without even turning to look at him, said, 'Adam, if you so much as touch the bag you will leave the premises this instant.'

Adam hesitated, and looked at Mrs Keane. 'Very well,' said that lady, 'I will not see a good servant lose his place.' She picked up the bag herself and placed it in the carriage, then went to climb up the steps.

'You had better climb up on top and drive it

yourself for no servant in my employ will drive you!' said Keane with a sneer. 'Don't be foolish, woman!'

She hesitated, and then stepped down with an air of dignity. 'Very well,' she said, calmly. 'I had assumed that you would allow me the consideration due to me as your wife, but I see now that you will not. So be it. I will carry my own bag and walk until I can get a hansom.'

She made for the gates, but Keane stepped in her way. 'I see you have lost all sense of decency,' he said. 'Do not forget that as my wife you are under my control and you will not leave my house if I have to knock you down and carry you inside.'

Despite the dreadful situation there was a muffled titter from the doorway, since Mrs Keane, though far shorter than her husband, undoubtedly outweighed him.

'Strike me, then,' she said dramatically, squaring her shoulders and offering her face for the blow. 'You have done everything else, why hold back from that?'

He smiled. 'I promise you, I will not.'

For a moment or two they stared at each other, both expressions set and determined, as if looks alone would make the other give way. Frances saw that Keane confidently believed that his forcefulness and the total command he had over his wife's fortunes would make her crumble. Perhaps it had done so many times before. He merely waited, therefore, for her to bend her head in submission, turn and creep back into the house. This time, however, was different. She started to walk around him and towards the gate, and Keane, with an expression of rage, raised his fist.

'Don't do it, Sir!' exclaimed Adam, suddenly.

'*What?*' said Keane, pausing in sheer incredulity.

'I said don't do it,' repeated Adam, who had now overstepped a servant's place so far as to be past caring what he said. His sturdy and muscular form was drawn to its full height, the shoulders back and impressive chest thrown out as if in a challenge. 'I have stood by long enough and seen you insult this good lady, and I can do it no more. If you try to strike her she will find a protector in me.'

'You impudent mongrel!' spat Keane, 'Get out at once!' He then became aware that the house servants were still watching. Both Ellen and Ettie had their aprons to their mouths to stifle exclamations of mingled horror and amusement, Mrs Grinham was scowling, though whether this was due to the scene or her lumbago was unclear, and Mr Harvey had taken the view that someone in the household ought to be dignified, and as no one else was it had better be himself. 'And you – all of you,' roared Keane, 'set about your duties at once or you will be on the street with no character, like this one!' He turned to Adam. 'Are you still here? I want you gone this instant!'

Adam pondered this for a moment. 'Very well, Sir,' he said calmly, 'I will go, and I wish well to Mistress, who deserves far better than you.' He turned, and stood quite still, facing the gate, but did not walk towards it. 'But there is one thing I must do first.' With that, he turned around and punched James Keane squarely on the nose.

Adam had a large fist and a brawny body

behind it. There was a crunching noise, and Keane's nose seemed to explode into something red and very ugly. He crashed backwards onto the cobbles, with dark blood streaming down his face and into his mouth. There were screams from Ettie and Ellen, while Mrs Grinham chortled, and Mr Harvey closed his eyes in distaste. Keane, sprawling on the ground, shrieked and spluttered incoherently, spraying blood and saliva over the front of his shirt.

It was Mrs Keane's reaction that was truly shocking, and with all attention suddenly on Keane, Frances, from her position by the gates, may have been the only one to see it. The unguarded naked look of admiration in the lady's eyes as she gazed up at her young protector was indecent, even carnal. Frances shivered at the sight, though she did not know why.

Keane, gurgling and spitting blood from his mouth, was calling for something to be fetched, though his words were indistinct and he was howling with pain and rage.

'Quick, get a towel and basin of water!' snapped Mrs Grinham. Ettie and Ellen hurried indoors, while Mr Harvey helped his master to his feet, taking care as he did so not to stain his own clothing. He and Mrs Grinham tried to assist Keane inside the house, but, almost at once, the stricken man started to shake, and before he reached the door, his knees began to give way. There was some danger that Keane might faint, so he was helped as far as the front steps, where Harvey saw he was seated, his head between his knees, blood dripping to the ground. Ettie and Ellen emerged, and a

195

towel was dipped in water and applied to what remained of Keane's nose, though even the gentlest touch made him almost weep with agony.

Adam, who appeared entirely satisfied with the outcome, came forward and took the bag from Mrs Keane and placed it once more in the carriage. She smiled at him, a kinder smile now that she had composed herself. 'Thank you, Adam. I hope you have not injured your hand?'

'Thank you, Ma'am, I have not.' He returned the smile, and for a brief moment they looked at each other. The scene of consternation about James Keane could have been happening a hundred miles away.

'Mr Harvey, shall I run for a doctor?' asked Ellen.

Keane coughed and seethed and moaned. 'Fetch –' I want you to fetch–,' he gasped, *'why will someone not fetch a policeman? Go and get a policeman this instant!'*

'I don't think that will be necessary Sir,' said a familiar sounding voice, and Frances saw Inspector Sharrock entering through the gateway, accompanied by Constable Brown. They had both seen her, pressed against the hedge, and she coloured immediately, but apart from a raised eyebrow from Sharrock and a smile and a polite nod from Wilfred, they did not give away her presence.

Keane sat up and pointed to Adam. 'That man! Arrest him at once! He has assaulted me!'

'All in good time, Sir,' said Sharrock. 'I do have one other more important duty to perform first. James Keane, I am placing you under arrest, and

196

require you to accompany me to the police station where you will be formally charged with fraud, forgery and embezzlement. Constable Brown, the cuffs!'

Wilfred stepped forward with a set of handcuffs and proceeded to put them onto Keane's wrists, oblivious to the astonishment all around him. The servants were suddenly immobile, like puppets who had lost their human operator. Keane could only gasp and choke with outrage, the red stain spreading on the towel at his nose. His wife, open-mouthed in amazement, watched the operation with a certain amount of pleasure.

'Good day to you, Mrs Keane!' said Sharrock as he and Wilfred took a firm hold on their prisoner and led him to a waiting carriage. 'That's a bit of a knock, you've got sir. Don't worry, we'll see to it down at the station.'

'What about that young criminal?' exclaimed Keane, stumbling along between the two policemen. 'He struck me! I want him arrested at once!'

Sharrock hesitated.

'Excuse me officer,' said Mrs Keane quietly. 'I think my husband must be mistaken. He tripped and fell just now, and struck his nose on the ground. It was an accident.'

'That is a *lie!*' bellowed Keane. 'He hit me!' He twisted his body round towards the servants. 'You all saw it! Tell the police what you saw!'

Ellen and Ettie hesitated and looked at each other, Mr Harvey took a deep breath, and then Mrs Grinham folded her arms, sniffed and said, 'It's just like Mistress said. He fell.'

Sharrock glanced round at the other servants,

197

who, one by one, nodded their agreement. 'Looks like you got confused, Sir,' he said. 'It often happens when you have a nasty bump.' Keane, now whimpering like a dog, was hauled out of the gate, his toes trailing on the ground, and pushed into the carriage. Frances hurried up to Wilfred.

'Constable Brown,' she said.

He looked at her, curiously. 'Miss Doughty – what brings you here?'

'I came to see Mrs Keane – though of course – circumstances – I was not able to speak to her. You know about what happened at the inquest this morning, I suppose?'

'I do, Miss,' he said, sympathetically.

'It is my belief that Mrs Keane was forced by the cruelty of her husband to lie to the court,' said Frances, earnestly. 'I do not blame her, she could not help herself.'

Wilfred smiled. 'I'll tell you a little secret, Miss. The police think so, too.'

'You do?' cried Frances, almost overcome with a great sense of relief. 'Oh and I had thought you would believe her and I would never be able to clear my father's name!'

'Miss Doughty – I know I shouldn't say it and it might seem an impertinent question, but – does your family have an account with the Bayswater Bank? Only, in view of what has happened here today–'

'I understand entirely, and thank you for that thought,' said Frances. 'Neither we nor anyone we know banks with them, as far as I am aware. We are London & Westminster.'

Inspector Sharrock had been ensuring that his

198

new charge was settled in the carriage. Keane, crumpled and half sobbing in one corner, was now utterly bereft of the manly bravado he had shown earlier. 'Miss Doughty,' said Sharrock, approaching Frances, a quick tilt of his head telling the constable to go and mind the prisoner, 'this is quite a coincidence finding you here. I hope you have not been attempting to do police work again, you will get yourself quite a peculiar reputation.'

Frances was unrepentant. 'Inspector, I have been almost driven distracted with worry, and I will do whatever I believe to be necessary. Now please tell me that you will not be arresting my father!'

'I should think that very unlikely,' said Sharrock.

'I am happy to hear it. He is a much injured man.'

'I must say, Miss, your family feelings do you credit. Now my advice is, go home, and see to your father's dinner.'

Frances watched them drive away. It was not yet over, but she was so near. The police would look into all of James Keane's business affairs and somewhere, she was certain, they would find the evidence of how and why he had murdered Percival Garton. Then her father would be cleared of blame, and everything could go back to what it once was. She walked home, idling a little in her happiness. Though it was still cold and grey, it seemed to her now that the worst of the winter chills had gone, ushering in a calmer season.

When she reached home, she saw Dr Collin's gig outside and wondered if he had called to discuss the inquest. Dr Collin had always had a great regard for her father and she looked forward to giving him the good news. As she mounted the stairs, there were rapid footsteps above, and Sarah appeared on the landing, her eyes filled with distress. 'Oh Miss!' she said, stifling a sob. 'It's your father!'

Afterwards, Frances could never recall how she had climbed the stairs to her father's room. The horror of those words lent her a strength she did not think she had, and she seemed to fly to where she was needed. The tall figure of Dr Collin was bent over the bed, and he looked up as she entered. 'Miss Doughty – I am very sorry,' he said.

She came forward, dreading what she would see, but her father looked the same as he had looked before, careworn and grey, the hair always needing her hand to tend it. He was fully clothed, dressed as he had been at the inquest, and had, as was his usual habit, lain down upon the covers to sleep a little. She sat by him, and touched his hand. It was warm, and she could not for a moment believe that this was anything other than a living man, but as she gazed at his face, so calm and peaceful, she saw that quality of unnatural stillness that showed her that life had fled. Dr Collin stood by her silently. He had stood by many such a bed, seen daughters, wives and mothers sit quietly beside the departed one, seen the last farewell touch and the lingering caress of the loving eye, and he gave her the time she needed to accept and understand.

'Tell me what happened,' she said at last.

'He lay down to take a rest, as I believe he often did. After a time the maid came in to see how he

200

was and found him with the handkerchief over his face. She recognised at once that something was wrong and called me. I know he liked to make use of a few drops of chloroform to ease him to sleep, and we have both cautioned him against the practice, but–'

Frances noticed that there was a slight reddening of the skin of her father's lips and nose. Dr Collin saw her peering at the marks and said, 'That redness is caused by the chloroform. It can burn the skin if one is not careful. Of course it is impossible now to know how much he used, and I have yet to ascertain if that was the cause of his death.'

'I should have been here,' she said. 'This is my fault. If I had only gone in to look at...'

'Chloroform used incautiously can kill almost in an instant,' said Dr Collin. 'You might not have been able to help if you had been standing by his side. Please do not blame yourself.'

'His hand sometimes shook,' she said, and sighed. 'Tell me you believe his death to be an accident.'

'I think that an accident is very probable, but I regret I will not be able to state my final conclusions without an examination,' said Collin. 'It will not be possible for me to provide a certificate today.'

Frances felt her heart lurch with dread. 'There must be an inquest?'

'I am afraid so.'

'Oh, and I came home with such joy!' she exclaimed. 'They have arrested James Keane for fraud and I know my father was to be cleared of all blame over Mr Garton!' She looked up at Collin, and saw an expression of pity pass over his face. She suddenly realised that she must sound distracted – Dr Collin knew nothing of her suspicions of James Keane, nor was there any reason he should.

'My dear Miss Doughty,' he said, softly. 'My advice to you is to send at once to some relative who may assist you; an uncle, perhaps, or a male cousin. There is always a great deal to do at such times, and you should not be alone.'

She nodded. 'Yes – my Uncle Cornelius.'

'I am afraid that there is nothing more I can do here today,' added Dr Collin. 'I will go at once and find a reliable man to assist me and return tomorrow morning at ten. I believe I shall be able to conclude my examination within the hour. I have no doubt that the inquest will be brief. It is a painful matter I know, and I will do all in my power to ensure that you are spared as much as possible.' He picked up the chloroform bottle carefully by the base, looked at it, sniffed it cautiously, and raised his eyebrows. 'It may help if I were to examine this further. Accidents sometimes happen where the bottle is at fault. I am sure you can provide me with an empty pill box.'

'Oh yes, of course!' Frances rose and called Sarah, who soon brought what was wanted.

Dr Collin put the bottle in the box. The handkerchief was folded and wrapped in a sheet of paper, and both items stowed in his bag. 'At least by tomorrow I will be able to arrive at the cause of death, and I very much hope that my findings will confirm that it was an accident. In cases where there may be doubt, inquest juries will always take into account the reputation of the deceased and the family, and will shy away from any verdict that will cause unnecessary pain. I can assure you that if circumstances require I will encourage them to do so.'

'Thank you doctor,' said Frances, gratefully. She fell silent, lost in thought. The memories of her brother's deathbed were so fresh in her mind that it seemed to her that it had happened the day before, and her father had expired from the sharp and poignant grief of his loss. Perhaps, she thought, in a way, he had, as his pain could hardly have lessened in time. Perhaps it might even have been for the best if he had joined her brother sooner rather than live in misery and confusion for only three more months.

'Until tomorrow, then,' said Dr Collin.

'Oh!' she rose. 'I'm so sorry, I–'

'Please don't trouble yourself, Miss Doughty. Your maid will see me out.'

He departed and she sat once more at her father's side. After a few moments she became aware of someone behind her. It was Herbert, his eyes bright with tears. 'Miss Doughty – what can I say! This is too terrible for words! I can hardly believe what has happened!'

'When did you see him last?'

'Just before he came up for his rest. He was his usual self. If it is any consolation, I think he cannot have suffered. He must simply have fallen asleep.' He wiped his eyes. 'There must be something I can do to assist you.'

'I need to send some telegrams, but apart from

that there is nothing to be done until after the inquest.'

'Inquest?' He seemed shocked.

'I am afraid so.'

'Oh Miss Doughty,' he exclaimed, sobbing, 'how I wish you might be spared such a thing.' Frances concluded that as a tower of male strength to whom she could look for guidance and support Herbert, was somewhat wanting.

She spent a few minutes arranging the bed more tidily, straightening the pillow underneath her father's head, smoothing the covers, and placing the spare quilt over him, as if he was merely resting and needed a little additional warmth. 'There,' she said. 'I will leave him now.'

Frances and Herbert descended to the little parlour. Sarah brought in a tray of tea things. 'I thought–,' she said.

'Yes, Sarah,' said Frances, gently. 'It was a good thought.'

Herbert, declaring manfully that he would do anything to be useful, was sent to get some telegram forms. Frances barely tasted her tea, but held the cup in her hands, taking some reassurance from its familiar shape.

'Mr Keane was arrested today,' she told Sarah. 'The charge was fraud but I am certain he will eventually be charged with Mr Garton's murder. That is the only thing that brings me some comfort. Imagine if the public were still to think my father had poisoned Mr Garton. Imagine what they would now suppose; that feelings of guilt and shame might have led him to–,' she shook her head. 'It is too horrible to think about.'

'Miss,' said Sarah cautiously. 'I hardly like to say it, but there is something you should know.'

'Yes?'

'Well, just before Mr Doughty went up to his room he seemed to remember something.'

Frances sat up. 'What was it?'

'All of a sudden he turned round and said, "Mr Garton's medicine, it wasn't," and then he stopped.'

'Was that all he said?' demanded Frances.

'Yes,' said Sarah regretfully. 'Mr Munson tried as hard as he could to get him to remember more, but it was no use. It was like as soon as it was said it was all forgotten again. I said as how if he took a rest and slept on it then maybe it would come back to him. So I took him up, but he never said anything more about it.'

Frances uttered a groan of regret. Had there indeed been something of importance her father had glimpsed before he died, or had it just been an irrelevant fancy? She would never know. Herbert's well-meaning efforts to try and get her father to remember might well have had the opposite effect to that intended.

The telegrams were written, and for a time Frances was busy with visitors, and Sarah made more tea. Mr Rawsthorne was the first to arrive, deeply shocked at the death of a man he had seen only a few hours before. He spent a few moments paying his last respects at the bedside, then offered Frances such help and advice as he could. It was agreed that the will would be read on the following day.

Uncle Cornelius arrived soon afterwards, and as

always spread his particular kind of calm. As executor of William Doughty's will, he proceeded to take upon himself all necessary duties, which Frances was grateful to give up to him. He sensed that the most important thing for him to do that day was to talk to Frances, and so they sat together amiably and exchanged stories of how things had been in better times. She told him of James Keane's arrest and her expectation that this would put an end to any imputations against her father, and he expressed his great hope that this would be so. The last to arrive was Mrs Scorer, who looked upon the body with an expression which revealed no emotion of any kind, and then glanced about the house taking note of any little items she thought ought to come to her.

Herbert was there, silent, strained and polite. He, like Frances, declined anything to eat, and eventually retired to his room. In the quiet little parlour there remained, towards the end of the day, only Frances and Sarah, and both sat together almost like friends, taking up a little mending to while away the time, until the moment came when Frances put down her work, and wept.

CHAPTER ELEVEN

The next morning, Sarah and Frances were about early. Lack of sleep was a part of both of their lives and they took it in their stride and set about fearlessly cleaning as if royalty itself was about to descend upon them. Frances very much doubted that anyone coming to wait for the outcome of her father's post-mortem examination would wish to eat either during or afterwards, but it would be impolite not to offer anything, and so Sarah prepared several plates of small sandwiches and little cakes. Herbert took himself away unhappily to his room. The business, bereft of qualified supervision, could not open, and a notice was placed in the window announcing the death of the proprietor.

With the work done, Frances changed from her everyday clothes into mourning. Elegant ladies, she knew, might have many sets of mourning, the sombreness of the attire depending on the closeness of the relative, or the time elapsed since bereavement. She had but one, and that would have to do. For the first three months after her brother's death she had worn no adornment, and only lately had she begun to wear the brooch with his portrait. Now she appeared in plain black, her hair simply dressed, her face more starkly pale than ever.

Shortly before ten, Frances inspected everything, and finding it to her satisfaction, entered her father's room for a final farewell. There had been a mad hope in her heart that it had all been a mistake, and she would see him stir and open his eyes, and declare what a refreshing sleep he had had, but his face was sunken and greyer than before, and the still cold of death could not be denied. Looking at him she could not help but recall Frederick's face after the long months of his decline, shrunken and aged with weariness, for the two had been very alike in features, if not in character.

Promptly at ten, Dr Collin arrived with his colleague whom he introduced as Dr Stevens, a much younger man clad in a new black suit and a strong sense of his own importance. His true role in the examination was apparent by the fact that he was clutching some sheets of paper and a pencil.

The doctors declined any refreshments and ascended the stairs to the bedroom, Collin carrying a stout brown leather bag, which Frances knew must contain specimen jars. Her Uncle Cornelius appeared shortly afterwards, and he reassured Frances that he had asked the undertakers to call at eleven to arrange and coffin her father's body. Everything necessary had been provided, and the funeral would be at ten on Tuesday. Herbert joined them and behaved very decently, shaking hands with Cornelius and thanking him warmly for his assistance. He seemed to be racked with emotion which he was barely controlling and this made him unusually quiet, as if he was afraid to say too much. Frances realised that she knew very little of Herbert and his family and wondered if there was some sadness in his own life which had made him unusually attached to her father who, it seemed, had had a place in his heart not unlike that of a parent.

Mrs Scorer arrived, outfitted in black crêpe with a heavy veil, and carrying a larger than usual bag, which she placed on her lap and clutched with an air of determination. Frances decided to watch her carefully in case she anticipated the distribution of assets. Mr Rawsthorne followed, rather later than expected, looking grim and distracted. Frances could not be sure if this was solely due to distress at her father's passing or if there was some other trouble that weighed heavily on his mind. He carried a leather folder of papers, which he held on his lap, and every so often some of them spilled out onto the floor and he was obliged to rescue them and push them back where they had come from, only not as neatly as they had been before, until the corners stuck out at peculiar angles.

There was little conversation. No one seemed inclined to eat at first, and Frances decided to place her visitors more at their ease by taking a sandwich, after which Cornelius gamely followed suit and Mrs Scorer boldly heaped a plate with food and gobbled it down. Only Herbert and Mr Rawsthorne ate nothing. There was little to say, but the waiting must have been a thirsty business, for everyone kept Sarah busy making tea and coffee.

Eventually Dr Collin and Dr Stevens reappeared. All eyes gazed at them anxiously. 'My preliminary examination of the body of Mr William Doughty confirms my original supposition that he died of inhaling an excessive amount of chloroform,' announced Dr Collin. 'Further tests which I will carry out today will indicate if there was any fatty degeneration of the heart which would have made him unusually susceptible to its effects.' He paused, and weighed his remaining words carefully. 'Nothing that I have observed to date suggests that the administration of the

209

excessive dose was anything more than an accident. Assuming that my tests do not indicate
otherwise, and there is no reason why they should,
that is the opinion which I will put before the
inquest on Monday. I will not intrude upon you
any further. The sooner I begin my work, the
sooner this sad business may be concluded. I wish
you all good-day.'

Frances shook his hand and thanked him, and
he and his colleague hurried away.

'As if it would have been anything else!' said
Mrs Scorer, contemptuously.

'I doubt that anyone in this room would have
thought so, but of course, the gossips will have
their say,' observed Cornelius. 'Thankfully, they
will soon be silenced.'

Everyone nodded emphatically.

'Well,' said Mr Rawsthorne, heavily, 'if everyone is content with my proceeding to read the
will? I would prefer to do it now as you are all
present, and there are other urgent matters
which will require my attention today.'

'Please begin, Mr Rawsthorne,' said Frances.

He unfolded the papers, and shuffled them into
order. 'Before I do I need to tell you all that this
will was made some three years ago, shortly after
Mr Frederick Doughty achieved his majority.
There is, as far as I am aware, no subsequent will.
During Mr Frederick's long illness I suggested to
Mr Doughty several times that he should consider
making some amendments to take into consideration the possibility that his son might predecease
him. He refused to do so. After Mr Frederick's
death I frequently entreated Mr Doughty to make

210

a new will, but he would not, and indeed his mental state was then such that he would have found such a task very difficult. Mr Martin, I believe you also approached him on the subject.'

'I did,' agreed Cornelius, sadly, 'but he would not be persuaded.'

'Well, to begin,' said Rawsthorne. 'Mr William Doughty appointed two executors, his brother-in-law Mr Cornelius Martin, and his son Mr Frederick Doughty.'

'I am more than willing to perform all the duties that befall me as executor,' said Cornelius.

'I am very grateful for that assurance,' said Rawsthorne.

'It seems to me,' interrupted Mrs Scorer, 'that if the will assumes that Frederick is living then it can't be valid.'

'It is perfectly valid,' Rawsthorne assured her.

'Well, we'll see about that,' she said, unconvinced. Frances guessed exactly what her aunt was thinking, that intestacy might result in her receiving more of the estate than might otherwise have fallen to her.

'Really, Maude, let Mr Rawsthorne speak,' said Cornelius.

'The will provides four specific bequests,' Rawsthorne went on, 'To Miss Sarah Smith, the sum of ten pounds. To Mr Cornelius Martin, the sum of two hundred pounds. To Mrs Maude Scorer, the sum of two hundred pounds. To Miss Frances Doughty, the sum of two hundred pounds to be held in trust by Mr Frederick Doughty until she should reach the age of twenty-one. All the remainder of the estate is bequeathed to Mr

Frederick Doughty.'

'Well!' said Mrs Scorer in astonishment. 'Mr Rawsthorne, what does this mean? Is Frederick's portion to be divided between the family?'

'No, his portion will pass to his nearest heir, that is, Miss Doughty.'

'Hmph!' snorted Mrs Scorer, not best pleased. 'And what is the value of the estate?'

'That is yet to be ascertained,' said Cornelius. 'But I know that William was always a very frugal man. I cannot imagine it will be less than five thousand pounds in all.'

Frances was silent, and found herself somewhat shocked by what she had heard. Money meant little to her, as long as she was able to live respectably, but even though the will had been made when she was sixteen, she could not help but feel a little slighted by it. Cornelius sensed what she was feeling and patted her hand. 'Do not distress yourself, my dear. I am sure that William always intended that Frederick would look after you, and I have no doubt he would have well merited that confidence.'

'I think William meant you to be poor,' said Mrs Scorer. 'He never liked women to have money of their own. Poor – and dependent on a man – that was what he planned for you – not this!'

'Now then, Maude, I think that is a little harsh,' said Cornelius. 'If he did not intend Frances to have the inheritance why did he not change his will?'

'Because he could never accept that Frederick was dead,' she retorted. 'I know my brother's mind. In the last few months he has done nothing but live in a past time when Frederick was alive and in health. It was as if Frederick had simply stepped into the next room and would reappear at any minute. To change the will would have disinherited him.'

Rawsthorne, apparently unnerved by this potentially embarrassing family discussion, was hurriedly gathering up his papers. 'If there is anything I can do to assist you, Mr Martin, do not hesitate to let me know,' he said. 'My deepest condolences to you all. Mrs Scorer, Mr Munson, I wish you well. Miss Doughty, please accept my best wishes for your future. I hope that the years in which I have represented the interests of your father will be followed by many more years in which I continue to serve your family.'

'Thank you, Mr Rawsthorne,' said Frances.

The solicitor departed, and Frances returned from seeing him to the door to find Mrs Scorer examining the sugar tongs with more than a passing interest. 'They're plate,' she said curtly, and her aunt coloured slightly and put them down on the table. 'There are some personal items of my father's which I will ensure are passed to you. I promise I will dispose of nothing until I have had the opportunity to go through his effects.'

'Two hundred pounds!' said Mrs Scorer contemptuously. 'After the years I spent as little more than a servant in this place!'

'Come, Maude, I will convey you home,' said Cornelius. 'You will not get your money today as I am sure you know. Frances, I have a little business to attend to but if it is convenient I would like to return this afternoon to go through

William's papers.'

'Yes, of course,' said Frances. 'There is a writing desk in his room where I think you will find everything you need.'

After her aunt and uncle had departed, Frances returned to the parlour to find Herbert sitting quietly with an untasted cup of coffee in front of him. He looked so miserable that she could not help but feel sorry for him. 'I am sure,' said Frances, 'that had my father made a more recent will he would have remembered you. He always had the highest opinion of your abilities. I know that there are some items he would have liked you to have, and I will see that they are yours.'

'Thank you, Miss Doughty,' said Herbert, gratefully. 'I suppose that you must have anticipated that you would be his heir.'

'It seemed very probable,' Frances admitted, 'though I could not be certain until I had heard the will.'

He paused. 'Please forgive me if this discussion is premature, but – I was wondering if you had given any thought as to the future of the business?'

She nodded. 'I understand your concern. It is my determination to do as my father would have wished and continue the business in the family name. Of course, it will be necessary to obtain the services of someone qualified to oversee the dispensary.'

'Oh, I am very happy to hear you say it!' he exclaimed. 'Your father would be proud of you indeed! And I think I can see a way in which I may be of service. Would you allow me to make all the necessary enquiries about a suitable man for the post?'

'Man or woman, Mr Munson,' she reminded him. 'As long as the individual is not Mr Ford, whom I admit I dislike.'

'It would only be until I am qualified, of course. And I understand that you were studying for your examinations before family duties prevented you. Would you consider resuming your studies?'

Frances had not given this any thought, but now he had mentioned it, she saw that it was possible again. 'I think that very likely.'

'Just imagine, when we are both qualified we could manage the business together!' he said, excitedly. 'How comfortable that would be! And – excuse me Miss Doughty for even alluding to such a subject at this sad time – but I had been thinking that perhaps – one day – in the fullness of time–'

'I pray you, Mr Munson, do not go on,' said Frances. 'It is not appropriate.'

He grew serious again. 'No. No, of course not. I am very sorry, I forgot myself. But I hope you may give me leave to refer to the matter again,' he added hopefully.

Frances had no intention of discussing the matter at this or any other time, but he looked so crestfallen that she did not want to add to his misery, and was as kind as was commensurate with a refusal. 'As you wish, but I offer you no hope of a favourable reply.'

How many young women would think her foolish now, thought Frances. A fortune of five thousand pounds and the offer of marriage from a respectable man with excellent prospects. She saw the years that lay ahead of her, years of solitude and study, perhaps in time having a shop of her own where she could train other young women in the profession that had scorned them for so many years. That'd be her gift to society. There was, in her imagination of the future, no marriage, no children. She'd never met a man in whose company she felt so content that she might've wished to marry him – at least none that was single.

Once the undertakers had come and placed her father's remains in a coffin, Frances began the task of tidying his room and sorting through his personal effects, of which there were few. From time to time, friends and customers, seeing the notice in the shop window, called to pay their respects, and Frances was kept busy, accepting their good wishes and sympathy without appearing to be wearied.

Shortly before five o'clock Cornelius returned. Frances pressed him to stay for supper and he agreed, then he retired to her father's room to examine the papers.

Frances and Sarah were preparing supper when another visitor arrived, Constable Brown.

'He says he is very sorry to intrude at such a time, only he had no idea until he saw the notice in the window, and he would be happy to come back again if you think it better,' explained Sarah.

'No, please, do show him in, I am very anxious to hear his news,' said Frances.

Wilfred looked very awkward as he entered. 'Please do accept my condolences, Miss Doughty. I'm very sorry to trouble you and would not have come today if I had known.'

'Please do not apologise.' She ushered him to a seat, and Sarah, unbidden, went to make more tea, and brought out such sandwiches and cakes as had not somehow fallen into Mrs Scorer's bag. 'Visitors are a welcome distraction at this time. Your arrival reminds me of a far happier occurrence, yesterday's arrest of Mr Keane, which I know will clear my father's name.'

'It will?' He looked surprised. 'I'm sorry, I'm not sure I understand. How can that be?'

'Because he will be charged with the murder of Mr Garton, of course,' she said, astonished that he had not realised this.

'Oh!' he raised his eyebrows. 'Well, at present he has only been charged with fraud and other financial offences. And I have to say, Miss Doughty, that it is very much down to you that he was.'

'Really? You do surprise me! How can that be?'

'It was your note about the address in Maida Vale which led directly to his arrest,' said Wilfred. 'One day I hope you may be able to tell me how you came by it.'

Frances decided not to take that particular bait. 'But I thought you found nothing there!' she said, offering the plate of food to the constable, and helping herself to a sandwich. He took a cake, and looked pleased as Sarah brought the fresh pot of tea.

'We found a great deal there, but I have not been allowed to talk about it until now. It was the key to the whole case. I know you will not be happy to hear it but Inspector Sharrock is to take much of the credit, although I have heard,' he added, unable to stop himself beaming modestly, 'that there is a smart and deserving young constable who may find himself made up to sergeant a little sooner than he had hoped.'

She smiled. 'I am pleased to hear that last news at least.'

'Yes, Miss, another three pounds eight shillings a year, that will be very welcome, what with the new baby.'

'Oh,' said Frances. She returned the sandwich to her plate. 'Your first child?'

'Second one, Miss Susanna, a little sister for Robert. He's just turned two.'

'I can see that you are very proud of them,' she said.

He nodded. 'I am.'

Frances suddenly felt very old. She could not have felt older if she had been a sixty-year-old spinster looking back on a dreary and unfulfilled life. The constable seemed to her to be very young to have the responsibilities of a wife and two children, and a long, hard and dangerous working day. She hoped that his wife was a good woman. When Sarah poured the tea, she accepted only half a cup.

'So,' said Frances, 'are you able now to tell me what you found in Maida Vale?'

'Well one of the neighbours remembered seeing a man of Mr Keane's description entering the house, and when we searched we found a number of items that suggested it had been used as a forger's den. Mr Keane was either a careless man, or in a very great hurry. He had tried to clear out anything that could incriminate him, but had not destroyed all that he hoped he had.'

Frances was reminded of Keane's appearance at

the gallery, the half-burnt papers, the few items tossed into the waste bin. A careless man, indeed.

'Of course we knew about his position at the Bayswater Bank, and we spoke to the managers. The bank was alerted and his papers were examined. It looks as if he has been selling forged share certificates and also forging property deeds as security for loans. There could be many thousands of pounds missing.'

'And what of the bank,' asked Frances, 'and its customers?'

'The doors are closed until further notice. There's a crowd of angry investors outside and rumours that the directors are in hiding. There have been some ugly scenes. Quite a few local businesses and charities had accounts there.'

'Oh my word!' exclaimed Frances. 'Has he confessed to his crimes?'

'In full, but he has been most adamant that Mr Garton was not a partner in his criminal activities and knew nothing of them. The only connection seems to be that it was through knowing Mr Garton that Mr Keane met the artist Meadows, who he employed to make the engravings. He says that Meadows has fled to France, and the police there have been alerted, but we think there is little hope of ever finding him. He has probably changed his appearance and his name by now, if Meadows ever was his real name, which we doubt.'

'But don't you see?' demanded Frances, 'If Mr Garton found out about Mr Keane's crimes, and Mr Keane thought he would be denounced to the police, that would be a motive for murder!'

'It would, Miss,' admitted Wilfred, cautiously,

219

'but it's hard to know how we might prove it.'

'You will I am sure,' said Frances, confidently. 'If, as you say, Mr Keane is a careless man, there may yet be other clues. Mr Garton may have confided the details of private conversations to his wife or other associates. What of Mr Berenger, the manager of the picture gallery, has he been able to assist?'

'Mr Berenger has been in the habit of taking a little more drink than is good for him. We found him in the Redan in a very fuddled state. He was not able to cast any light on Mr Keane's activities. But there is,' he added, 'one strange connection between this affair and the murder of Mr John Wright in Tollington Mill.'

'Oh,' said Frances, 'I had quite forgotten about poor Mr Wright. And I recall now that I asked you to discover why Mr Garton was not questioned in the case, when it seemed to me that he might be a suspect.'

'I have had a letter from the Gloucestershire police and it is simple enough. Mr Garton was in London at the time of Mr Wright's murder. He left Tollington Mill by train early on 28th July, before Wright was murdered. He was preparing to move his household there, and he was busily engaged in appointments with house agents, and viewing properties. Scotland Yard made some discreet enquiries at the time and were able to confirm his movements. Mrs Garton joined him there on 10th August. All the evidence suggests that by then Mr Wright was dead.'

'I see,' said Frances, disappointed. She wrote the details carefully in her notebook. 'But what

220

was the connection you spoke of?'

'When the Gloucestershire police were trying to identify Mr Wright they asked his housekeeper Mrs Cranby if he ever sent any letters, and if so, who they went to. She said that Mr Wright, being a gentleman who liked country walks, used to take his own letters to the post office, and she never saw who he wrote to except in one case. He sent a letter to a Mr James Keane of Bayswater. Naturally the Paddington police questioned Mr Keane at the time, and he admitted that he had received a letter from Mr Wright but he did not know the gentleman or how he came by his name and address. He had not kept the letter but recalled that Mr Wright had introduced himself and said that he wished to open an account at the Bayswater Bank and wanted Mr Keane to transact some business for him. Mr Keane thought this approach to be highly irregular and wrote back to Mr Wright saying he could not assist him personally and suggested he address his enquiries directly to the bank. He said he heard nothing more.'

'But that is an *extraordinary* coincidence!' said Frances. 'When Mr Garton was living in Tollington Mill he had never even met Mr Keane.'

'Perhaps,' theorised Wilfred, 'Mr Keane was recommended to Mr Wright by another gentleman, and then Mr Wright mentioned him to Mr Garton and when Mr Garton came to Bayswater he saw Mr Keane as being something of a mutual acquaintance.'

'And what of Mr Wright's family? Did the police learn anything from them?'

'About a month after Mr Wright's death, a lady

221

came forward who said she thought that he might be her brother. She was a Miss Mary Ann Wright of Bristol, and said that her brother John had been committed to an asylum about three years before. Since he was twenty-one he had suffered from delusions that he was a wealthy man, and the heir to vast fortunes. He was personable and convincing and was able to persuade a great many people of the truth of his claims. Legal men agreed to represent him, and a great deal of money was spent on searches for documents that existed only in his imagination. His family realised that he was squandering such little fortune as he had, and decided to have him sent to an asylum. But his sister, being an exceptionally kind lady and very fond of her brother, especially as she had no other, thought that she could care for him at home and keep him from harm. So she persuaded his doctor to release him and she and her brother lived together in Bristol very comfortably for a year. Sometimes he would tell her that he had been meeting with important men about his inheritance, even though she knew he had never stirred from the house. He also conceived the idea that he owned all of Hertfordshire, and often told her he had been there and back to pursue his claims, even though he had only been out for a short walk.'

'Oh, the poor lady! I do feel for her!' sighed Frances. Although Frederick's illness had been very different, she knew that in Mary Ann Wright's circumstances she would have done as much.

'Indeed, it was a very sad case,' Wilfred agreed. 'Most of the time he was in good spirits but sometimes he became very despondent, and said that he thought there were people sent to murder him for his money. But he always recognised his sister and was very affectionate.'

'But how did he come to Tollington Mill?' asked Frances. 'And why did his sister not visit him there?'

'In June of 1869 he suddenly appeared very distressed, saying that his life was in danger and he needed to hide away for safety. His sister thought it was only one of his strange ideas which he would soon forget, but the next day he was gone, and some items of family silver were also missing. She didn't tell the police because naturally she didn't want him arrested as a thief. She hoped that in time he would come back of his own accord. It is believed that he sold or pawned the silver and used the money to lease Tollington House, where he masqueraded as a man of wealth.'

'But in the following year,' said Frances, 'there was a month' – she looked at her notes – 'July 1870, when he was absent from Tollington Mill. Is it known where he was?'

'Yes. He returned to live with his sister in Bristol. She was very shocked to see the change in his appearance. He explained to her that there were assassins sent to look for him, and as his hair was a distinctive shade of red he had dyed it black to escape detection. She did not press him about the stolen silver, or even ask where he had been, but simply accepted him back into her home with gratitude for his safe return.'

'That is touching loyalty, and I can well under-stand it,' said Frances. 'But was it certain that the

223

John Wright who died at Tollington Mill was this lady's brother?'

'Of course the lady could not look at the body, but she saw the notebook and said it was in her brother's writing, also she recognised the clothes as the ones he had worn when she last saw him. Then she remembered that one day, while brushing his coat, she had seen a tear in the lining and mended it. Sure enough, when the coat was opened, there were her stitches.'

Frances nodded. 'But why did she wait some weeks before going to the police?'

'Poor lady, she felt that as long as she was not sure if he was alive or dead then at least she would have some hope. It was a relative who insisted she report the matter.'

Frances thought about the consequences of what she had just learned. 'So when Mr Wright reappeared in Tollington Mill and said he was going to an important meeting–'

'There may have been no such meeting,' agreed Wilfred. 'The mysterious M in his notebook may have been imaginary.'

'Or his murderer,' said Frances.

'We know that the money and watch he carried on his person were stolen. The police have always assumed he was killed by a footpad, and there is no reason now to amend that belief.'

'And yet the coincidences!' exclaimed Frances. 'The fact that Mr Keane has been associated with two men who have met a violent end and another who has disappeared! The fact that Wright and Meadows were both artists! What if Mr Keane had been employing Mr Wright to carry out his

224

forgeries for him and killed him when he thought Mr Wright would give him away? Suppose Mr Meadows has not gone to France after all but Mr Keane has murdered him?'

'Oh dear!' said Wilfred, alarmed at Frances' eager theorising.

'Just think,' said Frances, encouragingly, 'if you were to uncover those crimes you would be made up to Inspector on the instant!'

He smiled. 'Well, Miss, as you have been so helpful to the police, I will certainly think of what you have said when we are questioning Mr Keane.'

The parlour door opened, and Cornelius appeared, looking tired and strained. He was naturally startled to see Wilfred there, being regaled with tea, cake and sandwiches, and the young constable rose awkwardly.

Frances introduced the two men, and mentioned only that the constable knew her father and had called to give his condolences. Cornelius looked unusually relieved at this assurance, and Wilfred expressed his good wishes and hastily departed.

'I think there is still some tea, if you would like some,' said Frances. The cakes had been consumed and she offered her uncle the sandwich plate. 'Or I could ask Sarah to make a fresh pot.'

He shook his head, and sat down heavily on one of the parlour chairs. 'Frances,' he said quietly. 'Please sit down.' There was something in his tone that at once commanded her attention, and she obeyed. 'There is something I need to tell you and – my poor dear niece – I am afraid it is very bad news indeed.'

CHAPTER TWELVE

'Is this something to do with the Bayswater Bank?' asked Frances, faintly. For a moment she feared that, unknown to her, the Doughtys' business funds had been transferred there, in which case the bank's collapse would have had disastrous consequences.

He frowned. 'No.'

She breathed easily again. 'I am relieved to hear it. The constable told me there have been dreadful scenes outside the bank today, which has closed its doors. Many people are ruined. But I know we did not have an account there.'

Cornelius sighed. 'You might just as well have done.'

Again, she felt a chill of fear. 'Whatever do you mean?'

He shook his head in despair. 'There is no easy way to tell you. As you know, I have been trying to arrive at the value of your father's estate by examining his bank accounts. He has always been a careful man, and it seems that only a year ago there were several thousand pounds in the safest of investments. Today – and I am grieved to say it – there is almost nothing. It has all gone.' He turned his head away. He was unable to look into her eyes.

Frances stared at him. 'I don't understand. Gone? But where can it have gone? And how? Surely there has been a mistake. Uncle, you must go to the bank and make enquiries. He may only have placed the money in another account.'

'No, Frances,' he groaned, 'I am afraid there can be no mistaking what has occurred. It appears that your father was tempted into making some very unwise investments. By whom I cannot say. He began to withdraw funds, in small amounts at first and then greater, sometimes several hundred pounds at a time. It seems that the heavier his losses the more he withdrew to try and recover them, but as is so often the case with these things, his position became increasingly desperate. He threw good money after bad, as the saying goes. The stockbroker's accounts have told me the whole tale, and it is a very sad one.'

Frances felt hope draining away, leaving only a cold sensation in her stomach. 'And there is nothing at all?'

He gestured, helplessly. 'I think one account may have fifty pounds in it.'

There was a long silence. At first Frances thought she had become incapable of any emotion, as if she had been suddenly and sharply struck upon the head, and was sitting there in an icy and unfeeling trance. Then, just as suddenly, a jumbled mass of feelings began to flood though her mind – anger, despair, bewilderment, and a sudden insane desire to laugh hysterically. She realised that Cornelius was speaking to her. 'My dear, I pray you will calm yourself. It is a hard thing to bear, but I promise I will assist you in any way I can, and I know Maude will do her duty by you.'

The mention of her aunt was like a dash of cold water that restored her thoughts. At the back of her mind there was a voice telling her that it was not true, that it was a cruel joke, a dream, something said only to test her mettle, that in a moment she would awake, or Cornelius would tell her that the money was not gone after all, and beg her forgiveness. She pushed all of that aside. She had only to look at her uncle's face to know that it was true. 'Maude will only be grieved by the loss of her two hundred pounds,' said Frances, bitterly. She took a deep breath, and clenched her fists in determination. 'I must not give way. I must be practical. There must be things that I can do,' she said.

'My dear,' said Cornelius. 'I know it is a shock. Perhaps you should call Dr Collin.'

'No, please, I am well. I only need to order my thoughts. There are bills to pay but we can put them off a little. We must obtain the services of a qualified man so that we can open the shop again. Then there is the lease which is due to be renewed in two months' time. There is no hope of paying that. But I do think, if you were to help me, I could go to a bank and show them the accounts and borrow enough to see us through this time. There. All is not lost.'

Cornelius gazed at her pityingly. 'Frances, I am not sure if I have made the position clear to you. There is no possibility of your being able to borrow sufficient to recover. Quite apart from the business debts you have mentioned, there are others; to stockbrokers, to banks. These people will not wait for their money. You cannot borrow to pay them for you have no security to offer.'

'But the business–'

'Is encumbered by debt. It has no value as it stands.'

She stared at him. 'Then what must I do?'

'I am truly sorry,' he said softly. 'There is only one thing you can do. You must sell. The price of the business may well be sufficient to pay off the debts.'

'And then I will have nothing!' she said wretchedly.

He nodded. 'Very probably. But Frances, be assured of this, I will not desert you. You may make your home with me if you wish, or with Maude. I have a small investment which provides a little income and you are welcome to make use of it for your own necessaries.'

Frances began to tremble and he held onto her hands. In asking herself how she had come to deserve this, she could only answer that she did, that she had been at fault. When her father had been alone working on his papers she knew she was not to disturb him, yet would it not have been better if she had disobeyed him and done so? She might have seen enough to suspect what was happening. And, she realised, there was a moral fault also, the fault of greed. How could she hide from herself that in that short time when she had imagined she was mistress of five thousand pounds, she had felt a wholly unworthy satisfaction with her position, something for which she was now paying the price in full.

She looked around at the little parlour, so plain and so familiar, and thought of the shop and the smooth dark counter she had polished ever since she was a child, the storeroom where she had prepared the syrups and waters, the small kitchen where Sarah's cooking infused the air with warmth and delicious smells, and her own little bedroom. It was all she had ever known.

'I cannot give it up so easily,' she said. 'This is my home. It is what my father worked for all his life! How can I just sell it?'

He pressed her hands but said nothing.

'A month!' she begged him. 'Let me have a month!'

'But my dear, what can you do in a month?' said Cornelius sadly.

'I'll run the business!' she said desperately. 'I'll find someone to supervise; we'll open the doors again. We have well-wishers enough, and it is the winter season after all. In a few weeks we will have money.'

'But it will not be enough. At the end of that time the debts will still be there. You have no hope of paying them. Frances, I am talking of three thousand pounds just to clear the stock-broker's account.'

It was more money than she had ever seen in her life. She felt tears pricking her eyes, but fought them back. 'I'm sure you are right. But I need the time, if nothing else than for myself. I need to know that I didn't just throw it all away without even trying to hold on.'

He patted her hands and nodded. 'I understand. And now I come to think about it there may be an advantage in waiting. With hard work and economy the business may recover a little, and the dreadful events of the last weeks will, in the fickle public mind at least, be forgotten. You may well get a better price in a month than you could now. Very well. I will allow you what funds I can. At the end of the month we will talk of this again.'

When he had gone, Frances looked at her father's papers herself, and was unable to deny the truth of what her uncle had said. Her father was the only person who had the authority to draw the funds from the accounts. Why had he risked everything? Her aunt's words came back to haunt her. Had he done it so she would not inherit the business? Was this his way of keeping her poor?

If she had been the sort of woman to do nothing but dwell on her misfortune she might, thought Frances, have gone mad, but that was not her way. After the first cruel shock was over, she bent herself to exploring how best she could combat this twist of fate. Sitting at the parlour table, she put before her all the books of the business and household and studied them to see how she could pare expenses to the very smallest amount possible. She had, in truth, very little hope that these poor efforts would assist her, since it had always been their practice to watch every penny of expenditure, but the task did serve to give her the illusion that she was working towards the salvation of her fortunes.

It grew late, and as the light faded and her eyes dimmed, she laid her head down upon the pages and slept. It was Sarah who awoke her.

'Miss, it's very late.'

'Oh, yes.' Frances rubbed her eyes. She looked up into the face of the honest servant who had been the mainstay of the household for ten years, who had been, as she thought, rewarded with a few pounds, money which would probably have meant a great deal to her family, and knew that she would have to tell her the truth.

'Sarah, please sit down, I must speak to you.'

'If it's about the money Miss, I know these things can take a lot of time.' Sarah saw her expression, and paused. 'What's wrong Miss?'

'I have had some very bad news. My uncle has looked at my father's papers and found that – that all the money has gone.'

Sarah blinked. 'Gone, Miss?' To someone for whom ten pounds was a very material amount it was hard for her to imagine how the Doughtys' fortunes could have disappeared.

'It seems that my father made some bad investments,' said Frances. 'We are ruined. For the next month I am determined to keep the business open and see what I can do, but at the end of that time, I think I will have to sell in order to pay the debts.'

Sarah sat quietly thinking for a while. 'Where will you go, Miss?'

Frances smiled. Another servant would have been concerned about losing her place; Sarah's first thought was for Frances. 'I expect I will go to live with my uncle. He has already promised me that I can. Sarah, I doubt that I will be able to pay your wages. You may be best advised to look for a new place.'

'I'll stay here, Miss, if you don't mind,' said Sarah firmly. 'Who knows but that you may get a stroke of luck.'

'Oh I do hope so!' said Frances gratefully. 'I don't know how I could manage without you. If

232

the business is sold, well, the new owner may employ you, of course, and you will be given an excellent character.'

'Would Mr Martin not have a place for me, Miss?' asked Sarah. 'It's just that – I've looked after you since you were little, and–'

'I will ask him, I promise,' said Frances, but she knew that her uncle had a general servant and did not require another. One more thought crossed her mind. 'Sarah, there is something I have been meaning to ask you. What is the talk in the neighbourhood about my father's demise? Has there been any bad gossip about him?'

Sarah looked unhappy. 'There has, Miss, but I wouldn't care to repeat it.'

'I must know,' insisted Frances. 'Spare me nothing. I will have the truth.'

'Well,' said the maidservant reluctantly, 'they say that Mr Doughty was very unhappy, and took his own life from guilt about killing Mr Garton.'

Sarah gazed at Frances with some anxiety, as if the words might throw her into a paroxysm of grief.

Frances could only nod. 'That is what I feared.' She sighed. 'Sometimes, Sarah, I feel like a soldier fighting a battle. A lone soldier against an army of enemies. Some have faces, and some do not. That is why I have to know the worst, so I know who I am fighting.'

'You're not alone, Miss,' said Sarah. 'I'll never let you be alone.'

The following day Frances' work continued, and eventually she sat down with Sarah and instructed her on the harsh new rules of domestic economy.

There was to be no extravagance and no waste. There had been neither extravagance nor waste before, yet somehow they would find even more occasions where pennies could be saved, and nothing must ever be thrown away. Meals, Frances assured Sarah, could be made out of almost nothing, and coals must be strictly conserved.

Herbert was out arranging for a manager and returned in high spirits, announcing that a Mr Jacobs would be starting early on Monday morning. A poster was manufactured from a sheet of clean wrapping paper and placed in the window announcing the re-opening of the shop. Frances was unwilling to reveal to Herbert the full extent of her financial distress, but thought it only fair to inform him that she was considering selling the business after all.

'I don't understand,' he said, taken aback. 'You have never considered selling, not for one instant. It is your father's legacy.'

'His legacy was less than I expected,' she said dryly.

'How much less?' he blurted out.

She stared at him. 'Really, Mr Munson, I think that is entirely my business.'

'I meant – I am sorry – it was quite inappropriate, but believe me I spoke only from my concern about you, Miss Doughty.'

'Really?' Frances doubted it. 'And would you be more or less concerned if I had five thousand pounds or five?'

He blinked in amazement. 'I am not sure I understand you,' he said.

'Very well, I will be blunt,' said Frances, firmly.

'I have no money, Mr Munson. There, that is all you need to know.'

He stared at her, his mouth opening and closing like some strange barbelled fish in an aquarium. 'But you have the business,' he said plaintively.

'The business is encumbered. I am a pauper.' Frances could not avoid a certain note of triumph in her voice. Horrid as her situation was, much as she had determined to do all she could to maintain that little independence she had grasped just for a moment, she had been unable to resist seeing how Herbert would react to her reversal of fortune.

He was silent for a time, the colour draining from his face. When he spoke it was a whisper. 'That is terrible indeed.'

'I will not blame you if you do not choose to mention again the subject we discussed yesterday,' she added.

He buried his head in his hands. 'Oh, what you must think of me!' he moaned.

'I think,' said Frances, 'that like many another man, you seek to improve your fortunes in whatever way may present itself.'

'Yes,' he said, raising his head. His distress was all too apparent. 'That is true. But I believe that you have great worth in yourself, and now, even more than ever, you need – you *deserve* to have someone on whom you can rely. I think I may choose to mention the subject again.'

Frances was surprised, although no more inclined to look on his attentions favourably.

Cornelius called to see how Frances was, bringing with him a copy of that day's *Bayswater*

235

Chronicle. She read it eagerly. There was only a brief mention of her father's death, but two columns on the arrest of James Keane, who was due to appear before the police court the following Friday on charges of fraud, forgery and embezzlement. 'But not murder!' she said, frustrated at the inability of anyone but herself to see the obvious. 'Why do they not charge him?'

'He has as good as murdered many in Bayswater,' said Cornelius. 'Did you know that Rawsthorne's kept many client accounts in that bank, and he himself has lost a great deal of money.'

'Mr Rawsthorne is ruined?' exclaimed Frances, understanding now the reason for the solicitor's recent distracted behaviour.

'No, not so bad as that, but things will be hard for him for a time. I have just come from there and he is in a great state. He was distraught to hear of your predicament and said that if he had the means he would have lent you what you needed for the sake of your father's memory.'

'That was very kind of him to say so,' said Frances, wondering how many other old friends would tell her that they would if they could.

'I asked him if he might find some gentlemen who would be willing to invest in the business and he said he would see what he could do, but that gentlemen are not usually willing to wait indefinitely for a return on their funds. But I will continue to make enquiries on your behalf. For now, I am concerned with the arrangements for the funeral.'

'I suppose that my father will be buried beside my mother?'

Cornelius looked uncomfortable. 'I am sorry. I

have done my best, but it has not proved to be possible. But it will be a beautiful spot, I can assure you.'

'I am not sure that I can pay for it,' she said, the dreadful prospect of a pauper's grave suddenly arising before her.

'Oh, leave that to me, Frances,' he reassured her.

'But you have done so much for me already!' she said, unable to hide her relief and gratitude.

'You are my only sister's child,' he said. 'I will do whatever I can.'

'I must visit my mother's grave again,' she said wistfully. 'My father only took me there once and he was so distressed, I never dared ask him again. Will you take me there?'

'Poor dear Rosetta,' said Cornelius, with a far-away look. 'Yes, of course I will.'

Cornelius departed, not before he had ob-served Frances' very great interest in the news-paper, and, realising that not purchasing such an item was one of her many economies, he said that she might keep it if she liked.

The editor of the *Chronicle* was clearly in a state of great excitement, doing his best to convince his readers that here, in their very midst, was a crime of such enormity it would be recorded in the annals of the greatest frauds of the century. 'It is confidently expected that the trial, assuming there to be one, will be a sensation. The crimes of Mr Keane are said to rival even the iniquity of John Sadler, the cunning of Leopold Redpath and the cruelty of Lewis Cotter.' Frances had no idea who any of these dreadful persons might be, but felt sure that James Keane must be at least as bad as all three rolled into one. The editor also mentioned that forgery was not as it had once been, a capital crime, something Frances could only regret. The next step in James Keane's descent into the pit of retribution was the Marylebone Police Court hearing, when the charges would be heard and the decision no doubt made to commit him for trial. Frances was not prepared to wait until then. If only she could persuade the police to charge him with murder she would stop the hated gossips forever.

Frances prepared to go out, but before she did so, and after some thought, she decided that there was at least one thing she must attempt, and perhaps on this occasion it would be best to approach it in a proper manner. She wrote a note to Mrs Keane asking if she could call.

So much had happened to Frances since her first visit to Paddington Green Police Station that it held no terrors for her now. Was there any worse sight to see than the ugly brawl in front of the Keanes' house, any person less savoury in appearance than the Filleter, anything that could touch her heart more than the death of her father or crush her more than the loss of the home in which she had been born? She approached the sergeant's desk boldly, and as she waited her turn behind some women wrapped in layers of colourless and threadbare shawls, Inspector Sharrock came out of his office and saw her.

'Miss Doughty!' he said, and while it was obvious that he was not pleased to see her, the news of her bereavement clearly inclined him to indulge her a little. 'Come into my office and sit down. Whatever you want to say, I have a few minutes to listen.'

She followed him into the room and waited by the chair until he removed some papers from the seat and added them to the untidy pile on his desk. 'Thank you for seeing me,' she said.

'I am sorry to hear about your father,' he said bluntly, more for the purpose of disposing of that little politeness than any real expression of feeling, yet in a way it was more honestly spoken than the piteous ramblings of some of her neighbours.

'Thank you, Inspector. I have come to see you as a result of reading in today's *Bayswater Chronicle* about the charges against Mr Keane.'

'Oh dear!' he sighed. 'I know what this is about. You *have* got a bee in your bonnet about Mr Keane. Yes, he is a villain, but there is no evidence to say he is a murderer, and without evidence I can't charge him.'

'You had no evidence that he was a fraudster and all those other terrible things, yet you found it. I am sure if you looked–'

'Looked *where*, Miss Doughty?' he said, wearily.

'The murder of John Wright in Tollington Mill in 1870. The disappearance of Mr Meadows,' she declared.

'I know all about John Wright,' he snapped. 'You've got my constable wasting his time over it. John Wright was murdered by a footpad for his gold watch, and Mr Keane was in London when it happened. As for Mr Meadows, the French police are looking for him, but picking out one artist in France from all the others could be difficult.

Please, Miss Doughty, just go home and see to your own business and let the police see to theirs.'

'But this *is* my business!' she insisted. 'People are saying that my father killed Mr Garton and then took his own life! But Mr Keane had ample motive to commit murder!'

He rolled his eyes. 'Motive is not proof, Miss Doughty. Besides which, I should like to know how Mr Keane managed to put poison into a bottle of medicine which as far as anyone can see he never even came near.'

'Perhaps he bribed one of Mr Garton's servants to do it,' said Frances desperately.

'Oh? And which one of them do you suspect?'

'All of them! None of them! I don't know!'

He sighed heavily. 'You see Miss Doughty, it is all very well to throw out accusations like that but police work needs a logical brain, which, as I am sure you will agree, is not the forte of the fairer ones amongst us. That is why police and judges and lawyers are men, and always will be. Pharmacy is different, I will admit. Tending to the sick, making up a little mixture, tying up a pretty package, now that might well be ladies' work, but not this.'

'But you have never even considered that the servants might be involved in the crime,' said Frances.

'Which is where you are very wrong,' he said. 'We always consider the servants and in this case we took the precaution of looking in their rooms to see if there was anything of a suspicious nature.'

'And what did you find?' she asked.

'Well, nothing actually criminal,' said Sharrock,

pulling a face, 'dubious yes, but criminal, no. Not a suggestion that one of them might have had a hand in killing Mr Garton.'

'Will you tell me what you found?' she demanded.

He stared at her. 'You *astound* me, Miss Doughty. Do you think I would show you a confidential police document?'

'Since, as you say, there is nothing criminal in it, I don't see how it can do any harm,' she said boldly. 'And if someone had the means to introduce poison into the bottle without disturbing the seals, I might be able to recognise it.'

He paused and she saw his eyes flicker to the desk. His fingers drummed the edge. 'It would be highly irregular. Even if you were to agree that in return you would go home and not trouble me again, which, would, I admit be a tempting thought; even then, I doubt that I could allow it.'

'Inspector, please,' she begged.

'No, no, don't entreat me; I am immune to all persuasion. There are female persons who come into this station – I will not call them ladies – more adept at persuasion than you will ever be, and I have hardened myself against all blandishments of that nature. I am sorry if my decision distresses you, but so be it.' He frowned, and looked at her keenly. 'I hope you are not feeling unwell, Miss Doughty.'

'I am perfectly well, thank you,' she said, coldly.

'Only, it seemed to me that you might be in need of a glass of water, in which case I would go and fetch one for you.'

'I–' she stared at him.

241

'Glass of water, Miss?' He raised his eyebrows. 'Last chance to refuse.'

She understood. 'Yes please.'

'Wait there. I might be a minute or two.' He rose and left.

Hardly believing what had just happened, Frances hurried to the desk and quickly sifted through the papers, fortunately finding what she wanted near the top. She took her notebook from her pocket and quickly began to write. When she had done she replaced the paper on the desk in what she hoped was its original position, and sat down. Only a moment later Sharrock appeared with a glass of water.

'There you are, Miss Doughty, and it is not every lady who receives refreshment here without the preliminary of being locked up, something I hope you never come to.'

'You are very kind,' she said, sipping the water.

'I trust that you can now promise me that you will in future confine your energies to pursuits more, shall we say, appropriate to a young lady.'

'Thank you, Inspector,' she said coolly, 'but I regret that I am forced by circumstances to be my own judge of what is appropriate.'

He shook his head. 'I am sorry to hear it. You are, may I say it, very young and very inexperienced to be without a guide in life. I see many an individual go astray for that very reason.'

She put the glass down. 'One thing I *will* promise you. I will not trouble you again until I have in my hands proof positive of the identity of the murderer of Mr Garton.' She rose. 'And now I wish you good-day.'

He showed her to the door, and she sensed that her dignity and determination had at the very least earned his respect.

When she returned home, Sarah, in accordance with Frances' instructions, was preparing a frugal meal of grilled herrings and rice pudding with tea. Frances cared little what she ate as long as it was wholesome and nourishing, but Herbert looked at the arrangements with alarm, though he clearly felt unable to complain. Frances was able to find a little private time to study her notebook and wonder what, if anything, it told her. The servants' rooms naturally contained their own small personal effects such as clothing, toilet articles, family letters and a few gewgaws of cheap jewellery. None of the other items listed suggested that any one of them had received a bribe, though she could see why some might have been considered dubious.

In Mr Garton's house, an article of gentleman's under-linen, thought to belong to Mr Beale the coachman, had been found in the room of Mrs Grange the cook, while Mr Beak, a single person, with, Frances recalled, a fondness for ladies who knew their way about a kitchen, was the owner of a pamphlet entitled 'Sanitary Practices for the Married Man.' Flora, the nervous kitchen maid, had concealed under her mattress a collection of newspaper cuttings on the subject of burglaries in the neighbourhood, while Susan, the ladies' maid whom Ada had said was able to sleep through any amount of noise, had hidden away a small medicine bottle, empty but thought to have once contained laudanum. Ada's one secret possession was a photograph of a small boy – the police note had added '(very ugly)' – with 'Harold' written on the back. Mr Edwards, Mr Garton's manservant, would have been mortified to find that others now knew he possessed an elastic apparatus for the control of protruding ears.

The servants' rooms in the Keane household also revealed an interesting, though not incriminating, assortment of possessions. Ettie's secret vice was a small collection of dolls made from clothes pegs and scraps of knitting wool. Mrs Grinham, whose lumbago must have been worse than anyone had suspected, owned a large bottle of horse liniment, and a box of blue pills. At least Frances could now guess how Mr Harvey had gained such intimate details of the financial affairs of the Gartons. Hidden amongst his socks were some pictures of classical Greek statues and two postcards from Italy signed 'Affectionately, Cedric'. Mr Shilling the coachman had a collection of recipes for horse medicines, and Frances wondered if Mrs Grinham had been consulting him as more appropriate to her condition and a great deal cheaper than Dr Collin. Ellen had a neat little box of pretty seashells and a spectacle lens, and Adam had concealed under his pillow a dried corsage of flowers and a scrap of ribbon. Frances did not have to guess which lady had once discarded those items.

Tom arrived with a note from the Keane house. 'I got a message from Mr Knight and Mr Taylor as well,' he said. 'They say as how they're very sorry to hear about Mr Doughty and can they call on you to condole – or was it console?'

'I am happy for them to call, of course,' said Frances. She took the note. The writing was a looped elegant sweep, the letters 'i' not dotted, but ornamented with decorative whorls. 'Tom, I don't know if Sarah has told you about the new position, but there may be a difficulty with your wages.'

'Oh, that's all right, Miss,' he said, puffing out his chest with a grin. 'I'm a businessman, now. I c'n wait.'

When Tom had gone she opened the letter. It took a few moments for her to take in what it said. Against every expectation, Mrs Keane had said she could call at 4 o'clock that afternoon.

CHAPTER THIRTEEN

As Frances approached the Keanes' house again, she could not help but consider the difference between the outward show of respectability it presented and the dreadful reality within. She could feel only sympathy for Mrs Keane, the victim of a cruel husband who cared nothing for her, and indeed seemed rather to think of his wife with contempt more than anything else. To the residents of Bayswater it must have appeared that Mary Keane had an enviable existence. A fashionable journal might have held her up as an example of something to which every young woman might aspire, yet her situation was no less unhappy than that of Frances. A father on the brink of bankruptcy, a husband disgraced, she must even now be consumed with a dread of her own imminent ruin, and had probably agreed to see Frances more for some sympathetic female company than any other reason. It might even be, thought Frances, that no lady of quality would now wish to call upon her.

Clutching the note in her gloved hand, Frances rang the doorbell. It had already occurred to her that she could well be confronted with a servant who would know her under another name, but she would just have to make the best of that. When the door opened, she did not at first recognise the figure standing before her. Adam had the good sense, beneath his air of rigid dignity, to appear embarrassed. Whoever had chosen his costume had raided the worst excesses of the previous century's bad taste, and supplied him with an embroidered coat and braided waistcoat in burgundy and gold, burgundy knee britches and silver grey stockings, with shiny buckled shoes. If the object of the transformation had been to reveal to the world his exceedingly muscular calves then the exercise had succeeded admirably.

'Yes Miss?' he said, staring straight ahead.

'I am Frances Doughty. I have an appointment to see Mrs Keane.' She tendered the note.

'Please come in, you are expected.'

He ushered her in. The air was scented with best-quality beeswax polish. So this was the hallway where Percival and Henrietta Garton had entered the house for their last meal together. Frances noted the elegant paper decorated with tasteful designs of tiny beribboned flowers, the gilded glass lamps, a small table covered in trinkets which seemed to have no purpose other

246

than to demonstrate to the world that the owner could afford such things. There was an oil painting on the wall, framed in ornately carved and gilded wood, of a young couple in a classical garden. They wore almost Grecian garments consisting of filmy draperies so voluminous as to be entirely decent. The man looked like a stalwart warrior, tall and handsome with generous whiskers, but seemed to be paying more attention to some imaginary mirror than he was to the bovine lady who stood by his side, gazing at him in adoration, her flowing robes failing to disguise a figure of ample proportions. Beside them were two impossibly cherubic children. Frances had no difficulty in recognising Mr and Mrs Keane portrayed in a less unhappy time. She noticed in passing a slight alteration in the colouring of a rectangle of wallpaper, as if another picture had once hung in the hallway and been too recently removed to be replaced.

Frances suddenly saw herself as a player acting a part. Just as a play is performed many times, so she was now assuming the role of Henrietta Garton arriving with her husband to dine with the Keanes. She tried to imagine the circumstances of that evening. It would not have been Adam in the hallway to greet them that day, but most probably Mr Harvey, and the missing picture, almost certainly the drawing by Meadows that had been ordered for destruction, would have been there.

Adam did not offer to take her coat, and she understood by this that she was not expected to stay longer than the few minutes appropriate to a call. On the night of Percival Garton's death, however, it would have been different, and she saw a tall cupboard further down the hallway where the cloaks would have been put away for the evening.

'Mrs Keane will see you in the drawing room, Miss,' he said. 'Follow me.'

The drawing room, thought Frances, the place where the Keanes and the Gartons had retired on the fatal night to take small digestive drinks and treats after dinner. The room was, as she expected, a model of every kind of comfort. There was a well-tended fire, piled with as much coal as she might have expected to burn in a week, deep carpets, hangings of oriental silk, handsome furniture, and brightly polished lamps. Frances had supposed she might find Mrs Keane seated in the semi-darkness appropriate to her grief, but the room blazed with light, as if the most elegant guests were any minute expected, and the mistress of the house was arranged on a deeply upholstered sofa, her expression giving every appearance of satisfaction. A small table by her side bore a silver tray with a plate of small cakes, dishes of sweetmeats, and a decanter of sherry. As Frances entered, Mary Keane indicated an armchair with a languid sweep of her hand. 'My dear Miss Doughty, it is a very great pleasure to meet you,' she said, in that superbly rich voice, no less dramatic for being softly expressed. 'Will you take some refreshment?'

Frances, still aware of her role, asked for some aerated water, the same item Percival Garton had consumed in that very room on the night of his death. It was not a beverage she normally favoured, but Adam brought her a glass of sparkling liquid with an aroma of lemons, and she was pleasantly surprised by its flavour.

'Do not leave us, Adam,' commanded Mrs Keane. 'Stay by my side in case I require anything.'

'Yes Ma'am.' He took up his post by the side of the sofa, his face without any trace of expression.

'Adam has not been with the household long, at least, not in his present capacity, but I think you will agree that he is an ornament to any room he inhabits,' said Mrs Keane, admiringly.

'Indeed,' said Frances, politely.

Mrs Keane sipped a glass of sherry, and let her fingers hover greedily over the dishes of sweet delicacies, sighing in an agony of indecision. Frances felt sure that the entire contents of the tray would have been consumed by the end of the day. The fingers plunged, and plucked a morsel, which was popped whole into the lady's mouth. 'Delicious,' she said. 'And now, Miss Doughty, what can I do for you?'

'I hope you don't think it impertinent,' said Frances, 'but I have come here to make an appeal to you.'

'Oh?'

'We are both in a similar position, and therefore I think we understand each other.'

Mrs Keane gave a faint frown of perplexity. 'Similar? I am not sure to what you can be referring.'

This, thought Frances, was going to be even more difficult than she had supposed. At the risk of giving pain to her hostess she would have to speak more plainly. 'We have both suffered tragic occurrences in our families. We are both – I am sorry to have to say it in this blunt way – looked upon by society not as we were before.'

'That is certainly true,' Mrs Keane conceded, a touch unwillingly. 'And I was very sorry indeed to hear of your father's sad demise. Take comfort, my dear Miss Doughty. At least the breath of suspicion cannot touch him now.'

'He is past all care in this world, but those who remain still suffer,' said Frances earnestly. 'It is being rumoured that he – I can hardly say the words – that he took his own life. It is still widely believed that he made a mistake which poisoned Mr Garton!'

Mrs Keane sipped her sherry. The glass was empty and Adam stepped forward and poured another. 'I still do not see in what way I may assist you,' she said, calmly.

Frances, wondering now if the lady was deliberately not seeing her meaning, realised that she must be blunter still, and pressed on. 'Mrs Keane, I am aware of how cruelly your husband treated you, how he coerced you into saying what you did at the inquest. No one, and that includes myself, can possibly blame you for what you did. But now that he is in custody and the world knows his faults, it would surely do no harm to retract what you said.'

Mrs Keane sat back with her glass. 'That I shall never do,' she said.

'You need have no fear,' Frances reassured her. 'You can be in no danger of prosecution. The police know you were under your husband's control.'

Another sip of sherry. The lady pursed her lips and smiled in a way that was not entirely pleasant. 'Supposing I was to tell you that every word of my evidence was true?'

For a moment Frances shivered with horror, then, on a thought, she recovered. 'It was not true, you know it was not,' she said quietly. There was silence. Frances, little used as she was to mixing with the upper echelons of Bayswater society, still realised that to come to a lady's house by invitation and then accuse her of telling lies in court was not the most acceptable behaviour. She fully expected to be instantly, although politely, ejected.

Instead, Mrs Keane gave a little laugh. 'Of course, you are right,' she said. 'My evidence was a lie from beginning to end. I was never in Westbourne Grove that day, and I have *certainly* never entered your shop.'

'I knew it!' exclaimed Frances with intense relief. 'And it was your husband who made you say what you did?'

'It was. There are private reasons I cannot discuss here. Suffice it to say that just as you have come to me from a wholly commendable loyalty to your father, so I acted as I did from similar feelings. My husband played upon those feelings in a most unwarranted manner. He left me with no alternative.'

'If you explain as much to the coroner, I know he will understand,' said Frances eagerly.

Mrs Keane took a little cake from the selection before her. 'I have no intention of doing so.'

Frances felt her heart sink. 'I beg you – for the sake of my father's good name!'

'I am sorry for you, I am indeed, but what you ask is quite impossible. Even where he now lies my husband still has power over me and my father. He has not yet appeared in court. He is innocent in law and will remain so until such time as a jury says otherwise. Given the complexity of his crimes, that could be many months in the future. And if he employs a clever man, he may be acquitted. I cannot help you, Miss Doughty. And since you will be blunt, I must be so too. The consideration of my living father must take precedence over yours who is deceased.'

In the midst of that refusal, Frances found one word to which she could cling. 'You speak of crimes—'

'Oh yes, there is no doubt that my husband is a villain of the deepest hue. I married him for the good I saw in him, and at one time I believed there to be a great deal. Today, I know there to be none. The world would say that he has many grievous faults, but I disagree. He has but one – he is living. Were he to die tomorrow, he would, in my estimation, be perfect.' To Frances' astonishment, Mary Keane threw back her head and laughed out loud.

'Do you know of any other crimes he has committed?' asked Frances, as Mrs Keane partook of another sip of sherry. The awful feeling was growing that the lady of the house was more than a little intoxicated, and may have been so before the interview had commenced, the cruelty of her husband having driven her to this sad solace.

'No, though I would not be surprised to hear that there were many before I met him. I was so young then,' she went on, wistfully, 'younger than you are now, I suspect, just eighteen. It was in the spring or summer of 1869. I was out walking with my cousin Lydia. He was quite the handsomest man I had ever seen. A tiny flower fell from my hat, just in his path. I say 'fell'; it may have had a little assistance. He was gallant enough to restore it to me, and spoke to us very respectfully. I learned that it was his habit to refresh himself with a walk in that neighbourhood, and it was not hard to contrive to meet him again. I went out as often as I could in the hope that I would encounter him, and, before long, we met by appointment. Soon, a confidence arose between us. My father opposed the match since James had no fortune and was a mere clerk in a bank. Indeed, he once confessed to me that he was the son of a baker from Bootle. I remember being very glad my father did not hear of *that*. But I was in love, Miss Doughty; do you understand what that means?'

'I am afraid I do not,' Frances confessed.

'It is like a pain!' exclaimed Mrs Keane. She clutched a hand to her enormous bosom, her eyes opening wide and seeming almost to start out of her head. 'A pain in the heart that you think will never leave you unless you possess and are possessed by the thing you love. He could have told me anything – that he had ten other wives – that he was a juggler in the circus – I would not have cared. He did once, in an unguarded moment, reveal that James Keane was not his real name, but as soon as the words fell from his lips he regretted them. He said he wished he had never spoken of it, and begged me to entirely forget what he had said, and of course...' she paused dramatically, 'I did.'

Frances felt a great flood of excitement. If she could discover another identity and perhaps a criminal past for Keane, might that not direct the police to make further investigations? 'Did you ever learn his real name?' she asked.

'No, never.'

'Or what he did before he came to London?'

'He was a bank clerk before.'

Frances paused. She hardly dared go on, but she knew she must. 'Mrs Keane, you have said that you believe your husband to be capable of any villainy.'

'I think he is.'

'Even capital crimes?'

Mrs Keane frowned. 'I am not sure I understand. What crimes are these?'

Frances plunged on recklessly. 'Do you think it is possible that he could have been responsible for the death of Mr Garton?'

Again that disturbing, almost maniacal laugh. 'My word, no! James is not an emotional man, but he admired Garton and was most distraught at his death.'

Frances was unconvinced. 'What was *your* opinion of Mr Garton?'

'Oh, he was a man of great personal presence, handsome, of course, with the most captivating smile, he reminded me of how James had been in his youth – but I am done with all that, superficial charm cannot move me now; an honest worthy man is what I admire.' Her eyes swivelled to look at Adam, who had the decency to blush.

'Another sherry, Adam.'

Frances decided to take her leave before she witnessed anything more. She rose. 'I am afraid I must return home, now,' she said. 'But if anything should occur in the future which causes you to change your mind about retracting your evidence...'

'Those are circumstances I do not wish to contemplate. You understand of course that if you were to speak of this conversation to another person I will deny that it ever took place.' Frances glanced at Adam, whose face was stony. 'Adam hears or does not hear what he is told to. See Miss Doughty to the door. I wish you good-day.' As Frances left the room she saw Mary Keane sink back onto the sofa, clutching her sherry with a smile of satisfaction.

As Sunday dawned, Frances found it hard to believe that so much had happened in a week. On the previous Sunday, her morning had chiefly been engaged in getting her father ready for church, and now his coffined body lay cold in his room. A week ago, she realised, her absolute certainty that he was free from blame in Percival Garton's death had been a matter more of faith than absolute proof. Now, she was certain that she was right, but still a very long way from convincing anyone else. Once breakfast was done – bread, marmalade and tea – she devoted her time to helping Sarah get the shop ready for opening the next day, and the arrival of the new man, Mr Jacobs, who she had been assured was well qualified and industrious. There were floors to be mopped, the stove to be cleaned and prepared for lighting, counters polished, and glassware dusted. Everything had to gleam, everything had to appear most beautifully like a repository of all that was healthful and healing and good. With that done and the laundry sorted, it was time to dress for church. Sarah, now no longer required to spend her Sunday morning cooking a hot dinner for the family's return, was able to accompany Frances and Herbert, as was a sulkily unwilling Tom.

They walked to church. It was not far, and, with no invalid to protect, Frances had decided to save the cost of a four-wheeler. She knew that by walking, they declared themselves to be poor. Herbert protested, but she was adamant. 'Let everyone see us,' she said. 'They will see that we are not afraid to show our faces, that we have nothing of which we should be ashamed, that we have committed no crime, have no secrets. Let them see how proud we are, how firm in our resolve, how innocent.' Thus they walked, greeting those they saw on the way, never wavering in dignity.

As they stepped though the church doors, Frances realised that she was leading the way, and that this was how it should be. She was now the head of the family, from which its strength should be derived. For a moment, the thought frightened her, then she marshalled all her determination. She would meet the obligation, because she must. They took their places and opened their hymn books. Frances glanced about her. Herbert was staring at the pages very determinedly, as if the intensity with which he looked at the words would keep him from the eyes of others; Sarah was grim of face, and Tom was examining the book to see how much it was worth. 'Read!' ordered Frances, and Sarah corrected Tom with a light Sunday-weight cuff about the ear, took the book from his hands and set it back again the right way up.

It was, Frances knew, her duty to take comfort from the fact that her prayers would undoubtedly reach the One who knew everything. It would be too much to hope that there would be some great flash of enlightenment and that others would be able to see the truth as clearly as she did. God's help did not come so easily, delivered to her door like the penny post, but she believed that she was receiving it even now, giving her the strength of purpose she needed for what lay ahead. Reverend Day's sermon spoke well of her father, his long service to the sick, his kindliness; and the congregation remembered. She saw it all about her; people bending their heads in silent prayer. Afterwards they crept forward and approached her with sympathetic eyes, and offered commiserations. They pitied her for her loss, but underneath it all, even as their words recalled what her father had been to them, she saw behind their faces the ingrained image of an aged invalid, the poor shadow of a once fine intellect, the trembling hands and confused mind, the man who had made a terrible, deadly mistake and then, unable to bear the shame, had taken his own life. Last week her father had remembered something, but it had slipped away before he could speak of it. On the day of his death, less than an hour before, he had again nearly recalled some fact about Percival Garton's prescription. Perhaps it had been nothing of importance, but she felt desperately frustrated that it was beyond her knowledge forever.

They returned home, to a simple meal of potted meat, cheese, and bread. Even that frugal fare was almost more than Frances could stomach, and she had no trouble about offering most of her share to Herbert, who regarded the change of diet as an affront to his manly requirements. The kettle was boiling for a welcome cup of tea when Chas and Barstie appeared, with sympathetic looks, a posy of flowers and a box of buns.

'My dear, *dear* Miss Doughty,' said Chas, taking Frances' hand and applying an unexpectedly gentle pressure to her fingers. 'We pay our respects, to you and your family. Only a few days ago we drank a toast to your good fortune, and now, sadly, you suffer in a way that we can only try to imagine.'

'If there is any service we can perform for you, do not hesitate to ask,' added Barstie.

'Thank you,' said Frances. 'You are very welcome to stay and have tea.'

They sat around the table. Sarah brought tea and the box was opened, the buns much exclaimed over. Frances told her visitors of the circumstances of her father's death, and, after a while, Herbert, sensing quite correctly that his presence was of no interest to them, took his cup and a bun and retired to his room.

'My situation is worse even than you know,' sighed Frances. 'My father left me with debts I cannot meet. In a month from now, I must sell the business.'

'Oh! To lose your parent, your livelihood and

your home all at once!' exclaimed Barstie.

'I have tried to borrow money to keep the business running,' said Frances, 'but in my present position I can offer no security. I – don't suppose you know of anyone who–?'

'No one I would care to introduce you to,' said Chas. 'No one you would ever wish to meet. There are men who will lend you any amount of money on no security at all, but to default just once is to be as good as dead. I would not recommend it, but I will think very hard on your plight. If there is a way to help you I will find it. I promise.'

'Thank you,' said Frances. Hardly knowing either of the men, she felt unsure as to the reliability of the promise, but did not doubt that what was said was very much meant.

'There is one small piece of information we have discovered since our last meeting,' added Chas. 'I don't know if it will be of any assistance to you, but we pass it on, if only as proof that one should never believe without question anything one is told. Especially where money is concerned.'

'Any news would be appreciated,' said Frances, whose appetite had returned and was starting on her second bun.

'Now, I remember you saying that Mr Garton inherited his fortune from his grandfather who owned a shipping business in Bristol.'

'That is right,' said Frances, firmly. 'I have no reason to doubt it because I was told it by his own brother.'

'Ah,' said Barstie, mournfully, 'and it is a well-known fact that men always tell their brothers the *exact* truth about their finances.'

'Well there was a great deal in that story that was true,' said Chas. 'Mr Garton did indeed have a grandfather who owned a shipping business in Bristol, a Mr Horace Percival Garton. This gentleman died in October 1864 and left everything to his grandson Percival. But at the date of his death, Mr Horace Garton's entire estate was worth less than twenty thousand pounds.'

'Oh!' said Frances, in astonishment. 'But Mr Garton left a great deal more than that, and now that I recall...,' she took her notebook from her pocket and studied it. 'He sold the business when he came to London in 1870, only six years after he inherited it.'

'A very small business as these things go,' said Chas. 'His profit would not have been great. And as far as we have been able to discover he has undertaken no other business at all since then, unless one counts the gallery, which to all outward appearances can hardly pay the rent. Yet he died worth one hundred and fifty thousand pounds.'

'Perhaps he was fortunate with his investments,' said Frances.

'I have no doubt that he lived well from them,' said Chas, 'a household such as his will cost you your one thousand pounds a year or more to run, but only an adventurous speculator given great good fortune will multiply his holdings in that way. I have found that Garton's investments were safe, solid. He took no chances. So where did the money come from?'

'I don't know,' said Frances, 'unless he was involved with Mr Keane's crimes in some way.'

'We think that the gallery was more than it

appeared,' said Barstie. 'Crooked money going in, honest money coming out, and Mr Garton taking a percentage.'

'And how would that be achieved?' asked Frances.

'Oh, simplicity itself,' said Barstie, airily. 'The gallery was perfect for that purpose. In the art world it is possible for large profits to be made on a single transaction. False documents can easily be created to show that money was received through *bona fide* business, when in fact it was nothing of the sort.'

Frances, who prided herself on the shop accounts being correct to the last farthing, opened her eyes wide and said, 'How very wicked!'

'Contemptible,' said Chas, emphatically.

'Unpardonable,' said Barstie. They both shook their heads with expressions of grave disapproval.

'I think you have the answer,' said Frances. 'Perhaps Mr Garton demanded more money, or threatened to expose Mr Keane and so he was killed. All I need to do is prove how it was done.' She sighed, 'A difficult task, I think. I expect you have read in the newspapers of what happened at the inquest on Mr Garton?'

'You refer to Mrs Keane's evidence?' said Barstie. 'Please don't trouble yourself over that. With what has happened since, I doubt that anyone believes her.'

'I saw her yesterday,' said Frances, 'and she freely admitted that her husband had made her tell lies. I begged her to change her testimony, but she will not. I think he must have agreed to save her father from the bankruptcy court in

261

return for her perjured evidence. And she will perjure herself again if necessary.'

'Trust me, there will be things said at her husband's trial that will entirely undo what she has said,' said Chas. He rubbed his hands together, his face alight with anticipation. 'Oh yes, this promises to be very interesting indeed.'

'He enjoys a good trial,' Barstie confided.

'I do,' said Chas with great satisfaction, 'especially when it is about money.'

'He makes notes,' added Barstie, darkly.

'Only on what *not* to do, Barstie, only on what *not* to do.'

'The newspapers have painted Mr Keane as a very great villain,' said Frances, 'they have compared him to some of the wickedest criminals who ever lived, though I must admit I have not heard of any of them.' She showed her visitors the article in the *Chronicle*.

'Ah, yes,' said Chas, nodding his head sagely as he read, 'Mr Keane would be in fitting company with any of these three. Now Sadleir, he was before my time, '50s I think, but I remember my father talking of him. Mark my words, when future historians speak of the worst criminals of this century the name that will come to mind first will be John Sadleir.'

'Member of Parliament, wasn't he?' said Barstie. 'Double the villain, to my mind.'

'Yes, and the owner of a bank,' said Chas. 'He stole investors' funds to pay his stock market debts. Cleaned out the bank, thousands ruined, widespread misery.'

'I hope he was put in prison,' said Frances.

262

'Ah – no – he – I'm afraid he took poison,' said Chas in sudden embarrassment. 'Left letters saying he was sorry for what he had done, not that he was sorry about anything other than being found out. These types never are.'

'Oh!' said Frances. It was too close to what people were saying of her father, yet she was comforted by the fact that he had never expressed any feelings of guilt.

'*Swore* that his brother had nothing to do with it, and then it turned out that his brother was in it with him all along,' added Barstie. '*He* was a Member of Parliament, too.'

'Now Redpath,' said Chas, 'he was about Sadleir's time, I think. He was involved with a railway company; transferred the shares. Only he made sure that most of the shares he transferred ended up in his own pockets. He was transported for life.'

'I remember the Cotter case,' said Barstie, studying the article. 'Ten or twelve years ago – Liverpool way.'

'Now *he* was a nasty piece of work,' said Chas. 'Bank clerk, like Mr Keane. Forged share certificates and property deeds, again, very like what they think Keane has been up to. He had an associate, a poor man with a large family, tempted by the money no doubt. Well it seems they had a quarrel, so Cotter murdered his partner and ran off.'

'And was he put in prison?' asked Frances.

'Disappeared,' said Barstie. 'Never found. Five years later they arrested a man in Australia. A dozen witnesses swore he was Cotter so they brought him back to stand trial. Great sensation, police patting themselves on the back, lawyers adding up their fees. Turned out to be the wrong man.'

'What a terrible experience!' said Frances.

'He seemed happy enough,' said Chas, dismissively. 'Got more money in compensation than he'd ever seen in his life.'

'So Cotter is still at large?' said Frances. A thought was forming in her mind so extraordinary that she could hardly contain herself, yet she knew she had to keep calm.

'He is,' said Barstie. 'Abroad somewhere, if he has any sense.'

Frances could hear her heart thudding so loudly that it seemed impossible that the others could not hear it too. 'And you say he committed crimes exactly like those of Mr Keane?'

'Yes, very like.'

'*And* he came from Liverpool!' Frances jumped up so abruptly that both her visitors started with astonishment. She reached down an atlas from the bookshelf. Years ago, when Frederick had come home from his lessons, they had studied it together and learned the names of the principal towns of England. It was something that had never served her until now. She placed the atlas on the table and found the port of Liverpool. 'As I thought!' she exclaimed, then realised that her entire theory could fail on one very important fact. 'Tell me, how old was Cotter? If you say he was middle aged I shall be very disappointed.'

'No, he was a young man,' said Chas, puzzled.

'So today he could be the same age as Mr Keane,' she beamed.

They both stared at her. 'Are you suggesting that Mr Keane is Lewis Cotter?' asked Barstie.

'Yesterday I discovered that James Keane is not that gentleman's real name, and that he came from Bootle, which as you see on the map is near Liverpool. It is a very remarkable coincidence!' said Frances excitedly. 'Of course, I will need to find out what date Mr Cotter disappeared and when Mr Keane arrived in London, but if there is no conflict, they could well be one and the same!'

'And there's still a reward out for Cotter,' said Chas, thoughtfully.

'Is there? How much?' asked Frances, eagerly.

'Could be several hundred pounds, even a thousand, seeing as how the bank needed its good name back.' He smiled. 'Perhaps, Miss Doughty, you have found the way out of your difficulty.'

'Do they know how much Cotter got away with?' asked Barstie, frowning, 'because – and I don't want to say your idea is not a very good one – as far as we know, James Keane came to London with very little money to his name.'

'Unless he was a gambler or a speculator, these fraudsters often are penniless,' said Chas. 'Look at Sadleir. He could have lived like an Eastern potentate on what he took, but he lost it all on bad investments.'

Frances began to write earnestly in her notebook. 'I am making a plan,' she explained. 'I must find out more about Mr Cotter and his crimes. I have been too hasty running to the police and making accusations without evidence. I must have facts. And if the facts do not agree with my theory then I must accept that I am wrong, and look for more facts.'

There was an urgent knocking at the front door, which Chas and Barstie took as their cue to leave, repeating their condolences, and assuring Frances of their loyal service to her at all times. Sarah entered. 'It's Ada Hawkins,' she said, 'Will you see her, Miss? She seems very upset.'

CHAPTER FOURTEEN

Ada arrived in a great state of distress. She looked at Frances half afraid, as if she was about to confess to a terrible sin for which she knew she would be punished. Frances sat her down at the parlour table and calmed her, while Sarah brought a cup of water.

'Miss Doughty – I want to say – I was so sorry to hear about your poor father,' Ada exclaimed, 'he was such a good man, and so clever and kind.'

'Thank you, Ada,' said Frances. Her father had always, she thought, been a well-meaning man, but a stranger would never have observed the lack of warmth in his benevolence.

'I wanted to come sooner, but Mrs Garton's had us all turning out the house and not even an errand to run until now. And everyone's so upset, especially poor Miss Rhoda.'

The Garton's eldest child, Frances recalled. 'Is she very unwell?'

'As well as is possible, Miss, but you see, today is her birthday. And there was such a pretty little tea party planned, and of course Mrs Garton gave instructions that it was not to happen, and I know Miss Rhoda is quite old enough to understand, but still it has made what should have been a happy day into an unhappy one, if you see what I mean. And it means that every year her birthday will be unhappy because it will always remind her of losing her papa, who doted on her, and of course everyone is making a great fuss and bother about it which is making it harder for her, I think.' Ada, who had probably never had a birthday party in her hard-working life, was close to tears. Frances, whose birthdays had usually been marked by the gift of a shilling and a lecture on the importance of thrift, was less moved.

'I am sorry to hear it,' she said patiently.

Ada wiped her eyes. 'Oh but that isn't what I came to say. It's about the inquest. What Mrs Keane said.' Her lips trembled. 'I have thought and thought about it, Miss, but as much as I think, I just can't remember that the lady was there. I think what the coroner said was right, that if she *had* come in then the bell would have rung, and I *know* it was working because it rung when I came in. But I know as a court would sooner believe a lady like Mrs Keane then they would me. I don't know what to do, Miss!' Tears threatened again.

'Ada, please don't distress yourself,' said Frances, soothingly. 'I am quite sure in my own mind that Mrs Keane was mistaken.'

'Are you, Miss?' exclaimed Ada, her face brightening. 'Oh that's such a relief! I was so worried you might think me a liar, and I would never tell a lie.'

'I believe you to be very truthful,' Frances assured her.

'And I thought very hard about what Mrs Keane said about Mr Doughty going into the back of the shop, because I could see that that was very important,' Ada went on, 'and whether the lady was there or not, I am sure that he didn't. Not him or Mr Munson either. They just stood behind the screen, and after a minute or two Mr Doughty came out and gave me the package.'

For a moment, Frances pictured her father as he had been, the heart of the business, the symbol of all that was correct and trustworthy. His best moments were when he handed over the wrapped medicines to the customer; his manner and words always inspiring confidence. 'Did he say anything to you?' she asked.

Ada nodded. 'He smiled at me very kindly and said I was to hurry home as the night was so cold.'

But William Doughty had been on the brink of recalling something about that day. Herbert could not imagine what it might be, but could Ada, without realising it, have the answer? 'Ada,' said Frances earnestly, 'Do you remember anything else my father said, either to yourself or to Mr Munson when the prescription was being made up?'

Ada thought hard, but shook her head. 'I can't call anything to mind. I think Mr Doughty may have read out what was on the paper, not that I would have understood it. After that, all I heard was a sort of little sound. Not really talking, Miss. Just a sound, like in his throat.'

Frances had a sudden horrible feeling what that sound might have been. If she was correct then it

268

would change forever her understanding of what had happened that evening. She tried to retain at least an outward appearance of calm. 'Can you describe the sound?' she asked.

'It was a kind of "um-hum, um-hum" just a few times,' said Ada, innocently.

For a few moments Frances' throat was too dry for her to speak. She felt as if ice-cold insects were crawling up her spine and over her scalp. The very roots of her hair seemed to shiver. 'And – that was my father's voice? You're quite sure?' she said at last. Her voice sounded strange to her, but Ada seemed not to notice.

'Yes, Miss.'

'And you recall nothing more?' asked Frances.

'No, Miss. I'm very sorry, and I have tried so hard,' said Ada sadly.

But that was enough, thought Frances. More than enough. When Ada had departed Frances sat by the dying fire, lost in thought, wondering about the meaning of what she had just learned and what, if anything, she should say and do about it. But there were more important things to consider, the inquest on her father tomorrow morning, and the re-opening of the shop – on which her future hopes depended. Before she retired for the night, she prayed for the kind of crisp, bright day which would tempt people to come and shop in the Grove.

On Monday morning Frances awoke early, her face pinched with cold. Temperatures had fallen sharply overnight, the windows were thick with frost and outside everything was blanketed with heavy yellow fog. Sarah was already up and about making up the fires, and Frances quickly rose and made tea and lit the shop stoves, then gave the surfaces an extra polish. Mr Jacobs arrived promptly at seven, a soberly dressed and serious young man, who at once began meticulously to acquaint himself with the business. To Frances' relief he did not look upon it as his own, or even something that he might buy, but as a happy state to which he might one day aspire.

As the morning wore on so the gloom obstinately refused to lift, and temperatures remained below freezing. Frances wiped condensation from the windows and stared out onto a landscape so desolate she hardy recognised it. The sun was barely visible, and, across the way, only the steel-blue glitter of the Jablochkoff candles illuminating Whiteleys could be seen. From time to time, shadowy figures draped in heavy cloaks and shawls hurried past, and carriages brought a few determined shoppers, but the Grove was only a dull copy of what it ought to have been, and very few customers ventured into the chemist's shop. After a despondent hour, Frances went to help Sarah with the linen wash. They carried out the work almost in silence, Sarah respectfully supposing that Frances' mind was absorbed in thoughts of the inquest, whereas this was only a part of what troubled her.

Herbert came upstairs to get a hot cup of tea, and Frances decided that she could wait no longer to ask what she needed to know. He was about to return to the shop, cup in hand, when she asked him if he would go into the parlour. He was surprised, but agreed, and sat at the table. Frances followed him into the room, took the family bible from the bookshelf and placed it on the table in front of him. He stared at it in alarm.

'I know that you are a devout person, and therefore I believe that anything you swear on the bible will be true,' she said, and sat to face him.

He put the cup down, nervously. 'I tell the truth in any case,' he said.

'I think you do not,' said Frances, coldly. 'Now, place your hand on the bible.'

He was shaking visibly, the tips of his moustaches, pomaded to a fault, like little trembling wires. He obeyed. She looked directly into his eyes, saw fear, and knew that she was right. She too, was shaking, but with anger. She put her hands on her lap to conceal them.

'Now tell me,' she said. 'What did you do with the phial of *strychnia?*'

There was a brief moment of startlement, and almost a suspicion of relief in his expression, as if he had been expecting quite another question. He collected himself, quickly.

'As I told Mr Rawsthorne–' he began carefully.

'I care nothing for what you told Mr Rawsthorne,' she retorted. 'Tell me.'

He licked his lips, and squirmed in his chair. She stared at him, accusingly, and eventually an expression of guilt spread across his face and he capitulated. 'How did you know?'

'That doesn't matter for now. Tell me the truth, Mr Munson.'

'I swear there was nothing wrong with Mr Garton's medicine!' he blurted out.

'That was not the question I asked,' she said firmly.

He heaved a deep, shuddering sigh. 'I was afraid,' he said. 'The first time the police inspector was here he was asking me all about what we had containing *strychnia*, what was stored in the shop and what in the back, and I told him about the tincture and the extract of nux vomica, and he seemed satisfied with that. But I thought he might come back and search.'

'So you *did* know the phial was in the box?' demanded Frances. 'You lied to the inquest, to Mr Rawsthorne, to the police, and to me.'

He hung his head. 'Yes' he admitted, his voice so quiet it was barely audible.

'And how did you know?'

He seemed surprised by the question. 'Your father showed me the contents of the box when I first came here.'

Her father, Frances reflected, had never shown his own daughter the contents of the box, but then, he had left her a paltry two hundred pounds in his will. 'And has the box been opened since then? Has any of the *strychnia* been used? Please think carefully, this is of very great importance.'

'It was about six months ago,' he said, promptly. 'A prescription came in for *pilulae strychniae;* it was most unusual, and your father supervised me very carefully, the titration is very–'

'I know all about the titration!' snapped Frances. 'Did my father get the phial from the box?'

His body wavered back from her intensity. 'No, I did. He lent me his keys. We only used half a grain for a hundred pills,' he added plaintively.

'They weren't for Mr Garton?' said Frances, anxiously.

'No, nor anyone connected with him or his household.'

She nodded. 'And how much remained when you had done?'

'About thirty grains. The phial was half full. That was why I had to destroy it! Had it been full, then of course no suspicion could have attached to us, but as it was not—'

'You destroyed it,' said Frances grimly. 'I suppose you took my father's keys while he was asleep.'

He stared at the table. 'I know now it was wrong, but at the time, I am afraid I panicked,' he said. 'I poured the contents down the drain, crushed the phial and threw it on the fire.'

'So,' said Frances, trying to remain calm, 'between the making up of the pills six months ago and the day on which you destroyed the phial, none of the contents were unaccounted for.'

He paused. 'Yes.'

'A circumstance which would have greatly assisted us, and on which you might have given evidence!' she said, unable to keep the anger from her voice.

'I suppose so, yes, but of course they might not have believed me.' He spread his hands and gave her a wide-eyed helpless look, as if to say, what else could he have done?

'Instead of which...,' she paused and compressed her lips.

'I can see *now* why it might not have been the best thing to do,' he said weakly, 'but at the time

273

– I really thought – and of course I didn't think that your father would remember that we even had such a thing. If he had not then we would have been in the clear.'

'It was only for recent events where his memory failed him, as you well know,' said Frances sternly.

'True,' he admitted.

'And what of Mr Ford? Did he know of the box and its contents?'

'I believe not,' said Herbert. He sighed. 'I am really very, very, sorry.' He withdrew his hand from the bible and went to take up his cup, but Frances suddenly reached forward, seized his hand and put it back where it had been, so hard that he blinked.

'One more question, Mr Munson,' she said intently. 'Precisely when had you planned to tell me that it was you and not my father who made up Mr Garton's prescription?'

He gulped.

'Well? Your hand is on the holy book, Mr Munson, please do not lie!'

'I–'. The terror in his eyes was almost tangible.

'It was you, was it not?' she demanded. 'I spoke to Ada yesterday and she remembered that when she was waiting for the prescription she heard my father making that little 'um-hum' sound, as he always did when supervising one of us, but never did when he was dispensing medicines himself. When he saw his writing in the prescription book, he was confused enough to believe that it was he who had made up the medicine, but it was not him at all, was it, Mr Munson?'

Herbert bowed down, unable to face her.

274

'Was it?' she insisted, 'I am asking you the question! Look at me!'

After a short pause he raised his head. Tears were running down his cheeks and for a few moments he was unable to speak. 'I'm sorry,' he whispered at last.

Frances, a girl endowed with more than the general amount of sympathy for her fellow creatures in distress, felt none for the miserable object before her. 'Yet you allowed him to believe that it was he who had made the medicine, and he who was under suspicion,' she went on, angrily.

'There was nothing wrong with the medicine!' wailed Herbert.

She was almost shouting now. 'You allowed my father to be suspected; you said nothing to me, to Mr Rawsthorne, to the court or to the police!'

'But it made no difference,' he whispered.

'Oh?' said Frances in cold fury. 'Kindly explain to me how it made no difference.'

He wiped his face with the back of his hand. 'Whether he did it or I, he was the qualified man, and responsible. My hand, under his supervision is the same thing as if it had been his hand.'

'It was not the same thing at all to him, or to me!' said Frances.

'And—' he hesitated.

'Yes, do go on, Mr Munson, I am all agog to hear what you will say next!'

He swallowed, and tried to calm himself, taking a handkerchief from his pocket and wiping his face and nose. 'I think it was plain that your father would have retired very soon, and then the whole incident would have been of no moment.

275

I, on the other hand–'

She gave him a look of utter contempt. 'So now we have it. You let an ailing man take the blame in order to protect yourself. You never think of *anyone* but yourself. That was how I knew it was you who had taken the phial of *strychnia*. You were the only person with a motive to do so.'

He gazed at her pleadingly. 'I am very sorry. I know I should not have done it, but–,' there was a long pause during which he recognised by her implacable expression that he might better have tried to melt a block of cast iron. 'What will you do now, Miss Doughty?' he said anxiously.

She sighed. 'Believe me, I have given that a great deal of thought. And I have come to the conclusion that it would be of no benefit to tell another person of what has been revealed here. Whether or not my father made up the prescription, he imagined that he had done so, and the public will always suspect that he took his own life from guilt, something I will never believe. What I need is proof that Mr Garton's death was nothing to do with his prescription. That is what I will seek.' She rose. 'My uncle will be here in an hour to convey us to the inquest. Please ensure that you are ready.'

Herbert looked intensely relieved. 'You are very generous, Miss Doughty.'

'Not generous, Mr Munson,' she said coldly. 'Pleasant as it would be to see you arrested for the lie you told at Mr Garton's inquest, I do not think the business can afford publicity of that nature. Oh, and there is one further matter I should mention. The personal subject we discussed recently –

I would take it as a very great favour if it was never referred to again.' She left the room.

Cornelius arrived promptly at half past nine, accompanied by Mrs Scorer. She said nothing about the loss of William's fortune, but there was a noticeable air of triumph as she gazed at Frances, ill-concealed under a mask of pity. Her own loss of two hundred pounds was well compensated for by the knowledge that Frances would not enjoy a legacy to which she had felt at least partially entitled. In the interests of economy, Frances, her uncle and aunt, Herbert, and Sarah all managed to squeeze into a four-wheeler. The misty streets were almost silent, and Frances was thankful to see that there was no disturbance outside the court, although it was uncomfortably crowded within.

Cornelius asked her kindly if she wanted to sit elsewhere than the body of the court but she shook her head. She sat beside him, taking comfort from his calming presence. It was Dr Collin who gave evidence first, and testified that the lungs, heart and brain tissue of the deceased showed that he had died from inhalation of chloroform, and that there was no disease or any other condition that could have been the cause of death.

'Doctor, tell the court how long you have been the deceased's medical man?' asked Dr Hardwicke.

'More than twenty years,' said Collin.

'And had you noticed any change in his mental state in the last months of his life?'

'Mr Doughty's only son died after a protracted

277

illness in October of last year,' said Collin. 'He took it very badly, as one might imagine. For a time he was too unwell to work, but in recent weeks his condition had improved.'

'Was he very despondent?' asked the coroner. 'You understand the reason for these questions. It is distressing to the family, but unfortunately necessary.'

'He was, of course, greatly afflicted by grief, but not, in my opinion, in such a state as to give rise to any anxiety that he would take his own life,' said Collin, confidently.

Hardwicke nodded. 'As you are aware, in the last two weeks it has been suggested that Mr Doughty made an error in a prescription which cost the life of one of his customers, Mr Percival Garton. On the very day of his death, Mr Doughty attended the inquest on Mr Garton, which found that he was at fault in the matter. Clearly, this could have affected his mind. Do you believe that to be so?'

'No, I do not,' said Collin. 'Mr Doughty suffered from a defect of the memory in which he was able to recall perfectly events which took place in the distant past and also all his skills as a chemist, but on recent matters he was vague. I do not think the death of Mr Garton, tragic as it was, preyed upon his mind at all.' A whisper of comment flowed through the body of the court. Hardwicke peered at the onlookers and they fell silent.

'What is your opinion of the practice of inducing sleep by dropping chloroform on a handkerchief and placing it over the face?'

'I believe it to be extremely dangerous,' said the doctor, 'and always advise my patients against it.

Unfortunately many do not heed that advice, and this is not the first inquest I have attended of someone who has expired from this practice. The lay public is quite unable to judge how to use chloroform. They are lulled into believing it safe because it is pleasant to take, but in fact nothing can be further from the truth. It is extremely easy to administer too great a dose.' Frances saw the jurors glance at each other, and nod, and one or two of them scribbled notes.

'To your knowledge, how long had the deceased been using chloroform in this way?' asked Hardwicke.

'About two years, I believe. Occasionally at first, and then more frequently. He suffered greatly from headaches and toothache and found it brought him relief.'

'In your opinion, therefore, Dr Collin, do you believe Mr Doughty administered the chloroform to himself solely with the intention of procuring a refreshing sleep, or is there any evidence that he deliberately took his own life?'

'It is my opinion,' said Collin very firmly, 'that there is no evidence whatsoever to suggest that Mr Doughty intended to take his own life.'

'Very well, you may stand down.'

Sarah was the next to give evidence. She stated that on his return from attending Mr Garton's inquest, William Doughty had been tired and complained of a headache, and she had helped him up to his room. The last time she had seen him alive he had been lying on his bed fully clothed. About twenty minutes later she had gone in to see how he was and found him with the handkerchief over his face. She had removed it, and as soon as she did so realised that he was dead, and sent for Dr Collin. She and Mr Munson had both made valiant efforts to revive her employer while waiting for the doctor, even though they had been certain that the situation was hopeless.

Frances was next to be called, and found herself under the sympathetic gaze of Dr Hardwicke. 'Miss Doughty, I will keep this as brief as possible, and must apologise in advance for any distress it may cause you. Can you tell the court about your father's state of mind in the weeks prior to his death?'

'He was greatly grieved by the death of my brother, but in the last few weeks he was well enough to return to his work, something that meant a great deal to him. I saw many signs of improvement,' said Frances. 'I agree with Dr Collin that my father felt no personal guilt concerning the death of Mr Garton. There was nothing at all wrong with the medicine when it left our shop.'

'I must remind you and the court,' he said gently, 'that you were not present when the prescription was made and cannot therefore give evidence on that point.'

'Mr Munson said as much at the inquest, and he *was* present,' insisted Frances.

Hardwicke raised his eyebrows. 'Thank you, Miss Doughty,' he said. 'You may stand down.'

There were no more witnesses, and Hardwicke was just completing his notes prior to making his closing address, when, after a certain amount of conferring in the jury box, the foreman announced that they had come to a decision.

'Please write it down,' said Hardwicke, and a note was quickly scribbled and conveyed to him by an officer of the court. He glanced at it and nodded. 'Very well, please indicate your verdict.'

'We find that the death of Mr William Doughty was due to an overdose of chloroform administered by accident. And we further state that the public should be warned of the danger of the practice of sprinkling chloroform on a handkerchief to procure sleep.'

'I concur,' said Hardwicke. 'The verdict of this court is death by misadventure.'

'Well,' said Mrs Scorer, as they left, 'Thank goodness that is over! I am, of course, as distressed as anybody about poor William's death, but it seems to me that the indignity of an inquest and having one's private business discussed in the newspapers is almost as upsetting. Now let us have him decently buried and be done with it.'

On the way home, Cornelius advised Frances of the arrangements for the following day, the service at St Stephen's and the interment at Kensal Green Cemetery. When she confessed that she had nothing in the house suitable for refreshments after the burial, he instructed her to buy what was necessary and send him the bill.

On arrival at Westbourne Grove, Frances politely invited her aunt and uncle in, but Mrs Scorer turned up her nose at the cold sausage and bread and butter that was to be the midday meal, and Cornelius took her home. It was almost a relief for Frances to be able to turn to rinsing out the boiling linens. As she worked, she listed in her

281

mind all the things she felt she needed to know, and at the earliest opportunity transferred these thoughts to her notebook. When at last she was able to rest with a cup of tea she spread out the newspapers on the table and re-read them. One item that her eye had skipped over when she had first read it, suddenly stood out. When Garton's death had first been reported it had been said that his oldest child was aged eight. Assuming the newspaper to be correct – a very great assumption, Frances knew – that could have meant anything between just eight and nearly nine. It had been Rhoda's birthday the previous day, and, assuming it was her ninth, she was born on 25 January 1871, but Frances suddenly realised that this made no sense. According to Cedric, the Gartons had left Tollington Mill to consult a doctor about Mrs Garton's inability to become a mother. They had come to London in August of 1870 and the treatment had been successful, Rhoda, said Cedric, being born within a year of their arrival. Yet if what he said was true, her birthday would have been between May and July. Frances puzzled over this, unsure if it meant anything. Had it been Rhoda's eighth and not ninth birthday? Yet that made no sense either, as the interval between the Gartons' arrival and her birth would have been far greater than a year. Had she misheard what Cedric had told her? As soon as she was able to find Tom, she sent him to see Ada, and ask how old Rhoda was. He was also instructed to deliver a note to Constable Brown. Surely, thought Frances, there must be amongst his father's scrapbooks, some information about the criminal career of the infamous Lewis Cotter.

At the end of the day, Mr Jacobs departed, too polite to mention that there had been very little business. The fog still hung heavily over everything, and promised to continue to do so for some days. As Frances tried to do her mending by the light of a guttering candle, and Sarah rolled sheets of old wrapping paper into spills, Tom returned. 'Nine,' he said.

'She is quite sure?'

'Oh yes, remembers it like it was yesterday. No mistakin'.' He hurried away.

Frances put down her mending. She could only conclude that the child had been expected before Henrietta left Tollington Mill. She looked at Sarah, realising that on such matters the maid was possibly the only female she could consult.

'Sarah,' she said hesitantly. 'I know you have a number of nieces and nephews.'

'Oh yes, Miss, any number, can't count 'em sometimes,' said the maid, with a smile.

'Because I need the answer to a question on a delicate matter.' Frances took a deep breath, recalling a certain personal event in her life. She had been thirteen, and terrified. It was Sarah to whom she had run, crying, and not her aunt, Sarah who had comforted her and explained the common lot of women. 'Is it possible,' she asked, 'for a lady to be expecting to become a mother in less than six months and not to know it?'

Sarah suddenly dropped her work and gaped at Frances in horror, and Frances suddenly realised what the maid must be thinking. She felt her face flush hotly. 'No, Sarah, please be assured it is not

283

myself I am talking of – that is quite impossible.'

'Oh Miss, I am sorry I even thought it!' said Sarah with undisguised relief. 'But who is the lady you mean?'

Frances hesitated. 'If I say any more you must promise me to say nothing of it to anyone else. I am sworn to secrecy, and yet I need advice.'

'I promise, Miss,' said Sarah, earnestly. 'I hope I have never given any cause for you to doubt me in that way.'

'Never, Sarah,' Frances agreed. 'Well, I will tell you. Mrs Garton came to London in August 1870 to consult a doctor because she was very delicate and could not become a mother. Happily, her state of health improved greatly, and there are now five children. I was told that their eldest child, Rhoda, was born less than a year after they took up residence in Bayswater, and had assumed that she was born in the summer of 1871, but I have just discovered that Rhoda was born the previous January. Do you think it possible that when she came to London, Mrs Garton could not have known that she was in that hoped-for state?'

'Yes, I would, Miss,' said Sarah, emphatically. 'An ignorant young girl, with no one to advise her, might not know her condition till the pains began,' she added grimly.

'I see,' said Frances.

'Of course,' added Sarah, 'the lady might have been visiting London to see her doctor before she came here to live. Or it could just have happened naturally and the doctor took all the credit. Not that *that's* ever happened before.'

Somehow, thought Frances, everything always

came back to the Gartons' time in Tollington Mill. She wondered if Garton and Keane had been in touch even then. Perhaps Keane had visited Tollington Mill under an assumed name. The one person who would be able to answer all her questions was Henrietta Garton, a lady she felt quite unable to approach on any pretext whatsoever. As she considered what to do next, she realised that there was another possible source of information. Before the last candle died she took pen and paper and began to write a letter, but no sooner had she begun than she was in a quandary. How should she represent herself? At last she wrote, 'I am a private detective enquiring into the murder of John Wright in 1870.' She stared at the sentence. In a sense it was quite untrue but in its component parts it did describe her position exactly. She wrote again. 'I would be grateful if you were to agree to answer some questions I wish to put to you about Mr Wright and his friends in Tollington Mill.' There seemed to be nothing much more she could say at this stage. She signed the letter 'Frances Doughty' and deliberately left the 'e' ambiguous so that it might be read as an 'i' and give the impression that she was a man. It was comforting to know that this time her masquerade would not involve male clothing. She did not know the correct address to which to send the letter, but felt sure that it would reach its destination, assuming the recipient to be still alive. Boldly she wrote,

Mrs Cranby
Tollington Mill
Gloucestershire

and determined to take it to the post office the very next morning.

CHAPTER FIFTEEN

There was no respite from the thick, freezing fog. On the morning of William Doughty's funeral the sun had disappeared, and the world seemed doomed to an eternal wintry night. Frances, grimly determined to impose the daily routine as usual, opened the shop at 7 o'clock.

Cornelius arrived early, revealing that the chief mourners would, apart from the immediate family, be Herbert, Sarah, Mr Rawsthorne, and two elderly Miss Doughtys, Gertrude and Nora, William's aunts, who were coming down by carriage from Waltham Abbey. To Frances, the whole proceedings began to take on the aspect of a horrid nightmare. She had sometimes heard people speak of having dreams that repeated themselves, an affliction from which she had never suffered, but this was something far worse. Only three months ago, she had sat by her beloved brother's deathbed, and witnessed the final fading away of all that was bright and cheering in her life. Until the end, her father had not accepted that Frederick would die, and his howl of agony when faced with the unyielding truth still reverberated in her consciousness. For several days he had been as one struck dead, and only the faint

286

pulse of a vein at his temple had shown that he still lived. It had taken all her energy, all her care, to restore him even to that state in which he could attend the funeral. There had followed the inevitable gathering of black-clad relatives, the arrival of a hearse and carriages, the careful moving of the coffin down the precipitous stairs, the drive to St Stephen's for the ceremony, and then the journey to Kensal Green Cemetery and a return home to a miserable array of comestibles. On that occasion, too, Cornelius had assisted with the arrangements. Frances had mainly been occupied in attending to her father. That task, exhausting and difficult as it was, had at least given her something to engage her mind other than the unthinkable horror of consigning Frederick's remains to the ground. Frederick's death had been a long-expected event, although it was no less of a shock for that, but on the day of his funeral it had seemed to Frances as if, by the time his emaciated body was carried from the house, all her tears for him had already been spent, and the pain of his loss and that final farewell could never be exceeded by the pain of watching him slowly die. On the day of her father's burial, she found she had nothing to do but be conveyed from place to place, and her grief was suddenly doubled, as if she was feeling her current loss together with all the emotions that had not been released at the time of Frederick's funeral.

Mrs Scorer arrived in the full mourning she had worn for her husband, crisp and rustling like a great black meringue, her throat and fingers glittering with jet. The two great-aunts drew up in a carriage, and bustled quickly into the house, chattering to each other with excitement, as if a funeral was the only entertainment they now enjoyed, which may have been the case. They were so wrapped in cloaks, hoods, shawls and gloves, as to be almost spherical. Frances had rarely met them, but knew they shared a small cottage, with a very put-upon general maid of about their own years, between sixty-five and seventy. Mr Rawsthorne next appeared, and, with a great expression of dismay, went to each person in turn and pressed their hands, nodding and muttering something inaudible, as if he was too drowned in emotion to speak.

Before they departed, Cornelius suggested that Frances should have a small glass of brandy, but she declined, although Herbert gratefully gulped one down. The aunts twittered with anxiety about the advisability of such a draught, and decided after much debate to accept a small glass between the two of them, so as not to put anyone to too much trouble, by which time Mrs Scorer had finished her second.

The Grove was shrouded in a dull, yellow-grey twilight as they departed. Frances wondered, as the carriages followed the hearse, if there would be any marks of respect for the man who had served the citizens of Bayswater for twenty years. Blinds should have been lowered, shop windows festooned with crêpe and black ribbon, and people should have lined the way, with grim faces, hats removed, holding flowers to throw on the hearse as it passed by; but she doubted that this would be the case. To Bayswater, William Doughty was the pathetic invalid who had poisoned a man and then taken his own life. It was almost a relief not to be able to see.

The church was bitterly cold within, and only about twenty people shivered in the pews. Frances recognised some of her father's regular customers, who had not seen fit to patronise the shop for the last two weeks. A few had the temerity to approach the family with oily condolences. Frances would have very much liked to say, 'I trust we will see you back in the shop now that my father is dead?' but felt obliged to be icily polite. The aunts huddled close to each other for warmth, opened a box of herbal cough sweets and sucked them loudly, whispering audibly throughout the service, with comments on everything from the floral tributes to the reverend's complexion. Reverend Day did his duty. He had known William personally and spoke well of him, especially his learning and industry, which had set an example to all. He spoke of the death of Frederick, which had marred an otherwise contented life. 'As you all know, recent events have been distressing to William and his family,' he said. 'This is not the place to speak of them except to say that they should not be allowed to cloud the memory of a life spent in dutiful service to the community.'

As they made their way back to the carriages to go to the cemetery, Cornelius took Frances by the hand, and patted it sympathetically. 'It will be over soon,' he said, 'the poor fellow will be at rest. We might imagine him with Frederick, now, happier than he has been, happier than those he has left behind.'

'Far happier,' said Frances. She climbed into the

chill interior of the waiting carriage and drew a rug over her knees, wanting more than anything for the day to end. As they reached the main gate of Kensal Green Cemetery, she saw that a brougham waited outside, the groom in place, his greatcoat wrapped with heavy shawls, the horse breathing white plumes of vapour into the frosty air. Through the great arch she could just see tombstones looming out of the shadowy mist, and then a spectral figure appeared, a moving black ghost in the cloudy air, the form of a woman. As she neared, Frances saw that it was a lady dressed in the deep mourning appropriate to the recent loss of a close relative, and thickly veiled. She looked neither to the right nor left, and took no notice of the approaching cortège, but hurried from the cemetery, and stepped briskly into the brougham which drove away immediately.

Frances wondered what had brought the lady out on such a gloomy and inclement day as this, simply to visit a grave, when she might have waited for better weather rather than risk a chill. They descended from the carriage, Cornelius gave her his arm and she walked through the gate to the prepared gravesite. The day of Frederick's funeral had been dry and not too cold. Then, the cemetery had had the air of a formal garden, a place of quiet and repose, where one could visit and reflect, sad for the loss sustained, but with some comfort also for a life that could be remembered with joy, and with hope of being reunited in future. This day it was a grim and comfortless place, cold and dreadful, where hope was abandoned and only grief remained.

The service around the graveside was quickly done, out of deference to the ladies in view of the weather, and the attendants with frozen fingers managed with difficulty to lower the coffin into the ground. Frances scattered a handful of earth, and it was over.

'Come, my dear, let us get you back into the warm,' said Cornelius.

'If I may have a few moments, I would like to visit Frederick's grave,' said Frances. 'It has been too long, and I would like to see that it is in order.' Cornelius assented, and Frances took a small wreath from the hearse, and walked with him. As they did so they passed a row of recent graves, piled with hot-house flowers that had lain there for several days and were blackened with the cold. Frances stopped and stared, then looked closely at the tributes. Many of them had small cards attached, and she glanced at the messages. On one grave, she read, 'In eternal friendship, James' and 'To my dearest husband, until we meet again, Henrietta'. It was the grave of Percival Garton, and on top of all the shrivelled and wilted wreaths of eight days before was a single fresh posy that must have been placed there that day. Frances wondered if it had been left by the lady she had seen departing the cemetery. If so, then she could not imagine who the lady might be. To the best of her recollection the figure had been above medium height and of slender build, far too slender to be the widow, yet the mourning garments were appropriate to one who had been close to the deceased. A sister, perhaps – but Frances was sure that all the family lived in Italy – or even a mistress.

Cornelius waited patiently for her, then she took his arm and they walked on. She placed the wreath on Frederick's grave, and stood there for a few moments. 'He should have been with me,' she said. 'We had such happy times, and would have done again.' She tried to imagine life as it would have been with Frederick alive and the mourning period for their father over; the shop bustling again, with Frances working by her brother's side; Frederick meeting a young woman, who would be both a friend and a sister to Frances. Then a wedding, with herself as chief bridesmaid, and before long, a host of delightful children, and the house filled with laughter. She sighed. 'Uncle, could you take me to see where my mother is buried? Is it near?'

He hesitated. 'Oh, I thought you knew, my dear. Your mother is not buried at Kensal Green. But I promise faithfully as soon as the weather improves I will take you there. Now, I think we really should go. Your poor aunts are quite frozen. Any longer in this air and it will scarcely be worth our while to take them home.'

Frances nodded. Of course she had been so young when she had seen her mother's grave, and had gone there in a cab. She had assumed the burial was in Kensal Green, though now she thought about it she could not recall the imposing gates. There had been, she remembered, a beautiful chapel with a domed roof. There was another cemetery in Paddington, and she supposed it must be that one.

At home, the small gathering sat around the

parlour table while Sarah brought a satisfying repast of cold fowl, ham, pork pie, potted beef, bread and butter, cake and as much hot tea and coffee as anyone could want. Frances suspected that not all of the food bought for the event would appear on the table, and that anything uneaten would supply the family's needs for several days to come, while any partially used coals then blazing in the grate would be swiftly removed with tongs as soon as their visitors had left.

To Frances' discomfiture the conversation, now that everything regarding William appeared to have been settled, was on only one subject – herself.

'The question is,' said Mrs Scorer, piling more food on her plate than was normally considered polite, 'What is to be done with Frances?'

'Oh, I really don't think this is the time to talk about that,' said Cornelius.

'No better time, in my opinion,' said Mrs Scorer, firmly. 'We are all together, and who knows when we will be again. It had better be settled soon.'

Herbert looked alarmed, took his plate and cup and fled, with muttered apologies.

'Well *we* have neither money to spare nor any room for her,' said Gertrude. She shook her head with a great show of regret. 'It is very sad, but that is the case and there is no use pretending otherwise.'

'What *I* want to say on the subject,' said Mrs Scorer, 'is that I feel, and I am sure you will all agree, that I have more than done my duty already.' She looked around her for a hint of dissention. There was none and she nodded in a self-satisfied way, and bit into a slice of cold chicken.

'No one has asked you to do anything, Maude,' said Cornelius, gently. 'It is agreed that Frances can come and live with me as soon as the business is sold. I have more than enough room, and I confess it has been a lonely existence since dear Phoebe passed away. I would welcome the company.'

'I don't want to be a burden,' said Frances. 'I do hope to be able to make my own way in the world.'

'Perhaps,' said Nora helpfully, 'you might try the drapery trade. I have heard it can be almost genteel nowadays. That nice Mr Whiteley is very kind to the young girls who work for him.'

'I have several years' experience in the dispensary,' Frances reminded her. 'Surely that should not be wasted. I intend to take my examinations and seek an apprenticeship.'

'Oh dear,' said Gertrude. 'Such a nasty smelly business. I think the best thing for you, Frances dear, is to marry, and do it as soon as you can.'

'That might be the answer,' said Rawsthorne. 'A young woman without a fortune may still make a good marriage if she is an active, useful person. It so happens that I have a client, a widower with three small children, perhaps I could arrange an introduction?'

'In a year or two, Mr Munson would be an excellent prospect,' said Cornelius, 'and I do believe he admires you.'

'I am more concerned about Sarah,' said Frances, changing the subject. 'She has been a good, dependable servant for ten years, and as you know my father did intend to provide her with a small legacy. I would very much like to see her settled in a good place.'

'The *servant?*' said Mrs Scorer, witheringly, 'what concern is she of yours? Really Frances! If you think so well of her, then give her a good character and let her go, and that is all you need to do about *that.*'

'Frances, dear, I have just recalled that I know a gentleman looking for a governess,' exclaimed Nora. 'It might suit you very well. I don't think he can pay a great deal, but of course that is all to the good as it means he is not seeking anyone with many accomplishments. And his wife is very sickly and may not live long, and he is not so *very* much over forty as really matters.'

'If you don't mind,' said Frances, rising abruptly to her feet. 'I think I can feel the approach of a headache and it would be best if I retired to my room.'

The aunts made sympathetic noises, Cornelius nodded and rose to assist her, Rawsthorne uttered a woebegone sigh, and Mrs Scorer shrugged and helped herself to Frances' portion of pork pie. 'Shall I bring you up anything to drink Miss, or a cold compress?' asked Sarah.

'Thank you, Sarah, no, I just need peace and quiet.' Frances fled upstairs, but instead of going to her bed, she found herself entering her father's room, and, though it held the same furniture as when he had been alive, found it cold, spare and empty. She sat at the little desk where he had kept his papers, and began idly to look through them.

Cornelius had been thorough and everything was ready sorted into little packets. One packet held family documents and Frances looked through them with interest. There was the certificate of the marriage of William Henry Doughty to Rosetta Ann Martin on 10th January 1855, a date which caused her a moment of surprise. She already knew Frederick's date of birth, but it was interesting to see it on his certificate, 2nd July and she had always been led to believe that her parents had married in 1854. She raised her eyebrows. So many things were known only by word of mouth, so many things were discreetly hidden, yet these innocent-looking pieces of official paper told a story of their own. To her surprise she saw that there had been another child, a sister called Emilia born in November 1857, who had died only three months later from scarlet fever. Then there was the certificate showing her own birth on 15th September 1860. The last paper in the packet was Fred's death certificate, 4th October 1879.

Sarah peered around the door. 'They've gone, Miss,' she said. 'Is your headache better?'

Frances nodded with relief. 'Yes, Sarah, and it is about time I made myself useful. This room needs a thorough turning out and airing, so let us get started, and when that is done the linens can be starched.'

Much later, as they were enjoying a cup of tea with some of the left-over cake, there was a knock at the front door. Sarah answered it, and Frances wondered if it might be Constable Brown, although it was early for him. She was disappointed when Sarah returned, a small card held in her hand which she regarded with a certain air of distaste. 'It's a Mr Gillan,' she said. 'He's from the *Bayswater Chronicle*. I'll send him away, shall I?'

Frances considered this. Mr Gillan had no doubt been told to write a certain number of words in the newspaper. If she refused to see him, this would not, she thought, prevent him from doing so, but only encourage him to include suppositions and rumour in the absence of the facts. Worse still, he might already have interviewed persons who strongly believed her father to be guilty of error, and it was this point of view which would then prevail. 'No, show him up to the parlour, and make a fresh pot of tea,' she said.

Sarah looked surprised but complied. If young Mr Frank Williamson ever needed to appear in the Grove again, which Frances fervently hoped would never be necessary, she would, she thought, at least have more information on how he might best conduct himself.

Mr Gillan was about thirty, of respectable appearance, and neatly dressed, although Frances suspected that his clothes had been worn and refreshed for many years. Such thrift and diligence spoke of a careful wife or a fond mother. He knew that he was fortunate to be admitted, and bore the humble and sympathetic air of an undertaker, putting the best face on an unfortunate business. 'Miss Doughty, I am sorry to trouble you at such a sad time,' he said.

'Well, I expect you would not have troubled me at any other time,' said Frances, tartly. 'Do be seated, Mr Gillan. The maid will be bringing tea directly.'

297

'Thank you.' He had been relieved of his coat and hat by Sarah, and sat, shivering a little. He glanced at the parlour fire, where a few small coals glowed feebly, and rubbed his hands to warm them, before taking a notebook and pencil from his pocket.

'How may I help you, Mr Gillan?' Frances asked. 'And please do not hesitate to ask whatever questions you wish. If I did not want to answer them I would scarcely have agreed to speak to you.'

'I am very grateful indeed for that permission,' he said, 'and I would like very much to hear what you have to say on the verdict of the coroner's court on Mr Percival Garton?'

'I do not agree with the verdict,' said Frances, firmly. 'The court did not take into account the fact that Mr Munson was a witness to the making up of the prescription. There was no error, and my father did not at any time go into the back store-room.'

'But Mrs Keane's evidence?' said Gillan, scribbling.

'The lady was mistaken,' said Frances, promptly.

'Oh?' said Gillan, raising his eyebrows. He examined some notes made earlier. 'In what respect?'

She looked at him resolutely. 'In *every* respect. I do not wish to be unkind, but I can only assume she confused that day with another occasion.'

Gillan frowned and was about to speak when Sarah arrived with the tea things. He gazed at the teapot longingly, and Frances, who was fortunate not to mind the cold, furnished him with a steaming cup and a biscuit.

'I have spoken to Mrs Keane,' said Gillan, when Sarah had gone, 'and she has assured me that she has only ever entered the shop once. And at the inquest she correctly described the maid-servant waiting for the prescription, even to how she was sitting staring at her feet. So she could not have been in error either about the time or the place.'

'Mrs Keane, in common with every other person in court, knew that Ada was there because she only spoke *after* she had heard her evidence,' said Frances.

Gillan stared at her. 'Are you accusing Mrs Keane of making up her testimony?'

Frances hesitated. She had effectively done just that, yet realised it might be unwise to say so explicitly and without explanation. 'I suggest only that her memory was at fault. She may have been confused. I feel that this is far more probable than that the three other persons present were telling untruths,' she said.

'Mrs Keane has informed me that you have paid her a visit,' he said. 'That you begged her to change her testimony.'

'I asked her to acknowledge her error but she would not,' said Frances. 'I remain hopeful that one day she will think better of it, and do so.'

He made some notes. 'And – I know this is a painful subject, but...'

Frances felt that she was gaining some expertise in dealing with painful subjects. 'Please do not spare me.'

'The inquest on your father,' asked Gillan, 'what is your opinion on that verdict?'

299

'I agree with it entirely. My father had long been in the habit of using chloroform on a handkerchief to relieve pain and procure sleep.'

He nodded. 'Yes: headaches and toothaches, Dr Collin said. You believe that your father made a simple error with the dose?'

'I do.'

'But he did not make an error with Mr Garton's prescription?' he asked, slyly.

Frances saw how his questioning had led her on. 'The two things are quite distinct in character,' she said coldly. 'The excess dose of chloroform, a matter of a few minims, could have been due merely to a tremor of the hand, something he did suffer from in the last few months. As regards Mr Garton's medicine, there was the addition of a wholly foreign substance to the mixture. That is not something which can happen in a moment of distraction, or be caused by a trembling hand.'

'Are you saying that the strychnine was put there deliberately – that Mr Garton was murdered?'

Frances knew she must not be drawn into wild allegations which would find themselves in the newspapers, and alert any confederates Keane might have had. 'I make no suggestion of the sort,' she said. 'Without evidence, I can say nothing, and the *Chronicle* might deem it wise to say nothing also. In the case of my father, what I say is based on my personal knowledge of him, something other people cannot have.'

'But it is very clear,' said Gillan, 'that the strychnine must have been introduced into the medicine before it left your shop. It was wrapped and sealed, right up to the moment when Mr

Garton opened it and took a drink. There was no opportunity for anyone to introduce the poison.'

'I only know that my father could not have put it there,' said Frances, firmly. If her determination sounded like the blind faith of a doting daughter, then so be it.

'Perhaps,' he said, more kindly, 'you would favour me with a brief account of your father's life.'

'Yes, of course. He was born in 1830, and resided many years in Kilburn. He opened this shop in 1860. The Grove was not then the prosperous shopping promenade that you see today, but the area was genteel, and he thought the prospects good. My mother was the former Rosetta Martin. She died in 1864. My brother Frederick was to have been my father's partner in the business but he died last October after a long illness. Mr Gillan,' she added impulsively, 'my father has always enjoyed the respect and confidence of his many customers. All who knew him have only kind words to say, both of his character and ability in his profession.'

Frances suddenly felt a creeping of cold horror at the weak, pleading creature she must seem to be. She clasped her hands firmly together for a moment, willing herself to be strong. As she watched the reporter write, she wondered how many others he had interviewed; the police, perhaps, and what of Mrs Garton, or Cedric? She craned her head as far as was commensurate with politeness, to peer at his notebook, and saw to her disappointment an indecipherable collection of dots, lines and curlicues.

'Are you reporting also on the case against Mr Keane?' she asked.

He looked up with a smile. 'I am indeed; I will be at the police court on Friday to hear the case. That will be sensational reading!'

'What a terrible man he must be,' said Frances, 'and how he has fooled us all into believing him to be such a respectable individual.'

'Do you know him, Miss Doughty?' asked Gillan, pencil poised.

'I have met him only once, in the picture gallery, I thought his manners very unpleasant.'

Gillan smiled. 'Do you know he was a near neighbour of yours at one time?'

'No, this must have been before his marriage I assume?'

'When Mr Keane first came to Bayswater he took lodgings above the shop of Mr Beccles the watchmaker. That is a mere matter of yards from your door.'

'I cannot say that I recall him. When did he first come to live there?'

Gillan consulted his notebook. 'April of 1869; of course you would have been a child then.'

Frances restrained a small gasp of excitement. 'But after all these years, how can you be sure about the date?' He stared at her. 'Excuse me, but one reads so many things in the newspapers, and it is often a matter of great curiosity to me as to how anyone can find them out.'

'Ah, well in this case I was assisted by the fact that Mr Beccles is a very careful man who retains all his rent books. They show that Mr Keane first resided here on 19th April.' He rose. 'I will not trouble you further, Miss Doughty. You have been kinder than I had hoped.'

'Promise you will write nothing about my father except what you know to be a fact,' said Frances.

He smiled indulgently. 'But what are facts? And how can we ever hope to know them?' he said. 'Facts stare us in the face and we do not see them for what they are, yet so many of us choose to believe the impossible. What we know with all our hearts and souls to be true, even what is plain before our eyes, may still be false. I cannot deal in facts, I can only deal in what the public wish to read, secure in the knowledge that on the morrow my words will be used to wrap fish. I bid you good-day Miss Doughty.' He collected his hat and coat and departed.

There was just enough hot water for Frances to refresh the tealeaves. She took her notebook from her pocket and opened it, then carefully wrote '19 April 1869', and sat staring at the pages, sipping her tea. Frances thought of a new and useful way of arranging her information. On a sheet of clean wrapping paper she drew a chart of squares rather like an acrostic puzzle. Each row was labelled with a year, and divided into months, and in the relevant month she entered the information she knew. At the end of 1856, and Frances had to guess the month as December, Percival Garton arrived in England from Italy. In 1862 – again she had no precise month, and guessed April – he married Henrietta. Between those two dates he took up residence in Tollington Mill. In October 1864, Percival Garton inherited his grandfather's business. In 1867, possibly in September, John

Wright, who had been exhibiting delusional behaviour for several years, was committed to an asylum. In June 1868, he was released from the asylum and went to live with his sister in Bristol. On 19 April 1869, James Keane first took up residence in Bayswater. In June 1869 John Wright left Bristol for Tollington Mill. In July 1870 Percival Garton left Tollington Mill for London, and the following August John Wright was murdered. A few days later Henrietta Garton followed her husband to London. In January 1871, Rhoda Garton was born. Frances stared at the page for some minutes hoping to find inspiration, but there was none. She closed her eyes and for a moment imagined the squares moving about and forming another pattern, one that would make everything clear. Gillan, she realised, had been right about the power of delusion, the ability of human beings to believe only what they wanted to be true, and reject all else. Had she been guilty of that? She resolved to be firmer in future.

She could now only await the published article with dread. The family history she had given had been correct, and she hoped Gillan could read Mr Pitman's loops and lines accurately. Pondering briefly on what had been said, a thought came to her. During the interview she had mentioned her mother's death in 1864, yet could not recall having seen the relevant certificate in the packet that Cornelius had made. She went up to her father's room and looked though the packet again, but it was not there. Curious now, she examined the other papers in the desk, but it was not amongst them. She resolved to ask her uncle about it the next time she saw him. There was another comment that Gillan had made, something that pricked her memory and puzzled her, but it was probably of no moment.

That night Frances prayed for fine weather but the next day dawned cold and foggy once more. There was a little more custom, mainly servants who had been sent out to fetch cough mixtures and tonics for their employers, and a few prescriptions. People seemed to have taken to Mr Jacobs. He was young, smart and efficient, with the air of confidence that was always required of a man in his position. Some of the younger women simpered as if they found him handsome, which perhaps he was. Frances found her hopes increasing. As soon as the weather cleared a single man with good features could well be an advantage for business. When that afternoon a lady entered and asked for Mr Jacobs most particularly, Frances could not resist a smile. Herbert, who had been stern and sullen since their last interview, darted into the back where she knew he kept a jar of pomade on the shelf, and emerged a few moments later more pungent than ever.

As the darkness closed in, Frances returned to the parlour, lit a candle and took up some mending. She was sleepy, yet a knock at the door roused her into wakefulness. Sarah entered. 'It's Constable Brown,' she said. 'He's brought a big parcel of papers with him.'

'Show him in!' said Frances, excitedly. She put aside the sewing and composed herself, waiting for the young policeman's step on the stair. How she wished – but no, it was a thought she must

305

not permit herself. All her attention must be devoted to what was about to be revealed; the truth about Lewis Cotter.

CHAPTER SIXTEEN

'If you don't mind my asking, Miss,' said Constable Brown, as they sat at the parlour table and Frances started to unwrap the parcel he had brought, 'What is your interest in the Cotter case?'

Frances dared not answer that question, and could not help but feel ashamed of herself. To her utter mortification, she realised that she was, for the first time in her life, motivated by money, the reward for the capture of Lewis Cotter. If she voiced her suspicions to the police the chance of saving the business might be lost. 'Constable, I am very grateful for all the assistance you have given me,' she said awkwardly, 'and I know it ill-repays you not to be perfectly open, but would you forgive me if I was not to reveal my motives? After my last interview with Inspector Sharrock I have resolved to make no declarations to the police until I have evidence.'

He nodded understandingly. 'I can see that would be very wise.'

'Inspector Sharrock would regard anything I said as the ramblings of an hysterical female unless I was to bring him Mr Garton's murderer in chains together with a signed confession.'

He chuckled. 'Something I believe you to be

capable of, Miss Doughty. I should like to see that, I really should! Of course, I have read the newspaper with the report of Mr Keane's arrest which does compare him to Mr Cotter, and I was wondering–'

Frances fell silent, and lifted the newspapers from their wrappings.

'What I *can* say,' said Wilfred, after a thoughtful pause, 'is that Cotter's a Liverpool case, and not for us to look into. And I'm sure the Inspector has got quite enough on his plate what with Paddington criminals.'

Frances smiled, appreciatively, and unfolded a copy of the *Illustrated Police News* of 17th April 1869, which depicted, amongst other things, an unseemly fracas at a Methodist chapel in Batley, and an unfortunate clergyman being pounced upon by a large and hungry-looking tiger. Inside the newspaper Frances found a report headed 'Shocking Murder in Liverpool', and there were other papers which elaborated on the story. She felt a sudden thrill of excitement. The disappearance of Lewis Cotter had taken place only days before the arrival of James Keane in Bayswater. There was no obstacle to their being one and the same man.

Cotter's victim was forty-year-old Thomas Truin, a clerk in the Liverpool & County Bank. On the evening of Saturday 10th April, the bank had closed its doors as usual, but Truin, who was a punctual and orderly man, and not given to drink, did not return home. His wife, frantic with worry, had called the police, who at first assumed that Truin had been waylaid on his journey, but no reports having been received of anyone being robbed in the street, and no injured person or body having been found, it was next supposed that he might have become insane and be wandering in the city. Truin, it appeared, had ample reason to lose his mind. His salary was only one hundred pounds a year, his wife was in poor health and there were ten children, of whom several were very sickly. His eldest son was fourteen, and Truin had been doing his best to educate him for a good position in life, but the unequal task had, it was thought, been too much for him, and affected his brain.

On the morning of Monday 12th April the bank opened its doors, and, to the horror of everyone present, Thomas Truin's body was found in one of the offices. He was slumped across a desk, and the back of his head had been crushed with a heavy instrument. It was clear that he had been killed on the previous Saturday. There was no sign of a struggle, and it was assumed that Truin had been in the company of someone he knew or trusted, someone who had walked behind him on some pretext and committed the murder. By the end of the day it had been possible to name a suspect. The police had asked to interview all the staff of the bank, but one man was missing. He was Lewis Cotter, aged twenty-six, the son of a respectable tradesman, who had worked as a clerk in the bank for the last three years. Enquiries made at Cotter's home revealed that on the Saturday evening he had told his family he was quitting his post at the Liverpool bank for a better position in another city, only it was imperative that he pack his bags and leave at once. He had promised to write as soon as he was settled, but they had heard nothing further from him. His father and brother had been unable to agree on what city had been mentioned, but in any case the police were of the opinion that Lewis Cotter's story was untrue, invented to account for his rapid departure, and as the days unfolded, this was confirmed as no bank could report having offered him employment. Notices had been posted with a description of the fugitive, but no response had been received. Lewis Cotter had disappeared. His family was adamant that he would not have committed so dreadful a crime, but as the bank investigated its books, further facts were revealed.

Cotter and Truin had, it seemed, been in collusion to commit a fraud upon the bank. *The Liverpool Journal* asserted that both men were the most desperate villains, the *Daily Post* stated that the older, more experienced, man had led the younger into crime, but the *Mercury* believed that Cotter had been the instigator, and had tempted the impoverished Truin to assist him. Whatever the case, enormous loans had been obtained from the bank in assumed names, based on forged title deeds, forgeries of such excellence that it required careful examination by experts to declare them to be false. Share certificates had also been forged and sold to unsuspecting customers, and where genuine share transactions had been recorded in the books, the number sold had been falsified and additional amounts transferred to Cotter. Truin, it eventually appeared, had made very little from the crime, but there was a large and undisclosed amount missing from the bank's coffers. For a time it had been thought that the bank would have to close its doors, and there were scenes in the street of customers clamouring to withdraw their funds. Ultimately, however, the bank survived, although its operations were more modest than before.

Tragedy followed upon tragedy. Cotter's father, Solomon, on receiving incontrovertible proof of his son's villainy, had suffered a great spasm of the heart and expired in minutes. Truin's eldest son was withdrawn from education and found some honest employment, and a sixteen-year-old daughter sent into service, but their mother and the eight youngest children were obliged to remove to the public workhouse. A newspaper cutting dated six months later revealed that Mrs Truin and five of the children had fallen victim to an outbreak of typhoid, though it was hinted that Mrs Truin might have died of grief after hearing that her eldest son, disdaining to be apprenticed to a cheesemonger, had run away, and was appearing on stage with a travelling troupe of entertainers.

'How dreadful!' Frances exclaimed. 'And it seems that the murderer was never caught.'

'It is thought that he fled abroad with the proceeds of his crimes,' said Wilfred. 'It was two days before he was even suspected, so he had more than enough time. He could have sailed to America.'

Frances read on, and learned that passenger lists of transatlantic vessels had been examined, and the American police alerted by cable, but searches of incoming ships had not revealed anyone resembling Lewis Cotter. But Cotter, she

310

reasoned, was a clever man who must have known that to take a ship to America was the obvious thing to do. In many ways to be on board ship was to be trapped, with no hope of escape if suspected. Better surely to lie low for a while, and then slip away undetected some time later.

'I wonder why he killed poor Mr Truin,' she said. 'Such a cruel and unnecessary thing to do.'

'It seems that Truin was an honest man led astray for want of money,' said Wilfred. 'I think he regretted his crimes and told Cotter he would not help him again. Cotter might have feared that Truin would confess and, being a heartless individual, decided to remove him.'

Frances noticed that the newspapers had not said if it was Cotter or Truin who had committed the forgeries, but if Cotter had indeed become James Keane, the pattern that was now emerging was of Cotter masterminding the crimes and employing other men such as Wright and Meadows for their artistic ability. Whether or not Truin was the actual forger, the newspapers did not reveal. 'It says here that Solomon Cotter was a respectable tradesman,' she observed. 'Do you know what trade he followed, or where he lived?'

Wilfred shook his head. 'No, Miss. Is that important?'

She avoided his gaze. 'It is something I would very much like to know.'

'It might be in the Liverpool police records,' said Wilfred.

'Oh, I should not like to trouble them,' said Frances, quickly.

'Well, his death certificate would say.'

'Yes, of course,' said Frances. She knew that certificates were kept at Somerset House, but did not know how one might go about getting one. She imagined that there would be large books of certificates and clerks employed to search them. There would, she thought regretfully, inevitably be a fee.

The expense could, however, be well worth her while. The newspapers confirmed what Chas had said, the Liverpool & County Bank had offered a reward of five hundred pounds for information leading to the arrest and conviction of Lewis Cotter for his crimes, and an additional amount of one per cent of any missing funds recovered up to a maximum of five hundred pounds. Later editions of the *Illustrated Police News* and the *Police Gazette* had portraits of the wanted man, copied from family photographs, and therefore considered to be excellent likenesses. For some moments she was silent, studying the face of a murderer. Three deaths, she thought, three murders; Thomas Truin, John Wright and Percival Garton; all unsolved, and the last two with undoubted connections to James Keane. In the case of Truin and Wright, the method of murder had been the same. Add the missing Mr Meadows and that was a possible four murders and another man who knew Keane. Both Wright and Meadows were artists, and both the Truin/Cotter plot and Keane's crimes at the Bayswater Bank had involved forgery. There *had* to be a connection! But how, she wondered, had Keane succeeded in poisoning Garton's medicine? There was only one conclusion – he had an accomplice in the Garton

312

household. Recalling what Mr Gillan had said, she wondered if Henrietta was as loving a wife as she appeared to be.

'Are you feeling well, Miss Doughty?' asked Wilfred anxiously.

Frances realised that she had been trembling. 'Yes, I – I am disturbed that there can be such evil men in the world.'

'Perhaps it's not the best kind of reading for you Miss,' said Wilfred guiltily, 'I know Lily – that's my wife – wouldn't even want to think about such things let alone read them in the papers.'

'I expect she has a very kind nature,' said Frances.

'She does, Miss,' he said, smiling.

'I am not kind,' said Frances, 'I am upset and angry at what has happened to my father. Sometimes my emotions overcome me, but that is the lot of a female and I know I must resist it. I have work to do, and if some of it means I must read about dreadful crimes and suffering then I will not shrink from it.'

He hesitated. 'And you think that the case of Mr Cotter is connected with your father?'

'Am I mad?' she asked him. 'Am I distracted? Is that what you think?'

He stared back at her and after a moment, slowly shook his head. 'You don't seem it, Miss. You are one of the most collected ladies I know. But you have had great trials to bear.'

'And I will go on bearing them,' she said. 'Yes, I feel there may be a connection, but I need to clear my head and think about it. Someone said to me very recently that it is the habit of all

313

people to see only what they want to be true. You know too well that I want my father's name to be cleared, but I must try very hard to put aside all thought of how I want things to be and see only what is. That is my struggle. I am fighting myself, my own imagination, my frailties. When a man sees the truth he wants to see, he is said to be courageous, bold and determined, but a woman with such thoughts is weak and deluded, and in need of guidance. Why should that be?'

Constable Brown was obviously unused to conversation of this nature. 'I am sure I don't know, Miss.'

Frances stared once more at the pictures of Lewis Cotter. Young, yes, handsome, yes. Slender of build, and tall, with dark hair and richly curling whiskers. Was this the face of James Keane? She might almost be prepared to believe that it was, certainly there was nothing in the image that suggested it could not be he, or was this belief due to no more than a similarity of feature and wishful thinking?

When Constable Brown had gone, Frances turned to her notebook again, and drew up a chart of all the connections between the four possible murders, and tried, tried very hard indeed, to see only what was actually there. Wilfred had left the papers with her, and she studied them again. How she pitied the poor Truin children – how she felt for them – a father disgraced and dead, a mother gone, the family plunged into want, and the villain who had brought them to this, heaven only knew where. How much more bitter even than her own plight.

Thursday was as cold as before, with dense fog and hoar frost fringing everything with feathery spikes, yet the shop's custom had increased again. Frances calculated that takings were almost at a level with expenses, and likely to improve. The reason was not hard to deduce. Sarah revealed that talk was going around the Grove that young Mr Jacobs was a single gentleman, without a sweetheart, and that his father owned several chemist shops in various parts of London. Frances fervently hoped that her relatives did not get to hear of this, as they would have her married off to him in their imaginations ten times over before the month was out and very likely drive him away.

That afternoon Frances was in the back of the shop mixing up a batch of camphorated chest rub when Herbert approached cautiously. They had spoken very little since she had made it clear that his attentions were unwanted and he still regarded her with some anxiety, as if she was an unguarded dog who might snap at him any moment. 'There is a young person asking to see you,' he said. 'She is called Ellen, and has requested you most particularly. She will speak to no one else.'

Frances wiped her hands. 'I'll see her at once,' she said, and followed Herbert into the shop. Ellen, the Keanes' housemaid, was warming herself at the stove. She looked up and smiled as soon as Frances appeared. 'Miss Doughty, I'm so glad you could see me.' She paused, and a sympathetic look clouded her eyes. 'I want to say how sorry I was to hear about your father. I didn't ever meet him myself, but everyone who did says as how he was a very kind man.'

'Yes, he was,' said Frances, and it was true, ever since her father's death, everyone had been telling her that he had been a kind man, but only now was she beginning to see that he had never been kind to her. 'How may I help you?'

Ellen drew nearer to the counter. 'I want to talk about something in private. Is there somewhere we won't be overheard?'

'Of course.' Frances had a strong suspicion that Herbert would want to know what they were talking about and would sneak around the door of the storeroom if they went in there. 'Let us go up to the parlour.'

'I should only really stop five minutes, as I'm out on an errand,' said Ellen, 'not that I think I'll be missed, things are that bad.'

They climbed the stairs to the parlour, and sat at the table. Ellen looked about her, and she smiled, in an approving sort of way, seeing the small efforts at neatness and respectability rather than the vulgarity of show. 'I said I would come if there was any news, and there is. It's been such a to-do, with Mistress in hysterics and the doctor coming and dosing her, and I've been sent out to get her favourite smelling salts and a pound of Lumps-of-Delight.'

'Is this because of Mr Keane's arrest?' asked Frances. 'I called upon her not long afterwards and she did not seem distressed.'

'Oh no, Mistress was quite calm after that. It might not be right to say it, but I'd not seen her so happy in a very long time. Of course there were other reasons, but it's not the sort of talk I like to hear. No, this is all about her father, Mr

Morgan, who has the fancy millinery shop on the Grove, and we all supposed to be very rich. He came to visit her last night, and they had a long talk and then I heard them both crying, and now she has taken to her bed and is shouting out a lot and saying all sorts of dreadful things what I can't repeat. I have been looking after her as best I can, but she won't be comforted.' Ellen shook her head sorrowfully. 'It seems that Mr Morgan is ruined, and it's all to do with Master's situation, in some way that I don't really understand. Mistress blames it all on him, and keeps saying about the bank – I think she said "freezing his accounts", whatever that signifies. But I can't see what that has to do with Mr Morgan.'

'Oh,' said Frances, to whom these events were not wholly unexpected. 'I think I can. I have heard that Mr Morgan was not so successful in business as the world supposed, and Mr Keane, as a favour to your mistress, has been lending him money to help him, and has saved him from ruin many a time. I think–,' Frances hesitated, not wanting to say too much. She could see that Ellen was touched by her mistress's plight, and it would serve no purpose to accuse the lady of lying in court. 'I think that Mr Keane gave Mr Morgan some money very recently. But when Mr Keane was arrested, of course the bank must have suspected that the money in his accounts was all stolen, and so won't allow any more to be taken out. If Mr Keane gave Mr Morgan a cheque, then the bank will have sent it back and not given Mr Morgan his money.'

'Oh!' said Ellen in dismay. 'Then Mistress is

317

ruined also. She has been crying and saying that she won't give up the house, but I had just taken that to be her hysterics, Miss, I never thought it would happen. We – I mean all the servants – we'd been thinking that Mr Morgan would be able to help, but now, of course...'

Her heavy lidded eyes were bright with sadness. 'If Master is put in prison then I expect it will all be sold up.'

'I think so,' said Frances. 'And – I am sorry to say it – probably much sooner than that. There will be bills to pay, and with Mr Keane under arrest I doubt that tradesmen can be persuaded to wait.'

Ellen hung her head. 'Now I understand something else,' she said unhappily. 'There was a gentleman came to see Mistress two days ago, and when I was dusting the bedroom yesterday I saw that some of her jewels were no longer there. I thought she might have been having them cleaned, but now...'

'Pawned or sold,' said Frances. 'It seems probable.'

'Poor lady!' said Ellen, sighing deeply.

Frances noted that Ellen, surely about to lose her place in a matter of days, felt sympathy only for her mistress. It was a trait she appreciated. 'Perhaps,' said Frances, 'Mrs Keane will be able to remove to a smaller establishment, where she will be more content. Better alone in humble lodgings than with Mr Keane in a grand house.'

'You might be right, at that, Miss,' agreed Ellen. 'He is a very bad man.'

'He is worse than anyone supposes, I am sure of it!' said Frances. 'Ellen, I don't suppose you ever

318

heard your master and Mr Garton quarrelling? Did they ever fall out over money or business matters?'

Ellen frowned. 'No, Miss, as far as I could see they were always on the best of terms.' She paused. 'You can't think–,' her eyes opened wide with shock, 'Miss, you don't think Master poisoned Mr Garton, do you?'

'We know that he is a criminal,' said Frances. 'Moreover, he is cruel and unfeeling and, I believe, would do anything for money. I think he killed Mr Garton to get his legacy, and escaped detection by letting my father be blamed. So he must bear some responsibility for my father's death. I do not and cannot believe that my father would ever have taken his own life as people are saying, but his distress caused an illness, a shaking in his hands, which led to his dosing himself excessively with chloroform.'

'You know, Miss, now I think about it, I reckon you're right about Master,' said Ellen. 'Of course he had to pretend to be Mr Garton's friend or he would never have been left such a great fortune. I know you want so much to prove it wasn't your father's mistake that killed Mr Garton, and it's sad, but now that he's gone to his rest, I suppose you won't ever be able to find out the truth.'

'I still hope to,' said Frances. 'I still must. Even though my father is gone, and can no longer suffer from unkind words, there is still my family's good name to consider.' And, thought Frances, the one thousand pound reward.

'At least Mr Keane is where he deserves to be,' said Ellen, soothingly.

'In police custody, you mean?' Frances smiled derisively. 'Oh he deserves far worse in my estimation. And if he was to be found guilty of the crimes he has been charged with, which I am sure he will be, what would be his sentence? Eight, ten, twelve years? I have no knowledge of these things. And would he even serve all those years? I doubt it. One hears in the newspapers all the time of the most dreadful criminals being let free before they have served all their sentences. No, unless I pursue him, Mr Keane will never get what he deserves.'

Ellen looked at her, sorrowfully, and Frances wondered what there was in her manner, what distraction or pathetic clinging to false hopes, that had evoked such pity. 'Will you help me?' she asked. 'I need proof that Mr Keane is guilty of murder. Any little remark that you may overhear may be of importance.'

Ellen nodded. 'Don't you worry, Miss. I promise I'll do whatever I can.'

The following day was the police court hearing of the case against James Keane. Frances would very much have liked to be there, but she was needed both at home and in the shop. To travel to Marylebone Road and perhaps wait hours for the case to be heard, and then sit for half the day listening to the witnesses, was quite impossible. The day was suddenly brighter, the crisp whiteness of the frost gone, the air almost balmy. Those people of Bayswater who had not dared the stifling fogs and chills of the last few days emerged from their homes and enjoyed the sunshine, and the Grove came back to life. The shop was crowded again, with demands for tonics and lozenges, in-

320

halers, syrups, and capsicum plasters. Prescriptions were pouring in, too, and Mr Jacobs and Herbert were kept almost continuously busy while Frances was stationed behind the counter, wrapping little parcels as fast as her fingers would go, and Tom was running errands two at a time.

As the evening drew in, and business slowed, Frances could not help examining the takings for the day so far. They were good, and had she not had debts to pay and the lease renewal to come, they would have been more than adequate to keep the business running. With a sinking heart she knew that unless she had a very great stroke of good fortune, the business could not survive more than another two months.

'Well, my dear Miss Doughty,' said Chas as he and Barstie entered the shop with sunny smiles. 'I expect you will be very pleased to hear our news!'

'We were at the police court to see Mr Keane's case,' said Barstie. 'And didn't he look green in the face! Someone has pounded his nose flatter than a pancake!'

'*Very* interesting evidence!' said Chas.

'Chas took a *great many* notes,' added Barstie.

'I was told that Mr Keane is a very clever fellow and he might never have been caught but for Inspector Sharrock finding the house in Maida Vale where the forgeries were done,' added Chas.

'Really,' said Frances dryly. 'I am sure that Inspector Sharrock was very pleased with himself.'

'All puffed up and proud,' said Barstie, 'especially when Mr de Rutzen, the magistrate, said the police had carried out some very smart work, but he was not so complimentary about the bank, and the manager was very shamefaced that he did not find out what was happening any sooner.'

'And,' said Chas, 'now here is something which was a very great shock to many people, though not so much to those *like ourselves,* in the know; Mr Keane had obtained loans from the bank for his father-in-law, giving forged title deeds as security. And Mr Morgan was in court saying that he thought the loans were all *bona fide,* and, who knows, *he* might even be arrested as well.'

'People are saying that Mr Morgan, being a man of business, could not have been ignorant of the fact that he seemed to be getting loans for nothing, and was shutting his eyes to Mr Keane's villainy,' added Barstie.

'Also,' said Chas, 'our guess about what was going on at the gallery on Queen's Road was right! The manager, Berenger, gave evidence–'

'Looking like he'd just been freshly sobered up for the occasion, and wanting to know where his next bracer was coming from–,' said Barstie.

'I think his employers made sure to keep him in liquor all the while so he wouldn't ask too many questions,' said Chas. '*He* said that there were hardly ever any customers there, but Mr Garton and Mr Keane didn't mind that. They just told him to be there to keep the place open, and not to look too hard at what was happening. And there were books which he looked at once, and saw that a great deal of money came in and then the same money would go out again the very next day. But just after Mr Garton died, Mr Keane came round and took all the books away.'

'Mr Keane was very busy destroying things after Mr Garton's death,' said Frances. 'He made away with the picture the artist Meadows drew of himself and Mrs Keane. Was anything said about Mr Meadows?'

'Keane has made a statement to the police saying that it was Meadows who did all the forgeries,' said Chas, 'but he insists that Meadows has gone abroad and he does not know where. He has given the police a description of the man, but it sounds very like a thousand other men, and Berenger said that he had never seen Meadows.'

'And what was the outcome?' asked Frances.

'Keane was sent for trial at the Old Bailey. When it was announced, he fainted and had to be carried out,' said Barstie. 'He might have a long wait. There is always a great deal of paperwork in a trial of this kind.'

'But the evidence is very conclusive, and he will surely be found guilty,' said Frances. 'Do you know what his sentence might be?'

'Harry Benson was a very great swindler and he got fifteen years and his accomplices ten,' said Chas. 'That was three years ago. But these types are very clever. They never serve the full amount. These are your superior criminals. They know how to behave themselves. Keane will be out of prison in less than ten years.'

'Well, at least he will not be running away anywhere just yet,' said Frances. Ten years, she thought. If it was simply a matter of proving him guilty she would have had time enough, but if she was to save the business she had only a matter of weeks. There was a clanging of the bell, and a sudden influx of customers. 'If you will excuse me–'

'Of course! Business always calls!' They tipped their hats and departed.

The late post that day brought a letter, addressed to Mr F. Doughty. Sarah handed it to Frances without comment. Frances felt a great surge of excitement as she unsealed the letter. It was, as she had hoped, a reply from Mrs Cranby, addressed Ivy Cottage, Tollington Mill.

Dear Mr Doughty
It was with great pleasure that I read your letter informing me that you were enquiring into the murder of Mr Wright. As you know, I was his housekeeper for the year that he lived in Tollington Mill, and a pleasanter young gentleman one could never hope to meet. He was very well liked in the village and everyone was very distressed when he was so cruelly murdered. If it is possible for you to visit me I would be delighted to see you. My cottage is very comfortable and you would be welcome to stay. I could show you where Mr Wright once lived. I am sure the present owner who is a very agreeable and respectable gentleman would permit you to look inside. If you are able to come, please let me know. My son, Willie can meet you at the station.
Eliza Cranby

Frances viewed the letter with some dismay. Until now, she had imagined that her enquiries into the events at Tollington Mill would be conducted by letter, and had never dreamed for a moment that she might be invited there. She knew that it was impossible for her to go. She could not keep up the pretence of being a man for very long, and supposing she was asked to share lodgings with a man; that would never do. She could, she reflected, write to Mrs Cranby and explain the mistake, and country folk might well be persuaded that in London it was possible for there to be lady detectives. She shook her head. What could she be thinking of? She could never be spared from her place at the shop, and there were, in addition, all her household duties. Of course, she reminded herself, the Grove was very quiet on a Saturday afternoon, and she could depart at midday and return on Sunday. For the first time in over two years she had no invalid at home to care for, and Sarah could surely manage in her absence. Once again she shook her head. What a foolish, and possibly dangerous, escapade – to travel so far – to a village where there might be a murderer – to see the places where the Gartons and John Wright had lived – to meet with the very people who had known them and hear from their own lips an account of the events that so puzzled her. Horribly tempted, she knew there was only one way to satisfy herself that the journey was out of the question. With business quieter towards the end of the day, she walked up to Paddington Station and made enquiries. The journey to Tollington Mill would, she learned, take several hours and require two changes of train, but it could be done. As she bought her ticket she seemed to be in a dream. She felt the same pleasant dizziness as when she had danced with Frederick or taken her first glass of brandy. The telegraph office in London Street was open until late, and before walking home she sent a telegram signed 'Miss Doughty' to Mrs Cranby advising her of the visit. It was settled. She could not change her mind. She had spent several shillings she could ill afford and they would not be wasted. She was going to Tollington Mill.

CHAPTER SEVENTEEN

The Great Western Railway. To Frances, those few words could never fail to conjure up the prospect of adventure. When Frances was seven and had entered the great rail terminus of Paddington for the first time, her uncle had looked at her with an expression of concern, and said, 'Now Frances, there is nothing to be afraid of,' and Frederick had said, 'I'll look after her, Uncle,' and held her hand tightly. It would never have occurred to Frances to be afraid. To her childish mind the station, with its lofty columns and ornate traceries of ironwork, was a palace of wonders. The great vaults and arches above her head seemed to be as high as the sky itself, while the shining globe-like lamps hung like as many moons. Cornelius told her that the station had been built by a great man called Brunel, and she had wondered how one man could make such a very large thing all by himself.

And the trains – how her heart had fluttered with anticipation at the great green and gold monsters, gleaming with oil, uttering shrieks and blowing clouds of hissing steam like dragons. She was helped into a carriage, and found herself in something like a little house on wheels, with windows and beautiful padded seats, and polished wood and even curtains. Other people crowded in – two gentlemen with suitcases and a woman with a fretful baby – and she felt affronted by their impertinence at entering what she thought was for herself and Frederick and her uncle alone, but Cornelius explained that anyone who could buy a ticket could get on the train. There were more shrieks and whistles, then Frederick held her hand again, and the carriage lurched, and they started to move. Frances watched in astonishment as the station slid away, and she stared out of the window at the backs of houses, and maids running out to take in the washing. She was told that the Queen used to take the train when she went to Windsor and back, and Frances wondered if the Queen was on her train – she still thought of it as hers, despite the invasion – and if she would meet the Queen, and what she would say when she did.

Then she was travelling faster than she could ever have imagined possible, with trees and fields and houses going past in a blink of an eye. When they stopped it was always at a station so tiny it was like a doll's house of a station, hardly a real one at all. There were many such excursions; sometimes they would walk in a wood scattered with flowers, once they saw a water mill, once it was a beautiful large house with a garden, and once a river with all kinds of swimming birds with names she could not possibly remember. Each train ride had seemed like a magical adventure, but now, more than twelve years after her first, she was about to travel, not just a few miles but most

327

of the way across England, quite alone, to meet people who were perfect strangers, while pretending to be a detective, in order to discover the identity of a murderer. Now that *was* an adventure.

She was grateful to have started soon after midday, for it would be a long journey. Fortunately the guards did not seem to think it was unusual for a young woman to be travelling alone, carrying only a small bag. She was especially anxious that she should not be taken for a wicked sort of woman, and, if she had been asked, would have told her enquirers that she was journeying to care for a sick relative, but her fellow passengers seemed weary or preoccupied and she did not enter into conversation with them. Before she departed, Sarah had uttered dire warnings about men who might seem to be gentlemen, and offer to assist her, but might in the event turn out not to be gentlemen at all, but a predatory type of person of whom she should beware. She advised Frances to find a carriage populated mainly or even entirely by other females if she could, and this, Frances had taken care to do. She had brought some bread and cheese to eat on the way, but did not feel especially hungry. She read a newspaper that she had found discarded on the platform, and studied her notebook, then stared out of the window at gloomy fields with forlorn-looking animals. Of course, she realised, her childhood excursions had all been in fine weather; no wonder everything had seemed to her to be so bright and colourful. Now it was all in shades of grey.

The first stop was Bristol, whose station boasted a great iron roof like that of Paddington. She felt that the industrious Mr Brunel must have been at work there, too. Making anxious enquiries, she discovered where she needed to wait for her next train, and after half an hour of shivering on the platform, a small rattling collection of coaches drew up, and she boarded. By now, she was hungry, and ate the bread and cheese. An hour later she was deposited at a country station, open to the elements, with a dreary little waiting room that smelled of something unpleasant. The air was chill, and her coat was no protection against a stiff breeze. Fortunately there was only half an hour to wait and another little train hissed and creaked to a halt and she got on. It was late afternoon when she reached Tollington Mill, and the sky was darkening over, the tiny station encased in a filmy mist. As she stood on the platform with her little bag, no scrap of food to eat, and a few pennies in her purse, waiting for a stranger, she began to think she must be quite mad.

'Miss Doughty?' said a voice, as a lantern approached. The figure came closer and showed itself to be that of a man in his thirties, dressed in a neat, countrified way, with a stout greatcoat and a weather-beaten hat, large boots and a long muffler wound about his neck. He held up the light. He had a broad smiling face. 'I'm Will Cranby,' he said. 'Mother sent me to take you to the cottage. Here, this is the letter you wrote to her.'

Frances saw that he was holding her letter. 'Oh,' she said in relief. 'Thank you, that was very thoughtful.'

'The cart's just outside the station,' he said. 'It's only a mile or so. I'll take your bag.'

In the road outside stood a butcher's cart, drawn by a single horse, the back portion constructed like a box for carrying goods, the front being no more than an open bench for the driver and a passenger, although he had provided some rugs for comfortable seating and warmth. He held out his arm and she placed her hand upon it as she climbed up onto the cart. For a brief moment she thought she knew a little of how Mrs Keane had felt towards Adam, how reassuring it was to have such a strong male arm for one's support.

'So you're a detective, Miss,' he said, as they set off. 'I never knew there were lady detectives.'

'Ladies are entering into almost every sphere of society nowadays,' said Frances, but regretted saying it almost as soon as she had spoken. It made her sound like a proud sort of woman and she did not think she was proud.

'Is that a fact?' he said wonderingly. 'Of course I suppose it is different in London.'

'Tell me about Tollington Mill,' said Frances.

'Oh, well, not a lot to say, Miss. It used to be a lot bigger than it is now, what with the woollen mill, that's why we have the railway going up to Bristol, but the mill's all gone years ago, and we're no more than a thousand souls, mainly farming.' They were approaching a row of stone cottages, some of which had diminutive shop fronts. 'That's where I live, Miss, the butcher's shop there. Me and my wife Alice live over the shop. We do the best pork in Gloucestershire, I've heard people say.'

'I understand that Mrs Cranby no longer lives at Tollington House?'

330

'Oh no, not for a year now. After poor Mr Wright was killed, the place was leased by a Mr Armitage, and he engaged my mother as house-keeper. She was very happy to stay, but nowadays she has some trouble with her legs, and can't get about or manage the stairs as she used to do. So she lives in Ivy Cottage now with my sister Dora.' Just past the stone cottages was a handsome corner house, clad in creeper and clustered about with bushes. 'Up ahead there, is Old Mill House,' he said, 'where Mr Wright used to go to see his friend Mr Garton.'

Frances stared at it eagerly, trying to make out its features through the increasing gloom. It was far larger than the cottages of the village folk, and certainly in keeping with a man who owned a successful business, but a great deal smaller and less genteel than the Garton home on Porchester Terrace, Bayswater. 'We can take you to see Tollington House tomorrow,' said Will. 'Mr Armitage has very kindly agreed to show it to you. Now then, here we are!'

The cart stopped outside a stone cottage very like all the others Frances had seen, and Will helped her down and took her bag inside, calling out, 'We're here, Mother!' before he held the door open.

Frances peered inside. The door opened directly onto a small parlour. A modest fire blazing in the grate was somehow contriving to heat the room, a tiny oven, a kettle and a flat iron, while simultaneously boiling two pans of savoury smelling food on the iron plates at either side. A stout, elderly woman seated on an easy chair rose with some difficulty and came to greet her, walking with the aid of a stick. 'Miss Doughty! Oh I am so pleased to see you! I'm Eliza Cranby. You must be tired. Do come in, the kettle has just boiled.'

There was a curiously lumpy piece of furniture in the room, a kind of backless sofa much piled with rugs and cushions of all colours, and Frances realised that Mrs Cranby, no longer able to climb the stairs to her bedroom, had disguised her bed as quite another article.

A much younger woman, a slender copy of the first, was tending to the fire and the cooking. 'This is my daughter, Dora,' said Mrs Cranby. 'Now Will, I hope you have been making sure that Miss Doughty had a pleasant drive here, and showed her all the sights. Please take a seat, Miss Doughty. We have our supper almost ready and I know you must want something after so long a journey.'

'Thank you so much for your hospitality,' said Frances. 'It's a very pretty village. Such delightful cottages.'

'I could not be happy anywhere else,' Mrs Cranby declared. 'I was sorry to leave Tollington House, but this suits me very well. Dora goes in to do the laundry and cleaning for Mr Armitage, who has it now, and I turn my hand to the mending. And we are very comfortable here, very comfortable indeed.'

'I'll get on home now,' said Will, as he departed, 'but I'll be here to take you all up to church tomorrow morning. Good day to you Miss Doughty. I hope you have a pleasant visit.'

'Oh, Miss Doughty, you can't know how grateful I was to have your letter!' exclaimed Mrs Cranby, easing herself into a chair beside a square, plain wooden table.

'Talked about nothing else since,' said Dora with a smile, bringing a pot of tea.

'I was only Mr Wright's housekeeper for a year, but I can honestly say a better employer I could not have wished for. So thoughtful – such manners! And to think he met with a terrible end like that and no one brought to justice!' Mrs Cranby shook her head. Almost ten years ago it might have been, but Frances saw that the murder of John Wright was fresh in her memory.

'Is it his family who have asked you to enquire into the murder?' asked Dora.

Frances felt ashamed at having to be less than candid with these kindly and honest folk. 'I am afraid I am not permitted to say,' she said.

'His family!' said Mrs Cranby contemptuously. 'What do they care about him, whoever they are! There is a fresh posy on his grave every Sunday, Miss Doughty, and do you know where it comes from? From *me*. I put it there, because someone who knew him ought to do so, and never a member of his family have I ever seen tend that grave. I used to keep it tidy, when I could get about better, and now Will does it for me.'

'Mr Wright had a sister, I believe,' said Frances.

'Yes, and if I caught hold of her I would give her a piece of my mind!' said Mrs Cranby. 'Do you know, she told everyone that Mr Wright was mad?'

'And what do you believe?' asked Frances.

'That he was as sane as any of us sitting round this table!' Mrs Cranby exclaimed. 'All that talk

333

about how she cared for him and she has never been seen here to so much as pull one weed from the grave. And those stories she told about how he was supposed to imagine he owned great estates and said he went out for meetings when he stayed indoors. Well, I can tell you, I was shocked when I heard about that because I saw no sign of it at all.' She gave an emphatic nod, followed by a quick glance in Dora's direction as if she expected her daughter to say something, but Dora tended to the cooking and was silent.

'Did he have many visitors?' asked Frances.

'Only what one might expect. There was Mr and Mrs Garton from Old Mill House, and Reverend Jessup, and Mr Mullin the land agent, and Mrs Tate who used to collect for charity – she's gone, now, poor soul – but that was all.'

Frances suddenly realised that here at last was someone who she did not have to persuade to answer questions. Her hostess had probably been bursting to do so since receiving the letter. She took out her notebook and pencil and saw Mrs Cranby beam with pleasure. 'No one came to see him from outside the village?'

'Never, that I know of.'

'I understand he used to write a great many letters,' said Frances, scribbling.

'Oh yes, and posted them himself.'

'And you saw on one occasion that he wrote to a Mr Keane in London?'

Mrs Cranby was clearly impressed that Frances knew this. 'Yes, so I did. I don't know what came of that.'

'But this Mr Keane, he never visited Mr Wright

as far as you know?'

'No, Miss, as I said, I don't think anyone came there who I didn't already know.'

Frances nodded, thoughtfully. 'He must have received letters, too.'

'Oh yes, very regularly. I can't say who sent them, but I believe they came from London.'

'Do you know what happened to them? I suppose the police must have taken them away?'

'I didn't find any for them to take,' said Mrs Cranby. 'I think he burnt them all before he went away. Some gentlemen don't trouble to keep their letters.'

Frances wondered if those last hours before John Wright left Tollington Mill could hold a crucial clue to his death. 'Before he left – the last time you saw him – did he give any reason for his absence?'

'No, only that he would be going away on business. It was all done in a great hurry, and he didn't really have time to say much about it.'

This was, thought Frances, the first she had known that John Wright's departure was a sudden one. 'How much warning did you have that he was going?'

'Just a few hours. He told me, and he was gone the same day.'

'How did he seem – I mean his mood? Was he worried, or excited, or – did he seem to be afraid of anything?'

'He was not in his usual state of mind,' said Mrs Cranby, thoughtfully. 'He was always a very calm gentleman. The sort you'd think wouldn't be easily upset. He was flustered, I would say, rushing about a great deal. Like he'd had some troubling news. And–,' she paused. 'There was one thing I thought was strange.'

'Yes?' Frances held her breath.

'I'm sure you know he was a very clever artist, and he had a sketch book he used to take with him, and draw the countryside and houses hereabouts. The thing is, when he was getting ready to go, he took it and threw it on the fire. Burnt it up, Miss, quite deliberately. And I do remember thinking to myself at the time, why would he do such a thing? And the more I thought about it, the more the idea came into my head that he wasn't expecting to come back.'

'Did you tell the police this?'

'I did,' said Mrs Cranby, ruefully, 'but you know what the police are like; they thought it was just my fancy.'

'Did he take very much with him in the way of luggage?'

'One bag, that was all.'

Frances was astonished. 'When he expected to be gone a month?'

'He told me he would send for his other things, but he never did.'

Frances stared at her notes, wondering what it could all mean. 'How often did Mr and Mrs Garton visit?'

'Oh several times a week, or else he would go there. What would you say, Dora?'

Dora was bringing a platter of boiled ham and potatoes to the table. 'Oh yes, very friendly they all were,' she said. 'I used to do laundry and cleaning for Mr and Mrs Garton, so I was often there, and sometimes they asked me to help with the cooking, too. When Mr Garton and Mr Wright went off drawing together I used to put out a cold supper for when they came back.'

'Is it true, Miss, that Mr Garton died recently?' asked Mrs Cranby. 'I have heard talk in the village that he did.'

'Yes, I am afraid so,' said Frances.

'I haven't heard anything of them since they left,' said Dora, slicing the ham onto plates. 'Mrs Garton – do you know – did she have a little boy or a little girl?'

Frances stared at her for a moment. 'You knew her condition?'

Dora smiled. 'Well it wasn't that hard to see. She kept saying she was bilious, but it was plain enough to me.' She piled potatoes beside the thick slices of ham and pushed the plate over to Frances. 'You start on that before it gets cold. Don't wait on us.'

It was the best ham Frances had ever tasted, and she said so. 'You were quite right about Mrs Garton,' she added. 'She gave birth to a baby girl in the January after she left here, and since then she has had four more children, all healthy.'

It was Dora's turn to look surprised. 'Well, that *is* remarkable,' she said.

'Oh, you mean you knew there had been some – medical complication.'

'Yes, well it was obvious that there was something the matter, what with all the time they had been married, and no family,' said Dora. 'Dr McPhail used to come round and there were visits to doctors in Bristol, and then they went to see someone in London, and I think there was a man in Edinburgh, but they always came back looking very despondent so I expect they had been told there was no hope. Then Mr Garton took a sea voyage in the hopes that the air would do him good. He'd been looking very weary before, what with the business causing him a lot of worry, but when he came back he looked so much better, the very picture of good health, and it wasn't so long after that I noticed the signs of a child on the way.'

It was a few moments before Frances understood the import of what had just been said, and she gulped down a piece of ham almost unchewed. '*Mr* Garton took a voyage?'

'That's right, away for three weeks he was.'

'Not *Mrs* Garton?'

Dora looked puzzled. 'No, Miss.'

Frances chose her words carefully. 'You see – I had been told that Mrs Garton was a lady in very delicate health, and that the doctors had said she could never be a mother.'

Dora shook her head. 'Oh no, you've been told wrong. Mrs Garton was a very slim young lady but she was never unwell.' She paused. 'I hope you don't think I ever listen to private conversations...'

'I am sure you cannot be blamed for overhearing something by accident,' said Frances, with an encouraging smile.

'Only I once heard Mr Garton telling Dr Mc-Phail that he had been took very bad when he first came to England, and his doctor had told him then it could mean that he might never be a parent.'

Frances thought that she could see the reason for the error. She had been told about Henrietta's

338

poor health by Cedric, who in turn had had the story from his brother. Percival must quite understandably have been sensitive on the subject and preferred to let his family believe that the fault lay with Henrietta and not himself. She wondered if the sea voyage and Garton's improved health had indeed been the reason for the arrival of the longed-for family. Suppose, however, that Garton was not Rhoda's father. He could have suspected this himself, but the birth of four more children after the family's removal from Tollington Mill, and everyone they had known there, would have reassured him. Had there, Frances wondered, been an intrigue between Henrietta and James Keane? And if so, how would she ever prove it?

When the dinner plates had been cleared away, Dora showed Frances to the little room upstairs where she slept, and where a folding bed had been arranged next to her own narrow cot. Frances suspected that had she been a young gentleman, as they had at first thought, Dora would have had to sleep downstairs with her mother. Dora offered Frances her own bed, but Frances would hear none of it and insisted that she would be perfectly comfortable on the folding bed. 'My mother would be most mortified if she knew I had not given you the proper bed,' said Dora, 'not that she will know as she cannot climb the stairs now.'

'Miss Cranby,' said Frances. 'What did you think of Mr Wright?'

Dora smiled. 'Oh, I know my mother will hear nothing against him, and I will not say anything contrary in her hearing, but a handsome face does not always mean goodness of nature. There was something in his eyes that always seemed to be weighing and measuring and making unkind judgements. I know Mrs Garton did not care for him.'

'Did she say so to you?'

'No, only I once heard her say to Mr Garton that she would prefer it if he did not invite his friend to the house so often as she could not be easy in his company.'

'And what did Mr Garton reply?'

'He asked her why she did not like his friend but she would not say.'

'And did Mr Wright visit them less from that time?'

'No, I don't believe so. After all, it was Mr Garton's house and I suppose he could invite whoever he wanted.'

Frances felt uncomfortable about making an indelicate suggestion concerning Mrs Garton's friendships. 'What other visitors were there to the house?'

'There were business acquaintances of Mr Garton's. Elderly gentlemen; most of them had known his grandfather. They talked about trade and shipping, and more than once I saw Mr Garton all but fall asleep in his chair and Mrs Garton pinch herself to stay awake. Oh and Reverend Jessup used to dine there sometimes, and there is no sleeping in *his* company, for he seems to know everyone and everything and Mrs Garton found him very amusing. Mr Garton was a kind man, but rather dull in his conversation.' Dora paused, and made a great performance of smoothing the quilt. 'I can guess what many folk

340

might have been thinking in my place, but if every lady who found another man more interesting than her husband went and did something she shouldn't we would all be little more than animals and there would be no saving us.'

It was not hard for Frances to imagine Henrietta pining for company in the quiet village, with Percival often absent in Bristol, returning only with talk of business, or perhaps no talk at all. But then the Gartons had removed to Bayswater, which for all its dirt and noise was a constant bustle of gossip and incident. Both husband and wife had cheerfully plunged into society and then there had been the happy arrival of the children. The change had breathed new life into their fading affections.

As the last lights were extinguished and Frances made herself as comfortable as possible, she wondered if, in July 1870, Percival Garton had guessed the true nature of Henrietta's condition. It did not, she thought, matter whether or not Garton was the father, only that he might have believed that he was not and suspected Henrietta of infidelity with young John Wright. Had he then contrived, through someone hired for the task, to eliminate the man he thought was his rival, while he himself was establishing an alibi in London? Or had there been another motive entirely? If John Wright had confided in his new friend about his imagined wealth, he could have been killed for his fortune. Frances realised, just as she dozed off to sleep, that her mind was spinning off into wild theories again. Each time she learned something new she tried to make sense of it, but the facts resolutely would not make sense.

She awoke to the scent of frying bacon and despite the large supper of the previous night felt very hungry, and appeared at the breakfast table as soon as was commensurate with ensuring that she was presentable.

'This morning I will show you where Mr Wright is buried,' said Mrs Cranby, who was busy tying a bunch of supple branches into a small wreath. 'And you can talk to Reverend Jessup. He will say exactly what I have told you, that Mr Wright was a very pleasant young man, and not at all what his sister claimed.'

Frances wondered if pleasant manners and madness were necessarily incompatible, but did not say so. 'I know that after the murder it was some time before the police knew who Mr Wright was. Were there no clues when he lived in Tollington House about his life before he came there? Did he have no portraits, photographs, diaries, ornaments, jewellery, that said anything about him?'

Mrs Cranby shook her head. 'He took the lease of the house ready furnished, so everything was in place. He brought his clothes of course and toilet articles, but nothing else. He said he had been living abroad and most of his effects were in trunks at sea and would be following.'

'And did they follow?' said Frances, feeling sure that she knew the answer.

'Do you know, they never did, and I never liked to ask what had happened to them, as it was none of my business.'

Frances looked at her notes again. 'Did you not think it odd that he dyed his hair?'

'I didn't even know that he did until after he was murdered and the police found the bottle of hair dye. But I thought nothing of it, even then. So many gentlemen have their little ways.'

After the breakfast things were cleared, and had been well scrubbed by Dora in a little stone sink at the back of the house, Will came in the butcher's cart to take them to church. The day was dull but with a crispness to the cold, and a strange quality in the air which Frances could not identify at first. Eventually she recognised it for what it was, a complete absence of London grime. The church was not far, and she found it a handsome edifice, in keeping with the village's past glory, with a neatly kept graveyard. Will assisted Frances, his mother and sister from the cart then drove away to bring the rest of the family. Frances and the two women walked together up the path to the church door, Dora with her arm linked to her mother's very like the way that Frances had walked with her father in his later months. 'There,' said Mrs Cranby, pointing her stick. 'That is the grave.' It was a bare mound of grass, with no slab or head-stone, only a small wooden board carved with the name of John Wright. 'I asked Willie to make that for him,' she said.

They walked together to the graveside and Mrs Cranby dropped the little wreath on the grass, and uttered a sigh. Soon afterwards the remaining Cranbys arrived and Frances greeted Alice, Will's wife, a rosy-faced young woman in a loose gown that suggested an impending addition to the family, and four other healthy-looking children clustering about her, in their Sunday-best clothes.

After the service, Frances was introduced to Reverend Jessup, a stout gentleman in his early fifties with a handsome ruddy face and once flaxen hair fading to grey, and Mrs Cranby explained the reason for the visit.

'Yes, I remember John Wright very well,' said the reverend, nodding, 'and I agree with Mrs Cranby, he did not appear to me to be suffering from any delusions. I used to call upon him as I do all of my parishioners and found him always in good spirits and with no trace of insanity.'

'Of course,' said Frances, 'it may be that he was insane but was adept at giving the impression that he was not.'

'I have heard of such persons,' said Jessup, 'but it was not only his manner that convinced me. I have heard that his sister claimed he was convinced that he was the heir to great wealth and indeed owned all of Hertfordshire. I have had in my time to deal with some very unfortunate cases, persons suffering from the wildest of delusions. Had John Wright suffered in this way, I am convinced that he would have revealed it to me. His madness would not have permitted him to put a stop to the thoughts that, according to his sister, consumed him. But I was in his company many a time and I can assure you that never once did he tell me he was the heir to a fortune, neither did he make any reference to Hertfordshire, or indeed any other county. In fact I cannot recall that he ever spoke to me of money at all, but only how happy he was with his life in the village and the charms of the country hereabouts.'

'Who paid for his burial?' asked Frances, recalling that no money had been found in the possession of the deceased man.

'The parish coffers, I'm afraid. His clothes were distributed to the poor and there was nothing else of any value. I have a picture of his here that you can see, it hangs in my office. Would you like to look at it? It's a very poor thing, but it is of the church.'

'I should very much like to see it,' said Frances. He took her into a small office room, barely furnished with a desk and chair, and scattered with papers and pamphlets. There hung on the wall a pencil drawing of the church in a simple frame.

'It was found in the house after his death,' explained Jessup. 'No one else cared for it, so, in view of the subject and its associations...'

It was, thought Frances, undoubtedly a picture of the church in which she stood, but not by any talented hand. The artist had made a great effort to get the proportions and perspective correct, efforts made obvious by repeated pencil lines, but had only succeeded in producing an effect of untidiness and confusion. Was this the work of the supposedly talented Mr Wright? She peered more closely at the picture. In the very bottom corner was what might have been thought to be a small tuft of grass, but because she now had a very good idea of what she might be looking for, she was able to see it for what it was, a signature. The initials were PG. This was not the work of John Wright, but of Percival Garton.

The family was waiting for her in the church vestibule, where Mrs Cranby had been found a comfortable chair. 'Will has told me you are looking for the man who killed Mr Wright,' said Alice, eagerly. 'And after all these years!'

'It seems from what everyone says about him that he was very well liked here,' said Frances.

'Oh, he was, Miss. My sister Clara was a house-maid there, and she was so upset when he was found like that.'

'Does Clara still live here? I should very much like to talk to her.'

'No, Miss, she married a carman and they've gone to live in Bethnal Green. I still write to her. Shall I ask her if she would mind talking to you?'

'Yes, I would be very grateful.'

Will took Alice, Dora and the children home, then returned for Frances and Mrs Cranby, and drove them further up the main street to a hand-some manor house surrounded by gardens. 'This is Tollington House,' he said. 'It used to be the home of the mill owner back in the old days. I heard say he had a dozen servants or more, but was a very cruel man. Mr Armitage, who has it now, is a retired military gentleman.'

Mr Armitage was about seventy, but very active, and his wife was about the same age, dignified but amiable. They both greeted Mrs Cranby with great warmth, and made Frances very welcome. Although Mrs Cranby had been a servant, and in one respect remained so, it said much for the kind-ness and condescension of the couple that they now treated her as a favoured guest. Mrs Armitage sat with Mrs Cranby in the morning room while her husband showed Frances the house. 'The house is very beautiful,' said Frances as they toured the elegant apartments. 'Are the contents much as they were when Mr Wright was here?'

'Yes, the furniture is of excellent quality. The various decorative articles are our own.'

'I expect that when you first saw the interior it was in some disarray,' said Frances, 'Mr Wright having departed so suddenly and then the police coming here to search everything.'

'It had been very thoroughly cleaned by his servants, but as you say, all had been practically turned upside down by the search.'

'You yourself found nothing of his, I suppose? No letters or papers?' asked Frances hopefully.

'Nothing at all I am afraid.'

'What a pity,' said Frances. 'If I could only discover why he left.'

'And he had just renewed the lease for a whole year only a month before,' said Mr Armitage.

'Oh?' said Frances. 'Then he cannot have anticipated having to leave.'

'Yes, according to Mr Mullin, the land agent, Mr Wright initially leased the house for only three months from the first of June, but he liked it so much he renewed in September. Each time Mr Mullin thought Mr Wright would leave he renewed again and then in May he said he was so content that he would make it his home for good, and signed for another year.'

They joined Mrs Armitage and Mrs Cranby, who were conversing in the morning room, and their hosts insisted that the visitors stay for luncheon. Frances, who was anticipating a long train journey home that afternoon, was grateful for what might be her last meal for some time. She was, it had to be admitted, a little disappointed in

347

her visit to Tollington House. What had she been hoping for – a vital letter slipped down the back of a drawer, a trinket with initials coming to light years after the strange events of the summer of 1869? But the police had searched and there was nothing left for her to find.

Over soup and roast mutton and almond pudding, the conversation was mainly taken up by Mrs Cranby talking about her happy times at Tollington House. 'And I say it is such a shame that Mr Wright's sister has never even been here to visit his grave!' she said firmly.

'Neither has his brother ever visited,' said Mrs Armitage.

'Why, I didn't know that he even had a brother,' said Mrs Cranby, astonished.

'Nor I,' said Mr Armitage.

'Oh dear!' said his wife, 'I had really thought I mentioned it.'

'Did you meet this brother?' asked Frances.

'No, no, it was something Mr Mullin said. Let me think – yes, it was not long after we settled here and he visited on a day when Mr Armitage had been called away unexpectedly. We were conversing about how strange it was that we knew so little of Mr Wright and he told me that one day, when he called upon him, a letter was delivered. Mr Wright opened the letter and read it, and straight away flew into a terrible passion. He said, 'My foolish brother!' or some words of that sort. Then as soon as he had said them he apologised to Mr Mullin for such a display. 'There is never a chain that does not have a weak link,' he said, or something very like it, and he asked Mr Mullin not to reveal what had passed. Mr Mullin assumed that the brother was not very respectable, and agreed to say nothing. Of course after Mr Wright's death, he did not feel bound by the promise.'

'Do you know if Mr Mullin told the police about this conversation?' asked Frances.

'I really cannot say,' said Mrs Armitage, and Frances sensed that she had told all she knew.

'Would it be possible for me to speak to him?'

'I regret that he died some years ago.'

Frances was silent for most of the remainder of the meal. Taking her leave of the Armitages, she and Mrs Cranby were collected by Will in the butcher's cart. At Ivy Cottage she bid the Cranbys farewell and promised faithfully that she would write to them. As she left, Dora thoughtfully provided her with a slab of fruit cake wrapped in paper. She spent the journey studying all the notes she had made, but it was not until she was on the train to Paddington that the true import of what Mrs Armitage had said struck her. When Wilfred had told Frances about Mary Ann Wright, and she recalled this with great clarity because the poignancy of it had affected her at the time, he said that Mary Ann had told the police that she had cared for poor mad John because he was her only brother.

That night, back in her own cold bed, her last thought before she slept was that the mystery of John Wright – who he was and why he had come to Tollington Mill – which the police had thought was solved over nine years ago, was not in fact solved at all.

CHAPTER EIGHTEEN

Monday was the busiest day of the week; with anxious customers bringing their Sunday coughs and chills into the shop, and the weekly wash to be tackled. Frances had barely a moment to herself, but at last when the evening drew in, she ate her simple meal and decided what course to take next. It would mean more expenditure, and time away from the shop where she had more than enough to do, but she felt she had to visit Somerset House. It was late morning, after she had completed her household duties, that she departed, feeling some measure of guilt at not being in her appointed place behind the counter. It only occurred to her as she was on the way that she was essentially, albeit for a brief time, mistress of the business and could therefore do as she pleased. Nevertheless she did not wish to waste time, and deemed that to walk all the way there would take too long. It cost five pence to take the yellow omnibus to Chancery Lane. Crowded together with other ladies and an assortment of baskets and parcels, in the stuffy interior, she felt fortunate that the weather was dry, or the straw which lined the floor would have been churned to a muddy foetid slush by that time of day. Progress was slow, for the vehicle stopped every few minutes for the boarding and alighting of passengers. By the time she reached her destination, much cramped and stifled and jolted about, she wondered if the journey would have been faster and more salubrious if she had walked. From there it was just a short distance to the Strand. Somerset House, home to numerous Government offices, was a daunting building so large that, approaching it, Frances feared she might spend all day just walking around it to discover where it was she had to go. She entered by the main gates from the Strand, and found herself in a great courtyard with the buildings continuing on all sides around her. Fortunately, a list of departments was posted there, and she found that the General Register Office was in the front portion of the building on the first floor. She was aware that Somerset House had been designed a century ago to house artistic and historical institutions, and, inside, those origins were still apparent, with high ceilings, decorative plasterwork, graceful columns and a curved sweeping staircase – all, she thought, sadly wasted now on what was no more than a collection of documents.

On the first floor a sign directed her to the office, and she entered a large panelled room where numerous people, who all seemed to know exactly what to do, were busily intent on studying large books laid upon ranges of tall, sloping-topped desks. There was a long counter rather like that of a post office, with clerks behind it, attending to customers with their bundles of papers, and other smaller desks where black-suited gentlemen were at work. Large books, the largest she had ever seen, heavily bound in thick boards and marked with letters of the alphabet, were stored in ranges of deep shelves. Frances glanced at the pages of a book that was being pored over by an intent-looking lady with gold-rimmed spectacles, and saw to her surprise that it was not, as she had supposed, a book of certificates. The thick vellum pages were nothing more than long lists of names, each with a set of numbers and letters beside it and the name of a place.

She felt for a moment utterly bewildered, but then decided that if these people could master what was required, then she too could do so. She approached one of the gentlemen working at a desk, selecting one whom she thought looked kindly, and explained that it was her first visit and she was not sure what she must do to find what she wanted. He was not for a moment discomfited at having to put his pen aside, and rose to show her about the room. The books, he said, were divided into three ranges; births, marriages and deaths. Each year was divided into four quarters and within each quarter alphabetically by sur-name. The books recorded only the names of those registered, the district in which the regis-tration had taken place and the reference number of the certificate. It cost a shilling to search a series of five years. If she found what she wanted then a certificate would cost two shillings and seven pence. Frances' face fell. She had only a few shillings to spare.

'Do you know what you are looking for?' asked the clerk, gently.

'Yes, a man whose death took place in April or possibly May of 1869. I need to know where he lived and his trade.'

'You might find what you want in the probate record,' said the clerk. 'Did he leave a will?'

'I'm afraid I don't know.'

'Try there first, and if you don't find what you want, come back here,' he said, and gave her directions to the Principal Probate Registry. Frances descended the staircase and returned to the courtyard which she now had to cross. Fortunately, a sign showed her where to proceed from there, and she soon found another large panelled room with more ranges of huge books. She walked along the shelves, seeing that the volumes were in year order, and within each year were divided alphabetically. She selected the first book for 1869 and put it on the desk. This was better – much better. Each entry was a brief paragraph about the grant of probate. She hardly hoped that she would find it but suddenly there it was; the entry for Solomon Cotter, who died on 21st April 1869. Probate had been granted to his widow, Marianne, and the value of the estate was £254 10s 4d. This Solomon Cotter, moreover, was a master baker of Irlam Road, Bootle. She stood there for quite a few minutes, almost afraid to shut her eyes in case when she opened them again she would find the words had vanished and the paragraph had been a product of her own wishful thinking. She read it again, and again, her eyes almost caressing the words. There was no mistake. Lewis Cotter's father had been a baker from Bootle, just as James Keane had claimed his own father was. She took her notebook and pencil from her pocket and carefully made an exact copy of the words. It was not proof, of course, but it was highly suggestive.

She returned to the General Registry Office. It would be worth the search fee to find out a little more about Lewis Cotter and his family. The newspapers had described him as aged twenty-six in April 1869, so she would look in 1843 for his birth. She found the births range, and began with the book marked A to C for the quarter ended March, where she found the birth of a Samuel Cotter listed in the registration district of Liverpool. Without the certificate there was no way of knowing if he was any relative of Lewis. In the quarter ended September 1844 there was the birth, again in Liverpool, of an Eleanor Cotter. Frances decided to go further back, and in the quarter ended December 1841, discovered the birth of Lewis Cotter, in Liverpool. The newspaper had been incorrect about his age, but that was not in Frances' experience an unusual circumstance. Lewis Cotter would therefore now be thirty-eight years of age. There was one more thing she needed to know. She sought out the clerk who had helped her before and asked if the registration district of Liverpool included Bootle. He consulted a volume, and said that it did. It occurred to Frances that as she had looked in the years 1840 to 1844 for Lewis Cotter she could search the same range of time for the birth of James Keane. If Keane had been telling the truth in that unguarded comment to his wife, and he was living under an assumed name, then presumably there would be no James Keane born in those years. What was her surprise, therefore, to discover the birth of James Keane in Liverpool in the quarter ended June 1843.

She thought about this for a time. She had assumed that Keane's name was made up, yet reflected that if a man wished to live a full life under another name he needed documents such as a birth certificate. It was possible to forge one, she imagined, but how much better it would be to use one that already existed and that could therefore be checked and verified if required. Had Cotter perhaps known the real James Keane, and if so, how would he have felt secure that the man would never appear and contest the identity? There was, she reflected, one way. The real James Keane must be dead.

She looked into her purse. It was worth the risk. She found the Deaths section, started at 1868 and began to work her way backwards. She found what she wanted in 1866. In that year, in the quarter ended March, James Keane had died in Liverpool aged twenty-two. The age and the place were right, although to be certain the certificates were required. She now had enough, however, to go to the police. They could ignore her suppositions but not facts such as these. She felt sure that even if Inspector Sharrock laughed her out of the station, the very same day he would send someone to order the certificates. Frances then realised that the same range of five years would also contain her mother's record of death. It was not hard to find. The books prior to 1866 did not trouble to record the age at death, yet there could be no mistake. Rosetta Jane Doughty had died in the quarter ended March 1864.

Frances was too young to recall her mother's

death, but Frederick had sometimes talked about it, her long illness, how a house once filled with light and laughter had become sombre, his father solitary and withdrawn, sometimes in tears. Aunt Maude had come to live with them, and their parents' bedroom had for a time been a sick room, which the children were not permitted to enter. The nature of the dreadful disease, from which their mother had suffered bravely and in silence, had never been spoken of. Frederick also remembered the day when his father had told him that his mother had gone to live in Heaven. He had felt sad and angry. No one had explained to him why this had happened. He was only grateful that Aunt Maude had not tried to take the place of his mother in any respect other than the provision of material necessities.

As Frances gazed at the impersonal entry in the register, she suddenly realised that there was something strange about it. Westbourne Grove, she felt sure, would have been part of the Paddington registration district, yet according to the book, her mother had died in Chelsea. Could this be an error? Or had her mother been removed to a convalescent home, and died there and not at home? Was this why she had not been buried at Kensal Green? But if that was the case, why had Cornelius not told her about it? She was obliged to trouble the clerk once more, who confirmed that Westbourne Grove was indeed in the Paddington registration district. 'If someone died in the Chelsea registration district, where might they be buried?' asked Frances.

Another volume was carefully perused. 'I visited

the grave as a child,' she said, 'and all I can recall is a very beautiful chapel with a domed roof.'

'Ah, yes,' he smiled, 'that would be Brompton.'

Frances resolved to ask her Uncle Cornelius about the circumstances of her mother's death at the earliest opportunity. Then she considered again. Her uncle, she thought, a man whom she had learned to admire and trust, had not been perfectly candid about family matters she felt she had a right to know. She looked into her purse again. There was just enough if she walked home. She ordered her mother's death certificate. She would have to return in a week to collect it.

It was a long walk but she was more than equal to it, up Drury Lane to Oxford Street, across Oxford Circus, then on to the corner of Hyde Park, and up Edgware Road to Paddington Green and the police station. She composed herself before she went in so as to seem as calm and sensible as possible, and not like some beggar who had walked the streets without a penny to her name. 'I would like to see Inspector Sharrock,' she said to the sergeant at the desk.

'You've just missed him,' said the sergeant, who clearly recognised her. 'He went tearing out of here in a very great hurry about five minutes ago. I can't say when he'll be back.'

'I suppose Constable Brown is not here?'

'He is with the Inspector.'

Frances reflected. With James Keane safely under lock and key there was no great urgency to her news. 'In that case, I will return tomorrow,' she said, 'but you may remind the Inspector when you next see him, that I promised not to trouble him again unless I had facts of importance.'

Frances proceeded along Bishop's Road and then to Westbourne Grove, where she could not resist stopping to look into the windows of Thomas Morgan Ltd, crammed with bargains of every kind, none of which she could afford, and notices pasted everywhere declaring 'Closing Down Sale! Everything Must be Sold!'

'Good afternoon, Mr Williamson, we meet again!' said a hearty voice by her side.

She looked up in alarm. Cedric Garton stood beside her, a broad smile on his face.

'I'm afraid I don't–,' she murmured, turning her head aside in embarrassment.

'Now don't deny it, please,' he taunted, gently. 'I never forget a face.'

Frances blushed deeply.

'I have to admit I did suspect you at the time,' he went on. 'Oh don't mistake me, it was well done, you might have convinced many, and with a little coaching you would have convinced me, too. So,' he added conspiratorially, 'not so much a Mary Ann as a Tom.'

Frances did not know to what he was referring in his last comment and made a firm decision not to enquire. 'Please accept my apologies, Sir,' she said.

'None necessary,' he said airily, 'and don't worry,' he lowered his voice to a whisper, 'your secret is safe with me!'

Frances felt relieved. 'Thank you, Sir,' she said, 'and I promise you it will never happen again.'

'Ah,' he exclaimed with a toss of the head, 'how many times have I heard those words! Now then, as I have nothing to do at present, I suggest we have some tea. No brandy and cigars for you this time, eh? Unless of course, you prefer–?'

She shuddered and shook her head. 'No, thank you, I do not want such things.'

'Well, off we go then!' He linked his arm in hers and to her astonishment she found herself walking down the street beside him. He was so jolly that she suddenly felt guilty about deceiving him and resolved to do so no more.

'Mr Garton, I feel I ought to tell you–'

'The reasons you accosted me in that very fetching attire? I really wish you *had* been a boy, you were quite a handsome youth.'

'But you ought to know my name.' She stopped and turned to face him. 'Before we say any more, I must tell you that I am Frances Doughty, daughter of William Doughty of the chemist's shop on the Grove. I have been trying to clear my father's name of any imputation that he made an error in your brother's prescription. And I may have done some reckless and foolish and quite improper things but I regret none of them; except possibly the last glass of brandy.'

She waited for his reaction. His eyebrows had risen in surprise, and he stared at her silently for a few moments. She half expected him to utter a sharp remark and walk away, but instead he said, 'Well, what a girl you are, to be sure! Can't fault you on loyalty to your pa. Not sure you're right about him, of course, but – I must say you don't *look* the adventurous sort.'

Frances felt relieved at making the confession. Now it only remained for her to withdraw from his company with as much dignity as possible. 'I am very sorry I tried to deceive you. Of course, I understand that you will want to have no conversation with me ever again.'

She was about to walk away, but he stopped her. 'Please don't leave, Miss Doughty, I beg you!' he appealed. 'I have come all the way from Italy to this miserable climate, to a house full of screaming babies and a sister-in-law who can't speak for crying. I was hoping to return home where I am sure my sisters are pining away most dreadfully for my company, but now I suddenly find I have to attend long, tedious meetings with the most boring fellows on earth, and read all sorts of legal papers I don't understand. It is a nightmare from beginning to end. I *like* you, Miss Doughty. You interest me. Let us go and have that tea.'

To her astonishment, he linked arms with her again, and before she knew what had happened they were once again walking down the Grove.

For a few moments she was too startled by this development to speak, then she realised that one of his comments was of importance. 'Your sisters have not accompanied you here?' she said.

'Oh dear me no, they have a horror of the English climate and will not stir from home.'

Which meant, thought Frances, that the lady at Kensal Green Cemetery who had placed the posy on Percival Garton's grave could not have been a sister.

'So, Miss Doughty, or I could call you Frank if you were to prefer it,' he added with a sly smile.

She felt her face colouring again. 'Please, no, my real name will be best.'

'It is unnecessary, of course, to ask you why you believe in your father's innocence. I can have no comment to make on the matter. But what do *you* believe to be the truth of the business?'

She hesitated, then decided that she would learn more from him if she stated what was on her mind. 'I believe that your brother was murdered,' she said.

'You astound me! Why ever would anyone want to murder poor harmless Percy?'

'But what else can it have been? Pure *strychnia* is rarely taken by accident.'

'True,' he conceded. 'And I expect that those who can lay their hands on it would know its effect and would not elect to destroy themselves with it if there was anything else. Not that I believe for one moment that Percy took his own life. I saw nothing in his manner or in his personal affairs that would suggest it was possible.'

They arrived at the teashop, and were conducted to a pleasant table, where Cedric ordered tea, scones, and bread and butter. 'I have been pummelling my brain to think of the name of even one person who might have wished Percy harm, but without a single result,' said Cedric. '*Please* say you do not suspect Henrietta. The woman is distraught at his loss, and is quite genuine in my estimation. I have never seen such a devoted couple, especially after so many years of marriage. Sometimes one might almost have imagined them to be newlyweds, they were so affectionate.' He gave a slight shudder.

'I suspect James Keane,' said Frances.

'Hmm,' said Cedric, thoughtfully. 'Keane has

361

been a surprise to me. He is, essentially, a stupid and unimaginative man. He cannot, in my opinion, have committed the frauds on the bank without help. Of course there is this missing artist the police are looking for, who may be the key to the whole thing. Perhaps he was the clever one. The only thing is, say what one will against the egregious Mr Keane, he did hold Percy in the very highest esteem. I sometimes felt Percy did not regard *him* in the same light, but he certainly tolerated him.'

'Did they ever quarrel?'

He pursed his lips in thought. 'Not quarrel, exactly. I did once walk in on a conversation where Percy was accusing Keane of carelessness about something or other, but I never learned what it was, and they stopped talking as soon as I came into the room. But that was the only actual dispute I ever witnessed between them. No, the main reason I think Keane cannot have killed Percy is that it seems to me that if a crime was committed, then it was a very clever one.'

'Did your brother ever discuss Mr Meadows with you?'

'Only a passing mention. There were some pictures of his in the house, as one might expect. They've all been sold, now. At least I assume so, as Keane came round just after Percy's death and took them all away.'

The tea arrived, and for a while they sipped and ate thoughtfully.

'What were the subjects of the pictures?' asked Frances.

'Oh, landscapes, houses, castles, that sort of

thing. Nothing that appealed to me. I prefer – portraiture.'

'Do you recall the locations of any of the subjects?'

'I am afraid I did not pay a very great deal of attention to them.'

'But that could be an important clue!' said Frances, earnestly. 'If we knew where Mr Meadows drew his pictures, it might tell us something of his origins, or even where he is now. Please do try to remember!'

'You are very demanding of a fellow's brain,' protested Cedric. 'I am sure it is quite unhealthy to use it too often.' He chewed a morsel of scone and butter. 'There was, now I think about it, one that attracted my attention – Berkeley Castle – unfortunate incident in the history of our glorious Royal family – not for a lady's ears.'

'Do you know where Berkeley Castle is?' asked Frances, hopefully.

'Yes,' he said confidently. 'I believe it is somewhere in England.'

Frances wrote the name in her notebook, and resolved to find the answer when she reached home. 'Do you know how Mr Keane and your brother first became acquainted? Or indeed when or where?'

'You are full of questions, Miss Doughty,' said Cedric regretfully. 'I wish I had the answers.'

'I am sure Mrs Garton would know, but of course it would be most improper of me to enquire.'

'Even you have your limits of daring, I see.' He smiled. He sipped his tea. 'But to return to the matter under discussion, this supposed murder, assuming that it was one. The last time I spoke to Inspector Sharrock I was given to understand that the police had accepted the verdict of the inquest and were making no further enquiries. To your way of thinking, not only has the murderer escaped without being suspected of the crime, the police do not even believe that a crime has been committed. That to my mind is a singular achievement. If I was to attempt such a thing – and I am a far cleverer man than Keane, though I try not to let it spoil my enjoyment of life – I would hardly know where to begin. And I am sure I would make many mistakes and be discovered quite easily.'

'That is my difficulty,' said Frances. 'I can see that Mr Keane had a motive to commit the crime, but I am unable to prove how it was done.'

'To begin with,' said Cedric, 'where would one obtain a sufficient amount of pure strychnine? Surely only a doctor or a chemist could do so easily. *I* could not walk into a chemists' shop and ask for such a thing without it attracting *some* attention and if it was to be stolen that would surely be remarked upon. In fact, and you must forgive me for mentioning it, the only premises in the area which is missing a bottle of strychnine is Doughty's.'

'We have accounted for that,' said Frances sternly.

'Two or three grains the doctor said,' mused Cedric. 'But of course if the poison was in the medicine bottle, it would have to have been several times that amount, for anyone to take two or three grains in just a few teaspoonfuls.'

'Perhaps as much as thirty,' said Frances. 'I agree, it would not be an amount for anyone to obtain easily, and without detection.'

'What about those vermin killers Dr Collin mentioned at the inquest?' asked Cedric. 'He thought they could not have been used. Tell me about those.'

'They can be bought by anyone,' said Frances, 'but the drug is dyed with Prussian blue or mixed with soot so no mistake can be made in its use. No dye of any kind was found in your brother's stomach, so he could not have swallowed *strychnia* from that source.'

'Is it possible to remove the pure strychnine from the dye?'

'Yes, it can easily be done by–,' she paused, 'but only a chemist would know how to do it. Having said that, a person of education, able to obtain the right books, could learn what to do, but they would then need the right materials and equipment, and some private place where they would not be observed.'

'You couldn't just sieve it out or pick it out with a pin, or some such?'

Frances smiled. 'I wouldn't care to try,' she said.

'And then,' said Cedric, 'having somehow obtained the poison, it would have to be introduced into the bottle without disturbing the wrapping or the cork.' He shook his head. 'If Keane did all this unseen, while not even in the same house, he is a much cleverer fellow than I had imagined him. I am only surprised, Miss Doughty, that you do not

365

suspect me.'

'Why is that?'

'I had thought that I was mentioned in my brother's will, which gives me ample motive, and of course the fact that I was in Paris at the time of his death, is not, to your method of reasoning, an obstacle to my guilt. Then, of course, my origins must certainly enhance my status as a suspect – born in Italy, the land of the Borgias, where arsenic may be purchased on any street corner and used to dispatch your enemies with impunity.'

'Your brother left a very great fortune. Was the amount a surprise to you?'

'No. I knew he lived well in London, I saw that for myself when I last visited.'

'And the source of his wealth was the business he inherited from his grandfather?'

'Yes.'

Frances looked at him carefully but could find no indication that he was stating other than what he believed to be the truth about his brother's fortune.

'Did you see the business for yourself?'

'No, I am a great deal younger than Percy, and did not start my travels until after he came to London.'

'It must have been a very large business,' she ventured, 'since he seems to have lived very comfortably from the capital ever since.'

He smiled. 'Miss Doughty, you are not a lady who asks frivolous questions, just to make a noise. You have reasons of your own, ones which can be mysterious to others.'

Frances did not feel she could suggest to Cedric

that his brother might have been a part of James Keane's fraudulent schemes. 'I was wondering if your brother had other business interests in London, perhaps a partnership with James Keane. He may have uncovered Mr Keane's criminal activities and tasked him about them. Then Mr Keane could have got a confederate to poison him.'

Cedric leaned back, thoughtfully. 'Ah – I see – scandal, bribery, corruption, and the love of filthy lucre, all leading to murder most foul. What a mind you have, Miss Doughty! You'll be suggesting next that my brother had a beautiful mistress, who tried to poison Henrietta to dispose of her rival, only to mistakenly kill the man whose heart she most desired.' He placed the back of his hand to his forehead in a theatrical pose. 'She is, even now, declining in an attic room somewhere, just prior to throwing herself into the Thames.'

Frances looked at him disapprovingly.

'I know you will say these are fanciful ideas, but no less fanciful than the one you have suggested to me,' he said, more seriously. 'Sad to say, life is not a work of fiction. Drama is something that happens on the stage, melodrama doubly so.' He adopted a gloomy expression. 'How I wish that were not the case.'

'You are mocking me,' she said.

He threw up his hands in despair. 'Oh, what is a fellow to do in this place?'

'I am sure I cannot be the best entertainment London can offer.'

'Better than Mr Marsden with whom I had an appointment half an hour ago. How I dislike the man! My solicitor; who looks upon the world as

367

something he can suck dry. Would you believe, I am deputed by my family to try and overturn Percy's will, and must remain here until I succeed? Please, Miss Doughty, I beg of you, save me from boredom, it is a fate that harrows my soul.'

'I was unaware that you had pressing business and will keep you from it no longer,' said Frances, rising. 'Only brace yourself for the ordeal and think how much brighter the world will look when you emerge from Mr Marsden's office.'

She thanked him politely for the tea and he thanked her warmly for the company, but before they parted she extracted a promise that he would try to arrange an interview with Henrietta Garton.

Frances returned home to find the shop once again crowded and Herbert looking at her resentfully. At the very first opportunity she consulted her Atlas, and was able to discover that Berkeley Castle was in Gloucestershire, within a very few miles of Tollington Mill.

That evening she was reading through her notes, and thinking that she would go back to the police station as early as possible the following morning, when Wilfred called. She was naturally pleased to see him and hoped, just for a moment, that Keane had at last confessed. His expression as he entered the parlour told her that the news was troubling.

'Miss Doughty, I thought in view of your interest in the matter, you ought to be told – James Keane is dead. He was murdered earlier today.'

CHAPTER NINETEEN

'He was in the prison hospital,' said Wilfred, quite unaware of the effect his words had had on Frances, who had just seen her hope of the reward money she needed to save the business unfold its wings and fly away. 'The injury to his face wasn't healing well, and he was in a lot of pain. He was resting in bed, under morphine, very drowsy, and not considered in need of constant watching as he was hardly in any position to attempt an escape. Yesterday he had a visitor, a clerk from Marsden's solicitors, at least that was how the man represented himself, and he had all the right papers with him to prove that he was from there. And when he came to Mr Keane's bedside it was obvious that Keane recognised him. The man had a great bundle of legal papers and he laid them over the bed and talked about them to Mr Keane. There was a warder and a nurse in the room at the time, but I suppose they were not as watchful as they might have been. They are being questioned now. When the man left Keane appeared to be sleeping, which was not, in the circumstances, very surprising, but when the nurse next checked him, he was dead. A small thin-bladed knife had been run into his heart. It would have been the work of a moment, and the papers must have hidden what was happening.'

Frances was silent for a while. 'I disliked the

man very much,' she said at last, 'but I would not have wanted this. Much that I needed to know will now be forever obscure. Has the murderer been identified?'

'No, Miss. He was a tall young man, in his twenties, and appeared to be a respectable clerk of the type employed by a solicitor. He spoke well, seemed quite sane, and addressed Mr Keane by name. Naturally we spoke to Mr Marsden, who stated that he had not sent a clerk to see Mr Keane, and did not recognise in the description of the young man any employee of his.'

'I suppose,' said Frances, resignedly, 'that there is no reason now why I should not tell you that I believed James Keane to be Lewis Cotter, the murderer of Mr Truin in 1869. I discovered that Mr Keane first came to London only days after the murder, and I have proof, which I obtained only today, that he was living under an assumed name.' Frances showed the constable the information she had gleaned from Somerset House. 'Mrs Keane will, I am sure, confirm that her husband had once told her of his humble connections, and also confided to her that James Keane was not the name he was born with. I hope now that she will be able to re-think the evidence she gave at the coroner's court, and admit her mistake.'

'But who wanted to murder Mr Keane?' said Wilfred. 'Someone took a great deal of trouble to remove him.' He hesitated. 'Um – since you have taken an interest in his affairs – can you suggest what might have been the motive?'

'That,' said Frances, 'is very difficult, as I believe that so many people were eager to see Mr Keane's demise as to be sufficient in number to form a Society. Mrs Keane had every possible motive, as did her footman, with whom, I believe,' Frances lowered her gaze briefly, but it needed to be said, 'she is in a most irregular association. Mr Keane's employers at the bank will be glad to hear the news, as will any persons who assisted him in his frauds. Mr Meadows, for example, if he should still be alive. Then, of course, there are the relatives of poor Mr Truin, who, if they suspected Mr Keane of the murder, might, in the absence of any proof they could show to the police, have decided to take the law into their own hands. The man who actually committed the crime may have been someone hired for the task.'

Wilfred scribbled rapidly in his notebook. 'We are employing an artist to draw a portrait from the impressions of those who saw the murderer,' he said. 'When I have it, would you come to the station to look at it?'

'Yes, of course,' said Frances. She could not help but be flattered. Whether they liked it or not, all of a sudden, the police required her help and not the other way about.

That evening she sat down with the shop and household accounts, totalling with a guilty horror what she had expended on the now useless visits to Tollington Mill and Somerset House. Even with the business prospering, it was impossible to accumulate in just a few weeks what was required to pay the current bills and renew the lease. Several notes from creditors had arrived that morning. She had funds to meet the most pressing, but the others would have to wait.

On the following day she went to Paddington Green police station, where Inspector Sharrock was looking more than usually harassed. 'I understand you wished to see me?' she asked, unable to repress a slight smile.

'If you would come into my office, Miss Doughty, I will show you the portrait we have had made of the murderer of Mr Keane,' said Sharrock brusquely, leading the way.

Frances sat at the desk, and he dropped two pictures in front of her, then plumped down into his chair, which creaked loudly at this unwarranted treatment. 'Do you recognise the man?' he asked, then suddenly leaned forward, 'and let me add, Miss Doughty, that if you were a gentleman, you would now be at the very top of my list of suspects, and possibly already under arrest!'

'I assure you, Inspector,' said Frances, with great dignity, 'that though I would have been pleased to hear of Mr Keane's death, it would only have been if he had died at the end of a hangman's rope, after being found guilty in a court of law of the murder of Mr Garton. His death at this juncture gives me no satisfaction.' She perused the pictures. One was a full-length portrait of a slender young man, clean-shaven, with hair cut very close to his head, and wearing a sombre dark suit and spectacles. The second picture was a head and shoulders view.

'Both the nurse and the warder have agreed that the pictures are a very good likeness,' said Sharrock. 'Well? Is it anyone you know?'

Frances frowned. Her first impression was that she had never seen the man portrayed, and yet there was something familiar about him, a sleepy look about the eyes, and she wondered if she had once seen him dressed very differently. 'This man,' she said, 'may have disguised himself to commit the crime. He might have had whiskers which he shaved off and longer hair, and did not wear spectacles. Is the artist still here?'

'I'm afraid not.'

'Then give me a piece of clean paper and a pencil and I will see what I can do.' She saw him hesitate. 'I promise you I will not draw on what your artist has done.'

Sharrock looked doubtful, but after a search through the mound on his desk found what was wanted and pushed them across to her. He watched, puzzled, as Frances tore little strips of paper and used the pencil to colour them. It was hardly the right shade for hair as it was a bluish-purple, but it did well enough. She then rolled the strips like pieces of quill-work, and laid them on top of the larger portrait to resemble a moustache and side whiskers. After a moment's thought she added another piece for a beard. It was the flash of purple at the throat that decided her. 'I know who this is!' she exclaimed. 'It is Guy Berenger, the man who managed the gallery.'

Sharrock leaped out of his chair as if shot by a catapult, then leaned across the paper and stared at it intently. 'Well done, Miss Doughty,' he said excitedly. 'I see it now!'

'Has he been questioned?' asked Frances.

'He was not at his lodgings when we went to see him, and I suspect will not be there again. Clearly we must redouble our efforts to find him.'

'That does explain how he was able to obtain papers from Mr Keane's solicitor,' said Frances. 'Mr Keane had an office at the back of the gallery. He was careless with his documents and Mr Berenger was in a good position to take what he needed.'

'But the motive?' Sharrock suddenly slapped his hand to his forehead. 'Why yes, of course! It must have been Berenger who did the forgeries for Keane! It was Berenger who was Meadows all along, and under our very noses! He must have been afraid that Keane would peach on him in return for a reduction in sentence.'

'And he was much cleverer than he pretended to be,' said Frances. 'I suspect that the failed artist with a taste for alcoholic beverages was just as false a personage as the sober clerk.' A new thought struck her, about the real identity of Guy Berenger, but she did not voice it. She had no proof, and Sharrock would only dismiss it as one of her wild fancies.

'Well, I won't trouble you any longer, Miss Doughty,' said Sharrock, bustling, 'we have to do our best to find Mr Berenger, or whatever name he is using now.'

She rose to leave. 'Inspector, I must ask you one more thing. Will you be interviewing Mrs Keane again? In view of recent events she now has no reason to protect her husband or her father. I am hoping that she will admit at the very least that she made an error in her evidence at the inquest on Mr Garton. My father's memory is tarnished by this whole affair and I would have it bright again.'

'Ah,' said Sharrock. He paused, awkwardly, and

drummed his fingers on the desk. 'I am sorry, Miss Doughty, but I think it will not be possible to interview Mrs Keane for some very considerable time, and perhaps never.'

'What do you mean?' said Frances, seeing yet another hope being dashed to pieces.

Sharrock pulled a fat and battered watch from his pocket and studied it briefly. 'You'll have the news soon enough. Mrs Keane caused a great commotion when she was told of the death of her husband, and said a great many things which were found to be very shocking. A servant was involved, I believe, and I will say no more. Dr Collin took the view that the lady's mind had quite broken down and I believe that even as we speak she is being removed to some establishment which will provide her with the safe and secure place that she now requires.'

Frances uttered a small groan of despair. 'How then will I clear my father's name?'

He gazed at her, and even in his coarse face there was a faint tinge of sympathy. 'Well, I must get on to Mr Berenger's trail. Perhaps he will have something to say.'

Frances walked home, her eyes misting over with misery, but her mind would not let the matter alone, and at last she had a new idea. There was, she thought, just one more person to whom she might appeal for help.

As soon as she was able, she sent Tom with a note to Dr Collin, and, as a result, was granted an interview with him later that day. When Dr Collin showed her into his surgery it was with an expression of frank curiosity. 'I assume from your note that this is not a professional consultation,' he said.

'That is correct,' said Frances, 'and you must believe me I would not have spoken to you on this subject at all had it not been of the very greatest importance.'

He raised his eyebrows and sat back in his leather chair but said nothing, waiting for her to go on.

'I understand that you are Mrs Keane's doctor,' Frances began.

'I am,' he said cautiously, 'but of course you must realise that I can say nothing at all to you about her medical condition.'

'It was on another matter that I wished to speak,' Frances assured him. 'I appreciate that it may be some time before the lady can be questioned, but I hoped that you could tell me if she has said anything to you on the subject of her evidence at the coroner's court.'

'She has not,' said Collin, 'and I wouldn't consider it a suitable subject for her to be troubled with.'

'And neither would I expect you to,' said Frances, quickly, 'but if she should volunteer anything...'

'Even if she did,' said Collin, 'I am not sure that anything she said would be much attended to.'

Frances saw that it was time to be frank. 'I called upon her before Mr Keane's death. She freely admitted to me that her testimony was untrue and that she had never even entered our shop. But I cannot find it in my heart to blame the lady; I think she was forced to do it by her husband.'

Dr Collin looked sympathetic, but shook his head. 'Believe me, Miss Doughty, I can do no more than listen to what she says. I can hardly induce a lady who is very unwell into making an admission that she gave false testimony.'

'I have no desire for her to be punished,' said Frances. 'I would be quite content if she was simply to admit to someone other than myself that she made an innocent mistake. It would mean so very much to me,' she pleaded. 'Just a mistake that is all; nothing that she can be blamed for. Anyone may make a mistake; you yourself did so at my father's inquest.'

'I *did?*' said Collin sitting up straight in astonishment.

'Indeed you did, which shows how easily and blamelessly it may be done.'

'I am not aware of any error in my testimony,' said Collin a little stiffly. 'Perhaps you could enlighten me.'

'You said that my father suffered from both headaches and toothaches,' explained Frances. 'He certainly did have headaches, but toothaches, never.'

'I was quite sure that he did,' said Collin, mystified.

'He never complained of them to me,' said Frances firmly, 'and I think it is safe to say that if he did not complain of them, then he did not have them.' She rose. 'Please think of what I have said. One word from Mrs Keane, one expression of regret for the slightest of errors, and my father's reputation would be restored.'

She took her leave, observing a touch of strain

377

in Dr Collin's noted affability of nature.

On the following morning, Frances' mind was occupied in the necessary task of composing a letter to Mrs Cranby. How guilty she felt at raising that lady's hopes that an answer might be found to the mystery of the death of Mr Wright, and how impossible it now seemed that she would ever find it. She could do no more than assure the Cranbys that the man who was probably responsible for the death of Wright had gone to find his punishment in some place beyond human retribution. Before she could find time to put pen to paper, however, a letter was delivered to her. It was from Clara Simmons, Alice Cranby's sister, who had once been a maid at Tollington House and was now married to a carman in Bethnal Green.

Dear Miss Doughty
Alice has written to me all about your visit, and how you are looking to find who killed Mr Wright. I have often thought about this as he was a very fine gentleman, and I was very sad when he was murdered. On Saturday morning I will be taking the children to the Museum in Cambridge Road, and if it would be convenient we might meet there, and I will tell you what I remember of Mr Wright, and hope that it will help you. We may meet by the fountain at 10 a.m.
Clara Simmons

Frances read the letter and sighed. Only a few days ago the words would have filled her with great excitement at the prospect of uncovering new clues, but now, how useless it all seemed. Nevertheless, she thought it only polite to go. The

378

cost of the omnibus would only, after all, bring her a shilling or so nearer to ruin. She wrote back to Clara agreeing to meet her as requested.

Frances had never visited the museum at Bethnal Green, but had heard people say it was a very fine thing, and provided a wholesome diversion and salutary education for persons of all walks of life. There were maps of London on her father's bookshelves which told her where it was located, and pamphlets from the omnibus companies which she studied so as to find her way.

On Saturday morning, Frances took the yellow omnibus as far as Cheapside and was then able to hail the chocolate brown which would go to Bethnal Green Road. It was not a part of London she knew, except that it had had at one time a reputation for unhealthy dwellings and criminal activities of every kind, and for all she knew, still did. She comforted herself with the thought that any robber who took her bag would be ill-rewarded for his trouble.

The omnibus kept to the larger public thoroughfares, and, by doing so, Frances suspected that she was being protected from the sight and smells of the dirt and misery in which she knew some persons passed their lives. Whatever circumstances she might be reduced to, she thought, she knew that such abject distress would never be hers. She would be dependent upon her uncle, but at least her home would be warm and clean and she would not go without food. Alighting on the corner of Cambridge Road, she found a not unpleasant commercial street, thronged with people who, while far from the most elegant of persons, had some pretensions to being well-dressed. It was in many ways reminiscent of Westbourne Grove, though not, of course, of the same class. There were drapers, milliners, bakers, coopers, tin plate shops, booksellers, and even to her amazement a dairy, where the owner thought nothing of keeping his cows in what should have been his front parlour, and offering to draw off a pint of milk into the customers' own jug as if he was a tapster drawing beer.

In a few minutes she found herself outside the museum, a handsome building of warm red brick, with decorative murals representing the worlds of art, science and agriculture, suggestive of the educational nature of its contents. Outside was the largest fountain Frances had ever seen. Some thirty feet in height and still larger across, it was faced with ornamental pottery tiles and topped with a statue of St George slaying a dragon. Frances thought it utterly splendid. There were crowds of people of every rank of society all wanting to be admitted to the museum, but a young woman was standing waiting by the fountain, with two neatly dressed children of about seven and eight years of age. She looked similar enough to Alice Cranby to be her sister, but as Frances approached she saw with some concern how thin the children were, and the fragile, troubled look of their mother, and a fading yellow bruise on her cheek.

'Mrs Simmons? I am Frances Doughty.'

'Oh,' said the young woman, her face brightening in a becoming smile, 'I am so happy to meet you – Alice told me all about how you had gone all that way to see Mrs Cranby. Did you have a pleasant visit?'

'Very pleasant indeed, everyone could not have been kinder.' Frances smiled at the children, who looked up at her with distrust and clung to their mother's skirts.

'Now then, Eddie and Johnnie, you say hallo to Miss Doughty,' said Clara. The boys mumbled what might have been a greeting and turned their heads away.

'They can be a little shy, sometimes,' said Clara, apologetically. 'Would you like to go into the museum?'

'I would like to very much,' said Frances, wondering how much it might cost, and was pleasantly surprised to find that it was free. The interior reminded her of a railway station, with a high arching roof graced, and indeed probably supported, by slender iron columns. There were two galleries running the length of the building with decorative iron railings, and a very handsome marble mosaic floor.

'The museum itself is a thing worth seeing,' said Frances.

'I come here when I can,' said Clara. 'There are lots of pretty pictures and nice furniture and china. And there is an exhibit all about food, but most people find that very dull.'

Frances stopped by one of the many glass cases ranged along the floor to look at some delicately crafted oriental porcelain. 'I would like to hear all that you can remember about Mr Wright,' she said.

'Oh, he was a very fine looking young man,' said Clara. 'Very clever with all his drawings.

Beautiful drawings, Miss, all kinds of things, he could make them look just like the real thing. Better than a photograph.'

'Did you ever hear him say anything about where he had lived or what he had done before he came to Tollington Mill?' asked Frances, hopefully.

'No, never, Miss. He never spoke about his life before.'

Perhaps, thought Frances, the villagers of Tollington Mill were used to wealthy gentlemen who liked to come there so they could forget the world of commerce and obligation. 'Did he ever entertain visitors from outside the village? People you didn't know?'

'No, Miss, nothing like that.'

'He posted his own letters, I believe?'

'Yes, always. He said he enjoyed the walk, even if the weather was very bad. I said I didn't mind going, but he wouldn't have it.'

'And he received many letters, too?'

'Yes, but I don't know who sent them. I thought–,' Clara paused.

Frances felt a leap of hope. 'Yes?'

'I thought that whoever wrote to him it was always the same person, the same writing.'

Such a tiny clue, thought Frances. 'Can you think of anyone who might have wanted to kill him?'

'Oh, no, Miss, and if I had known such a thing, I would have told the police straight away.'

Frances was finding it hard to hide her disappointment. Had she really come all this way to speak to a woman who knew nothing?

'What is your opinion of the statement made by his sister that John Wright was insane? Did you think him to be so?'

'Not at all, Miss, I never saw any sign of it,' said Clara indignantly. 'All that nonsense about him being afraid of an enemy and dyeing his hair, I never heard such a story in all my life! If you ask me, it was the sister who was not right in the head.'

'Well, it seems he did have an enemy,' said Frances.

'Maybe, but he never dyed his hair. It was natural black.'

Frances had been staring at a carved jade snuff-bottle, but this suddenly lost its attraction. 'Why do you say that?'

'Because it's true,' said Clara firmly. 'I never saw a hair dye that didn't leave marks on the pillow cases, and his were always white as white.'

'But the police found the bottle of hair dye in his cabinet,' Frances reminded her.

'They may have done, Miss, but that was after he was dead and the house had been closed up for over a month. I cleaned that bathroom many a time, and turned out all the cupboards regular, and I never saw a bottle of dye anywhere. And I gave the house a good clean before it was closed up and there was no bottle of dye there then.'

'Did you tell this to the police?' asked Frances.

'I did, but they never believed me. They said that it was there as plain as plain could be, and I must have missed it. I'll tell you now, if I was to go into a court and swear on the bible, I would say just the same.'

Frances wondered what that could mean, if

indeed it meant anything. It was, she thought regretfully, easy enough to prove a fact, that something had been present, but very hard to prove its absence.

Clara sat down on a bench facing a display of small paintings, and the children clustered at her side. 'I brought something for you to look at Miss,' she said, and drew a small parcel from her bag. Frances sat by her and watched in curiosity as the string was untied and the paper opened to reveal a book. It was bound in dark red leather, and the covers and the edges of the pages were very badly charred. It took a moment or two before she guessed what it was. 'This is Mr Wright's sketch book,' said Clara proudly.

'I was told he burnt it up!' exclaimed Frances.

'He did put it in the fire, just before he left, and he said to me, "now Clara, be a good girl and make quite sure that it is all burnt to ashes," but as soon as he was out of the room I got the tongs and pulled it out. I felt a bit guilty afterwards, I suppose in a way it was stealing, so I didn't tell anyone I had it, but I just couldn't bear to see all those beautiful pictures gone forever. Do you think I was wrong?' she said anxiously.

Frances opened the book, and stared at a drawing of Tollington House. 'No,' she said at last, 'I think you did just the right thing.' As she studied the picture, the deft workings of the artist's pencil, which had, with just a few strokes, created an unmistakable image, she suddenly felt a prickling sensation at the nape of her neck. She turned the pages, and saw a view of the village street, a farmer driving past in his dog-cart, and some young women in their Sunday best walking up to the church. What she was seeing was, she knew, impossible. The subjects of the drawings were unimportant, except that they showed the artist's taste, but the style was most strangely familiar. Could it really be that the missing Mr Meadows and the long-dead Mr Wright could be the same man? But if that was the case, Guy Berenger – who would have been no more than fourteen when the drawings were done – could not possibly be Meadows.

'They are lovely pictures,' said Clara, breaking a long silence. The children huddled close to her, making little whimpering noises. Frances suspected that they were hungry. She groped in her purse and found two pennies she could hardly spare, and gave them one each. 'Oh thank you, Miss, I'm sure that's very kind. Say thank you to the kind lady!'

The children mumbled their thanks, and looked at Frances with less suspicion than before. Frances turned another page and found a picture, which was undoubtedly that of Mrs Garton. Younger and very slender then, it showed a woman of great beauty and grace, with a tender smile on her lips. Frances wondered what Henrietta had been gazing at. She had seen the look before, she recalled, when the Gartons had walked together on the Grove, and Henrietta had smiled up at her husband, but her husband was not present in the portrait and she seemed to be looking directly at the artist. She turned another page. This was a street scene, and Henrietta was walking arm in arm with a gentleman who Frances did not recognise. He was thin, aged about forty, with a narrow face, short side whiskers, a well-trimmed beard and a serious expression.

'This is another very good likeness of Mrs Garton,' said Frances. 'Who is the gentleman with her?'

'Why, that is Mr Garton, of course,' said Clara.

'Surely not,' said Frances. 'Some friend of his, perhaps. This does not resemble him in the slightest.'

Clara looked at the picture. 'No, that is Mr Garton, and I would say it was very like.'

Frances could only stare at the page before her. Try as she might, imagining the passage of time that could have changed his features, and the accumulation of flesh which had come with good living, even allowing for those things, it was clear to her now that Percival Garton of Bayswater, the man who had died in an agony of poisoning with *strychnia*, was not the same Percival Garton who had lived with Henrietta in Gloucestershire. For a moment she felt utterly confused, wondering which of the two men could be the real Garton, then she reflected that it must be the London man, for Cedric Garton had identified the body of his dead brother. Then she recalled something that Cedric had told her, and finally she knew the answer. She was obliged to stifle the urge to laugh.

'Are you feeling well, Miss?' asked Clara, with a worried frown.

'I – yes – I am just surprised at these portraits. May I borrow this book? I think it contains some important information and should be shown to the authorities.'

Clara opened her eyes wide. 'Really, Miss? Well I never! Yes, of course, you may take it and welcome. Will it help discover who killed Mr Wright?'

'I hope it may,' said Frances. 'At any rate, I am now sure that I know who killed Mr Garton.'

As she travelled home, trying to erase the sight of the two boys with their pinched frightened faces, and their anxious mother, Frances reviewed the notes she had made. In the last weeks she had learned a great deal, but each succeeding fact had been no more than another piece in a great puzzle which she had been quite unable to assemble. Something had been missing from the heart of the puzzle and its absence had meant that none of the other pieces would fit together. The new information was acting as a catalyst in her mind, and everything was starting to draw together to form a picture. She took out her notebook, and began to write, and by the time she reached home, had almost completed composing an account of what she now felt sure had occurred.

As she passed by the shop on her way to the front door, she glanced in, seeing that there were numerous customers within, and hurried up to the parlour, determining to finish her notes and then go to the police. Wilfred was waiting for her, and seemed relieved when she entered.

'Constable Brown,' she exclaimed. 'I am so glad you have called, I have some information of very great importance.'

'Miss Doughty,' he said seriously, 'I have been sent to bring you to the station at once.'

CHAPTER TWENTY

As Frances was ushered into Inspector Sharrock's office, a man seated there rose and greeted with her a slight bow. She had not met him before, but saw that he was of middling years, and respectably dressed in a dark suit, with the air of formal deference appropriate to a very superior class of servant.

'Miss Doughty,' said Sharrock, briskly, 'this is Mr Robert Edwards, who was formerly manservant to Mr Percival Garton. I think you should hear what he has to say, and then I will ask you to examine the item he has brought.'

On the desk Frances saw a large gentleman's winter cloak, of the best quality, folded neatly on its wrapping paper.

'Miss Doughty, I wish first of all to express my deepest sympathies at the many tribulations you have suffered recently,' said Edwards. 'I hope that it may be my lot to bring some alleviation to your distress.'

Frances secretly thought that the best alleviation at that moment would be about three thousand pounds, but she merely thanked him politely.

'When my poor Master died so tragically, Mrs Garton was too distraught to attend to anything in the way of household business, but in recent days she has been seeing about disposing of certain items to deserving charitable causes,' explained

Edwards. 'I have been pleased to assist Mrs Garton in going through the Master's possessions. In recognition of my services over the last several years, Mrs Garton has very kindly told me that I could have Master's cloak as a gift. It is this that I have brought here today. As you see the cloak is new, in fact Master wore it only once, on the night he died. It seemed to me in perfect condition but when I examined it I discovered something unusual, and at once saw that it had some significance.' He unfolded the cloak, and showed Frances the interior of a pocket, which was crusted with a whitish crystalline substance.

Frances drew nearer and stared.

'Miss Doughty, I would ask you not to touch whatever is on the cloak,' said Sharrock, 'but if it is what I think it is, you are better placed than most to express an opinion as to what it might be. Of course, we do intend to send it to the public analyst this afternoon.'

'It appears to be dried syrup,' said Frances, who had often had to clean encrustations from the necks of the stock syrup bottles in the shop. She leaned forward and sniffed. Even days later the pungent aroma was still in evidence. Oil of oranges, cardamom, cassia, and a hint of nux vomica. 'It is Mr Garton's digestive mixture,' she said. 'I have no doubt of it. The syrup is our own blend. Yet how did it come there? The bottle is supposed never to have left his bedside after it was brought home. He is not supposed even to have unwrapped the bottle until after he returned from dining with Mr Keane.'

'My thought exactly,' said Sharrock.

Frances sat down and considered the implications of what had just been revealed. Inspector Sharrock, Wilfred and Mr Edwards were all silent until she spoke again. 'The fact that the syrup leaked from the bottle at all shows that it must have been opened,' she said. 'When we dispense a mixture the cork is first mechanically compressed so when it is put in the bottle it ensures a tight fit. Once the bottle has been uncorked for its first use it will never fit as well. Do you have the original wrapping? I would like to examine it.' Frances could not resist a glance at Wilfred, who was staring very determinedly at his shoes.

Sharrock complied without a murmur, and watched her carefully as she unfolded the paper.

'Yes,' said Frances, who knew the answer but was not about to reveal that she had seen the paper on an earlier visit. 'See – there is no staining anywhere. The medicine leaked from the bottle after it was unwrapped. You realise what this means?'

'Er – yes, of course,' said Sharrock, looking less than enlightened. 'But perhaps – in your own words...?'

'Mr Garton suffered from indigestion and he was about to go to dinner. What more natural than he take his medicine with him? He cut the string and unwrapped the bottle, but it was not after he returned home, as we have supposed, but before he departed, and then he slipped it into his pocket. But the cork was firmly seated, and the bottle would not have leaked unless he uncorked it to take a dose of medicine. Remember that Mr Garton was seen drinking from a bottle as the carriage was drawing away. We all assumed that he was drinking from his brandy flask as that was the only bottle we knew to be there, but what if it was not the brandy, but his medicine? If he failed to securely re-cork the bottle, some of the contents may have leaked into his pocket.' Frances turned to the servant. 'Mr Edwards. I believe it was you who saw Mr Garton drink when he was in the carriage?'

'Yes, I did,' he agreed.

'Did you see what kind of bottle or flask he drank from?'

'I am afraid I did not, it was far too dark. But of course, Mrs Garton was in the carriage with him and would, I am sure, be able to enlighten you.'

Sharrock furrowed his brow. 'Well that will be all, Mr Edwards,' he said quickly. 'Make sure we know your new address if we need to speak to you again.'

Edwards looked regretfully at the cloak.

'Don't worry; you'll have it back when it's no longer evidence.'

After the manservant had departed, Sharrock strode up and down deep in thought. Frances had half expected she would also be dismissed but he seemed to be content for her to remain. She realised that it was the mention of Mrs Garton's name and the suspicion that the lady had not been entirely truthful about some events – at least on the night of her husband's death – that had led to the abrupt ending of the interview with Mr Edwards.

'Now then, what did Mrs Garton say about her husband drinking in the carriage?' said Sharrock. He glanced at Wilfred, who obligingly burrowed into the heaped papers and extracted a folder, which he opened and perused. The constable shook his head. 'She said she was too upset to remember anything,' he said.

'But wait a minute,' exclaimed Sharrock, 'he *couldn't* have drunk the medicine in the carriage or he'd have been taken ill at the Keanes' house.'

'Yes he could!' exclaimed Frances. 'He could have drunk the medicine with impunity if there was no poison in it.'

Sharrock stared at her.

'Don't you see?' she went on. 'The poison was put in later.'

He folded his arms and narrowed his eyes. 'And when exactly do you think that happened?'

'Well,' said Frances, 'if the bottle remained in the cloak pocket, and the cloak was hung in the hall cupboard at Mr Keane's house, there was an interval between the bottle being opened and Mr Garton taking the fatal dose when the bottle was left unattended for some five hours.'

'That may be true,' said Sharrock, dubiously, 'but how did this supposed murderer even know that the bottle was there?'

'Only three people knew that the bottle was there,' said Frances. 'Mr Garton, who, I think we agree, did not take his own life, Mrs Garton, and one other – the person who took the cloak and who might have noticed the weight of the bottle in the pocket.'

'And who just happened to have a lethal amount of strychnine about their person?' said Sharrock sarcastically.

Frances paused, her eye suddenly caught by a

picture on the desk that had been uncovered by Wilfred's search. It was the head and shoulders portrait of Guy Berenger, the upper part of the head partly obscured by an overlapping sheet of white paper. Why had she never seen the resemblance before?

'I assume the Keanes' house is closed up now,' she said regretfully.

'I think Mr Morgan is over there arranging for the sale of the contents,' said Wilfred.

'What about the servants?' exclaimed Frances.

'I think some of them are still there.'

Frances rose to her feet. 'Then we need to go there at once,' she said, 'there's just a chance.'

'A chance of what?' said Sharrock.

'Don't you see?' she said, gesturing at the portrait of Berenger. When that brought about no enlightenment, she put the sheet of white paper over it folded in the shape of a maid's cap.'

'Oh,' said Sharrock suddenly, then *'Oh!'* He looked up at Wilfred. 'Well constable, what are you waiting for? Order up a cab. You'd better come with us Miss Doughty. You've a lot of explaining to do, and you'd better begin right away.'

As the four-wheeler rattled its way towards Craven Hill, Frances had barely time to arrange her thoughts. When she began to speak she was extremely gratified to see that both the Inspector and the constable were listening with rapt attention.

'The important thing,' she said, 'and I have both documentary proof and witnesses who will swear to it – is that the man who was living in Bayswater with Henrietta Garton as her husband was not Percival Garton at all.'

'Then who the Dev– I mean, who was he?' exclaimed Sharrock.

'I believe,' said Frances, 'that he was Lewis Cotter.'

'Lewis who?'

'Liverpool case, Sir. 1869,' said Wilfred, promptly. 'He was a bank clerk involved in a forgery case – murdered his accomplice, a Mr Truin, and then ran off.'

'I see,' said Sharrock in astonishment. 'But wait a minute – didn't Mr Garton's brother identify the body? How come he didn't spot it was a different man? Or is he involved in some way?'

'Cedric Garton is very much younger than Percival,' said Frances. 'He was just a child when his brother left Italy for England. Cedric next saw his brother – or the man he thought was his brother – when he came to London last year, an interval of twenty-three years from their last meeting. When he made the identification it was on the basis of the man he had met only a year ago.'

Sharrock frowned. 'And you don't suspect him? He seems like a rum sort to me.'

Frances smiled. 'Indeed, but he is not a murderer. All this time, I had been wondering who would have wanted to murder Mr Garton, but now I believe he was killed because the murderer knew that he was Lewis Cotter. I was misled because Cotter was ten years younger than Garton. No wonder the false Mr Garton always seemed less careworn than a man of forty-eight. He was really thirty-eight, under a great deal of whiskers.'

Sharrock looked more confused than before. 'But how did the killer know Garton was Cotter?

394

And where did the strychnine come from?'

'I think this murder has been planned for many years,' said Frances. 'It was just a matter of waiting for the opportunity. To us it seems mysterious and improbable because we see it as the work of a moment, but once we realise that there was a carefully laid plan it is not so remarkable after all.'

Outside the villa in Craven Hill, a man was pasting up a sign announcing the sale by auction of the contents. Frances and the two policemen marched boldly up to the door and rang the bell-pull. Ettie answered the door. She looked dusty and unhappy. 'Oh!' she exclaimed seeing the policemen, then gaped in bewilderment to see Frances.

'Is Mr Morgan at home?' demanded Sharrock, abruptly. Ettie looked at the two policemen standing on the doorstep, then her face crumpled and she burst into tears.

Frances hurried in at once and comforted the maid, quickly. 'It's all right, Ettie it's not what you think; the police just want to talk to him, that's all.'

Ettie sniffed. 'I'm so sorry – only I – do come in Sir, – if you'd just like to wait in the front parlour, I'll tell Master you're here.'

As Ettie conducted the policemen to the parlour, Frances said, 'Ettie, I can't explain now, but I must know. On the night of Mr Garton's death, when he arrived – who took his cloak?'

Sharrock nodded. 'Answer the question now, there's a good girl.'

Ettie blinked through damp eyes. 'Well – let me see – I was laying the table and Mr Harvey was seeing to the wine. I suppose it must have been Ellen.'

'As I thought,' said Sharrock, as if the idea had been his, 'and where is Ellen now?'

'I don't know, sir. She's packed her bags and left.'

'If you ever locate Guy Berenger,' Frances told Sharrock, 'they may well be together. I am sure they are brother and sister. There is a look about the eyes which is so similar as to suggest they are related.'

Mr Morgan, a weary-looking man of about sixty, entertained his unexpected visitors in the front parlour which was already festooned with dustsheets. The auctioneer's men, who had been milling about taking notes, were persuaded to go to another room. Mr Morgan was unable to help the police a great deal. He had no information about where Ellen had gone, and knew nothing of her origins. When introduced to Frances he did have one admission to make; his daughter had confessed to him that her evidence at the inquest was untrue, something for which she blamed her husband. He promised that he would make a formal statement to that effect.

On the way back to the station, Frances was deep in thought. She was beginning now to see how everything had happened and why, and even the tiny fragments of fact which had puzzled her were being explained. 'Once I realised that Mr Garton was not Mr Garton at all, almost everything became clear,' she said.

'Clear as mud to me,' said Sharrock, 'but go on – if you can make sense of this, I'm prepared to listen.'

'In 1862, Mr and Mrs Garton were married

and went to live in a village called Tollington Mill in Gloucestershire,' said Frances, feeling as if she was about to tell a story.

'When you say "Mr Garton?" queried Sharrock.

'The *real* Percival Garton. He came to England from Italy in 1856 in order to manage his grandfather's shipping business in Bristol. In June 1869 a man came to live in Tollington Mill. He called himself John Wright, but he was really Lewis Cotter. After he murdered Mr Truin in April he hid for a time. He then took a new identity and leased the house in Tollington Mill.'

'Didn't you think that Mr Keane was Lewis Cotter?' said Wilfred.

'Yes, and I was wrong, but very close. I think James Keane was Samuel Cotter, Lewis' younger brother. Keane was not as clever as his brother, and when he took a new name he assumed that of someone he had probably known and who had died as a youth. It was a careless thing to do, and his brother was not pleased with him. If Lewis Cotter was John Wright then he was a very talented artist. I think he committed the Liverpool forgeries and used Mr Truin to gain access to the bank papers. After the murder he planned to live quietly in the country for a time, and eventually establish himself in London. His brother Samuel had gone ahead to London as a part of that plan. But then the unexpected happened. Lewis Cotter met Henrietta Garton and they fell in love. He stayed on in the country and had even decided to settle there, and then in June or July 1869 Henrietta found that she was going to have a child. She must have told Cotter then that this would mean discovery. I doubt if Cotter had known it before, but Mr Garton had been told by his doctor that he could not be a father.'

'How do you know all this?' exclaimed Sharrock suddenly.

'By asking the right questions of the right people,' said Frances. 'I believe that Cotter and Henrietta decided to murder Mr Garton and make it look as if John Wright had been murdered. Then Cotter could go to London with Henrietta as her husband. There were a number of difficulties – while Garton and Cotter were of a similar build they looked quite different – Cotter's hair was darker and Garton had whiskers whereas Cotter was clean shaven. It was part of the plan that Cotter should go to London as Garton to establish an alibi for the death of John Wright. He probably didn't want to risk going about wearing false whiskers, which would have given him away if anyone had noticed, so he left Tollington Mill for a month until they were grown. Then he returned, and killed Garton. Garton was dressed in John Wright's clothing, his face was shaved and his hair dyed black. Then Cotter planted the bottle of dye in the house to make it look as if Wright had always dyed his hair.'

'It's a bit of a melodrama if you don't mind my saying it,' said Sharrock.

'I can give you a witness who will say that the bottle of dye was never there when the house was closed up,' said Frances. 'And she told the story to the police at the time, and they wouldn't believe her. Perhaps it's still in the notes they took.'

Sharrock raised his eyebrows but said nothing.

'Cotter planted a notebook on the body to make it look as if Wright was still alive on 30 July,' Frances continued, 'but he was actually killed some days before, then Cotter went to London and kept appointments to establish an alibi. Since no one thought Wright was missing there was no search, so the murderers felt sure that the body, left in an abandoned quarry, would probably not be found for some time. It was the only chance they took and it paid off. The body wasn't found for two weeks, and the summer heat had ensured that it would be identified by clothing alone.'

'But what about the sister who said Wright was insane?' said Wilfred. 'She must have been telling the truth as she knew about the stitches in his coat.'

Frances thought about the slender lady she had seen coming out of the cemetery in the deep mourning appropriate for a brother. 'I think that she may have been Cotter's sister, Eleanor. If he had stayed with her during the month he was away from Tollington Mill, she might well have mended his coat then. He must have been hoping that the police inquiries into the identity of John Wright would slow down, but they were continuing more vigorously than he wanted and he decided to put an end to them, so he asked his sister to go the police and tell a story that would explain the mystery. Her story also placed John Wright with her in Bristol at the same time as Lewis Cotter was in Liverpool, thus averting possible suspicion that they were one and the same man, and reinforced the suggestion that John Wright dyed his hair. I suggest you make enquiries to find out where the lady was living in 1870. I would be very surprised if she was not then in Bristol.'

'So – Lewis Cotter killed Mr Garton in Tollington Mill in 1870,' said Sharrock. 'What about Mrs Garton? Are you accusing her, too?'

'The actual murder was undoubtedly committed by Cotter, but Mrs Garton lied to the inquest on John Wright. She said she had met him in the street on 30th July, in order to establish the date of death at the time when her supposed husband was in London. I don't know if she knew who John Wright really was, but I believe she knew that he had killed her husband, and that the knowledge did not revolt her.'

'Then Mrs Garton and her – gentleman friend – came to London and thought they were safe,' said Sharrock, 'and they *were* safe, for more than nine years. So who killed Cotter and how?'

'Two of Mr Truin's ten children were bent on revenge,' said Frances. 'Ellen was only eight when she and her mother and brothers and sisters were sent to the workhouse, and she saw most of her family die there. I expect that when she was older, her brother, the one who had declined a career as a cheesemonger for one on the stage, told her the whole story. Somehow, and it may have taken them many years to do so, they discovered who Lewis Cotter really was, and where. Then I think it was just a matter of positioning themselves to commit murder. Ellen managed to find a place in Keane's household, and her brother, calling himself Berenger and posing as an artist, worked at the gallery. They were very patient, and very careful.

They wanted to get away with it.'

'But why not just tell the police their suspicions?' asked Sharrock.

'Would they have been believed?' said Frances. 'A servant and an actor claiming that a respected citizen of Bayswater was an impostor and a murderer? I hardly think that probable. In any case, I suspect that they might have thought death by hanging to be far too merciful an end for the man who had destroyed their family.'

'And where did they get the strychnine?' asked Wilfred.

'Do you think it was stolen from your shop?' asked Sharrock.

'We have accounted for the missing *strychnia*,' said Frances, with a touch of embarrassment. 'It was inadvertently destroyed some time ago. But I agree, that is a difficulty. The pure article is a hard thing to obtain in such quantity without attracting attention. I suggest you make enquiries at all the chemists in the district to see if one of them has sold any. But of course, the supply could have been obtained elsewhere and over a long period of time. I hope you do eventually catch up with them because I would like to ask about that myself.'

'What about Mr Meadows?' asked Sharrock, 'Where does he fit in? Or was Guy Berenger Meadows?'

'I think that Lewis Cotter was actually Meadows. It was he who produced the forgeries and his brother's only involvement was to amend the bank records. After his death, Keane was afraid of discovery and destroyed as many of his brother's drawings as he could in case anyone

401

made the connection.'

'And then Berenger killed James Keane,' said Sharrock. 'Why? Because of his association with Cotter? But he had nothing to do with Mr Truin's death!'

'No,' said Frances despondently, 'and I have a horrid feeling as to why they killed him. I think it may be something to do with me.'

Sharrock opened his mouth in surprise and Wilfred looked alarmed.

'You see,' explained Frances, 'Ellen knew I suspected that James Keane had killed Mr Garton. She came to visit me, apparently to give me information that might help, but of course what she really wanted was to find out how near I was to discovering her. She thought that the fact that Mr Keane had been arrested would stop my enquiries, but I told her it would not, that I would never stop until it was proved that Mr Keane was a murderer. She must have decided that one way she could stop me was to dispose of Mr Keane.'

'But,' said Wilfred, clearly appalled, 'she might also have asked her brother to kill *you*. You were in very great danger!'

Touched by his concern, Frances felt a fluttering at her breast, like the filmy beating of an insect's wings. 'Yes,' she said, 'I see it now. Maybe they did consider killing me, but they chose to kill Mr Keane instead. And I think I can see why. First of all as we know Mr Keane was a very great villain, and to a pair of people bent on retribution for crimes, he was therefore a more satisfying target. Also I believe that Ellen felt some sympathy for me. Her father had been maligned and disgraced, as was mine.'

Wilfred was shaking his head. 'You must promise us that you will never do such a thing again,' he said.

'Well, I do think it most unlikely that I shall ever need to enquire into another murder,' said Frances with a smile.

Two days later the police caught up with Ellen and her brother. A sharp-eyed lodging house keeper who was well aware that many of her customers might be criminals in hiding and therefore have a price on their heads, alerted the police to the couple posing as husband and wife, and a suitable force was sent to the address. Ellen was secured quickly but Guy was able to get away and made the mistake of trying to dodge his way across the Strand in full flood of traffic. Misjudging his path in his desperation, he fell under the wheels of an omnibus and was frightfully mangled. When the police picked him up he was dead.

The next day Wilfred called upon Frances. 'We've been trying to question Miss Truin,' he said, 'but she won't speak a word unless you are there. She says that you are the only person who would understand.'

Frances was shown into Inspector Sharrock's office where Ellen was seated looking unnaturally calm, although her eyes were red with weeping. She was gazing at the artist's drawing of her brother. Frances wondered why she had not noticed the family resemblance before, but realised that Berenger's heavy-lidded eyes, so like those of his sister, had simply given the impression he had intended, that of a man steeped in alcohol.

Sharrock and Wilfred stood by as Frances sat opposite the girl.

'I'm glad you are here, Miss Doughty,' said Ellen. 'You will know why I did it, you will understand. I was only eight when my father died but I remember him like it was yesterday. No matter what cares he suffered from, he always had time for us. He was a loving father who'd have done anything to see that we were comfortable and safe. How it would have grieved him to see what we came to! Mother was always ill, and all the memories I have of tenderness and affection are of my father's love. I'm sure you will know what I mean.'

But Frances knew she did not. Her father, though dutifully providing for his family, had never been a warm presence in the household, and had never treated her with affection. All his love and pride had been directed towards Frederick.

'My mother died very soon after we went to the workhouse and of my little sisters and brothers all but two died also. Only my sister Jane and brother Stephen lived; they were very little older than me. Jane went into service when she was thirteen, as did Stephen. They are still in Liverpool and are doing well, I understand. My oldest sister Mary went into service soon after my father's death. She gave birth to a child a year later and was turned out of the house. Both she and the child died not long afterwards. George – that is my older brother – he called himself Guy,' she paused, and a tear ran down her face. They gave her a moment of respectful silence in which to compose herself. 'George had run away to go on the stage, and later when I went into service

404

he came back and told me everything that had happened. He didn't think we could do anything about it, but I said we could and we should. He said he would help. Of course the first thing to do was to find Mr Cotter.'

'How did you do that when the police had failed?' asked Sharrock.

'The police thought he had gone to America; I don't think they were even looking for him. But remember I was in service. People say things in front of servants in the same way as they would give away their secrets in front of furniture. The first thing I did was to find a place near to where Mrs Cotter lived. I made friends with the servant of the house. In time the servant left and I was recommended for the place. I worked there – actually worked for the Cotters – and I watched and listened. At last I found that Mrs Cotter wrote letters to a man in London called James Keane who lived in Bayswater. I wondered if Mr Keane was really her son. So I came to London and found a place in Bayswater. In time, I learned where Mr Keane lived, and I got a new place somewhere very near to Mr Keane's house, and made friends with the servants. It was a very unhappy house and the servants didn't stay long, so I was soon able to get a place there. I wrote to George and told him what I had done and he came to London. I knew about the gallery and he went there pretending to be an artist. He wasn't able to sell any work, but he did get a position as manager.'

'How did you find that Mr Garton was Lewis Cotter?' asked Frances.

'I had worked for Mr Keane about a year. I wasn't certain he was my quarry but thought it very like. He was visited by Mr Garton very often and there seemed to be a brotherly affection between them. Once I overheard Mr Garton berating Mr Keane for choosing to call himself Keane, after a friend. He said he had always been careless even as a child. He said he would have been better choosing a commonplace name as he had done. I was surprised about that as I did not think Garton to be such a commonplace name.'

Frances smiled, knowing that this was a reference to the name John Wright.

'But that did tell me that neither man was living under the name he had been born with. So I suspected them both,' added Ellen.

'You thought that they were brothers?' said Frances.

'There was a resemblance, though of course it was hard to be sure, as both gentlemen had very ample whiskers and wore them differently. Then one day I walked in as they were sitting together over a glass of wine and found them raising a toast to their father. I pretended not to have understood them.'

'What made you realise that it was Mr Garton and not Mr Keane who was Lewis Cotter?' asked Frances.

'I had read everything about the case I could. George had been collecting newspaper articles and we studied them together. One thing we knew was that Lewis Cotter was older than his brother Samuel. I was serving dinner one evening and there was a conversation where Mr Garton made some joking allusion to being older and wiser than Mr Keane, and Mr Keane laughed and said that Garton was only two years older and he didn't think it signified. That was when I knew. I told George and he said that he ought to be able to kill Mr Garton when he next visited the gallery, but Mr Garton was hardly there and when he was he was always in the company of Mr Keane and sometimes others, too. I pleaded with George not to take any risks. We wanted revenge for what Cotter had done but not at a cost to ourselves. I told him he had only to kill Cotter when he could escape free and not be suspected.'

'I met your brother once,' said Frances. 'I went to the gallery. I pretended to be unwell so as to be conducted into the office where I could sit down. He was very kind.' Out of the corner of her eye she could see Sharrock shaking his head in disapproval.

'Yes, he was kind,' said Ellen appreciatively. 'And talented, also. He appeared to the world to be no more than a failed artist with a fondness for drink. He once played such a part on stage, and, I am told, did it to perfection. He even carried a little flask which was supposed to contain alcohol. In fact it was water. He used to rinse his mouth with a little whisky from time to time so as to give people the impression of alcohol on his breath. Mr Keane and Mr Garton were doing something very criminal at the gallery and George was able to run the business for them and make them think that he was too fuddled to spot that anything was amiss. That suited them very well.'

'And the murder of Mr Garton?' said Frances.

'How was that done?'

'When I took his cloak I felt that there was a bottle in the pocket. He had carried such bottles many times before but they had always been tightly sealed. If the bottle had been sealed I would not have done anything, as he would have at once known that someone had opened it. But this bottle had already been opened and some of the contents taken and there was quite a bit spilt. It was only about half full.'

Frances could not resist a smile of triumph towards Sharrock, who threw up his hands in capitulation. 'All right, Miss Doughty, you win!'

'So,' said Frances to Ellen, 'what did you do?'

'The hall was empty most of the time,' said Ellen, 'I ran up to my room and got the strychnine, then came back and put it in.'

Frances realised that since the bottle had not been full, the amount of poison required was far less than had been supposed. 'Why did you choose strychnine?' she asked, 'and where did you get it?'

'George suggested Prussic acid but that has a strong smell – anyone would have noticed it – then there was arsenic; but I did recall hearing once that strychnine was a very painful death. You see, I wanted him to suffer great agonies. He deserved it. We have had ruination and pain for many a year and he was not to die easily. But getting the poison was hard. I couldn't just go into a chemist's shop and buy it. I asked George to pretend to be a doctor, but, when he tried, the chemist asked all sorts of questions he didn't know the answer to, and was very suspicious, so we gave up that idea. Of course there was no difficulty about getting vermin

408

killers; there were some at the Cotters' house in Bootle, but they were mixed with dyes. George tried to get the strychnine from the powder but he never could. Then one day he got a vermin killer without dye, it was mixed with soot. I had an old spectacle glass of my father's. He used to amuse us by looking at things through it – pebbles and shells and the like. It was very thick and made them look larger, and you used to see all the pretty patterns. When I looked at the powder with the soot I could just see the little crystals of pure strychnine. If I was very patient, I could pick them out. So that was how we did it. It took a long time, but then we had time, and gradually I collected together what I needed.' She smiled. 'You understand, don't you? I know you do. The thing is, Miss Doughty, I think that really we are very alike.'

Frances suppressed a shudder.

CHAPTER TWENTY-ONE

It was a day, if not for celebration, then for a quiet expression of pleasure. Two weeks after the arrest of Ellen Truin, Frances received a letter from the directors of the Liverpool & County Bank stating that her enquiries had enabled them to discover a hidden account in which Lewis Cotter had concealed funds, undoubtedly the bank's, and enclosing a cheque for £200. It relieved her most pressing financial needs, and enabled her to give Sarah her £10, although it was not, alas, sufficient to prevent the sale of the business. Young Mr Jacobs' father had already made enquiries on his son's behalf which Frances was inclined to view favourably, since the price would be sufficient to settle her debts and leave her with a modest sum. That day, however, with the late February gloom hanging over the Grove, Frances had other matters on her mind. She was sitting at the parlour table. In front of her was a cup of tea, untasted, a large jam tart, uncut, and a manila envelope. There were footsteps on the stairs and her uncle Cornelius was admitted.

'Frances, dear, you wanted to see me,' he exclaimed. Cornelius's emotions were always transparent if one knew what to look for and there was a trace of anxiety behind his smile. 'I hope all is well.'

She smiled faintly. 'Yes, Uncle, I require only information.' She poured tea and cut a slice of tart. He settled himself across the table with an expression of anticipation. Sarah's powerful hands had a well-known lightness of touch when it came to pastry. He glanced at the envelope on the table, but Frances rested her fingers upon it and made no reference to its contents.

'I was examining the family papers in my father's desk,' said Frances, calmly, 'and I could not help but notice one item that is missing – my mother's death certificate.'

'I see,' said Cornelius, thoughtfully, 'well it might be amongst my papers. I did assist your father at the time of Rosetta's death. I promise I will look for it as soon as I am home. But surely it is not something you require urgently?'

'Uncle,' said Frances, with a pained expression, 'I know that you have always had my interests at heart, but don't you think I am now old enough to be told the truth?'

The slice of tart in his hand never reached his mouth. It trembled and dropped to the plate. 'Oh,' he said.

'When I was nine years old my father took me to place flowers on my mother's grave,' said Frances 'He found the visit so distressing I never spoke to him of it again. Until recently all I knew about her death was the date on the tombstone: 1864. So I went to Somerset House and purchased the certificate.' She opened the envelope and removed a sheet of paper.

'Oh dear,' said Cornelius, terrified not only by what Frances now knew, but by the coolness of her manner.

'And here it is,' said Frances. 'The death of Rosetta Jane Doughty, 10 March 1864, at an address in Chelsea. I have made enquiries and the place is a lodging house. Cause of death: fever and convulsions; age – two months. I see also that there is no father's name given but the mother's name is Rosetta Ann Doughty. I have been foolish and unobservant. My only excuse is that my mind was otherwise engaged. But I see from my parents' marriage certificate that my mother's middle name was indeed Ann. Uncle–,' she leaned forward to Cornelius who was ashen-faced with shame. 'This is not the death certificate of my mother; it is that of my mother's daughter. So – this is what I wanted to ask you – is my mother still alive?'

411

Cornelius bowed his head and ran the fingers of both hands through his greying locks. He was almost afraid to speak and yet, Frances suspected, relieved to be obliged to speak after so long.

'I don't know,' he said, looking up at last, 'I haven't seen her in sixteen years.' He groaned with regret. 'You are right; you are old enough to know. Frances, I am so very sorry, there is no way to put it delicately – there was a man. When your mother knew that a child was due she went away in this man's company and left your father a letter to explain her actions.'

Frances had already guessed at what had happened, but even so, to hear the truth cut deeply at her heart. She had always thought that she would have loved her mother dearly if she had known her, but it was painful now to find that both she and Frederick had been abandoned by her. 'Who was this man?' she asked.

'Please believe me, Frances, I don't know – no one does,' said Cornelius, unhappily. 'Naturally your father was distraught and deeply ashamed. He was also most anxious to protect both yourself and Frederick from the knowledge of your mother's disgrace. We talked and decided that it was best for you to believe that she had died.'

'Frederick could remember being told that she was ill,' said Frances. 'He said that there was a sick room.'

'There was,' said Cornelius. 'For a time your father entertained the hope that Rosetta would be discovered and brought back so we created the impression that she was still there but was too ill to be seen.'

'He would have taken her back?' exclaimed Frances in astonishment.

'Oh yes, and the child too, in an instant. He loved her very much. But when all hope of her return had gone he told Frederick that his mother had died. You, of course, were too young to understand. Some months later your father heard through an acquaintance that there had been a child who had died. I found out the burial place in Brompton Cemetery, and we agreed that if ever you or Frederick were to ask to see your mother's grave you would be taken there.' He sighed deeply. 'There you have it. To this very day I don't know if we did the right thing.'

'I see,' said Frances. She drew a second certificate from the envelope. 'Then you knew nothing of this?' She slid the paper across the table to her uncle, who perused its contents with astonishment. 'When I saw that the Rosetta who died in 1864 was my sister, I looked in the register for her birth and I discovered that there was another birth in the same district and on the same page; Cornelius Martin Doughty, Rosetta's twin. That is the certificate of the birth of my brother, and as far as I am aware he is still living.'

'Frances,' whispered Cornelius, 'you must believe me – I didn't know – my heavens, if I had – if I had only known...'

'You would have acted differently?' said Frances, not at all sure that this was the case.

'I hope so. Not at the time, perhaps, but I think I would have said something sooner. Do you intend to try and find your mother and brother?' asked Cornelius, anxiously.

'I do,' said Frances. 'I don't yet know how to set about it, but then when I determined to find Mr Garton's murderer I had no idea at all how to begin, and I think I enjoyed some success with that.' She was unable to prevent a note of self-satisfaction from creeping into her voice.

Cornelius shook his head, disapprovingly. 'My dear – have you thought – your mother may still be in the company of the man for whom she left your father – it would be a most irregular household.'

Frances smiled. 'I have entered worse places; and the man, whoever he may be, is of no consequence to me.'

To her surprise, Cornelius suddenly buried his face in his hands. Then he took a deep breath and looked up at her with an expression of resolve. 'We have gone this far,' he said, 'I suppose you ought to know everything.'

Frances felt suddenly dry-mouthed with anticipation.

'Frances,' he hesitated awkwardly, and she saw his fingertips tremble, 'have you never wondered why it is that you are taller than both your father and brother?'

She stared at him in bewilderment. She had sometimes regretted her height, but had never wondered about it, supposing that her father had been bent with care, her brother stunted by illness. It she had thought about it, then she would have imagined that her mother was a tall woman, and very like herself. She remembered suddenly her masquerade as Frank Williamson in her brother's clothes, the trousers that were too short in the leg.

'As you know, Frederick's features resembled

William's very closely but yours do not, and I can tell you that you do not appear in any respect like Rosetta,' said Cornelius. 'I think it is very possible that William was not your true father.'

For a moment Frances thought he was talking about an impossibility – but then she thought of the unknown man with whom her mother had run away. Could it be that she was the daughter of this man and not William Doughty? It certainly seemed that Cornelius believed so. She should, she reflected, have been grieved at the discovery, but somehow she was not. Her sense of duty towards William was unabated, and she would always, no matter what, think of the man who had done his duty to her as her father, but the ties of blood could not be denied. 'Did he suspect too?'

Cornelius nodded. 'Yes, we spoke of it. It could never be proved, of course, but from the time your mother departed, he thought that you were not his daughter. He once saw Rosetta conversing with a man, a tall man of very distinctive appearance. It all seemed perfectly innocent at the time and he thought nothing of it, but later he suspected that this was the man she had left with, and he sometimes said that he saw the man's face in yours.'

Frances suddenly understood a great deal. She recalled a life in which her needs had always been not merely secondary to Frederick's but of virtually no consequence, and in which, now she thought about it, she had been valued only in respect of her usefulness, much as one might have regarded a servant. She had never resented this or thought of it in any way other than this was the usual way of families, since she was a daughter.

Many other girls, she was quite sure, were treated the same, or even worse, an afterthought in the affections, always subservient to their brothers; but perhaps in her case there had been a little more to it. Then there was the slightingly small legacy, hardly more than one might have left a housekeeper.

Cornelius looked wistfully at the certificate before him. 'This youth, who will be sixteen now, will be your full brother, and my nephew,' he said.

'All the more reason why I should find him,' said Frances.

Diffidently, and with more than a trace of apprehension, he reached across the table towards her and took her hands. 'I hope you will find it in your heart to forgive me,' he said. 'We did what we thought was best.'

'It is forgiven,' said Frances, and she meant it.

The following morning, Frances was enjoying a frugal breakfast of bread and jam, when Sarah brought her two letters. One was from Mr Rawsthorne, saying that the papers for the sale of the business to Mr Jacobs senior had been prepared and it only remained for her to present herself at his office that morning to append her signature. She set the letter aside with regret, but knew that she would have to complete the sale, and there was no point in any delay.

The second letter was from Dr Collin.

Dear Miss Doughty
I apologise for not writing to you sooner on this subject as I have been out of town. I have given some thought

*to your suggestion that I may have inadvertently made
an error in my evidence at the inquest on your father,
and as a result have re-examined my notes. I accept
that Mr Doughty did not complain of toothache either
to yourself or to me, but he had most certainly been
treating himself for that ailment with the usual remedy,
oil of cloves. When I examined the bottle of chloroform
found by his bedside, there were fingermarks on it in an
oily substance which smelled most distinctly of clove oil.
I trust that you can now agree that I did not make an
error, I remain, your most obedient servant
Arthur Collin, M.D.*

Frances stared at the words, trying at first to push
aside their full meaning. For a moment she was
almost paralysed with shock. If she could have
gone through her life ignorant of that letter and its
import, then she thought she would have preferred to do so, and yet what an appalling ignor-
ance it would have been, leaving her at the mercy
of everything that was vile. As the emotions broke
through her defences, and flooded her body, the
distress and rage and sense of deep betrayal were
enough to make her feel violently ill. Her hands
shook, and she dropped the letter on the table as
if it had been a venomous snake. It was impossible to keep still; she rose and began to pace
about the room, clenching her lips together,
making little whimpering sounds, clutching at her
stomach to try and stop the hideous heaving. She
was breathing so hard she felt dizzy and faint, and
went to the window overlooking the Grove and
held onto the frame to support herself. Outside,
people were walking about as if nothing had hap-

pened. There was a soft tinkle of the shop bell. Someone had come in to ask for a cough syrup or an aperient, someone with no concept of the horror that was now hers. The very normality of it all almost persuaded her that she was dreaming, and she breathed gently for just a moment before the agony began again.

She heard a footfall behind her, and thinking, with a great sense of relief that it was Sarah, turned around and saw Herbert at the parlour table, about to help himself to a slice of bread. His moustache was freshly pomaded, and as the unmistakable scent of oil of cloves reached her nostrils she was unable to control a physical recoil of sheer revulsion. Hot tears of grief and rage suddenly welled into her eyes and rolled down her cheeks. He looked up at her, and was startled by what he saw, then noticed the letter on the table. He picked it up, and read it, then he slowly raised his eyes to her again, and as she saw his expression she knew that the unthinkable thought was right.

'You monster!' she cried, hardly knowing where the power to speak had come from. 'How could you! A defenceless old man! A man you thought of as a second father!'

Herbert said nothing, but crumpled the letter and put it in his pocket.

'Please don't say you did it for the business!' she raged, 'and please, above all, don't say that you did it for me!'

He was about to speak but she suddenly held out her palm towards him. 'No – stop! Don't move! I want to hear you admit you did it!'

He licked his lips, thought for a moment, then

nodded. 'I looked in on him. It was already in my mind that it had to be done. Everything he had built in the last twenty years was being destroyed, and there was only one way to stop it. Yes, I admired and venerated him – that was what made it so hard, but I thought – if I do it, then he will feel no pain, he will be at rest. He had the handkerchief over his face and he was asleep; deep stertorous breathing – maybe he had already had too much – maybe if I had done nothing at all he would still have died.'

'If you had removed the handkerchief he might have lived,' said Frances, bitterly.

'Yes, I think so,' he admitted. 'But I did not. I added more chloroform to the handkerchief.'

She closed her eyes for a moment. It was almost a relief to hear it. She wiped the tears from her face. 'If you have one shred of decency left in you then you will go to the police at once and confess what you have done.'

He shook his head. 'Oh no, I will not do that. The letter is not evidence against me. It is only important to you, because only you can see its significance. Dr Collin obviously cannot.'

'Then *I* will go to the police!' said Frances, boldly.

'And what will you tell them? That I am a murderer because I pomade my moustache? They will hardly arrest me for that. It will seem like the wanderings of a hysterical female mind. I will say that you have been afflicted with melancholy. The death of your brother, the death of your father, and now the loss of the business have all been too much for you to bear. And then of course, there is your disappointment in love.'

'My – what are you talking about?'

He puffed out his chest with a smile. 'Your ambition to become my wife; your unhappiness and jealousy on learning that I have set my heart on winning another.'

There was a loud snort from the doorway. 'Stuff and nonsense!' said Sarah. She had, as Frances knew, been standing there long enough to hear all that had been said. Frances' order to remain still had been directed at Sarah and not Herbert.

He spun around and his face paled with fright. 'I'll deny everything!' he squeaked.

'We'll see what the police have to say,' said Sarah, calmly. 'I've already sent Tom for a constable.'

Herbert yelped and made a grab for the bread knife, but was hardly able to hold it for trembling. 'Get out of my way – let me pass!' he ordered, holding the wavering blade inches from the broad front of Sarah's apron.

'You want to watch that, Mr Munson, you might cut yourself,' said Sarah. What followed took only seconds. Her large fist closed around the hand that held the knife and gave a violent outward twist. There was a loud cracking sound and Herbert screamed, but only for a moment, as her other fist collided with his jaw, stretching him unconscious on the floor.

Frances gasped, in mixed horror and admiration, and staggered back against the window, clutching the sill for support. Sarah shrugged. 'I got eight brothers, Miss, I'd to survive somehow.'

To Frances, everything suddenly seemed to happen very slowly. The room gradually darkened, as if night was drawing in and a series of increasingly drab curtains were being pulled across her eyes. What she was still able to see started to move about her in a strange, sickening waltz. Sarah came towards her as if she was wading through mud, yet still managed to reach her before she fell, and Frances found herself, as she had sometimes been as a child, enfolded in the maidservant's stout arms. The strength had gone from her and without that support she would have fallen. Sarah smelt of starch and polish and dust and sweat. It was, Frances knew, the best smell in the world. She found herself floating effortlessly upwards, as if on a cloud; Sarah had picked her up as easily as one might a baby, and she was carried to her room, and laid upon the bed with such gentleness that the transition between the warm strength of the maid's arms and the firm but familiar support of the mattress was almost imperceptible.

She looked up at that plain but comforting face. 'When I saw you standing there,' she whispered, 'I knew that I would be safe.'

Sarah smiled. 'You know, Miss, don't you, that I'd die before I let anyone hurt a hair on your head.' Nothing more was said, and she watched over Frances as a mother might watch her child until the police arrived.

Two days later, Frances gave evidence at the police court hearing which concluded with the committal of Ellen Truin for trial at the Old Bailey on a charge of murdering Lewis Cotter, otherwise known as Percival Garton. To Frances it was merely a matter of duty, but as the hearing proceeded she became aware of two things; first of all the enormous public sympathy for Ellen which would, she felt certain, ensure that the girl would not hang, and secondly a distinct and unexpected interest in herself. It was not necessary for Frances to reveal more than a small fraction of what she had done in order to uncover the mystery, and yet that part which she was obliged to describe brought gasps of astonishment from the packed courtroom. As she left, people pressed about her; some tried to shake her hand and there were even some cheers. One face she recognised was that of Mr Gillan, the *Chronicle* reporter who succeeded in extracting from her the promise of an interview.

The next edition of the *Chronicle* carried a paragraph stating that the police had decided not to prosecute Henrietta Garton. There were many things that only she could explain, but she had remained close-mouthed under police questioning. It was, of course, impossible to prove that she had known that her lover had murdered her husband, and only if she had known could she be charged as an accessory. Of one thing Frances remained in no doubt; Henrietta Garton and Lewis Cotter had loved one another. Frances pictured the dying man, his mind alert and lucid in the midst of his pain, his one thought, to protect the woman he loved. Cotter knew he had been murdered, and that the poison could only have been in the bottle, but had the police suspected a crime, his life would have come under close scrutiny, and had his true identity been revealed Henrietta might have been accused of the murder of her husband.

Cotter's last agonised words would have been to urge her to do everything she could to ensure that his death appeared to be an accident, a chemist's error. Henrietta's insistence that there had been a mistake with the prescription, her lies about when the bottle had been unwrapped, her deliberate concealment of the fact that her supposed husband had taken the medicine in the carriage on the way to the Keanes' house, had further misdirected enquiries. The one difficulty was that after Cotter's first dose in the carriage, the spillage in his cloak, and the second dose at home, the bottle contained only an ounce or two of medicine. Henrietta, thought Frances, must have dropped it deliberately as she handed it to Ada so it might seem that only one dose had been taken, and later poured water from the carafe onto the stain to make it larger. The lady, still in possession of her secrets, had already left Bayswater with her children for an unknown destination.

The other notable piece in the newspaper was headed '"My Remarkable Career" by a Lady Detective as told to our own reporter.'

It was some moments before Frances realised that this was a sensationalised version of the interview she had granted Mr Gillan. She comforted herself with the thought of how much worse it'd have been had she refused to be interviewed.

Time was running out. The business was effectively sold. In another week she would remove to her uncle's house, and Sarah would have to find a new place. Tom also was looking for employment. The Filleter, who had recently been entertained for a month at one of Her Majesty's more secure establishments, had returned to his old haunts, and Chas and Barstie had abruptly closed down their London business. Tom had last seen them running full tilt down Bishop's Road in the direction of Paddington Station while pelting each other with bread buns. Despite this, Frances couldn't help feeling that she would see them again before long.

Cedric Garton had decided to remain in Bayswater. The complexities of his family's inheritance could take years to unravel, and he had decided to make the best of it and had taken an apartment on Westbourne Park Road, employing Mr Harvey as his personal servant. Frances had an open invitation to call and take tea whenever she liked.

Frances was still intending to try and qualify as a pharmacist, and had applied for a number of apprenticeships but had been unsuccessful in each instance. She suspected that despite her considerable experience she was being passed over for other less knowledgeable but male candidates. Her association with several murders also gave her the kind of notoriety that a respectable business could well do without. Herbert's arrest had created a vacancy in Mr Jacobs' employ for which she considered applying, but she soon learned that young Mr Jacobs had a brother eager for the position.

Herbert was currently awaiting the police court hearing that would no doubt commit him for trial, and Frances felt sure that in the fullness of time, he would achieve, albeit briefly, a long hoped-for ambition, an increase of some two inches in his height.

One afternoon, as the last of the February chills

departed giving way to a balmier March, Frances was completing the last of the packing together with Sarah, who was leaving it to the very last moment before she sought another place. Frances felt humble to see how very few possessions she actually had. One small trunk would take her effects and there were some books in a bundle and that was all. Unexpectedly, there was a knock at the front door and Sarah answered it. She brought back a card, with the name of Algernon Fiske, M.A.

'He wants to see you on a personal matter of express importance,' she said.

'I do not know Mr Fiske, but you may show him into the parlour,' said Frances.

Mr Fiske was a respectable-looking man of middle age, who swiftly removed his hat and shook Frances warmly by the hand.

'It's an honour to meet you Miss Doughty. You are quite the sensation in these parts!' he said.

'I expect that will pass,' said Frances politely. 'What can I do for you, Mr Fiske?'

'I am here on behalf of the Board of Governors of the Bayswater Academy for the Education of Young Ladies. Our school provides instruction appropriate for the daughters of professional gentlemen.'

'Oh,' said Frances, hopefully, assuming that she was to be offered a post. 'I have no experience of teaching young ladies, but I am more than willing to do so if you wish.'

'Ah, no, that is not the reason I am here,' said Fiske in embarrassment. 'The fact is, there is a matter of some delicacy, a strictly private matter, which needs to be looked into, and we feel it requires a lady's touch.'

Frances was quite taken aback. 'Am I to understand, Mr Fiske,' she said at last, 'that you wish to employ me as a detective?'

He nodded emphatically. 'That is exactly it!' he exclaimed. 'The reputation of the school is very much at stake, but it'd not, we feel, be appropriate to allow male detectives to question our girls.'

'I really don't know what to say,' said Frances, 'I have never even thought of–'

'You would be paid a generous daily rate,' he interrupted, 'with all necessary expenses, the first week payable in advance.'

The more Frances thought about it, the more impossible it seemed, but he was so engaged by the idea that she felt she had to find a gentle way of sending him away disappointed. 'I am truly sorry, but–'

He mentioned a figure. Frances was shocked into silence.

'Of course, if that isn't enough, it could be increased,' he added.

Frances suddenly saw stretching ahead of her two quite distinct lives, one of genteel idleness in which she was dependent upon the kindness of her uncle, and one of diligence and even danger, in which she was answerable to no one but herself. The advance fee offered by Mr Fiske would be more than enough to pay a month's rent of a small but comfortable apartment sufficient for a single lady and her maid. She settled back in her chair and folded her hands on her lap. 'Perhaps,' she said, 'if you were to begin at the beginning.'

AUTHOR'S NOTE

Strychnine, first isolated in 1818, is a highly poisonous alkaloid extracted from the seeds of the *strychnos nux vomica* tree. It has a very bitter taste. As little as half a grain has been known to be fatal. Medical professionals and pharmacists would have called it by its Latin name, *strychnia*.

In apothecary's measure, one fluid ounce was the equivalent of 29.6 ml, and there were eight drachms to the ounce. One grain was 1/480 of an ounce.

While William Doughty's chemist's shop is fictional, as are most of the characters in this book, many of the people and locations including the public buildings, streets in Bayswater, the Redan public house, and Paddington Green police station, are real.

William Whitely, a Yorkshire draper, opened his first shop on Westbourne Grove in 1863, and by 1880 his empire had expanded to a row of ten shops, the frontage lit by bright blue lamps known as Jablochkoff candles, with further large premises around the corner in Queen's Road (later renamed Queensway). In January 1880, he was locked in a dispute with Paddington Vestry regarding the conversion of eight houses on Queen's Road into warehouses and shops.

In 1880 many Paddington inquests were held at Providence Hall. Dr William Hardwicke (1817–1881) was the coroner for Central Middlesex.

Benjamin Day was a Paddington curate who looked after the parish of St Stephen's for the vicar, Revd T.J. Rowsell whose court appointments meant he had duties elsewhere.

Isabella Skinner Clarke, who lived in Paddington, became in December 1875 the first woman to pass the major examination of the Pharmaceutical Society, although she was not admitted to membership until 1879.

Sam Lynn, chemist, appears in the 1881 census at 123 Queen's Road.

William Powell Frith (1819–1909) was a popular artist.

The tragic death of Lilian Selina Holt was reported in the January 1880 edition of *The Chemist and Druggist.*

Dr John Whitmore (1821–August 1880) was the public analyst for Marylebone.

John Sadleir (1813–1856) was a Member of Parliament, banker and property dealer. He suffered massive losses, raised money on forged papers, and milked the Tipperary Bank of funds. When his crimes were exposed he committed suicide.

Leopold Redpath (1816–1891) was a clerk who defrauded the Great Northern Railway of some £220,000 by falsifying the books and selling fake stocks. He was transported for life in 1857.

Albert de Rutzen, (1831–1913) was for many years the chief magistrate of the London police courts. He was knighted in 1901.

Harry Benson was part of a gang of fraudsters

who induced people to place enormous wagers on fake horse races. In 1877 he received a sentence of fifteen years, but was released on licence in 1885.

Chas and Barstie are of course fictional characters, although they may bear a slight resemblance to two people of similar name who are brilliant sports!

The publishers hope that this book has given you enjoyable reading. Large Print Books are especially designed to be as easy to see and hold as possible. If you wish a complete list of our books please ask at your local library or write directly to:

Magna Large Print Books
Magna House, Long Preston,
Skipton, North Yorkshire.
BD23 4ND

This Large Print Book for the partially sighted, who cannot read normal print, is published under the auspices of

THE ULVERSCROFT FOUNDATION